The Uroboros Saga

The prince beyond the Veil

KARINA NOVAK MONSONEGO

To the one who is always there for me, in body, soul, and advice,
thank you for letting me turn my reality into a fantasy.
You have forever conquered my heart.

Warning – Explicit content, violence, death.

GLOSSARY

Dökkálfar and Ljósálfar – Norse mythology, light elves, and dark elves.

Samhain month – November.

Buck Moon – July full moon.

Tvímánuður - mid-*August* to mid-*September*

Yggdrasil – The world tree that connects the realms.

The Ice Lands – Modern-day Greenland.

Véfrétt – The high priest in the service of the serpent.

Jörmungandr – The world snake that encircles the world.

Midgardr – The capitol or Islandia – the realm of man.

Islandia – Modern-day Iceland.

Rôst – 1 mile – 1.6 kilometers.

Náströnd – Afterlife of the guilty.

Álfheimr – The light elves home world.

Álfur – An elf.

Lundi – old Norse for Puffin.

Dauðadýr – Death-bound creature- a mortal.

Hnefatafl – A board game, Viking chess.

Dróttning – A queen.

Runes – An ancient writing system.

ISLANDIA.

B.

Principum Ins. et Belgice decennali
Abriel anno 1585.

Straum
nes

Almingar

Addalwig Langabak.

Iokalstrut.

liifford.

Grumvig.

Ar...fuella strand.

Amaruedford.

Snafberg.

Dyrefiord.

Armanford.

Glama.

...fuerda..k.

Borders.

Hualo nes

Occidens

C.

Breydafiordur.

D.

Onluertent.

Sneuels Iokul.

Laxaburg

Staps akil.

Sudurlant.

E.

J.

Gre furlafker.

BLOE.

Oligford.

Beids
Insa.

VVESTFIORDVNG

Perpetua
nives.

Pelle Strand.

Huams huert.

Huams
fiori.

Bald Iokul

Fons syrregulialis qua ob-
mando od da mdm fac
Auarcti   fans foilens
mucina.

Staphalt.

Hiatus terra
fastentes.

Kirlyr.

Halfuorberg

G.

H.

Ellre

Gre ene

I.

Scala milliarium Ilerdorum.

3   10   15   20

Septemtrio.

Grims ey.

Rauda gnupe

Langanes prom.

Rodefkufn

Faxangarga

Kolker

Flatey

Laudey

Grimsefiord
Maffiord
Ranefiord
Sandroy
Duganes

NORDLEN
DINGAFIOR
DVNG.

Strinde

Hvfvvig
Grenefid
Mal
Suar nore

Sand
lokul.

Arnafelds lokul

His nota distinguitur limes inter vtrumq dioecesim

AVSTLENDIN
GAFIORDVNG.

Aradal

Floredalir

Garvig

SVNDLEN
DINGAFIOR
DVNG.

Hekla perpetuas alimentia
pariat et ab horrendis boatu
lapidu evomit

Hiorsfiyd

Brid

Medalland.

Corvi, et falcones albi.

ILLVSTRISS. AC POTENTISS.
REGI FREDERICO II DANIAE,
NORVEGIAE. SLAVORVM. GO
THORVMQVE REGI, ETC. PRIN
CIPI SVO CLEMENTISSIMO.
ANDREAS VELLEIVS
DESCRIBEB. ET DEDICABAT.

IN THE BEGINNING.

e hung, strung up in darkness, while his world crumbled around him.

CHAPTER 1
THE STAG

Buck Moon rises in Islandia.
2163 B.C.

hey called him a trickster but captured him, a fool, a victim of deception, and made him her prisoner. He was at her mercy, but she had none to spare. Slipping through their wicked fingers, he lay hidden, dormant, forgotten until the heinous beings who lost him craved to seize him again.

A prominent figure walked the silent streets of the sleeping town. He appeared out of the darkness and set his sight on the city's fringes. The moon illuminated his metal gold-plated armor, and his crimson cape billowed in the wind behind him as he stepped up to the water at the mouth of the fjord.

His one eye flashed in golden light, and the air sizzled with electricity. For a moment, all remained silent, and then the sea rose to meet him. A corrupted stellar fissure opened in the sky above the water, and a hoofed beast of radiant light stepped out.

"Find him." The golden warrior commanded the animal. "Find him before he has a chance to call forth his true might."

The fissure closed as the beast entered the city, its empyrean aura thundering through the bay while up on the hill in the west wing of Blackstone castle, a youth with long ebony hair and bronze skin was plunged into a terrible dream.

Buck Moon sets,

A celestial display of violet and emerald lights danced across the late evening sky.

High above the sleeping town's cobbled streets, the divine illumination of dancing fiery lights seemed to converge on the black stone castle. Inside his room in the west wing, the second son of Lord Freyr, Úlftýr, lay in bed under the beamed ceiling, sweat-stricken, caught within a nightmare he could not awake from, staring without seeing at the sky through his arched window.

In his nightmare, Úlftýr had flaming scarlet hair and emerald eyes that shimmered in the darkness surrounding him. A complete contrast to his ebony locks and amber eyes he was known for.

In his line of sight, his beloved redhead maiden screamed his name. He had never met her, but he knew with all certainty that she was his. His wife, his life, her light shone, gone before he could reach for her. Amongst those who sought to extinguish his happiness stood his friend, mentor, and betrayer, Baldur, who looked at him with contempt in his azure eyes. Úlftýr's whole demeanor changed at the sight of him, his eyes narrowed, and his body tensed.

Belated, Úlftýr realized Baldur's treachery. Only when the minor deities surrounding him brought him down to his knees and thrust him through the fissure in the crackling sky did he understand the full extent of Baldur's betrayal.

He fell on the other side; a comet plunged to Earth from the heavens. The stars exploded around him as he plummeted down.

He could not stop his descent to Abaddon or free himself from her clutches. A maiden with golden hair that followed his as he fell, a glint of evil in her eyes, and his blood on her hands. The night and the winter, the frost and the death that followed him as he plummeted downward.

They called him a trickster but captured him, a fool, a victim of deception, and made him her prisoner. He was at her mercy, but she had none to spare.

Úlftýr took sick pleasure despite his anguish watching the golden-haired maiden's ire rise. She realized too late that she could not drain his powers without destroying herself along with him.

The heavy iron shackles she cast on his limbs burdened his flesh and soul.

The venom she poured into him burned his insides, the acid ate at him, and her laughter drowned out his screams.

Úlftýr felt the toxin coursing through his veins, poisoning him, pulling him through the veil to seal him away so deep the light would never reach him.

His mind was a jumble of thoughts, and most vividly was the treachery of the one he trusted.

In the distance, Baldur bellowed. It was full of agony and rage as he faced the truth. That the one he betrayed was not to blame. Úlftýr thought Baldur would see his candor, but in Úlftýr's dream, Baldur believed his tormentor's lies.

Úlftýr struggled for breath. And he kept on falling.

He could not escape the nightmare. It hurt too much, and he had no choice but to succumb to the pain.

Úlftýr awoke screaming, still in the clutches of the horror he envisioned. Stunned, he lay on his back, the world tilted on its axis, breathless and disoriented; he tried to remember how to breathe again, the horrors he experienced in the dream too real to deny.

Outside, on the outskirts of town, the wind whispered familiar lullabies through the wide mouth of the fjord. Úlftýr shut his eyes, but the darkness behind his eyelids frightened him. Something called out to him, called him to get up and walk, dazed, outside.

His long, ebony hair billowed in the wind. His somewhat toned arms swayed uselessly at his sides as he shuffled his bare feet. He knew not where the wind was taking him or how long he walked. His footsteps on the lonely, cobbled streets carried throughout the night.

No one saw him as he was drawn further away from the paved streets and into the lonely fields, but he was not the only one awake that night. His shadow fell upon a house.

Dizziness struck Úlftýr. He leaned against the cold brick of the house and listened. In the sweet howl of the night, he could clearly distinguish two different types of breath. One deep and shallow and one high and rapid.

Úlftýr glanced inside from the side window. He wanted to call out to the one inside, but he couldn't; his mouth felt as if it was filled with cotton, and in his brain was a fog he couldn't lift. He remained planted where he stood, watching, while the scene inside unraveled before him.

"Hoder." The pearl-blond youth named Baldur on the bed uttered the name and sat up.

Baldur's hair was disheveled; he exhaled and bent down to look under his wood-framed bed.

Úlftýr caught a glimpse of a pair of azure-colored eyes gleaming at Baldur from the darkness. "What are you doing?" Baldur sat back. "Come out."

The youngling, only seven years of age with flowing golden locks, huffed and pulled himself out from under the bed.

Úlftýr knew the child. Baldur smirked at his little brother, standing in his cream-colored, linen night robes.

They looked similar, with shimmering bright bronze skin and light eyes, but while Hoder's features were soft and delicate, Baldur had already grown to the full height of two meters, with a lean muscular body, and having gained the firm set jaw of a grown álfur. He had azure-colored eyes and a jewel shard the color of rain at the apex of his pointed ears.

"I've heard him again," Hoder whispered, and Úlftýr strained to catch what he said.

Baldur visibly frowned. "Then, why do you not alert mother or father?"

Hoder squirmed under his brother's gaze. "I can't. They're not home; they went to a council meeting."

Now it was Úlftýr's turn to frown. He knew nothing of this late-night council assembly.

Baldur raised his left eyebrow. "A council meeting this late? What about?"

Úlftýr nodded to himself, wanting to have an answer to that as well.

"The stag," Hoder revealed in a high-pitched whisper. They think it's sick, and some unknown illness has made it run around and crash into the houses these last few weeks. And it's here now!"

"Hoder, it was only a dream." Baldur grabbed his hand and pulled the boy closer.

Úlftýr shook his head. "It is not a dream, you fool." He muttered.

For weeks, the stag had been terrorizing the town, breaking down fences and denting the sides of the stone wall houses. Only the night before had the massive animal trampled a farmer. The poor bastard barely escaped with his life as he scrambled before his lord father in a plea to save his crops.

Baldur sighed. "Hoder, you know that Mother would want me to reassure you that there is nothing to fear. The animal, sick or otherwise, cannot harm you. Go back to sleep. It was nothing but-"

A loud thud cut him off. Hoder's eyes widened in fright.

Úlftýr's breath caught in his throat, and he felt the house vibrate. Panic set in as he quickly realized the deranged stag had smashed into the house.

Another thud followed the first, further away from Baldur's front-facing window and closer to Úlftýr.

"Don't move." Baldur told Hoder.

Hoder released a yelp and climbed into his big brother's bed, diving under the covers.

Úlftýr witnessed the exchange and almost laughed.

Baldur rolled his eyes. Clothed only in loose linen trousers, he reached for his double-edged sword slung over the bedpost. Releasing the large blade from the sheath, he stalked closer to the window. Úlftýr watched Baldur, gripping the carved hilt featuring the tree of life until his knuckles whitened, Baldur's muscles tightened, and his tunic rose as he held his breath and peered outside, searching through the semi-darkness.

"It's him!"

"Damn!" Baldur jumped at Hoder's loud whisper behind him. He grabbed Hoder and pinned him to the wall.

"I told you not to move."

"But it's him! It's the stag." Hoder struggled against him.

Baldur released him, and both brothers crouched down and peered through the crack in the open window.

Úlftýr moved past the side window and followed their gaze. He saw the beast too close for comfort.

It looked like an elk, but no elk like Úlftýr had ever encountered. It was big. Too big. Twice the size it should have been. The giant animal huffed, sniffing the air. Suddenly, it raised its head and bolted away from the house back into the sanctuary of the forest.

Úlftýr heard shuffling in the house. He imagined Baldur standing up, sword in hand.

"No. What are you doing?" Hoder whispered loudly; he must have tried to pull Baldur back down.

"He's gone," Baldur said plainly. "It was just an elk. A large elk, yes, but nothing more than that."

"That thing is not normal," Hoder insisted. "He is more like the stag from father's legends than a regular beast."

Baldur snickered. "The legendary stag?" He smirked. "Father should not tell you tales of our ancestral home before bed, brother."

Hoder huffed. "I know what I saw." He sounded like he was about to cry. "He is special, but he is different somehow from the myth. There is something wrong with him."

"Hoder -"

"I don't care if you believe me. I will prove my claim; you'll see."

Úlftýr heard Hoder storm out, slamming the door shut behind him.

Baldur sighed.

Úlftýr stared into the tree line where the stag had bolted to. He couldn't track it down at night, even if he wanted to go after it now. He had tried that already. No, he would have to wait until it's morning again.

Red mist came down over Úlftýr's eyes, something deep in his soul called out to him again. He moved as if hypnotized towards the trees. At some point, he turned around and met Baldur's gaze. The two locked eyes as Baldur held his breath. He squinted at the sight, his eyes widened, and the scene felt too surreal to be true.

Baldur blinked once. Úlftýr was not aware of the strange emerald glowing eyes he now possessed that held Baldur's gaze, and then Úlftýr was drawn further into the forest, leaving green mist behind him as he walked. To Baldur, he seemed to dissipate as he appeared, a mirage in the blackness of night.

CHAPTER 2
THE HUNT

In the morning, Úlftýr and Ingrid, his elder sister, joined Baldur as he stood at the wall of his manor, inspecting the damage. The two siblings stood at similar heights, slightly shorter than Baldur. Five winters separated Baldur and Ingrid, while eight lay between him and Úlftýr.

Úlftýr's ebony hair came down to his waist, while his sister's locks were the color of dark chocolate and stopped mid-back. Both had lean, muscular bodies and amber eyes that followed intently after every move Baldur made.

"You think it was the stag from the legend?" the ebony-haired youth asked.

"Not likely, Úlftýr," his sister said. "He is a myth. Baldur, your father told Hoder one too many tales before bedtime about our shrouded histories." She looked intently at her brother.

The night before had been odd. She found him wandering around the castle, barefoot, his feet muddy, as if he had been walking through the woods. She led him, a sleepwalker, back to his room, and when she helped him to bed, he looked at her, unblinking, and said in the lowest voice she had ever heard from him, "Baldur needs us."

In the morning, when a carrier delivered Baldur's message, calling them to the fields, she had to wonder why she was not surprised.

Baldur looked the teen over; nothing about his stance to indicate he was aware of the night before. Perhaps it was just a mirage. "I don't know." Baldur reached to touch the indented patch on the stone where the stag's colossal antlers had struck the previous night. "Who can tell now what is true but the elders, for they keep their secrets behind closed doors in their dark minds, but I checked the fields this morning, and it got to the crops. I followed the stomped-out path to the cliffs above the valley, then circled back into the forest. Someone must stop it either way. If only to give me a night's rest from Hoder cowering under my mattress."

They all laughed.

Baldur met the prince and princess when Ingrid was shy of eleven winters.

She followed her adventurous brother as he dove under the cliffs at the edge of their city to explore the caves below. Úlftýr's remarkable ability to hold his breath for as long as seven minutes, even at a young age, earned him somewhat of a reputation for displaying the characteristics of a fish.

Ingrid was caught in the surge and was pulled under; Úlftýr didn't notice her follow him, but Baldur did. He got her out but was then swept away himself. If it weren't for Úlftýr, who had just resurfaced and knew how to surf the currents to safety, they would have all drowned.

"We need to hunt him down," Úlftýr said. "Are you in, Ingrid?" He looked at his sister.

"Us three alone, you mean?" Ingrid raised her eyebrow. "Or do you suggest we set out with the council-appointed hunting party?"

"What hunting party?" Úlftýr raised an eyebrow.

Ingrid shook her head in dismay. "You never listen when our father speaks, do you?"

Úlftýr smirked. "What hunting party, Ingrid?"

"The one they established last night." Baldur guessed.

Ingrid nodded.

"Your father will never let you join the hunting party." Hoder piped up from the open window.

Úlftýr, Ingrid, and Baldur glared at the boy in the window, unaware he was there until he spoke.

"What are you doing in my room?" Baldur asked, frowning. "Are you eavesdropping on us?"

Hoder bit his lip. "King Freyr won't let his heirs go," he said in a small voice.

"I'm not an infant." Úlftýr crossed his arms and puffed out his chest.

"Nor am I." Ingrid agreed.

"Even if you are right, we refuse to accept the truth in your words, little one," Úlftýr said.

But Hoder was right. They were babes in the eyes of their people, but caught in the grasp of youth, the words of warning spoken by their elders fell on deaf ears.

That afternoon found them standing in front of the council. A heavy wooden door led into the council chambers. Long, arched windows loomed above them, and Úlftýr's family crest, the two green serpents coiled around a blue rose, decorated the walls. The youths stepped onto the podium, surrounded by fair elder lords and ladies adorned in crimson robes embroidered with gold serpents.

Baldur, the oldest of the three, spoke clearly and passionately of their will to hunt down the beast that stomped out the fields and terrified their young.

"You are not ready." Was the consensus of the assembly. "It is too dangerous," their guardians said.

"I forbid you from taking on this endeavor." The king looked pointedly at his children.

The tall King sat on his golden throne; serpents were carved on either side, their bodies curved forward as if protecting their lord. Lord Freyr was adorned in golden robes, his dark wood-colored hair came down to his shoulders, his face was lean and stern, and it felt like life itself was held in his deep amber-grey eyes.

"I will leave the decision regarding Baldur's participation in this hunt to his father, but you two are staying here where you are safe."

"We are ready." Ingrid protested.

"Even if I considered Úlftýr's' participation, yours is out of the question, Ingrid." The king's words had a finality that Ingrid could not accept.

"You think I'm lesser than my brother." She knew her skin flushed red and hated her emotions for exposing her so clearly.

"You are the next leader of our people. You are to succeed me in due time, and risking yourself for such an endeavor is selfish and childish, Ingrid." the king said with heavy air.

Úlftýr clenched his fists yet said nothing.

However, King Freyr unfailingly caught the gleam in his boy's eyes. In his mind, this affair was far from concluded.

The warriors appointed by the King retired to discuss the best way to capture the animal, and the youths used the commotion to sneak into the main hall behind the royal podium.

"We are still going, though, right?" Baldur asked, making sure they were out of everyone's earshot.

"Yes, my friend," Úlftýr whispered back. "I will not spend my days seated on the council, clad in golden robes, weighted down by royal affairs." He looked at his sister.

"Our place is out amid our land, not between the safeguarded walls of our father's castle." Úlftýr glanced at the end of the hall where several council members still lingered. "We go tomorrow, with or without our father's blessing."

"Yes." Ingrid agreed.

Baldur nodded. As a son of a council member himself, the need to stand tall in his own right was not lost on him.

Before the sun rose the next day, Baldur sneaked out of his house and met the siblings at the unguarded servant's entry into Blackstone Castle. When Baldur was certain no one was about, he signaled Úlftýr and Ingrid when it was safe to come out.

Although Úlftýr and Ingrid were sure that the guards at the main gate would be sympathetic to their endeavor and probably pay no heed to their actions, they did not wish to put them in such a position facing the king. For the guards' sake, they'd better leave them in the dark.

The youths, armed with a short spear, a sword, and an axe each, tracked the elk through the valley. Baldur was aware of the farmers watching them as they inspected the wood fences the beast struck down in its path of destruction.

"Baldur, Ingrid, over here." Úlftýr signaled the two to follow him, following the path of the broken branches at the edge of the fields.

The first light of day shone on the tracks leading out of the timber into a thoughtfully cleared grazing area that ran from the valley to the Grove erected under the castle. The beast's tracks circled as if it were looking for something. A chill stood in the air. In some places, grey patches of dry soil outcropped through an otherwise green field. The branches of the trees surrounding the clearing hung unusually low.

Baldur thought about mentioning the lifeless greenery, but then he saw the beast. "By Odin's eye, he's enormous." Baldur gaped at the beast while it basked in the crystal stream.

It was tremendous for an elk, its fur rough and bushy with twisted antlers resembling a thorny bush. Parts of its fur had fallen off in patches, and where the skin was visible, it appeared wrinkled and blistered.

"Even the surrounding birds ceased their song," Ingrid observed.

Baldur listened intently. "What is this dead silence? That's not right." Baldur began questioning their adventure and the immediate danger he put the King's heirs in. "Perhaps we should get out of here. Let's leave him for the hunting party." He pulled at Úlftýr, crouching closest to him, but the latter remained frozen where he sat.

"*He should not be there. He is corrupting the water*." Úlftýr said, his voice deeper than usual.

Baldur and Ingrid exchanged worried glances, and Baldur looked at his friend. "What?"

"*I see the poison dripping from his antlers*." Úlftýr continued in the same low, deep voice.

Baldur laid a hand on the prince's shoulder. "Úlftýr, what are you talking about?" Unnatural heat emanated from his skin under the black, gold-trimmed tunic he wore.

Úlftýr glanced at him, and Baldur gasped, attempting to shuffle back. Only Úlftýr grasped his hand, his touch scolding.

"Ingrid! Look!" Baldur gulped. "Úlftýr — your eyes,"

His friend never had glowing emerald eyes like the ones that bore into him now.

Ingrid laid her hand on her brother's back but removed it immediately. "Úlftýr?" She, too, felt the heat emanating from him. "What's going on here?"

"*Crossing through the veil corrupted him. He made a mistake*," Úlftýr said, unblinking.

Unease set inside Baldur. "What is happening?" he asked Ingrid. "Is the stag responsible for Úlftýr's odd behavior? What is this creature?"

Úlftýr let him go. "*You, it is you. You are finally by my side, but you don't know who you are*." He closed his eyes.

Baldur caught him when he staggered.

"Úlftýr!" Ingrid moved forward to catch her brother before he hit the ground.

Something in the air around them shifted, a dark energy that wasn't there just a moment ago.

"Ingrid, don't move." Baldur stilled her, the hairs on the back of his neck standing on edge.

The elk raised its head from the water and sniffed. He knew they were there. The silence heavily cloaked the air; not even the wind stirred.

The beast swung its large head in their direction, eyes with no living light pierced into them. Baldur drew his sword out of its sheath with a sharp hiss, prepared to defend them all.

The animal came for them; hooves beat against the forest floor closer and closer, only it suddenly changed course and charged, blind with rage, right past them.

"Where is it going?" Baldur and Ingrid helped Úlftýr up.

For a moment longer, the prince looked confused, and then his eyes returned to normal. Amber and gold.

A scream echoed through the clearing. Baldur cursed under his breath.

"No! It's Hoder." *Did he follow us? Damn him.* Baldur left Úlftýr's arm, and Ingrid lowered her brother back to the ground while Baldur bolted toward the clearing.

"Hoder, run!" He yelled and waved his arms, attempting to catch the wrath of the stag.

Hoder remained planted where he stood in fear. The stag snarled and advanced toward the boy.

"Baldur!" Ingrid broke into the clearing. She whipped her head towards the stag, then back at Hoder, skidded to a stop by the boy, scooped him into her arms, and ran towards the town.

Baldur blinked, taken aback by the Princess's response. Sweat gleamed on his brow. He breathed a sigh of relief and briefly nodded toward the princess, a thin smile on his lips. Then he turned back toward the matter at hand. "Over here, you stupid animal!" Baldur bellowed, drawing the stag's attention towards himself.

It worked. The stag turned on Baldur. Baldur slashed at the animal with his sword, the blade grazing off the massive antlers, Baldur yelled and slashed again, hitting bone. The stag reared and budded the sword right out of Baldur's hand, cutting his wrist in the process.

Baldur drew his spear and launched it at the elk's head. It struck its skull and remained in its fur, dripping thin, grey blood. The elk snorted

15

in rage, more blood trickling out of its nose. He charged in full force, giving Baldur no time to get away.

The beast rammed his massive horns into him, piercing Baldur's shoulder through and remaining in his flesh, protruding from the other side.

The impact with the young álfur did nothing to stop the stampeding animal.

The elk plowed forward with Baldur still skewered on the jagged spikes growing out of his head.

Stomping the ground, sending clumps of earth flying, the elk charged through the valley until it smashed into a nearby tree and stood, its horn trapped in the tree trunk, caught by its own volition.

Baldur grunted, unable to move.

The sound of his friend's pain snapped Úlftýr back to his senses, and he rushed forward, his spear drawn.

The beast saw him coming. It thrashed, attempting to escape, its horns going deeper into Baldur's flesh and drawing more screams from the trapped álfur.

Úlftýr drew closer; his thoughts jumbled up. He wasn't sure how to do it, but he had to get Baldur free. He avoided the elk's powerful back legs with the mistletoe spear raised, kicking the air to bash him. He sidestepped to the right, but not far enough.

A mighty hoof connected with his shoulder, and the impact threw him back. He growled and dove forward; he knew now when the hoof came at him. Ready for another impact, he sidestepped again, leaped off the ground, straddled the beast, and struck the wild animal in its neck, thrusting the spear deeper until the stag stopped moving, slumping where it stood, dead.

Úlftýr jumped down from the stag's dead body, put the spear down, and tugged at the antlers to liberate them from the tree, along with Baldur.

"Are you all right?" Úlftýr reached for the wounds in Baldur's shoulder.

The impact with the stag covered Baldur in sprays of his blood. His breath came in heaves, but he nodded.

"Where is Ingrid?" Úlftýr asked, realizing with a start that there was a gap in his memory.

"Hoder," Baldur breathed in ragged gasps. "The damn kid followed us. I lured the beast away, and Ingrid got him to safety. I hope."

Úlftýr wanted further information about his memory gap, but he would have to wait for a better time. He looked down at the stag's corpse. "Even with all this dead weight, he got himself stuck there." Úlftýr nudged the dead elk.

"My axe," Baldur growled through blood-splattered, gritted teeth.

Úlftýr nodded. He reached for Baldur's belt, pulled out the small battle axe, and started hacking the tips of the antlers. Baldur suppressed his screams and grunts with every hit Úlftýr made as his friend's action caused him great pain. Baldur's eyes darted in every direction as he attempted not to cry. "Úlftýr," Baldur stayed his hand after a few blows to the velvet-coated bone. bone. It moved." Baldur gasped.

"Yeah, I moved it." Úlftýr swung the axe again.

"No, it's alive," Baldur whispered.

Úlftýr glanced at the animal, steam rising from its nostrils. It salivated green goo onto the ground, withering the grass and flowers.

"Shite." The stag's dead eyes opened; the pupils were completely white. It made a screeching sound, lurching up with such ferocity that it knocked Úlftýr to the ground.

The stag screeched again, reeled back, and threw Baldur off his antlers at Úlftýr's side. The elk stomped, enraged at where he fell.

Úlftýr, still on his back, kicked out and pushed Baldur out of the way.

The unmistakable sound of hooves crushing bone echoed through the clearing. Úlftýr yelled, his right leg shattered.

Baldur lifted his head off the ground, coughing out blood.

The elk lowered its head, intending to ram its antlers into Úlftýr. Úlftýr threw his arms up, seized the antlers of the elk standing above him, and, with a swift motion, while the elk bucked and flung his head up, Úlftýr used the beast's own momentum to straddle the monster.

The elk launched forward, and Úlftýr held on for dear life. He covered the elk's eyes with one hand. He desperately held onto the animal's thrashing antlers with the other as the elk raced forward in crazed gallops. Its maniacal movement had one purpose — to toss Úlftýr off.

The stag whined, rose on its hind legs, and Úlftýr held himself from toppling over. He gagged, the stench of sulfur coming from the stag overwhelming.

In the last moment, he grabbed the stag's shaggy neck and opened himself to a vicious bite, the stag's saliva stinging like acid.

He only had one shot. He knew where they were headed- he recognized the path. The cliff at the edge of the clearing drew nearer.

Something took hold of Úlftýr then. A tint of red clouded his vision. Something primal, an ancient force, stirred awake within him.

He plunged his injured arm deeper into the stag's mouth, squeezed his neck with all his might with the other, and ripped the head of the stag towards him while the precipice loomed before his eyes.

The next moment was a blur of crashing limbs and sounds of struggle. Úlftýr punched the animal, wrenched his arm from its mouth, and leaped off. The stag snapped at him, toppled over the precipice, and fell to the rocks below.

Úlftýr lay on the ground, panting, his right leg numb, his arm stinging but, miraculously, alive.

He must have blacked out because Baldur, Ingrid, and Hoder were beside him when he opened his eyes again.

"Úlftýr!" Baldur loomed over him.

"That was spectacular!" Hoder stared at the prince, his eyes gleaming.

Baldur shot him with a disapproving glare. "Mad. The words you are looking for are completely mad. Úlftýr, that stag could've killed you, and I would be to blame."

"Nonsense." Ingrid shoved him playfully. "It would be on this lunatic." She pointed at Úlftýr. "I'm glad you're alive, little brother." She said, smiling.

Úlftýr chuckled and squirmed to find the proper position for his injured arm. "Don't take it to heart, dear Baldur." He attempted a smile.

Baldur shook his head. "Think you can sit up?"

"I'm not sure — what about the stag? Is it dead for good this time?"

"We couldn't see beyond the shrubbery at the bottom when we looked over the edge. We can return for it when you feel better and find out." Ingrid looked at the cliff. "But I think it's safe to assume it wouldn't survive a drop like that, and he won't be climbing back up."

The tension ebbed from their minds; they smiled to each other in relief for surviving this endeavor, and in the silence that followed, the sound of nearing hooves rang in the air.

"Úlftýr. Ingrid." King Freyr, mounted on his grey mare, followed by the King's guard, appeared at the edge of the clearing. The royal procession made haste to reach them.

When the guards told King Freyr that Úlftýr and Ingrid had gone from their chambers, he knew precisely where the youths were going.

They found them fast, tracking the carnage the stag's rampage left through the valley.

King Freyr halted by Úlftýr, still lying flat on his back. The boy looked up at his father.

"Anything you have to say for yourself?" The King asked calmly, sending chills down Úlftýr's spine.

Baldur balled his fists and sprang up. "King Freyr, it was my idea; I lured the princes here with the promise of adventure…."

The king silenced him with his gaze. Baldur shuffled back.

"What about you?" Freyr asked Ingrid.

Ingrid bit her lip but then stood up. "I did what I thought was right and am glad at the outcome."

"She saved me!" Hoder bubbled excitedly. "She plucked me from before the monster and carried me to safety."

A gleam of pride crossed the King's face before his station concealed it. "We shall discuss this further at a later date. Now, to the infirmary. All of you." He signaled to his King's guard. "Take him first." He gestured at Úlftýr.

"Baldur." Úlftýr groaned.

"I'm right behind you," Baldur said. Ingrid stepped up to him, and along with another guard, they helped him up to a grey mare.

King Freyr ordered his men to leave the beast where it lay.

Days passed, weeks followed, and the healers finally deemed Úlftýr well enough to leave the castle grounds.

When Úlftýr and Baldur set out to retrieve the beast's remains this time, it was with the King's blessing.

"Ingrid won't be joining us," Úlftýr told Baldur when the latter came to collect him from the castle. "She is sitting on her second council today after she rather enthusiastically advocated for us to see our mission through."

"After its nearly deadly outcome," Baldur smirked.

Úlftýr smiled; he was proud of Ingrid. She was where she belonged in the castle while they belonged in the wild. With that, the youths came back to the cliff.

They scavenged for the stag's remains through the rocks and shrubbery at the bottom until they found it.

"Oh, what…?" Baldur was reluctant to touch the remains. "How strange."

"You're right," Úlftýr agreed. "Even though only a month had passed, only bones remained. Look at this; this grey skin that covers the remains and that green sludge-like substance; what a horrible stench." He stepped closer. "Ah! The antlers are intact."

Baldur looked at him sideways. "So, what about it?"

Úlftýr's eyes flashed with excitement. "I am going to collect them and hang them in the throne room of Blackstone Castle."

"Are you sure that is wise?"

"Of course," Úlftýr edged closer. "Mounted on the wall for all to see, they will remind me of my, Ingrid's, and your first hunt together and the bond of friendship that saved us."

"I hope nothing bad will come of it," Baldur whispered, watching the prince lift the sharp bone out of the sludge.

CHAPTER 3
THE SETTLEMENT

Four centuries passed since Baldur, Ingrid, and Úlftýr chose to stand together against the evil stag that plagued their land.

Hoder, dressed in earth-tone robes trimmed by green snakes as a scholar of the serpent, came to the barracks behind the castle to speak to his brother, Baldur, who was pleased with his new post as captain of the royal guard.

They stood in front of each other, sizing each other up before they spoke. Baldur watched his little brother, who was not so little anymore. Hoder grew as tall as him; his face was no longer slim but fuller, and his muscles came in, although not as prominent as Baldur's were. For some reason, he kept his hair shoulder length. Perhaps it was to differentiate himself from his brother further.

Baldur recognized unease on his little brother's face. The way Hoder shifted his eyes, darting every which way, his hand touching the blue shard embedded in the apex of his ear. He might have seemed at ease standing like that to everyone else, but Baldur knew something stirred beneath the surface.

He attempted not to show his anger at Hoder's recent actions, which did not include him.

They stood inside the black walls. Hoder was reluctant to reveal his reason for coming, so Baldur did it for him.

"You should have told me you are going in front of the council. Why do I need to hear of it when the deed is already done?"

Hoder shuffled his feet. "Would you have supported my cause, or would you have stood against it?"

"Does it matter now what my thoughts would have been? Markian told me you are leaving already." Baldur said.

"And you won't attempt to talk me out of it?" Hoder asked.

"I would if I believed my speech would yield desirable results." Baldur crossed his arms. "An expedition to explore the Ice Lands headed by our brightest scholars. Courageous, daring, or foolish, and I haven't decided which yet."

Hoder chuckled. "You are so formal, Captain."

Baldur rolled his eyes. "I just need you to explain your desire to go," Baldur said. "What do you want there that you can't find in our land?" He grabbed Hoder's arms. "Join my ranks, and I'll give you excitement if that is what you seek. We shall explore this whole island together."

"I was a frightened child," Hoder looked away, avoiding Baldur's questioning eyes. "Content in the peace of my little patch of land, but I feel now that we might as well be prisoners in a gilded cage. Any question, any thought we have of the outside world, is shut down by the elders. They keep reminding us of the darkness they escaped in our homeland, and we spend our lives forever in debt to the ones who sacrificed themselves to bring us to these safe shores. I do not want to diminish their memory, but there must be more in this world for us to discover."

Baldur shook his head. "What exactly do you hope to find, Hoder?"

Hod's eyes turned distant. "I feel the force that sustains our land and guards our long lives is dwindling; something is coming for us. Perhaps not now, but we must be vigilant for enemies we have yet to encounter. Most of all, I am looking for a reason, Baldur. I am looking for a reason the great ice serpent saved us and brought us here, but it is not here that I will find it. There," he gestured at the window. "Is where I may discover it. And, perhaps, once I leave, my path to the truth will become clear."

Baldur laid a hand on Hod's shoulder. "Can I do or say anything that would convince you to stay?" Baldur inquired, knowing the answer before his brother provided it.

Hoder looked at him. "Is there anything I can do or say to convince you to come with me?"

A sad smile tugged at the corner of Baldur's lips. "I cannot go where your spirit calls you, Hoder. As much as I crave adventure and exploring the unknown with you, my duties lay here. When you return home, brother, I will welcome you with open arms."

Hoder laughed wholeheartedly, embracing his brother. "Where else would you go?"

Several decades later, Ice Lands settlement.

The days were peaceful in the little village they had built for themselves.

Although, at first, the terrain gave them no mercy, they found a way to tame it.

They built their settlement on higher ground close to the coastline, with reasonable boat access for fishing, which thankfully was plentiful. The area they chose was a flat, well-drained region, and several large farmsteads were erected within its limits.

The scholar Markian, in his earthtone robes, sat by a roaring bonfire in an outdoor communal fire pit. He had a chiseled jawline, slightly pouty lips, and striking green eyes.

His mate, Hoder, sat behind him. He had just finished braiding the side of Markian's head.

"I shall go tend to the animals," Hoder said.

Markian nodded; he leaned back into him and sight contently when Hoder kissed his head and rubbed his shoulders before he got up to continue the chores of his day.

Alongside Markian, several others were busy with different activities; some made food and some carved tools, a pastime they had established to teach the younglings to adapt to the resources the land provided.

Markian held a wood slab in his hands, and on it, he carved the royal family's crest in bright color: two green serpents intertwined around a blue rose.

He was showing it to a group of younglings who attempted to copy his design on their own slabs.

Hoder walked past them with his livestock, intending to lead them to their grazing field beyond the hill. He smiled at Markian, and the latter blushed. Markian averted his eyes towards the path leading to the beach and gasped.

Several mortal creatures stood there, heaving. Markian had seen them before when they arrived at the beach in their small wooden vessels. They kept to themselves for a while, and Hoder warned that their peace with the strangers would not last. At first, Markian wanted to believe they could find a way to live together, but now here they stood, their red and yellow hair disheveled and their flushed bodies covered in various animal hides.

For the quietest and most horrible moment, the dauðadýr —as Markian came to call them—faced his tall, innocent people. Then, a bellow of attack rumbled through the mortals, a call to arms to claim this land as their own.

"Markian, the younglings!" Hoder shouted. He was the first after Markian to notice the mortals at the edge of the camp.

Chaos erupted. The Ljósálfar fled their attackers while the dauðadýr pursued them—butchering, slaughtering, slaying, and cutting down any Ljósálfar that got in their path.

The dauðadýr slaughtered everyone. The grown males, the females, and their offspring, no one was spared.

Soon, blue blood had covered the stomped-out ground.

Those who remained alive after the slaughter fled their settlement, with Markian leading the survivors to an agreed-upon hideout deep in the mountains.

Hoder decided to turn back despite Markian's protest. The courageous warrior volunteered to return home to his beloved city to call for help.

Markian understood why he volunteered to go. Hoder had to ensure the safety of those who followed him, a true sign of a leader, and he had to ensure Markian was safe. For the briefest of moments, Markian got to secure Hoder in his arms, and then it was over.

Hoder said goodbye to Markian on the dirt path. They embraced, and Markian mouthed words of love to Hoder while their heads were bowed against each other. Hoder kissed Markian's tears away while his heart clenched. They both knew that this might be the last time they would see each other alive.

Elska hid until she could hide no longer. When the attack came, she was knocked out and woke up sprawled atop bodies in the prayer house. She wanted to cry, to call out for help, but she couldn't, and the door kept opening as the mortal monsters tossed more of her brethren in.

She lay with her long red hair covering her tear-stricken face and watched the light of day going down outside.

Finally, when she was sure they had all fallen asleep, she stumbled away from the fallen and carefully opened the large wooden door. Charred square-shaped stone foundations marking former houses met her eyes. The stench of burning flesh and fresh blood stood in the air.

Such miserable lone indicators there was once life here.

It seemed only the one building she was in remained standing. An enormous rune stone depicting the voyage of the Ljósálfar from Ljosalfheim on the back of the great ice serpent stood as a monument at the entrance.

The sacred ground was overturned with the Ljósálfar's desperate, fleeting feet and with the marks of the barbarous advancement of the mortal warriors upon them.

Elska breathed hard, her eyes darting in every direction. She stepped forward, and a large shadow fell on her small frame. She turned and screamed. The brute seized her by the throat and lifted her up; the mortal wearing a bear's fur growled and shook her. He flung her to the wall of the prayer house. She hit the stone and slid down, winded. Her ears rang, her heart raced, and when she looked up, the bear man was upon her. His claws racked through her arm, leaving behind throbbing, painful red claw marks, three gashes open, and bleeding in her flesh.

She screamed, and suddenly, the brute was pulled from her.

"Run!" Hoder ordered. He struck the bear man on the head and tackled him to the ground. "Go!"

An uproar from the mortals brought her back to her senses. Elska pushed away from the wall and ran, tears streaming down her face. She didn't want to see the mortals capture Hoder.

The dauðadýr pursued him to the beach. Their arrows pierced his flesh. Miraculously, he endured several direct hits to commandeer one of their small boats and propel it into the sea.

Blood poured from his wounds. Elska's sensitive ears could not drown out Hoder's cries of horrified surprise and then heartbreaking anguish and the thud of his body collapsing, hitting the bottom of the boat with a sickening wet thud while the waves carried him away.

They followed him, attempting to crash into Hoder's vessel before he made port, but something took them from the deep. Something large in deep purple and shimmering blue slithered from under the waves and took out most of them before they had a chance to pursue Hoder further.

Midgardr, Capital Region, Islandia.
The end of the Samhain month.
1708 B.C.

Úlftýr, the second prince of Islandia, tossed and turned in his wood canopy bed in the west wing of Blackstone castle.

Sweat stricken, he opened his eyes and reached for his neck. An invisible hand had held him in a vice grip. Úlftýr gasped and struggled, the weight of the unknown assailant squeezing the life out of him.

Suddenly, as if someone lifted him, he was flung out of the bed. He hit the wall and slid down, winded. His ears rang, his heart raced, and when he looked down, he witnessed a throbbing, painful red mark appear on his arm, claw marks, three gashes open, and bleeding in his arm.

Úlftýr sat for a while, rattled, sucking in the air. He had experienced such terror before, and his fog-filled mind, like before, guided him to Baldur.

He left the castle barefoot, wearing only his black linen pants. His steps barely made a sound on the stone pavement.

He appeared out of the fog like a mirage, and his guards raised their swords to face him before they realized who he was.

Baldur, the fair captain of the Ljósálfar guard, heard the commotion the prince's arrival created at the barracks entrance and hurried down from his room to guide him in.

"What happened?" Baldur asked the prince, referring to the marks on his neck after they were seated behind closed doors, and Baldur gave the order to keep quiet about the prince's presence amongst his soldiers. "Who attacked you?"

Úlftýr shook his head. "I don't know, a dream, a demon from my night terrors that followed me back from the sleeping world."

"You are already healing," Baldur said, inspecting the claw marks. "Have you seen something? A vision?" Úlftýr's strange eyes from centuries before still Haunted Baldur. "Is something coming for us again? Another beast?"

"I don't think the injuries are actually mine." Úlftýr rubbed the red marks. "It's more of an echo, but I felt her. I felt her fear and her pain." He said, his eyes glazed over as if he was still inside that dream.

"Her?" Baldur raised an eyebrow.

"What?" Úlftýr blinked.

"You said 'her,'" Baldur confirmed.

Úlftýr hummed. "Did I? I didn't realize..." He gasped and grabbed Baldur's hand. "She needs me." He declared.

"Who?" Baldur demanded.

Before Úlftýr could speculate on the answer, the ancient bronze bells at the outpost of Engey island, north of the capital, summoned the warriors in sharp alarm. The wind carried the sound howling through the town set by the long, narrow fjord.

"Get your armor," Baldur commanded. He ran to the door. "Everyone up!" He bellowed down the hall.

Soon after, they were ready. Mounting their steeds, their horses galloped through town, arriving at the city's docks, sword at hand, flanked by their battalion.

The docks were deserted when they approached, the bells calling anyone who was out and about - inside.

The sound of the sea was the only noise louder than the Ljósálfar warriors. The waves crashed against the weathered boards, resonating with the clanks of the metal they wore.

Captain Baldur's blue eyes caught sight of a small dory boat swaying back and forth, helpless to the waves carrying it to shore.

His ears twitched, and the yellow jewel shard embedded at the apex of his ears gleamed, catching the dying light of day.

He signaled his troops to follow suit with Úlftýr by his side. They rode, mounted on dun fjord horses, slowly advancing closer.

Dark blue blood stained the small boat, and it pooled at the bottom of the wooden craft, giving it the appearance of tar-black water.

A motionless figure wrapped in a blood-soaked cloth lay in the murky puddle of the boat's water. "He must be of álfur descent," Baldur told Úlftýr, dismounting. Úlftýr nodded.

He and their warriors advanced carefully, with measured steps toward the boat.

Before they reached it, however, a movement shifted the broad-leafed reeds on their right. Baldur turned just as a rabid savage burst through the tall grass and charged, frenzied, at them with his short metal blade raised above his head.

"Baldur!" Úlftýr drew his sword in a flash. He sidestepped his captain, grabbed Baldur's shoulder, pulled him back, and plunged the blade into the charging man, dispatching him of this life.

The man collapsed. Laying on his back, blood spilled out of his mouth as he gurgled his last breaths. His red hair was coarse and filthy, and his clothes were a patchwork of animal hides.

"Search the reeds," Úlftýr ordered. "There might be more. Baldur," He looked at the captain, who had his eyes set on the motionless figure in the dory boat.

"I have to see," Baldur said.

The captain planted his right hand on the boat's gunwale and vaulted in, landing by the still form. He sheathed his blade and crouched in the filthy water, where the smell of seawater and metal assaulted his nostrils.

For a moment, he hesitated, summoning his courage. He reached out his hand and lifted the dark material.

"No!" A horrified cry ripped out of Baldur's throat.

His warriors shifted and gasped behind him; they recognized the injured álfur.

A face much like Baldur's, framed by damp, golden curls, lay bloody and beaten under the fabric.

Baldur clutched the dirty cloth in his trembling fist, terror gripping him. He brushed aside the messy locks from his brother's unconscious face.

"Hoder! Hod!" Without thinking, Baldur pulled his brother into his arms and shook him in a desperate search for a sign of life.

The bulk of the arrows stuck under the fabric and came into full view when Baldur tore away the cloth wrapped around Hoder. The captain revealed Hoder's mangled body, pierced through with arrows of such size and build as Baldur had never encountered before.

"Bal..." Hoder exhaled in a shuddering breath. His pale blue, bloodshot eyes fluttered open, "Am I... I'm back?"

"What happened?" Baldur held him tighter, willing Hod's fleeting life to remain within him.

Hod shivered.

Baldur looked at his brother's contorted face. "Hoder, what horrors broke your brave soul?"

"Attacked," Hoder coughed violently. "The outpost, I left them." He grabbed onto Baldur's tunic. "I had to," Hod whispered. "They slaughtered my people, and they've destroyed - everything." He closed his eyes, and Baldur thought he wouldn't open them again, but then Hoder rasped. "Bal, Markian is still alive." Hoder spoke, blood trickling from his mouth.

He reached a shaking hand into his robes, but it faltered and fell back to his side. Baldur followed his movement, reached into Hoder's robes, and produced a leather-bound map.

Baldur released the strap, and the etched leather fell open.

"Here..." Hoder marked the spot with his blood past Mirpur rósaviður forest in the south valley. "Please, they need you. Don't let - Markian die." His eyes shone with unshed tears.

Baldur eyes stung, and he gripped the tattered cloth harder. "Hod?" His voice came out faint, cracking before he could finish his name. The stillness of his brother's mutilated body told him enough, but he squeezed the cloak until his nails broke the skin of his palm. "Hoder!" he pleaded. He didn't dare to hope anymore for an answer.

Hoder returned his soul to the great serpent of the sea.

Baldur looked down at Hoder's still face. He crushed his brother's limp body to his chest, his hands trembling. His throat thickened, and shuddering breaths racked through him as Baldur barely held himself together. Pain violently swept over him. He made a desperate plea then to the great serpent waiting for them in the depths of the sea. "Grant us favorable winds and swift victory, and give me the strength to fulfill the vow my blood calls for."

Úlftýr, second in command to Baldur by his own choice, laid a hand on his captain's shoulder. His long, ebony hair fell to his waist, and his amber eyes held the deep-cutting pain he felt.

"We must make my lord father aware of this," he said. Baldur remained silent for a while longer, his gaze fixed on the still features of his dead brother, forevermore destined to remain unchanged, and then he sharply nodded.

He got up with his brother in his arms, refusing the help of his subordinates. He placed the body onto his grey mare and solemnly mounted the beast. He briefly nodded at the fists the company held tight to their chest. The show of respect was not lost on Baldur, and a new determination burned inside him.

Úlftýr signaled their troops to step back with his hand, acknowledging their distraught and sorrowful expressions. They found the second boat the foul creature used, which had been overturned in the water. There was no one else besides them, and Úlftýr ordered the mortal to be taken away and back to the castle to be examined later for questions he still had.

The streets were eerily empty when they rode through the town, and those still out hastily cleared the path for them before disappearing behind beautifully carved wooden doors and robust iron latches.

Baldur kept his face devoid of emotion. The gazes peering through the creaks of open windows witnessed Baldur ride with Hod's dead body in his arms and follow him through the paved streets; Hod's head lolled against his chest.

Baldur ignored the cries of horror, the gasps of astonishment, and the mournful wails the dreadful sight of Hod conjured.

Without another word, Baldur carried his brother's body through the town to the safeguarding walls of his lord's castle, home of King Freyr and Queen Gerðr.

CHAPTER 4
THE COUNCIL

News of Hod's death spread through the valley. One by one, the Ljósálfar gathered to pay him their last respects.

The court's maidens arranged Hoder's body in the middle of the inner courtyard, on top of a stone table, on a bed of blue roses. They cleaned and clothed Hoder in the finest, shimmering cobalt-blue silk robes that fluttered in the light breeze of the evening, and the movement gave the illusion of breath in his chest.

Hod's long, golden locks shone in the dwindling sunlight. His face remained peaceful.

Baldur didn't stay to observe them as they removed the arrows deeply embedded in Hod's flesh. He mourned his brother in constraints reserved for a trained warrior.

Taking measured steps, Baldur left his brother's body in the castle's courtyard in the care of the sorrowful maids.

Baldur kept a glacial gaze, holding himself back from his will to wail to the heavens. For Hoder's sake, Baldur refrained from showing his weakness publicly, for he needed to set on his quest for retribution.

Conversations hushed as Baldur walked stiffly past the many who gathered. Eyes avoided him, and the air grew thick like the blood that clung to his clothes. In the new quiet, the sound his feet made amplified and thundered on the stone pathway as he strained to keep moving forward without falling.

Baldur spoke to no one when he entered the black stone barracks behind the castle, and others knew not to disturb him. Hoder's blood stuck to him like a beacon of sadness.

Baldur never thought of how claustrophobic the black granite bathroom was. He stood there in the confined square space, his thoughts in the tomb Hoder's body was destined for—the nothingness that awaited him, the void that threatened to devour Baldur along with his brother. Hoder was to be locked away too soon, sealed from the light of the sun forever.

He peeled the bloodstained garb clinging to his skin. The rind repulsively refused to fall away.

He threw the clothes to the ground, and they made a sickening sound hitting the granite.

Hod's last moments flashed before his eyes. Baldur still felt him in his arms, his life draining, slipping away through Baldur's fingers. The heaviness of the cloth he was wrapped in, like a death shroud weighing him down, dragging him into the darkness of the underworld.

The horrible arrows that brutally mangled his body stuck out through his clothes. Baldur didn't want to know where all the blood came from; he didn't want to look past his brother's eyes, but he felt Hoder's shattered body in his arms and the wheezing in his dying breaths.

Baldur's trembling fingers found the lever, and he pushed it over and released the water pumped from the hot springs that ran parallel to the castle. It churned through the lead pipes with deep rumbling until it burst from the overhead stone faucet onto his skin.

Baldur didn't flinch. He stared, unseeing, at the blue blood trickling down his hands and chest, carried away into the drain while the scalding water beat against his limbs. Baldur cried out and drove his fists into the wall, too distraught to experience the pain of the impact. He grunted and collided with the wall behind him.

Steam rose from his skin, where the water released him of Hod's partially dried blood. Baldur breathed hard. The burning fumes stung his eyes, invaded his nose, and suffocated him. He heaved and fell, beating the wet floor repeatedly with his fists until his trembling hands no longer supported him, and he collapsed, turning over from the offending stream that still relentlessly poured from above.

He had only one thought: lying in a fetal position.

More than anything, he wanted vengeance because regret would eat him alive if he allowed it to take hold of his mind.

Úlftýr wanted to wait until Baldur got out of the barracks to speak to him, but when his sensitive ears picked up Baldur's anguished shout, he rushed in.

Úlftýr found Baldur lying on the wet floor, his eyes shut and a stream of scorching water beating his shaking body. Without thinking, Úlftýr stepped into the narrow space and crouched beside him.

"Baldur?" Úlftýr's voice seemed to make the proud warrior shrink further into himself.

Úlftýr got up, shut off the stream, and crouched back to take hold of his friend. Baldur allowed Úlftýr to pull him to his feet and leaned on him as Úlftýr led him to the changing chamber.

"Hoder...the outpost...we have to – " Baldur uttered.

"I know," Úlftýr said. "Let me help you."

Baldur nodded. He stood, unsteady on his feet, while Úlftýr helped him to put on his formal attire. The crimson robes weighed on him more than his silver ceremonial armor, symbolizing the mental battle he was about to endure.

"Thank you," Baldur said on their way out of the barracks. "But I have to do this next part by myself."

He entered the castle to request an audience with the King and the Council of Elders. He had a job to do.

The royal court swiftly granted his request.

Twelve hours hadn't passed since Hoder took his last breath when Baldur stood before the assembly in the middle of the circular room, illuminated by the sunlight.

The center of the circular room where he stood grew hot as the rising sun beamed in from high arching windows. Baldur imagined himself slowly roasting alive at the bottom of a cauldron under the scrutinizing gazes of the elders seated on white marble benches that encased the room. He stood before the raised podium of King Freyr, determined to fulfill his brother's last honorable wish. The conversation had all but halted as they awaited Baldur to convey his intentions to the expected council.

"My Lords." Baldur bowed, and his posture appeared firm, but if someone had stood beside him, he would have seen Baldur tremble. "I beseech you; allow me to take command of the full extent of our armed forces," he urged the council. "Let me march against the savages that destroyed our settlement in the Ice Lands."

Murmurs of agreement rustled throughout the council chamber, but no one voiced their opinion. Sixty-six lords and ladies of the court sat in the council chamber, and all waited for the Elders to cast their votes.

Nine Elders gathered to call forth the great Ice Serpent who rescued their kin from the oncoming darkness. Four remained now to tell the tale. They were seated high above the other members of the council. Mounted on sovereign rests, each space entwined by the color of their jewel shards etched in crystals inside the marble. Red, yellow, and blue.

Old and weathered skin couldn't hide the wisdom and life that still sparkled from their assessing eye like the gems that surrounded them.

One of the four Elders donned in golden robes like his brethren, who witnessed Jörmungandr, the great serpent, address Baldur first.

Svarta, the ancient among them, earned the place of a well-respected council member throughout the centuries. From where he stood, Baldur perceived the sunlight hitting Svarta's silver hair, which had long lost its luster, creating a wave of luminance that danced behind him.

"I am sorry for your loss," Svarta looked down at Baldur.

All fell silent and listened to the wise old álfur speak.

"Your brother," Svarta said. "May he find Álfheimr again; knowing the risks involved in his journey and ignoring our warning, he still set out."

Baldur had to bite his tongue to stop himself from interrupting the Elder's words and lashing out at him.

"When Hoder stood here before us," Svarta continued, "we warned him and those who followed that they did so at their own peril."

Baldur's body trembled, his fists clenched, and he longed to grip his sword. He had to fight back the heat rising to his face. He knew that if the King and the council refused him, he would gather those loyal to him and go off on his own. He begged the gods not to put him in that position.

Another Elder, Siran, had risen to address the assembly.

His dark eyes could pierce anyone through with his gaze alone. His stare burrowed into Baldur's rigid mind, attempting to penetrate his hardened soul.

"We, who journeyed here from Ljosalfheim, set on that fateful voyage to escape the darkness that consumed our homeland." He shook his head, "And Hoder – " He paused. "You shall forgive me for saying so, Baldur; set out on his quest to quench his spirit's thirst for adventure."

A rumble of agreement, siding with the Elder's wisdom, passed through the assembly.

"I do not doubt the Elders' purpose in leaving our home world," Baldur said, his voice low, the rage boiling inside him contained only by the honor of his station. "You came here for the safety of your offspring, yet you confined us to these shores. You granted us freedom from the darkness, yet you discouraged us from ever attempting to find another source of light. I can only wish that I possessed the same courage my brother had. Perhaps, then, he would still be alive. A ship in the harbor is safe, my lord, but that is not what we build a ship for."

Baldur turned to King Freyr in the silence that gripped the council. The King looked at him from the royal podium, his golden robes shimmering with threads that moved like serpents.

"I beg you, my King," he bowed low. "I beg my lord and this council to grant me the mandate to preserve our freedom."

The King looked down at his loyal captain. "I am weary, Baldur," Freyr said in a solemn, considered manner.

"I am wary of the prospect of putting any more of our people in danger over this endeavor. What proof do we have that I would not be sending you and those who follow you to perish at the hands of the foul creatures who snatched your brother from the living? What proof do you have that the settlers Hoder left behind are still alive, and you can save them?"

The pain on Baldur's face struck Úlftýr deep.

Earlier, Úlftýr accompanied Baldur from a distance as he laid Hod's body on the stone table in the inner courtyard. Úlftýr morbidly thought about what he would have done, what he would have felt if that had been him saying goodbye to his older sister, Ingrid.

Úlftýr clenched his fists. He glanced at Ingrid.

"Go." His sister mouthed.

Úlftýr took a deep breath. Ingrid always knew what thoughts plagued him.

Encouraged, and before anyone could stop him, Úlftýr stepped down from the royal podium and marched up to Baldur, catching him off guard. Úlftýr positioned himself beside Baldur and turned to face the assembly to the astonished gasps of the court's lords and ladies.

Their laws dictated the exact order of presentation of one's request to the council and the sequence in which the royal family and the council members cast their votes.

It was unheard of for a royal Prince to take a stance against his lord father.

Úlftýr glanced at Baldur, who looked back at him, puzzled, and then turned to face Freyr, ignoring the outraged hum of the council for his blatant disregard for protocol.

He stared at his father with apparent defiance in his eyes. "I believe that, no matter how far they are, how bitter the cold is on the road that leads there, and how few they were or how steep the mountain they erected their outpost upon, we would always be there for our brethren. Because they are us, and we are them." He said, poised in front of the King, a kindred spirit to Baldur, determined in Baldur's quest he now regarded as his own.

"As my memory serves, Father, you taught us to stand by our people."

Úlftýr looked at the silent assembly, the lords and ladies that stared at him in admiration and some with disdain.

"The sea is just another road for us to cross, another mountain to climb. The Ljósálfar still alive in the Ice Lands are our people, Father, and they are a part of us." Úlftýr looked hard into his lord Father's eyes.

"I know that if it was Ingrid or me, bereft of life, lying on that stone table, and it had been our dying wish, you would not hesitate to fulfil it at once."

Úlftýr caught the shudder his father attempted to conceal.

Úlftýr looked at his mother. The chestnut-haired Queen sat by his lord's father's side.

He was pleased to discover her hands intertwined against her chest - a smile of pride on her face.

His older sister, Ingrid, who had grown to resemble their mother more than his father, sat slightly flushed and embarrassed by the sudden attention Úlftýr's remark drew to her. Despite her long life and abundant years sitting beside her father on the council, she was not adept at having total command of the crowd. Despite this, she knew her influence mattered, and so she, too, nodded in approval.

She smiled at Úlftýr; her smile carried genuine warmth, and Úlftýr smiled back.

Ingrid often told her younger brother she wished she had the boldness Úlftýr maintained to act recklessly enough for life to be interesting. At the same time, she was content to limit her travels to the scrolls of their library and her poetry books.

Freyr let out a sigh and regained his composure.

He stood from his throne, and Baldur took a knee, readying himself for the King's verdict.

"I can't deny the truth in my son's words," Freyr said. "Baldur," The King's booming voice carried through the council chamber. All eyes were on him; all ears hung on what lord Freyr would say next.

Baldur stood to attention and bent his head in respect.

"I will give you command of three of our finest ships. You shall choose a crew of Ljósálfar loyal to you and set sail to the Ice Lands to retrieve our people." He spoke those last two words with an emphasis and a faint smile directed at Úlftýr.

Baldur bowed to Freyr and then to Úlftýr. "Thank you." He whispered to the prince.

"My lords and ladies, I dismiss you," Freyr said. He looked down at Baldur. "Captain, a word before you go." He rose to step down into his private passage.

"Yes, my king." Baldur bowed again to the prince and followed the King to the corridor behind the royal podium. "Before you depart to prepare for the journey, Baldur, I bid you swear an oath to me," Freyr said when Baldur joined him.

Baldur bowed. "Anything, my King."

He noted that Bileygr, the one-eyed elder, and the King's chancellor, stood within earshot distance.

During the debate they had just participated in, Bileygr stood silently behind the King. He was running a hand down his white beard while contemplating. Baldur knew he was being watched, feeling the weight of the one-eyed observer's piercing gaze, always assessing with a depth that surpassed most with two eyes.

Baldur believed that Bileygr could easily persuade the King to change his mind if he opposed his journey.

Apprehensive about his support, Baldur decided not to question the Elder's motives.

"Knowing my son," said the King, "Úlftýr will offer himself to battle, and seeing his power of persuasion firsthand, he will try to convince you to bring him with you. Under no circumstances are you to agree to his request. Do I make myself clear?"

Baldur nodded. "My King, I understand your worry about your daring, bold son." Baldur resisted the urge to smile as memories of their youth flooded his mind.

"I won't let you down, sire. I will resist his words; my quest shall not harm him. Úlftýr will remain home." He swore, readying himself for an inevitable fight.

That night, while Baldur packed for the voyage in his bedchamber and contemplated a battle plan, a knock on his front door startled him out of his thoughts.

Baldur went to the door with growing concern and opened the lock.

"Úlftýr," he breathed out. "My dear friend, your sight does put my heart at case. I feared the King might have changed his mind."

"How are you holding up?" Úlftýr stepped over the threshold and embraced Baldur. They parted, and Baldur beckoned him in.

"You must allow me to come with you. I know you intend to leave me behind." Úlftýr insisted. He closed the door behind him and followed Baldur in.

"No, my Prince." Baldur stepped back, bowed his head, and looked into Úlftýr's golden amber eyes. "You have done more than I could have ever asked of you or dared to hope for, and I will forever be grateful to you. But I will not, in good conscience, allow you to accompany us, and I will not have your blood on my hands."

Úlftýr frowned. "That is not the answer I hoped to hear; my blood is my own to do with as I please," Úlftýr said, frowning.

"That may be so, but my blood is your father's to do with as he pleases," Baldur guffawed.

Úlftýr snorted.

"Please, Úlftýr, do not make me go against my King. He had been lenient with us in our youth, and it almost cost you your life. I doubt he will forgive now if I put you in mortal danger again." Baldur continued, smiling at the prince's reaction. "Your life is a bright beacon of light and hope for our people." He breathed. "I do not intend to offend or disappoint you,"

Úlftýr's golden gaze never wavered from Baldur's eyes.

Baldur knew the young Prince did not want to appear weak. After decades Úlftýr spent training along with those now considered brethren, Baldur understood. He secretly hoped Úlftýr would defy his king and join them, but he could not say such things out loud.

"May I speak what is really in my heart?"

Úlftýr smiled halfheartedly. "I wouldn't have it any other way."

Baldur nodded, reassured.

"My prince-"

"Úlftýr." Úlftýr interrupted him. "How many centuries must I ask you to address me by my name? We have been through too much together for these formalities to stand when we are alone."

Baldur half smiled. "Úlftýr," he relented. "I sense that one day, you will be the leader your álfur kin will turn to in our most dire hour when the enemy finds their eventual way to our shores. You are pure of heart and honorable, and such strength in one so young will inspire others to follow your command, my Prince."

Baldur then placed his arm against his breastplate.

"By my honor, I pledge my life and loyalty to you if you shall have it, Prince Úlftýr. I beg you to allow me to do my part in keeping you safe."

Úlftýr's eyes widened in shock. "What are you doing…? Your pledge to me… I am not the Crown Prince; Ingrid is… It is inconceivable, Baldur."

"I know I have broken the chain of the royal succession by pledging fealty to you, and I know leadership is not the goal you strive for," Baldur said. "I know that, under our laws, only the King may choose his heir. To overrule his bidding, reserved for the great ice serpent of legend and no one else." He confirmed. "And still-"

"I am the youngest of your King's offspring, and the honor of pledged allegiance by the warriors should go, after the King, to my older sister, Ingrid," Úlftýr said, still in awe of Baldur's gesture.

Úlftýr sighed. "If word got out of your vow to me, the elders would reprimand you for it, demote you even. I will do nothing that would put your mission in jeopardy."

"I understand your eagerness for battle. I also liked the games of war while Hod was alive and by my side." Baldur said.

"You say that you would follow my command if fate put me in that position," Úlftýr said, "The prospect does little to appeal to me; however, I shall follow your command now. It would honor me to fight by your side, yet I won't risk your mission. You will not see me leave this land."

"Thank you, my Prince." Baldur nodded, awestruck that the King had predicted this moment in his wisdom. Something nagged in the back of his head. Somehow, this exchange went a little too easy.

"I only have one request, if I may," Baldur said.

"Name it."

"If I don't come back," Baldur began, Úlftýr's eyes widened. The mere thought sent chills down his spine. Baldur continued, "I humbly ask that when the ships return, whether I am with them, you shall take care of the settlers without judgment. After the atrocities they faced, they deserve we welcome them home as all our people do."

Úlftýr nodded, extending his hand. "By my honor, you have my word. I will see to it that it shall be done."

The platoon was ready to set sail at daybreak. They stood on the dock, fine warriors clad in red hoods, with their mirror-polished steel armor shining through.

The silver armor sat atop quilted crimson leather gambeson. The breastplates were etched with the royal family's coat of arms, two giant serpents wrapped around a frost-touched rose.

Baldur boarded the main ship after his men, and Úlftýr did not come to see them go.

"I am saddened I would not part with Prince Úlftýr - if the gods see fit that we live through this battle, I hope I might greet him as a friend again." Baldur bowed to Ingrid, who arrived to send them off in the royal family's name.

"If it is all right, please convey my sincere gratitude and apology to your brother, Princess,"

Ingrid all but rolled her eyes. "You know it still feels horribly odd when you address me in such a formal manner, *Captain.*"

Baldur smiled. "I will keep the formalities only when we are in a public setting, I promise. The elders insist upon it." Baldur said. "I am half expecting him to be on board when we arrive at the Ice Lands, but that, I am ashamed to have wished so," Baldur admitted. He failed to reveal to the princess that he avoided from searching the ships before their departure for this exact reason.

Ingrid extended her hand to shake that of Baldur.

"Do not worry. Wherever you go, Úlftýr will be with you." She told the captain before the latter smiled sadly, bowed again, and departed.

"Safe travels," Ingrid whispered.

As the enormous vessels exited the mouth of the fjord into the unknown sea, Úlftýr quietly said goodbye to the shore through the small round window in the ship's bowels, observing until it vanished from his sight.

Baldur walked the deck above him, unaware of his friend's deception, and while he lay hidden in the ship's belly on a cot of straw and fur, Úlftýr fell into a fitful sleep. The dream he soon experienced was nothing like he had seen before. A frightful vision enveloped him, and in it, Úlftýr's reflection appeared in a body that wasn't his own in a strange city, perched atop a tall building made of black glass.

His body seemed thinner, shorter, and more fragile than he ever knew it to be. The air reeked of smoke and something else. Úlftýr could not place the smell; however, it stung his throat and burned his eyes. It felt unnatural.

The once tall, ebony-haired, and bronze-skinned álfur Prince contemplated the body he inhabited through foreign eyes and stepped onto the ledge. He spread his arms wide, akin to wings, and pushed off the edge, plummeting down like a comet.

'I'm falling.' was his first thought.

'I'm soaring through the air.' The ledge faded from his memory. *'The wind is blowing into my face. My eyes water, but I will not close them. I want to see this.'*

The evergreen leaves of the immense trees passed him by. The ground got closer.

'I'm falling.' The voice that echoed through his mind was not his own.

His arms were heavy at his sides. *'I am bound to my decision to jump.'* He thought. *'I will not attempt to stop my impact with the ground.'*

A terrible crack resounded through the air. In Úlftýr's dream, Úlftýr lay on the searing ground. His face pressed into the rubble; some small stones mixed with the blood in his mouth.

'I can't move.' Pain invaded his senses. *'I hurt from the inside out.'* He whispered. *'Not from the bones I must have shattered, but from something deeper within...'*

He rolled onto his back, letting out an anguished cry. He panted, his heart erratic, threatening to burst out of his chest. His limbs refused to move after the exertion it took to turn.

In his dream, Úlftýr lay in a pool of his blood, looking up at the heavens. The clouds passed overhead; the rustles in the green trees were familiar music to his ears.

A moment ago, a lifetime ago, he leaped and plummeted down like a comet.

'Why would I do that?' He questioned. *'Why can't I remember what brought me up there? My eyes are closing on their own. I want to wake up from this nightmare; the darkness feels so peaceful.'*

The sun shone through his fluttering eyelids, blinding him. He had no strength to fight to keep them open. Patches of light were gleaming through the tree canopy against his skin.

'I need to know what brought me up there. Why can't I remember? This thundering pain in my heart, a gaping hole I cannot fill.' He tried to cry out. *'Is this a dream? I beg the gods to wake me from this nightmare!'*

His senses got duller; his eyes refused to open. Nothing existed but the darkness, the rustling foliage in the evergreen trees, and the sun.

The scorching sun, its bright burning light, forced its way through the leaves to caress his broken body.

Úlftýr woke up with a start. His heart pounded against his heaving chest. The echoes of pain from broken bones and torn-up skin rippled through his body. The clutches of the foul dream refused to let him go.

He hastily clamped his hand over his mouth, his eyes darting around him. He waited, agitated, yet nobody came. He lay numb, his body stiff and lifeless.

Úlftýr took a deep breath and glanced up, frightened his own would discover him before they sailed far enough into the open sea.

Through a small window beside him, Úlftýr witnessed the world plunged into darkness; it hadn't yet been a day since they left.

Úlftýr placed his right hand on his chest.

'*What a horrible nightmare. It feels like centuries have passed since I last dwelled on the fruitful shores of Islandia. Will I ever see them again?*' He thought. He looked out of the small round window.

The wind howled through the sails like a hungry wolf while the pit in Úlftýr's heart refused to close.

CHAPTER 5
THE ICE LANDS

The voyage to the south side of the barren land proved fraught with unforeseen dangers.

The sea took no pity on Baldur and his crew, and they struggled against the harsh weather and the monstrous waves.

The three ships groaned and creaked, threatening to come apart with every crash of the waves against the bows of the massive wooden vessels.

'I know the great serpent and my brother's life essence guide us through this storm. Their spirits alone prevent our ships' destruction.' Baldur thought to himself, standing by Snakur, the helmsman.

Baldur made sure to tie a rope to the lad's waist and through the wheel to the pedestal to ensure he wouldn't be thrown overboard. He would have liked to secure the rest of his crew as well and felt irrationally guilty that he could not guarantee them the same as he did for Snakur.

Strong gales howled through the sails, penetrating the toughest of armors. Involuntary shivers ran through Baldur's bones; his cloak clipped to the armor billowed around him, whipping at his body with the harsh wind.

The ship lurched ahead, and Baldur's fingers dug down, his knuckles turning white from the force he used to hold on to the ornate, serpent-shaped railing.

The restraints that lashed Snakur to the wheel creaked and groaned from the strain of him being thrown around, his hands frozen to the wheel as he forced it against the ocean's push. If he went down, the ship would surely go down with him.

Fear was evident in the faces of the troops around him. Their eyes were wide as if to reflect the depths of the sea.

Baldur wished Úlftýr was there with them. He never questioned the blatant honesty of his close friend; only with him did he speak openly about his own reservations.

Baldur looked at the ocean, the old scars tingling in his skin.

A monstrous wave towered over their ship, crashing down with terrifying speed. The surge propelled them forward. It violently threw Baldur and several others, halting in a sprawl like a rag on the cold, wet deck. Baldur's stomach dropped.

Baldur lifted his head to a platform set in the upper part of the mainmast where Vanir was heavily harnessed lest the ship's lurch catapulted him into the sea.

Vanir, the youngest among them, was barely one and a half a century old and a quarter of Baldur's age.

Although initially reluctant to bring young Vanir on this dangerous journey, Baldur acknowledged Vanir's reputation as a celebrated crow master. He was brought mainly on him by Úlftýr, who had pushed Vanir towards the elusive position.

Each recruit tried his hand at becoming their new crow master after the last one dove off a cliff on a dare; they never recovered his body. A special connection had to occur. The crows had to accept the chosen álfur as the leader of their flock. But none of those who tried before Vanir escaped theirs throughout pecking.

When they saw Vanir, the lad failed to hide his terror of the birds, but Úlftýr trusted his intuition and the sparkle in the birds' eyes.

So Úlftýr led Vanir to the cages, opened them, and sat with him, never letting him go until the crows came to him nearly three hours later.

The winged animals accepted the young álfur by bringing him a golden trinket they had stolen from the castle, and thus, their new crow master was born.

"Vanir!" He shouted to the álfur, who kept a lookout for land and other treacherous hazards the sea might thrust upon them. "Release the crows!" He ordered.

Vanir looked down at Baldur and nodded. In one swift motion, he pulled himself up to the black steel cage, lashed to the mast, and set the night-colored creatures free.

The crows cawed loudly and departed.

Baldur hoped the crows would fly true, for land drew them even with low visibility. The crows disappeared into the fog, and his gut twisted.

Evil thoughts invaded his mind.

"Is this mission ill-fated and doomed to fail before it even began?" He asked the wind and gritted his teeth. "Am I, in my eagerness for vengeance, about to be responsible to the claimant of my loyal warriors' lives?" Baldur asked the heavens, glad the howling storm masked his fear.

In the murky water of Baldur's gloom-stricken mind appeared a vision of the Ljósálfar bodies washed on the rocks by the ominous surge and then dragged down to eternal rest in the dark, deep, watery grave.

Baldur struggled to get back on his feet. Rain poured into his eyes, and it matted his hair, going down into his armor in big globs of icy cold slashes of frost biting his skin.

He blinked to clear his vision. His eyes stung from the splashes of the rough waves still beating against the ship. He shook his head off the unsettling thoughts and wiped his eyes.

Three days had passed since his beloved shores disappeared from his sight, replaced by the towering waves, and Baldur begged the winds to keep their course true.

And under the deck, while the ship creaked and groaned, Úlftýr was tossed around like a rag doll. "Calm yourself," Úlftýr willed the sea. "Please, heed my call; release this vessel from the clutches of your raging waters." He pressed his back against a wooden beam, his head pounding with the sound of churning water.

"Please," Úlftýr fell forward. Standing on all fours, he breathed in the damp sea air.

Úlftýr dug his fingers into the floorboards. His arms felt like ice, and his fingertips glowed blue. A call for power gripped his gut; he could feel the ocean's unrest as if it fought to keep them from reaching their destination.

Úlftýr closed his eyes, allowing the might to build within him; it snaked up from the bottom of his feet and held his throat in a vice-like grip.

"Protect us." Úlftýr opened his eyes; they glowed in blue fire, his hair flew around him, and a scream tore apart the bonds that held his throat, a vortex of raw power violently erupting from his veins, and the sea fell to rest.

The floor rushed to meet him, and Úlftýr collapsed; the room swirled into the darkness around him.

Above his head, Baldur stared at the blue sky. The clouds parted, and the ocean that, until a moment ago, appeared black became clear.

"Thank you," Baldur whispered. He knew not who he thanked, but he felt them, the powerful spirit of their protector, and it was a familiar one. "Thank you," Baldur said again.

"Land!"

Vanir shouted from above. Baldur focused his gaze beyond the horizon. There, between the heavens and the sea, their destination loomed like a shadow on the water.

Here it lay.

The cursed land materialized out of the mist akin to a ghostly plain. A land of ice and fog. A land of shadow and death.

Baldur's eyes darted over the ice-covered mountains, his lips a thin line, his eyebrows knitted together. He couldn't seem to draw a regular breath. Whatever happened next, they'd done it; they'd reached the shore of Niflheim.

The ship slowed; the steady movement indicated they were now on low waves.

Úlftýr slowly opened his eyes, his head pounding. He glanced out of the tiny window at his side; it revealed the desolate shore the ship came upon. They arrived, and there was no turning back now. The movement of his troops was evident through the cracks in the wood above him; dust shimmered in the air, water bit against the boat, and splashes rose up to the small window beside him.

Úlftýr took a breath and pushed himself up from where he lay among the crates of provisions.

He took slow, careful steps, listening to his troops going to and fro on the upper deck, preparing the small, wooden boats for their departure.

Baldur's voice carried down to his ears. His friend was giving the last words of command to those who'd remain on board, and Úlftýr knew this must be his moment.

"Lower us," Baldur said, sitting down in the last rowboat.

"Wait!" Úlftýr stepped onto the deck, and a collective gasp followed by a thundering silence gripped the troops, interrupted only by the low-lapping waves.

The silence didn't last. The warriors exploded in cheers, morale elevated by the appearance of their Prince.

Úlftýr met Baldur's eyes, an array of emotions passing inside him. Astonishment, disbelief, twisted happiness even, and a horrifying realization struck him. A fool he was to wish for this. In his mind's eye,

Baldur was struck with an image of Úlftýr, grey, mutilated, broken, and deprived of breath in his arms, the same as Hoder was.

"No!" He whispered under his breath. "No, you were meant to stay safe!" *'What if I can't protect you like I failed to protect Hoder?'* Baldur added, distraught in his mind. Baldur stood up sharply; the boat rocked on its cords. "Úlftýr! I ought to throttle you! I should have known! I was so naive to believe I convinced you."

Úlftýr smirked, walking up to the boat to the gleeful pats on the back he received from the other warriors. "Forgive my deception, dear friend. I had to, for you refused to disobey my father, and I could not accept his decree."

"I hate the happiness I feel at seeing your face. If anything happens to you, the guilt will devour me whole. You know I am done for. Your father will wring my neck. By the Yggdrasil, Úlftýr! Everyone has the right to be stupid, but you are abusing your privilege."

Úlftýr smiled, "I missed you too."

Baldur grunted exasperatedly and grabbed Úlftýr's arm. "Get in, you bastard," he said, pulling the unruly Prince into the boat, and Úlftýr sat beside him.

"If you are here, then what about the vow you made to me regarding the return of our people?" Baldur asked in a more solemn tone.

"Ingrid knows what I have done. If I die, you can trust Ingrid to keep the oath I gave you, and you can hold her to it when you go home."

"If you die, there is no going home for me," Baldur said.

Úlftýr clapped him on the back. "Then, I guess we both will have to stay alive."

Baldur growled but said nothing.

Heartened by the beaming faces of their warriors, he gestured to the deckhands' crew to lower the tender boat into the sea.

The landing party docked on the hard, icy soil. Baldur noted the daylight was unusually dark, and grey clouds covered the sun. The air stood heavy in their lungs. Baldur could scarcely believe that anything would grow here. There was no flora in sight save for the lichens that clung tenaciously to the rocks. Marks of erosion littered the ground, indicating its incapability to yield crops. He wondered how the settlers survived here as long as they had and what they relied upon to nourish them.

"There is no time to waste," Baldur said.

"Snakur," He turned to the warrior. "Take nine of your warriors and scout the beach for any patrols the mortals might have stationed."

Snakur nodded once, his right hand on his breastplate, and then he dispatched with the selected few while the rest, over two hundred strong, prepared for the looming battle.

"We found no one in our immediate proximity," Snakur said when he returned some thirty minutes later. Vanir arrived with two crows perched on his right arm and another one soaring above his head. Their black, glistening, abyss-filled eyes watched Baldur inspecting his warriors' preparations.

Vanir whispered a command to the winged creatures. They made a single croak in unison and then silently rose and settled once more into their steel cage.

Baldur produced the leather-bound map Hoder gave him. Devouring emptiness overcame him while he examined the map and scoured the terrain, doing his best to ignore the bloody fingerprints forever embedded in the skin, portraying the maledict land.

Úlftýr stood beside Baldur.

"Are you ready?" He asked in a low voice, careful not to diminish the vision of the powerful leader in the eyes of Baldur's troops.

Baldur gave a sharp nod and turned to look at his armor-clad brethren.

"We all know why we are here. I'm grateful to you all for following me to see through Hoder's quest and bring our people back home." The warriors stood to attention.

A sudden rumble went throughout the battalion.

"Someone is coming!" The scouts ahead announced in urgency. The noise of dozens of blades sliding out of their sheaths simultaneously grazed the air.

Baldur stepped forward. He looked ahead at the terrain before them. What little light illuminated the ground bounced off what looked like crystallized rocks scattered ahead. From this distance, Baldur could not be sure if they were ice or actual crystals. A shadow passed behind the rock formation.

He signaled the archers to string their bows. For a moment, they were in complete silence; then, there was a shuffling of feet and a yelp.

"Stop!" Baldur lowered his sword. "Nobody fires! Lower your weapons!"

The platoon parted, and Vanir and Úlftýr ran forward to meet the tiny figure stumbling out from behind the crystallized rocks ahead.

The child stared at the platoon with wide eyes. He reached for them and collapsed.

"Bring water!" Úlftýr got to him first.

He removed his cloak, wrapped it around the child, and picked up the boy in his arms.

"Here," one warrior handed Úlftýr a water skin.

"Drink." Úlftýr sat down on the ground, allowing the child to lean against him. The boy opened his sunken eyes.

Úlftýr brought the leather pouch to his lips, and the pale-skinned boy drank in big, hungry gulps. Baldur tapped his supplies belt, signaling to one of his men to get him a dried piece of fowl for the boy to eat.

Once in his hands, the child devoured it whole. He coughed and then looked up with pleading eyes.

"Is there more?" he rasped.

Vanir reached into his belt and produced another piece, and he handed it to the boy.

Baldur inspected him.

The child's blond hair lay flat, caked in mud, and stuck to his scalp in odd directions. His clothes were nothing more than rags hanging loose on his body, and someone tore up adult clothes and tied them over him to keep him warm.

"Where did you come from?" Baldur asked gently.

The boy pointed in the general direction of the settlement.

"Are the bad ones still there?" Baldur asked, and the boy whimpered, afraid.

"It's okay," Baldur assured him. "You are safe now, and they can't hurt you anymore." Baldur got down on one knee close to the boy. "You were hiding in the rocks until you saw us coming, didn't you? You are very brave. Can you tell us exactly how you've managed to escape?"

The boy let out a sob, and Úlftýr held him tighter. "Mama…" the young álfur said. "Mama pushed me under the fence and told me to run and hide behind the prayer house and then sneak away when she called those monster men to her." Tears streamed down his face. "Mama said Jörmungandr would protect me."

Baldur nodded. "And so, he has."

"Take him back to the ship and remain by his side," Baldur ordered a young warrior. The álfur's sour expression spoke volumes of his dismay that he wouldn't be allowed to fight. "Garuk, You won't be deprived of battles in your life," Baldur said, his voice calm. "But, for now, you have a chance to protect one." The young warrior nodded; his cheeks colored bright red at his disobedience. He scooped the boy up from Úlftýr's arms and made his way to a nearby dory boat.

Baldur looked at the soldier beside him, proclaiming with renewed vigor. "Scout ahead, I want to know where the prayer house is. We will come from behind it." He told the runners, who briefly nodded and forged ahead.

Baldur turned to his troops. "We have seen what these savages are capable of, and we know now more than ever why we are here, and I suspect we know exactly what they are. Are you ready to fight, my brothers?"

In a silent agreement, the entire company put their fists to their breastplates. It sounded like the rumbling of distant thunder.

Baldur almost smiled.

"After me," he ordered loudly and marched to the head of the company to lead the way.

Two hundred and seventy-nine troops fell into equal pre-arranged parties, and silent, they followed Baldur up the rocky shore.

Swiftly, they moved through the cold dunes and frosted crystallized rocks littering the ground.

Without uttering a word to disturb the stillness of the bleak land, they made the nine-mile hike from the sea down into Tasermiut fjord.

Baldur sent out three scouts to forge ahead of the company. It took only a short time until they returned with news of the invading convoy.

"Mortal men," they confirmed Baldur's suspicion. Following the trail the scouts mapped out, they found the mortals stationed at the ruins of what used to be Hod's settlement.

Baldur knew he would have picked this place himself when he saw it.

It stood to reason to choose a location close to the coastline with reasonable boat access for fishing. The area was a flat, well-drained region planned to contain several large farmsteads within its limits.

Charred square-shaped stone foundations marking former houses remained, lone indicators there was once life here. The smoke from the fires that burned them still lingered in the air.

Only one building remained standing.

Baldur recognized the enormous rune stone depicting the voyage of the Ljósálfar from Ljosalfheim on the back of the great ice serpent. Their people had erected it in what must have been the inner courtyard of the serpent's Jörmungandr prayer house.

The sacred ground appeared stomped through with the Ljósálfar's desperate, fleeting feet and with the marks of the barbarous advancement of the mortal warriors upon them.

Baldur cursed his thoughts for straying to set the image of Markian, Hoder's soulmate, in his mind. He hated the idea of the beautiful álfur lying inside, savagely murdered, another life Baldur failed to save.

Markian was a véfrétt — a devoted scholar whom the Kingdom entrusted with keeping the histories and legends of the Ljósálfar race.

Baldur sighed. Even eternal creatures cannot halt the fading of memory.

Baldur forced himself to look at the wooden door of the serpent's sanctuary. He gulped. The door stood smeared with faded remains of blue blood.

The battalion approached the crumbling settlement, and Baldur understood why the mortals were easy to spot.

The smoke rising from the makeshift mortal camp turned the morning sky dark, mixed with the fumes of their carnage in the settlement.

Death and decay stood akin to a wall in the air. Half-eaten game and skinned muskox carcasses littered the ground. Their bloody coats covered the hides of the filthy mortals who sat by a dying fire and others who lay where they fell on the ground in a blissful drunken sleep.

Those who kept upright were busy slicing meat and rummaging through the possessions they removed from the beautiful beings they slaughtered. Baldur recognized the shimmering fabrics and the delicate silver jewelry.

Worst of what they saw was the Ljósálfar, the ones not slain by the mortal beasts.

At least nine females Ljósálfar sat imprisoned in the animal enclosures near the campfire.

They were tied up, dirty, and smeared with crusts of blood, and almost all the wonderful fabrics that were used to adorn their skins were nothing but rags.

It was an obscene sight. Hot, rage-filled patches appeared at the corner of Baldur's vision.

One woman lay with her face in the dirt at the mortal's feet, her arms twisted, bound behind her back, exposed to the elements, and her neck placed at an unnatural angle.

Another woman sat on a log by the flames, heaving and shivering. Too scared to move, her face streaked with tears and dirt, her bare chest half-hidden beneath clumps of dirty hair.

Baldur's honor would have never permitted him in good conscience to attack an unarmed, inebriated adversary throughout his long life. However, Baldur gave no meaning to an honorable fight on this day, not against the monsters who murdered his brother. *'To hell with honor,'* he thought. *'Today, my sword will taste blood, and tomorrow the great serpent will forgive me for my wrongdoings.'*

When Baldur set foot onto the cold sand of this mist-stricken land, he entered a world of shadows where his good conscience could not play any part in his decisions. Here, he had to face an unnatural foe.

The sight of the mortals sucked all reason out of his tormented mind. On this day, his vengeance led him. It festered inside him from the moment Hoder drew his last breath in his arms. It grew throughout his journey and now threatened to consume him. The craving to spill red blood pulsed through his blue veins.

Following Baldur's sign, the warriors crept on the mortals. They silently spread out around the encampment. They relied on the shine of their ear jewels to ensure they had taken the best position to lay siege around the mortals.

When they were nearly upon them, Baldur released a bloodthirsty battle cry. "Tyyyrrr!" The company descended on the mortals, attacking with all their might.

The female álfur screamed and tumbled off the log.

Baldur smiled with the satisfaction that he had never marveled at before, slashing at the surprised savages. His face contorted with hot white rage and self-loathing at this newfound disgusting sensation.

"I should have joined you on this journey of discovery, brother!" Baldur yelled ferociously, his sword hacking at the mortals. "Rid me of this loathing I sense at the chance I missed exploring this unknown world with you!" He begged the heavens. "Hoder, forgive me. I failed to keep you alive."

At the back of his aching mind, Baldur knew he had acted recklessly. He charged forward with bitterness overpowering all other emotions, decapitating one mortal on the spot.

The heathen, with its manic smile spread over its bloody features, tumbled into the sizzling coals.

A billow of flaming sparks rushed into the frigid air.

A mortal, sitting by the smoldering ashes, burst out laughing at seeing his comrade's head in the reignited flames.

He fell to the ground, convulsing with mirth, and Baldur looked at him with pity.

"What sort of poisons have you taken, you monstrous beast?" he asked with revulsion, burying his blade into the chest of the foul-smelling mortal.

The man gurgled, spitting out blood, and his painted laughter died on his cracked lips.

Baldur pulled his blade out of the dead man.

All around him, the brutal battle of his Ljósálfar kin with the loathsome fighters raged on. Crows dove in from above, a mess of flapping wings and loud squawks, pecking and tearing at the mortals at the crow master's command.

The mortals were chaotic in their combat style; they attacked with the ferocity of wolves and the tenacity of savage bears.

They possessed astonishing stamina, and even after the Ljósálfar warriors' blades cut them deep, they kept on coming despite their injuries, on some occasions, without several of their limbs.

Some only died when they lost so much blood that their bodies could no longer sustain themselves.

The chaotic human rampage came from all sides in an exploit of crazed mania. Baldur needed to find out where the sudden reinforcement was coming from. Had they been waiting for them? Had they laid in hiding to ambush his troops?

"How?" Baldur whispered. "Vanir!"

Baldur shielded Vanir with his blade, hindering a savage from plunging his spear into Vanir's gut. He grabbed hold of the mortal's wood-carved spear, flipped it around, and drove the weapon into the surprised man's neck.

The ruffian fell to the ground, emanating undistinguished gurgling sounds. He attempted to seek Vanir, reaching his bloodied hand towards the young álfur. Still, the wound he sustained proved fatal, and no matter what drove those terrible adversaries, it was not enough to keep them from their inevitable grim end.

Baldur glanced at the fire.

The head still sat, watching him through the flames.

"It's mocking me," Baldur said through gritted teeth. "Its open eyes torment me as if the creature still lives." The dead eyes stared at him until they burst; the flesh melted off, and a grinning, charred skull remained.

A chattering of teeth alerted Baldur to the danger emerging from behind him. He turned and came face to face with both man and beast fused into one.

The creature reeked of drink and death.

The abominable being had a bear's fur draped over his ripened, heaving body.

The mortal appeared in a deep trance. His limbs shook, his mouth foamed, and his face turned purple. He opened his bloodshot, dilated eyes, gaze focusing on Baldur, and snarled. The purple-faced human roared ferociously. He launched at Baldur, erratic and mad.

Baldur raised his sword and slashed the mortal across his chest, but the metal that cut into his flesh did not bother him at all.

The mortal continued his path of destruction despite the affliction Baldur brought down on him. Baldur yelled to stop one of his own coming to his defense and watched in horror as the berserker lifted him up and tore him apart.

The lout tossed the dead aside and advanced toward Baldur with inhuman speed; his eyes glazed over. Baldur spun out of his reach and stabbed the lout, his sword slicing through pelt and flesh. The Berserker pounced on Baldur while his back was turned and went to grip him in a vice from behind. Baldur anticipated the attack. He lowered his head and sunk his teeth into the arm that came around his neck.

The berserker seemed surprised. He snarled and thrashed to shake Baldur off. He knocked Baldur's sword out of his hand, tackled him off his feet, and fell on top of him, pressing down on Baldur's neck with astonishing strength.

The mortal squeezed Baldur's throat with rough, hairy hands, ending in sharp, broken, claw-like nails that dug into Baldur's skin. The brute crushed Baldur's hands under his weight and growled, his mouth slightly opened. Baldur winced with revulsion, seeing the beast bite down on his own tongue. Red blood spilled through the mortal's clenched teeth and dripped down from his mouth onto Baldur's face, tainting his flesh.

Baldur failed to notice the metal claws fused to the bear's skin in his attempt to escape the Berserker's death grip. The Berserker submitted Baldur to the ground with one massive strike and then, with a roar of victory, grabbed hold of the blades and plunged them into Baldur's side.

Baldur gasped, and the Berserker drove the claw knives further, twisting them while they went in. He cried out, his spleen ruptured, and blood spewed out of the cavity the claws left behind when someone roughly dragged the mortal off him.

Baldur's ears rang, and a metallic taste invaded his mouth.

Baldur panted in misery, his vision tunneling into black. Deep in his confused mind and beyond his blurry vision, a raven's blur of long hair and silver armor clashed in a ferocious battle with the bear man. *'Figures...'* Baldur thought while the world swam away. Closing his eyes, he reserved himself for returning his spirit to the great serpent and joining Hoder.

CHAPTER 6
THE SHIELD

Úlftýr saw Baldur go down under a massive clump of animal hair and human teeth, and Baldur's blue blood spilled onto the battlefield. Úlftýr roared Baldur's name and charged at the beast man, first slashing the brute's back with his blade. Then Úlftýr tossed his blade aside and grabbed the monster. He dug his fingers into the brute's face and dragged him off Baldur and onto the ground.

The crazed mortal was immensely large. He tossed Úlftýr off him, and as Úlftýr rolled to the side, he grabbed his sword off the ground and cut the man ear to ear. The mortal groaned, heaved, and snarled like a wounded animal.

Úlftýr kicked him and punched him, tearing and slashing at every part of him he was able to reach until the mortal lay where he fell, hopefully, passed to the hell that awaited him.

Úlftýr sheathed his sword and ran to Baldur's side. He turned him over and screamed. Baldur's previously radiant bronze skin was ashen, and the tint of his lips was almost white. Around them, the battle raged on. He called on the ice and fog to still the horrid gash and the blood still spilling.

"Don't die," He willed Baldur, whose soul was slipping through his fingers. "I told you that we both must live."

Baldur woke to agony. His ears still rang. The air reeked of burned flesh and fresh blood, assaulting his nostrils. He howled, deep, searing pain claiming his senses. His limbs went rigid, and the pain pounded through him, binding his body to the cold, hard ground.

"Hold him still." Someone said,

Baldur yelled, straining to set himself free of his captors. He struggled, but it hit him; he knew the sentries that were holding him down. Strong, familiar hands pressed on his arms, and another pair held onto his legs.

Cold hit his stomach, pulling the pain of the deep gash out of his body. Baldur yelled again, scorching heat following the cold, rupturing in waves across his abdomen.

He tried to catch his breath while the feeling of heat slowly subsided.

A strange heaviness akin to a plate of armor lay across the area the mortal had cut open, and when Baldur attempted to move, the armored plate moved with him, fused to his skin. A moment later, his friends released him. The pressure on his limbs vanished, and the searing pain that claimed his torso dulled into a distant ache. Baldur opened his eyes to meet Úlftýr's worried gaze hovering over him.

"What...?" He touched the smooth, hard surface integrated with his stomach.

He looked at Úlftýr. His pale blue fingers slowly returned to normal, and the ice at his fingertips melted away.

"What is this?" Baldur asked, pointing at his stomach.

Úlftýr placed his arm around Baldur's shoulders and helped him upright. With Úlftýr's assistance, he leaned against the large log set by the fire where his warriors moved him. Baldur did his best to ignore the grinning skull sitting in flames.

Thanking his friends for working on keeping him alive, Baldur scoured the rest of his warriors, watching them release the prisoners he saw earlier in the animal enclosures.

Their dead lay covered by his warriors' red cloaks. One female álfur sat by the bodies, silently crying. The other survivors huddled together, and one wailed for her child.

"My heart goes out to her," Baldur rasped. "I hope her child is the boy who found us, and I desperately crave to reunite him with his blood." A groan escaped him when he attempted to pull himself further up. "At least someone would get a happy ending in this magic-forsaken land." He said.

Baldur turned back to Aesir. Beads of perspiration covered the red-haired brow. Sweat trickled, glistening, down the sharp line of his jaw from the effort of invoking his elemental powers.

Aesir held the strength of control over the fire.

Few álfur possessed dominion over the flames, but those who did have a spirit identical to the fierce blaze they conjured in their hands.

Baldur knew Aesir to have a grand passion for everything he took on in life. He displayed the same enthusiasm in battle or celebration, like when he made a fiery stag in the sky when Baldur and Úlftýr returned with their prey.

"So, what is this?" Baldur asked, pointing at his stomach.

"Obsidian," Aesir explained. "I summoned volcanic rock from the ground to form a crystallized structure around your wound."

"That's…" Baldur grassed his fingertips over the dark, hard, glass-like crystal. "Creative." He finally let out a smile. "Thank you."

"I am no healer," Aesir said. "But you were bleeding out, and I sensed the volcanic rock in the ground under our feet. It is only a temporary fix, and it won't last long, especially when you start to move around."

"Hopefully, it will last long enough for us to get you to a proper healer," Úlftýr clapped Aesir on the back.

"That thing that attacked you...." Úlftýr began.

"A Berserker," Baldur whispered.

Úlftýr nodded in agreement. "Yes, I thought so. I read about these abominations in our library, and I understand you have as well."

"Yes," Baldur said. "I know the story," he said. He felt feverish just thinking about it. "In myth, the Berserkers were bear-skin-clad fighters of various races. They worshipped the old vengeful gods celebrating death and destruction above all else."

"Do you remember the entry from the book?" Úlftýr raised his eyebrow, trying to make light of the situation.

"Why would someone want to live like this?" Vanir asked.

Baldur sighed. "I am glad your heart is still filled with youthful innocence."

Vanir blushed.

"Some folks were devout enough to sell their freedom for power, too simple-minded or blind to realize their souls were what they had given up," Baldur replied. "I remember the graphic images depicted in the books of the various Berserkers, tearing up pieces of themselves and each other. Blood, nails, and teeth mixed with the flesh of the wild animals they skinned and whose untamed pelts they bore on their filthy bodies, gone up in flames as a sacrifice." He spat. "It makes me sick repeating the passages I read. It revolts me that I can remember them so clearly."

Úlftýr pressed on Baldur's shoulder.

"It was a tribute to the old gods." Úlftýr continued in his stead. "Once accepted," he looked at Vanir. "Indicated by the smoke rising into the heavens, the old gods made the mortals believe they gained the strength and the spirit of the animal whose coats they adorned."

Silence fell while Aesir and Vanir took in the unsettling information.

Baldur gazed into the distance of the once again eerily silent icy plain. Blue and red blood desecrated the ground. The bodies of mortals lay scattered around them, and his own warriors lay side by side, honored and arranged by their troops.

"What happened while I was out?" he asked solemnly. "How many dead?"

"Twenty-three perished from among our ranks," Úlftýr said, crestfallen, his lips a thin line. "Seventeen injured. Most nonfatal wounds, I thought it was best to send them back to the ships."

"What about…?" Baldur began.

"The mortals?" Úlftýr spat. "Most of them are dead. Those we have not slain scattered toward the mountains. Let them find their maker in a frozen grave."

"Those purple-faced rabid creatures fought themselves to extinction. In the end, they simply went mad. I swear their blood sizzled, spewing out of every orifice of their bodies." Said Aesir.

"It boiled them from the inside," Vanir added in disgust.

Úlftýr nodded in agreement.

Baldur looked at his old friend. He read the grave expression on Úlftýr's face.

"There is something you're not telling me." He waited for an answer, the silence stretching into an eternity before his patience shattered. "Out with it!"

"Baldur, we found the dead settlers." Úlftýr finally revealed.

Baldur fell silent. He nodded slowly. "Where?" he asked, although he already knew.

"The mortals discarded the bodies inside the prayer house," Úlftýr confirmed Baldur's suspicions.

Baldur took in a shuddered breath. "Markian?" he asked regarding his brother's mate.

"We didn't see him," Aesir said but quickly added. "However, the mortals piled them up in such a way… we cannot be sure."

Worry and guilt stabbed Baldur's gut. "I need to know." He said, attempting to get up.

"Whoa! No." Úlftýr grabbed Baldur's arm, and Vanir and Aesir hurried over. "There will be time to put our people to rest," Úlftýr said, his hands on Baldur's shoulders. He looked into his friend's eyes while he held him down. "If Markian lives, we will find him. If he passed, you need not see this horror right now."

Baldur sighed; their journey was far from over. With or without Markian, there were still Ljósálfar in this godforsaken land in need of their help.

And Hoder told them exactly where they were.

"How far to where Hoder said the settlers were headed?" Baldur asked.

He produced the leather-bound map out of his damp tunic and handed it to Úlftýr to examine.

Úlftýr opened the parchment, his brow creased. "Myrkur rósaviður forest?" Twice now, blood stained the map, first by Hoder and now by his brother.

Úlftýr wondered how many more would leave their bloody mark on the face of this cursed ground.

Úlftýr looked at Baldur. "Another twenty-two rost* to the forest from where we sit."

Baldur closed his eyes; his ears rang again. "I feel as if I am seasick." He attempted to blink the vertigo sensation away as the world liquefied before his eyes.

"Are you sure you can make it?" Úlftýr frowned.

"I have to try," Baldur whispered.

Úlftýr looked at him, sighed, and turned his attention to the map again.

"There must be a way around these mountains." Aesir pointed at the map in Úlftýr's hands.

The long, narrow valley nestled between two giants whose summits had risen to a height of approximately ninety-three rost*. Climbing it with our troops and then going back down into the valley will take too long. My patchwork on Baldur's stomach won't withstand the journey, and it will surely crack, and I don't know if I can summon enough material to make another one."

"There is a way around these mountains," Vanir pointed out, taking the map from Úlftýr's hands. "If we return to the boats and sail into Tasermiut Fjord, we can disembark right at the edge of Tasersuag Lake draining into the fjord and hike the rest of the way into the valley where the forest is."

He looked at Baldur, who blinked at him, surprised by his innovative thinking.

"What do you think?" Vanir asked.

It took Baldur another moment or so to gather his strength to reply. Baldur let the youth sweat at his audacious plan as he worked to sit propped up on his elbows. Taking another long moment to process a few painful breaths, he looked at the hopeful eyes surrounding him. "That can work," he said at last, pleased.

Úlftýr rebounded the map and stashed it in a cloth pouch attached to his breastplate.

Baldur planted his hands against the log he leaned upon and attempted to stand, and Úlftýr and Aesir both caught him under his arms and heaved his injured body up from the ground.

Baldur clenched his teeth, fighting through the pain.

"Do you want to stay on the boat when we hike into the valley?" Úlftýr asked, his question meant for Baldur's ears only.

Baldur shot Úlftýr a glare. Anger burned in his eyes. He knew Úlftýr suggested the idea out of concern for him, but he could not allow himself to sit out the rest of the journey, no matter how badly he wanted it to be over.

"We must find our people still left in this wretched land." Baldur groaned. "I must honor Hoder's dying wish."

"You won't honor it with your death," Úlftýr grip on Baldur's arm tightened.

"Is this how you know me, my friend?" Baldur managed a weak smile. "I shall not give up until we reach our destination. But I will attempt to honor his wish as long as there is breath in me." Baldur looked into Úlftýr's worried eyes.

The ebony-haired Prince was easy to read and never tried to conceal his emotions. "You shall not give up until we reach the end of this journey," Úlftýr relented. "You must stay alive to lead us home."

"I swear to do just that." Baldur agreed, and, in his mind, he added, *'Or the task will fall to you.'*

With the captain on his feet, supported by Aesir and Vanir, Úlftýr gathered the troops and put their plan into action. They boarded the large wooden craft, and to Baldur's delight, he witnessed the young boy who found them reuniting with his mother. Determined to complete their quest, they set sail into Tasermiut Fjord.

CHAPTER 7
THE TEMPORARY SANCTUARY

The journey proved hard on Baldur. Each time a wave hit the boat, he let out a ragged breath, and his injured body shook, yet Baldur stubbornly kept himself up.

They left the slain settlers at the prayer house. Baldur wanted to find the living first before he had to deal with the dead.

Two hundred able-bodied Ljósálfar descended ashore when the boats docked in the calm water. Grey-leaf willows dipped their branches low into the water at the mouth of Tasersuag Lake. The sun shone high above them while the company trotted up the path from the lake through shrubs of Mountain Ash under trees of Downy Birch and Green Alder. The air under the trees was cold and surprisingly pleasant.

Baldur breathed heavily as the road into the valley became steeper the further they went.

"We should stop to rest," Úlftýr said after noticing the beads of sweat on Baldur's forehead.

"We can't stop," Baldur replied in a guttural voice.

"Look at yourself," Úlftýr frowned. "You can barely keep on your feet."

"I…" Baldur protested when the vegetation's rustling up ahead gave way to reveal a pewter-colored robe and a tall dark blond álfur carrying a long hand-carved hiking staff. The staff bore a design of a Celtic braid and featured the tree of life.

The dark blond's eyes widened at the sight of them, and he hastily made his way down the path.

"Markian!" Baldur exclaimed, forgetting his ailments. A grunt of pain healed his excitement, and at the sight of Hoder's mate, unharmed and breathing, Baldur allowed himself to slide down to the ground.

Baldur looked up at him. Markian has stayed the same since the last time Baldur laid eyes on him.

Markian's dirty-blond hair came down past his shoulders and braided on one side of his head. Baldur admired his chiseled jawline, slightly pouty lips, and striking green eyes.

"Baldur." The álfur dropped to his knees in front of Baldur. He laid his staff on the ground and embraced his old friend. "Hoder made it home," he said, relieved. "So, he…" Markian halted. The look in Baldur's eyes told of the sad truth Markian longed to deny. "They got him." Markian closed his eyes. "I felt his demise in the air." He murmured; he bowed his head, his hands still on Baldur's shoulders. "I did not want to admit it, but his spirit brushed against my heart when it departed this world. I know Hod returned his essence to the great serpent."

"I'm sorry…." Baldur didn't know how to put his grief into words. "If I'd come with you when he asked…."

"Then, you might have suffered the same terrible fate he had," Markian concluded. "I have no animosity towards you, Baldur. When it mattered, you came to our aid. I know you are an álfur of honor, and Hoder would have done the same."

"Hoder would have done better. All I could do was to avenge him, and even that task I have left incomplete."

Markian frowned. "What do you mean?"

Baldur lowered his gaze. "It shames me to answer."

"Some got away." Úlftýr stepped up to fill Markian in. "We defeated most brutes that attacked you, but a few fled into the mountains."

A glint of recognition crossed Markian's eyes when he glanced at Úlftýr, and he nodded. "You did more than I could ever hope for. I pray the great serpent will take their souls to his icy depths."

He let go of Baldur and took up his staff, getting back up to his feet.

"We need to head back. Those who escaped the savage raid are down in the valley from this hill, and they will worry if I delay for too long."

Baldur nodded and attempted to rise after him when a crack akin to a bone-breaking rippled through the air.

"Huh." Baldur looked down and lifted his tunic to reveal a long fissure in the dark obsidian.

Before their eyes, the crevice filled with fresh, bright blue blood.

"What…?" Markian frowned. "Volcanic glass?" he touched the hard surface.

"He got hurt fighting a berserker," Úlftýr explained, taking Baldur under his arm.

Markian inspected the wound. He tapped on the glass.

"I can help you, Baldur. Or, at least, mend the wound enough to withstand your journey home," Markian said. "But whose bright idea was it to fuse glass to his skin?" He raised an eyebrow.

Markian knew full well since there was only one fire elemental among them.

"I did what I could to stop the bleeding." Aesir divulged. "Seemed like the right thing to do."

Markian looked at him with a piercing gaze, and Aesir swallowed. Markian smiled. "You saved his life." He said, and Aesir visibly relaxed.

"Follow me. I will take you to the colony," Markian said, leading the way.

They followed the dark blond up the path and soon exited the tangled forest. A vast valley unfolded before their eyes.

Baldur stared, dumbfounded.

The valley had an extensive grazing area for the few sheep, goats, and horses the fleeing Ljósálfar absconded with in their escape from the mortal barbarians.

"How did you get the resources to do this? I thought you fled when they attacked?" Baldur looked ahead.

Tents of fresh Birchwood frames stood skillfully constructed throughout the valley. Most of their flaps, made of a canvas of stretched linen, were raised.

"They did not attack us upon their arrival," Markian explained. "They watched us, and we watched them for days. More than a week passed until we felt they might become a threat. They were content at the beach at first, hunting, smoking, but then-" He sighed. "Hoder pointed out that this truce between our camps could not last. He encouraged us to get ready to leave. We had time to gather our provisions. We did it in secret, at night. The humans didn't know we suspected their pending attack."

Baldur looked at the tents the settlers built in the mountain's shadow. Inside stood sturdy rope beds, adeptly woven, a skill Baldur himself had been proficient in. They covered the floor of the triangular tents with moss and boar fur. The communal large, circular, stone fire pit stood at the edge of the camp, situated inside an open mouth of the mountain.

"You knew they weren't coming after you?" Baldur stepped forward.

"We sent out scouts after we arrived here," Markian said, "Most of the women and children are still inside the mountain, but I am almost certain the mortals have no interest in coming after us."

Baldur shook his head. "Then, why would they do this, Markian? Why go to all this trouble to attack you if they didn't mean to drive you extinct from these lands?"

"I don't know," Markian said as he led them to the fire. "They might have acted on the command of some malicious god or strove to take possession of our resources, and we might never know their real motives for attacking us."

A group of Ljósálfar raised their gaze to greet Markian and the troops who approached them. Most of them sat near the flames, and some ground-up berries and Baldur knew the sort. Crowberry.

He remembered his mother baking them into pies and using them to smoke fish. The flavor always seemed slightly bitter to his taste, and many preferred to consume the berry as wine. Baldur knew it to better teeth, as it helped keep wounds clean of disease and contributed to strong bones and healthy blood.

A few kept busy by teaching the younger Ljósálfar to carve out arrow shafts while some grown Ljósálfar were busy stringing bows.

A pleasant aroma of meat reached the warriors' nostrils.

It spread in the air, rising from the sizable pieces of meat cooking on solid, triangular, iron structures above the flames.

"You look comfortable here," Baldur frowned. "You don't intend to stay here and build a more permanent site, do you? I want to leave this place soon and take you all with me."

Markian gazed at his fellow survivors who sat by the fire, and he was responsible for their well-being.

Baldur held his tongue, anticipating Markian's decision regarding what they should do next. "Your journey will soon see its end," Markian said.

Markian's eyes were dim with pain and sadness. Baldur remembered them being so much brighter.

"I cannot guarantee our safety here," Markian admitted. "And, even if this valley offers us this temporary sanctuary, we cannot be sure it will remain hidden for long. Other mortals could invade at any moment. Those you let escape with their lives might survive in the mountains, and I suspect they will come to seek vengeance for the men you killed."

He sighed. "To tell you the truth, I would like our orphaned youngling to grow up in the beauty of Islandia and not in the harshness of this barren land. I will not let them die here."

Markian looked at Úlftýr, who accompanied them along with Aesir and Vanir. "I remember you. You were on the royal podium when Hoder made his request before the council. You are lord Freyr's younger son, are you not?"

"You were there? You never told me that." Baldur looked at him.

Úlftýr suddenly felt hot under the collar. "I didn't know what the council was discussing that day, and father wanted me to attend for a long while. I implored him to tell you after it was done without delay. I am sorry I could not give you ample warning."

Baldur sighed and nodded.

Úlftýr turned back to Markian. "As for your question, yes, I am Lord Freyr's son," Úlftýr confirmed. "I rarely participate in matters of state, but Hoder's speech moved me. Never have I met someone so determined, so brave in the face of unsentimental blindness to anything that was a disturbance to outdated rules."

Markian smiled, his hand resting against his chest. "May I inquire what you are doing here? I wouldn't expect Lord Freyr to let you go happily. Or take a risk with your life."

A look of amusement passed between Úlftýr and Baldur.

"Along with my Princely duties, I am a warrior. My place is by my commander's side, where my people need me."

"So, he does not know, or didn't when you set out on this journey," Markian said heavily.

"No," Úlftýr confirmed. "The troops know me, but few of your colony will recognize me in uniform, and I would like to ask you, Markian, to keep your discretion regarding my identity and my presence here. I do not want to become a spectacle and a cause for turmoil in this delicate time."

Markian bowed his head and then looked at Úlftýr's amber eyes.

"I shall not reveal your identity until you command me otherwise, my Prince. If I may ask, please tell your troops to rest. You can gather your strength while we disassemble the camp. We should spend one more night here and set sail early tomorrow morning. That way, we can also make a few runs to the boats you sailed on up the river during the daylight that remained and set our provisions in order."

Markian leaned over an old female álfur in red robes sat by the flames, vigorously writing in a leather-bound journal.

"Friia." He whispered, not to startle the old álfur. "Friia." He seemed uneasy to disturb her. The woman sighed and finally put down her carved wood, quill, and inkwell. She looked up at Markian and then at Baldur.

"We agree then," she did not phrase it as a question. "You can tend to your matters, Markian. I will rally some Ljósálfar and look over our preparations for tomorrow."

"Thank you." Markian laid his hand on the old álfur's back and helped her up. She smiled weakly at him and made her way to a cluster of tents, followed by several of the younger Ljósálfar.

"I believe she's been around long before the great serpent revealed itself to us. She might have been there at the start of our home world," Markian said. "She is my mentor. More Ancient in years than the Elders themselves. No one possesses greater knowledge of the serpent than her."

Baldur nodded. He had only heard of Friia until now, for she would rarely leave her house on Eyjafjallajökull mountain.

But when Markian set out to the unknown land, she surprised everyone by going with him. The King was not pleased with her leaving Islandia, but Friia said she needed to be closer to the desolate land, for within it lay secrets she did not yet understand. Something pulled her there, and even the Elders could not deny the gift of foreknowledge she possessed.

Baldur grunted in pain. He began feeling faint again. The wound in his stomach refused to stop pulling life out of him in slow gulps of bright blue blood.

"Úlftýr," he said. "Make sure our warriors have eaten. Then, take some provisions to the injured at the boats."

"Don't worry about your wounded warriors. I will gather my healers, and after I tend to your wound, we will go down to the fjord to take care of your soldiers." Markian looked at Aesir. "If you don't mind, please join us. I will require your assistance."

The redhead nodded, and Markian led Aesir and Baldur further from the fire. They helped Baldur settle down on a carpet of downy cotton grass.

It was the most comfortable Baldur had felt since he found out his brother had died.

Markian handed Baldur a crystal vial he produced from a pocket in his robes. "Yellow Poppy infused by my magic," he explained when Baldur eyed the little bottle in his hands. "To help put you to sleep."

Baldur nodded and allowed Markian to prop up his head and pour the yellow liquid into his mouth.

The potion took effect gradually yet powerfully. Baldur knew it would help him fall asleep and keep him asleep for the gruesome task Markian intended to perform. 'Good,' Baldur thought. He did not want to be awake for what came next.

Baldur's eyes fluttered under his closed lids, and his breathing slowed to a deep, steady pace.

"We can begin," Markian said.

Aesir crouched on the ground by Baldur's still frame.

Markian called on another dark blond healer, and together, they began applying Brittle Bladder Fern paste inside and outside of Baldur's wound, infusing it with their green earth magic by weaving the paste with the warmth coming out of their hands. A breeze formed around them; Baldur's body was enveloped by a low glow as his skin softened to accept the remedies.

In contrast, Aesir's fingers glowed red, sweat accumulated on his brow, the air shimmered, and he slowly began detaching the glass from Baldur's skin.

Half an hour later, with the obsidian safely removed and the wound on Baldur's stomach looking substantially better, Markian asked Aesir to boil Pyrola leaves and apply them around Baldur's wound to keep the inflamed skin at bay. Aesir took great care in separating the dark green, wavy-edged leaves from the stem and discarding the waxy flowers.

Markian then gathered the rest of his healers. There were five in all. He armed them with various herbs and remedies, including Dwarf Birch and Betula Nana, for pain and what he used on Baldur.

Relying heavily on their magic to clear the air of any substances that could hinder their abilities, Markian led his medicine Ljósálfar down the path out of the valley and onto the ships to treat the rest of the wounded soldiers. The healers that accompanied him formed a barrier of warmth around them and kept the air humid and moist to assist in their endeavors.

The following day, the small camp bustled with activity.

The Ljósálfar were going back and forth, taking apart the tents, breaking up the fire pit's stones, disassembling the camp to be ready for transport, and herding the animals down to the boats.

After the Ljósálfar, both young and old, split between the three massive vessels, Baldur's troops took him on board, and Markian came on board to say goodbye.

"You are not coming with us?" Baldur would have jumped up to shake the smiling álfur to his senses had he regained his strength and his body allowed him unrestricted movement.

He groaned in pain instead.

Markian laid a gentle hand on his chest and pushed him back down to the red velvet cot he lay on.

"I am a véfrétt of the serpent," Markian said, holding Baldur's enraged gaze.

"Friia and I will stay here. She senses there is more this ice land is yet to reveal to us, and, as a scholar of the serpent, it is my duty to return to our desolated settlement and properly return the essence of our dead to the ground."

Tears came to Baldur's eyes.

The warrior could not fight him. "I promised Hoder I'd save you, and I wanted…" he whispered. Markian took Baldur's hands and placed them on his stomach; he laid what felt like a book underneath Baldur's clasped fingers.

"But you have," Markian said, leaning over Baldur until his brow was to his.

"Friia's book," Baldur whispered, and Markian nodded.

"A brief history of our scant time here and personal observations. She said to give it to you. There are passages here that are for your eyes only; I haven't even looked them over as per her instructions. I trust she has a good reason to prevent me from reading what she addressed to you." Markian straightened up. "I am afraid she will not survive the grueling journey home," he squeezed Baldur's hands. "Besides, she already confided in me before we even came here. She foresaw this voyage to be her last."

Baldur did not reply. He hoped he would not be the one to break the news to the King.

"The mortals desecrated this land," Markian continued. "Either in the name of some malevolent god or their savagery, it would take an unspeakable amount of time and the good of our people to restore this land. I will remain to make sure they did not perish in vain."

Baldur opened his mouth. He wanted to beg, threaten, and shout at the beautiful álfur, but the gaze in Markian's warm eyes took all the fight out of him.

"Take this." Markian held up a blue rose, and it glowed brightly in the rays of the sunlight. "Hoder cultivated the blue roses himself," He revealed. "He cared and raised each bud until it bloomed and revived the magic long forgotten in these parts of the world." His voice became soft and emotional.

Baldur sighed. "I see the love you still bear for my brother, Markian."

Markian bit his lower lip. "I believe Hoder was in tune with the great serpent, more than I could ever hope to be. This rose had grown from the seeds Hoder brought from our homeland. Like him, it should come home."

Baldur couldn't answer; the lump in his throat cut off his ability to speak. Markian gave him a knowing look.

"My healers will administer Pedicularis for the fever to all your badly injured warriors. I will give you all Yellow Poppy to induce sleep and help you heal. Hopefully, when you awake, it will be between familiar walls."

Baldur allowed Markian to raise his head from the cot so that he could give him the yellow elixir.

"I will not say goodbye, Markian. I will see you again." Baldur whispered, drifting off into a dreamless slumber.

Markian laughed lightly. "Yes, I suppose you will."

Baldur awoke to the shouts of his sailors, fighting to keep them afloat. The journey back home seemed as perilous as the one they experienced getting there.

With every sway of the boat, the waves crashing into their vessels, and the gasps of their new passengers, Baldur fought to stay awake. He did not want to go under, never to see them make port.

"Úlftýr-" his hoarse voice didn't even sound like him.

Snakur was the one who heard his call. He made his way to where Baldur was bound to the cot, grabbed his hand, and leaned over him to try and make out his words through the storm.

"Úlftýr…" Baldur gasped. "Help him get us home."

Snakur looked at the Úlftýr, who was at the stern, the ropes of the sails wrapped around his arms while the wind battled against his attempts to fasten them down.

"Here!" Snakur shouted to the sailors at his side.

By this time, Úlftýr got the ropes tied off, and he rushed to the middle of the deck, hitting his back against the main pole as the waves tossed them forward, his fingers digging into the wood and the ship lurched with the current, out of anyone's control.

Rain poured into Úlftýr's eyes, and it matted his hair, going down into his armor in big globs of icy cold slashes of frost biting into his skin.

He blinked to clear his vision. His eyes stung from the splashes of the rough waves still beating against the ship.

"Calm yourself," Úlftýr commanded the ocean. "Heed my call; release our vessels from the clutches of your raging waters." His fingers glowed blue.

A pulse thundered through the water.

"You…" Baldur stared at the prince. "It was you…You kept us safe."

Úlftýr locked eyes with Baldur; Úlftýr's orbs glowed in blue fire, and his hair danced around him. Snakur and two others from their company grabbed onto Úlftýr's arms to try and help him channel his power.

A scream tore through Úlftýr, a vortex of raw power violently erupting from his veins, and the sea fell to rest.

This time, when he collapsed, several hands were there to catch him.

Baldur watched them lay the unconscious prince on the deck.

Above their heads, Baldur stared at the calm scene. The clouds parted, and the ocean that, until a moment ago, appeared black became clear.

"Thank you," Baldur whispered, allowing himself to drift off; now he truly believed they would make it home.

Two hundred and seventy-nine set sail from their homeland of Islandia.

Among those soldiers, twenty-five were dead, and fifteen were injured. Two more succumbed to their fatal wounds on the journey back. They, too, would never get to see their home again.

Baldur himself hung between life and death when they reached their fruitful land's safe harbor.

They saved three hundred and ninety-five souls on their quest. The rest, nearly twice as much, perished in the land of ice and fog.

CHAPTER 8
SAFE HARBOR

When Úlftýr told Ingrid of his plan, the first words out of Ingrid's mouth were, "What am I going to tell our father?"

Úlftýr frowned at that. "You are not to say anything. Swear to me, Ingrid, on our bond as siblings, that you would not utter a word of my deception until the ships are long gone with me on board, and it would be too late to stop me. Swear it!"

And Ingrid did.

As it happened, Ingrid didn't have to tell the King anything.

Freyr summoned her and her brother to the throne room not long after the ships set sail. "Where is Úlftýr, Ingrid?" Freyr asked, rising from his throne.

Ingrid's silence was the answer their father dreaded. He sent Ingrid away, and once the doors to the throne room shut behind her, the unmistakable sound of ice forming on the inner walls of the chamber crackled in the air, crystallizing until it ruptured, sending sharp icicles into the wooden door.

Now, Ingrid waited.

She stood on the dock and watched the approaching boats flicker across the dangerous surge of the angry sea, steadily drawing closer.

At first, they were dots of light gleaming in the smothering darkness.

Her heart skipped a beat every time the shimmering lights disappeared from her sight, obscured by another monstrous wave. The waves crashed against the stern of the water-bound vessels and threatened to drag all the souls on board to a watery grave.

A lengthy sigh of relief left Ingrid. The three ships finally made port.

The first to disembark were the troops ferrying in the injured. Then, out of respect, the dead.

Among the injured, Ingrid found Baldur, his eyes shut, his face pale, and his armor stained by blue and red blood. They carried him on a cobalt crimson velvet stretcher.

"Baldur?" Ingrid felt a pit open inside her. She had yet to see her brother, Úlftýr.

Now, with the sight of Baldur, she feared the worst.

"He is alive, my lady," Snakur, a cobalt-haired warrior holding onto one side of the cot, told her. "He fought valiantly, my lady. He led us against the mortal beasts to avenge his brother and the lost colonists."

Ingrid nodded. "Make haste to the infirmary." She said, "We cannot let the brave heroes of the Ice Lands perish now that they made it back home. Do you know where Úl-?"

"Ingrid," Úlftýr stepped onto the dock after them, his ebony hair blowing in the wind.

They embraced, and Ingrid looked her brother over, holding him at arm's length. "By the blessing of the great serpent, you seem unharmed. Are you all right?"

"Was father mad at you for hiding my secret?" Úlftýr answered her with a question of his own as he did want to think of the dreaded ice lands now that they were back.

"Furious," Ingrid shrugged. "But you will be happy to know your actions, while frowned upon, were not a startling revelation to him."

Úlftýr smirked. He turned to the other boats emptying onto the dock and the survivors making their way slowly down the road to the beach. Some older Ljósálfar recognized him from afar and came to greet him and Ingrid and express their gratitude. They revealed that the soldiers on board their ships had told them of the brave prince's benevolent stand against the council and his fight to bring them home, both diplomatically and physically.

Úlftýr shook their hands and smiled politely. He endured the awkwardness of being the center of attention, a fact Ingrid did not miss.

"Guilt is gnawing at me, telling me I do not deserve their gratitude. Baldur is the one that should be the recipient of their high praise." He confided in Ingrid when the older Ljósálfar were out of earshot.

"I understand," Ingrid remarked in a low tone. "But you have to accept their gratitude if only not to offend them."

Úlftýr sighed, nodded bitterly, and forced his mouth to form a pleasant smile that failed to reach his eyes.

Úlftýr felt her before he saw her. Like a pulse, a heartbeat starting anew.

A red-haired maiden. His red-haired maiden. He never thought of anyone as his before. He noticed her the moment she appeared on the gangway. A fair maiden with flaming red hair stood against the crowd of dark mahogany and bright yellow strands. He thought her skin had a sickly greenish tint and her expression grave.

Úlftýr gathered she had been seasick from the harsh waves that rocked the vessel before they made port. He kept her in his sight. She came up the rocky beach with the crowd of his fair people. He recognized more and more of the older Ljósálfar who were returning home after a decade away in the Ice Lands. The few children among them were all unfamiliar faces to him, save those he recognized from the Ice Lands. Those younglings had never seen the beauty of Midgardr's most glorious fjord.

"I will see what I can do to help." Úlftýr parted with his sister before he went down to the beach. "Snakur," he turned to the warrior who came to stand beside him. "Was Baldur taken to the infirmary?"

Snakur nodded. "Several horse-drawn carriages departed to the infirmary, and I ensured the captain was among the first to go."

"Can you take over in Baldur's absence? Ingrid told me they had prepared warm clothes on the dock and assigned dwellings my father allocated on the north side of Tjörnin lagoon, opposite the harbor. The wood cabins meant to house visitors from the town of Ísafjörður from the north side of the island will go to them."

"Leave it to me, sire," Snakur said. He looked at Úlftýr.

Skilled, tireless hands built the beckoning homes the prince spoke of, including Úlftýr's.

"By the time the Ljósálfar of Ísafjörður village arrives to serve the hákarl at the midwinter celebrations, we will build new accommodations. We shall expand our beloved city further." Úlftýr said, smiling.

Snakur nodded. He bowed to Úlftýr and took his leave, signaling to two of his warriors to follow suit.

After the initial chaos and confusion subsided, the night grew more profound, and the stars shone on strangers and family gathering around makeshift fires they lit along the beach.

In perfect harmony, beautiful voices arose in song; their melody carried on the light evening wind, echoing through the fjord. They sang in remembrance for their fallen brethren, in gratitude for their saviors, and with hope for a brighter tomorrow.

For a while, the red-haired maiden vanished from Úlftýr's sight in an ocean of faces.

Úlftýr found her, making his rounds at the campfires. He greeted his fellow Ljósálfar, those he had not encountered before they disembarked the boats, and attentively listened to their hardships in the Ice Lands and on their way back.

The young lady seemed lost when Úlftýr laid eyes on the maiden again. 'Perhaps,' Úlftýr assumed, 'she lost her family among the crowd.'

Her expression appeared sad. The loss in her eyes didn't speak of the deaths she witnessed or the harrowing journey she endured; it spoke of loneliness Úlftýr only knew to recognize in her heart because it echoed his own, rooted too deep to find the seed that sprouted it.

Until that moment, Úlftýr had never believed in the concept of love or finding your other half. He had only experienced passion, lust, a thrill that ended as fast as it began. He was young by his people's standards, yet many fine maidens courted him throughout the centuries, and none of them lasted to test the span of his heartbeats.

However, in sight of this red-haired maiden, Úlftýr acknowledged the solitude that plagued him all his life.

At that moment, he did something he had never done publicly before. He joined the other Ljósálfar in song.

He knew he sang for her.

The flames transfixed Elska. Her thoughts were of her old home. She wondered if, now that she had come back, her father would welcome her and if she would even have the courage to knock on the familiar wooden door.

She did not live up to what her father expected of her. Her father wanted her to join the council and take a suitable mate, which he would choose for her. Elska disagreed with his way.

Respected and wise among his peers, her father wasn't as loyal to her mother as he was to his work. That fact was widely known.

Elska always felt her father found comfort away from them. Consumed by his apparent fear of becoming irrelevant, he surrounded himself with adoring followers and failed to notice the tension he wore like a cloak inside their home. Akin to a caged animal, his eyes constantly darted to the door, his body language always slightly turned away from them, ready to leave at the first call of his duty.

Eventually, close relations convinced her mother it was time to move on and seek a new life in a new land. She still had deep respect and affection towards the one she pledged her life to, but no love existed.

Elska left with her. She could not bear the thought of leaving her mother to fend for herself, and she wasn't sure that her father ever forgave either of them for their choice.

As for her mother, she found comfort in the arms of another, an álfur she met on their journey to the Ice Lands. They headed together now to their new home with their offspring born in a foreign land.

Elska made peace with the notion that there was no place for her in the new life her mother built for herself, but she felt no animosity towards her for it.

Instead, relief filled her, freedom to venture out on her own. She had no desire to awe her makers.

Elska raised her head to look into the crowd.

An enchanting melody carried on the evening's light breeze, settling in her sensitive ears.

The voice filled her with warmth before the light of the flames revealed his face to her. The musical piece drifted with the flares from the fire into the stars, and her heart soared with them higher than the night sky.

She stood up and followed the harmonious tune until it led her to a roaring fire. Her heart skipped a beat when her eyes fell on the tall, young álfur who had drawn her in with his voice.

Their eyes met, reflecting the flames dancing to Úlftýr's enchanting melodies. A blush rose in both of their cheeks, but Úlftýr didn't stop, and Elska never wanted a moment to endure longer, more than the one she experienced now.

She had encountered the tall álfur before; she was sure of that, yet she could not place him. In the castle, perhaps? In her father's chambers? That wasn't relevant right now.

He watched her approach with eyes the color of amber. His hair shifted in the wind, a dark halo framing his perfectly sculpted face and body he could not hide even under his long, leather cloak.

She stood and listened to his song until the tune died out on his lips. They gazed at each other for a moment until the silence became unbearable.

"Hello," she let out a nervous chuckle and attempted to regain her composure. "I am Elska." She introduced herself.

"Hello, Elska," the beautiful álfur answered, extending his hand to her. "Would you like to come and join us?" He smiled.

She nodded and took his hand, "I've never seen a more beautiful smile." She said,

Úlftýr blinked and then laughed. Elska's eyes widened, and she clamped her hand over her mouth. "Did I just say that aloud?" she asked, blushing.

"You have," Úlftýr confirmed. He beckoned her to sit by him on a long log set by the flames.

She sat, shy at first. Úlftýr noticed she kept her hands concealed awkwardly, tucked in her sleeves, and then placed in a manner that kept his view of her right hand obscured.

Being so close to someone that beautiful, it felt heavy, like the gravity of the earth multiplied and merged to a tiny point beneath him - making him skip one heartbeat after another just when he thought he found a new rhythm to life.

Looking at her sitting beside him, he was not at all prepared to be involved with someone so unique. He wasn't ready to be in love at all, but there he was, captivated.

"Are you cold?" Úlftýr asked, noting her shrunken demeanor beside him.

"No – " Elska tightened her grasp on her right arm. "It's nothing, it's – " she didn't finish.

Úlftýr laid a hand on her arm. "May I?" he gently pulled her towards him. He lingered a moment and then slowly raised her sleeve up, revealing four nasty gashes across her forearm. The cuts looked as if they were ripped out of her flesh.

Úlftýr's vision blurred. He knew these marks. He knew these gashes. How they felt. His eyes darted to her neck. Her skin was clear, but he knew what was there before. He felt it happening.

"Who – " Úlftýr breathed. "Who hurt you?" he demanded in a low menacing voice. Ire rose within him; he longed to dispatch the culprit's head with his sword.

Elska pulled her arm back and hid it again, tightening the fabric of her sleeve around her injury.

"It was one of them," She whispered. "The grave-bound, he tried to grab me as we ran. He looked like a mad animal in his bear skin. I almost couldn't tell if he was man or beast." She bit her lip. "After we made it to the sanctuary, I couldn't sleep; I kept thinking he might come for us. The thought of him still being out there – "

Realization thundered through Úlftýr. The bear beast was almost Baldur's demise.

When they finished working on closing his wound, Úlftýr discovered the man was gone. He could only hope the mortal went off to die in the mountains, but if he didn't and Úlftýr let him go...

"He won't," Úlftýr said.

"What?" Elska blinked, and the beautiful álfur by her side held her gaze.

"He won't come for you," Úlftýr stated.

"How do you know?" Elska frowned.

Úlftýr took her hands. His skin was hot, his touch soothing, healing. "Because I will rid the world of him, my maiden. I promise you this. You can sleep soundly tonight."

A dam opened between them, their conversation from that point on a gushing waterfall. They spoke of Elska's journey to the Ice Lands, "The first time I saw the ships, they seemed so large and ominous," Elska admitted. "Only when I climbed on board I felt a new being would emerge when I stepped off. I remember my father in the crowd that came to see us off. It was perhaps one of the only times I received an embrace from him. At least, I am finding it difficult remembering him showing me any affection throughout my childhood."

Úlftýr asked about the day the mortal beasts attacked the place she used to call home and was glad to know she did not witness the bulk of the massacre that took so many of them. She then asked him to change the subject and asked him about his life in their land.

He obliged, somewhat unwilling to reveal too much about himself and hoped it did not show, but told her about his mischievous childhood, about his sister, and his favorite pastime - strapping blades or animal bones to his boots and slipping on ice and rock in the cold.

She tried to stir the conversation back to his father. Úlftýr divulged the tail of them hunting together, but it was clear he was closer to the mother who dedicated herself to raising him and his sister.

Despite Úlftýr's somewhat guarded demeanor, they felt comfortable with each other, and both experienced a sense of calm they had not had with any other álfur before.

Úlftýr was tempted to keep the obscurity of his station because he finally found someone who saw *him* first, not the prince. But somewhere in the back of his head, nagged the voice that called him a liar despite him not actually lying, just keeping some facts about himself private. He knew, though, that he could not keep this up for much longer in their present company.

He noticed the glances he got from the Ljósálfar around him, but he was glad to see Elska was oblivious to them, and her gaze was reserved solely for him.

Elska did not ask the álfur's name, for she feared it would break the night's enchantment. However, she asked the álfur to pull her closer, to shield her from the cold with his warmth.

Úlftýr held the redhead maiden in his arms, praying she would not notice how fast his heart was beating.

"Come with me," Úlftýr said at last when the glances of others became unbearable. He got up, took Elska by the hand, and pulled her after him.

They stepped away from the light of the fires, swallowed by the shadows of trees. Elska didn't question his motives to retire from the crowd. She, too, was a solitary being. She leaned into his embrace, her small, curved frame aligned perfectly in the sanctuary his firm body created. Drunk with happiness, she boldly snaked her arms under his coat and marveled at the smooth frame of his warm body.

An alluring blaze emitted from within him, hot and enticing. Elska allowed her hands to travel up his scolding skin and into his voluptuous hair, and then, she pulled him to her and, with all inhibitions gone, kissed him.

His lips were soft and warm, his taste - sweet nectar. At that moment, Elska stood on the edge of a cliff. One more step, and she would fall over. Elska feared that if she sunk into this emotional abyss, she could never climb back up. She stressed that she would not want to, and she would lose herself by doing so.

Elska had never known such a deep connection or such powerful intensity before. Something awakened within her—a primal, irrefutable craving for the godlike being that tenderly captivated her heart.

"Who are you?" Elska asked while she stood enveloped in his embrace, searching for his lips again. The slightly blushing álfur opened his mouth to speak, but a loud, cheerful voice disturbed the enchanted silence before he uttered another word.

"Úlftýr! There you are."

All color drained from his face. Úlftýr's gut twisted. His sister approached them, accompanied by two royal guards.

A look of utter disbelief obscured Elska's attractive features. She abruptly detached herself from him.

A hollow feeling filled Úlftýr.

"Prince Úlftýr…?" She whispered in disbelief.

Úlftýr just stood there, lost.

He didn't mean to lie to her, but it was much easier when she didn't know the truth about his station. The deception allowed him to let her see the álfur he was inside without the mask of the prince.

"Elska, this is Ingrid." He introduced his sister through gritted teeth.

"Hello, Elska," Ingrid took her hand for a moment, bowing her head in a respectful greeting.

Elska followed suit. "Highness."

"I've been looking everywhere for you," Ingrid said, addressing her brother. "Mother became worried and is eager to see you well."

"I was here," Úlftýr said, trying and failing to avoid glancing at Elska. She looked away, embarrassed.

A smile tugged at the corners of Ingrid's mouth. "I see."

Úlftýr wanted to punch her, knowing full well she could take him on without breaking a sweat; her powers had long awakened. He clenched his teeth, then took a breath to regain his composure and turned to Elska.

"Elska, may I offer to take you to your new home?"

Elska, flushed in red that appeared strongly on her snow-pale skin and spoke of deep embarrassment was reluctant to act rude; she bit her lip, sighed deeply, and agreed.

"Yes." She said in the mousiest voice and followed the siblings to the docks, where their two-horse carriage awaited.

Siran, the dark-eyed Elder, watched from the shadows of the trees that grew near the beach, Úlftýr and Ingrid leading the red-haired maiden away.

After they disappeared into the carriage, he, too, departed—his destination - the infirmary. An arched cloister portal made of black marble etched with ancient runes greeted him. He rode his spotted grey-black horse through the entrance of the two-story white sandstone building.

He was there the day the great serpent that brought the Ljósálfar from their destroyed homeland to these safe shores bestowed the gift of the rune knowledge upon them.

Swirling symbols danced along the walls, imbued with old elemental magic. The inscriptions of these runes invoked protection from the elements and channeled the power of wind, sun, and earth towards replenishing the life force of the wounded Ljósálfar within the infirmary walls.

Upstairs, in a large, rectangular room supported by high ornate columns, a fire burned in the hearth, distributing heat throughout the space. The tall, arched glass windows stretched to the domed ceiling, bringing abundant light. The infirmary was naturally lit during the day and hardly needed any artificial lighting at night when the stars and the moon shone in like lanterns set in the inky sky.

On the first floor, the healers evenly spaced apart cots of a wood frame covered with crimson velvet along a vaulted solarium. Siran had designed the room's shape to make it easy for the Ljósálfar stationed in the infirmary to respond quickly to those in need of their care.

They built the infirmary on a raised platform, allowing vaulted stone tunnels to run underneath. The tunnels supplied mineral-rich water from the underground natural springs the healers used in their remedies.

It was common to meet red deer grazing the green lawns surrounding the property in the summer.

Their sleek coats glistened in the sun as they gracefully leaped around the area.

"Magister." Eir, a young healer in training, greeted him when he entered the vaulted solarium. "We were not expecting you this early. May I be of service?"

Siran smiled with a smile reserved only for his students. "Yes," he answered in an indistinct voice.

"They brought here a group of the royal guard last night. Those returning from the Ice Lands. Do you know if the captain is well enough to speak?"

Eir nodded. "If you follow me, Magister," she said, leading him to the chamber's far end. "We repaired the damage to his internal organs. I expect he will recover fully, and we will release him from our care in a few days," she said.

"Here we are," she took hold of a heavy linen, grey-blue curtain and moved it aside to reveal a crimson velvet cot.

Baldur, half sat against several pillows. In his right hand, he held a wood chalice engraved with a howling wolf's head containing a yellow liquid. In his left, he had a worn-out leather-bound book. His bruised torso was exposed, tightly bandaged by a woven material, and his long golden hair was disheveled.

"Lord Siran," Baldur said, startled. He put the book down. "I did not expect your visit."

An irrational thought entered Baldur's mind. Could the elder hear his thoughts? He feared the book's content would be revealed before he had a chance to understand it.

As an elder, Siran could claim the writings for the archives. The last lines Baldur read still stood clear in his mind.

'*He who was betrayed shall be again at the mercy of a friend, a lover, and a brother, and only the blood shall decide his faith. But not from the womb shall come his redemption, for the bonds that hold him are stronger than them all.*' Baldur could not fathom who the text spoke of, but he could guess, and his assumption frightened him.

Baldur looked at the elder.

"That will be all, Eir," Siran said to the young healer, who bowed and left at once. Siran pulled at the heavy curtain, obscuring him and Baldur from curious eyes.

Baldur looked at him, unease swirling in his gut.

Did the Elder come there to reprimand him for the lives lost in his quest to fulfill his brother's dying wish? The passage he had just read in Friia's book ground across his thoughts. *'He who possesses this tome shall glimpse his fate but know that he is destined to perish on the mount of friendship.'*

He squirmed uncomfortably in his bed. Siran examined him with his somber gaze. "I…" Baldur swallowed. He wasn't sure what he should say.

"The Ljósálfar that came home tonight told of the cruel enemy that has invaded the small settlement they erected in the Ice Lands," Siran said. His gaze wandered to the arched window.

The rising sun's first rays created light hallows upon the damp ground. "Our people call them *'The dauðadýr'*; A mortal beast and grave bound. I understood from their account that those creatures acted barbarously, and our kin observed they were a petty kind."

"The settlement scouts on board told me they were killing even their own," Baldur put the chalice down on the bedside table.

"Not for the resources they could easily find," he groaned, pulling himself further up the mattress. "But out of sheer envy and pure greed. It took several weeks from when they arrived at the Ice Land until they finally attacked, so our people had ample time to study them and learn their customs."

"It is a wonder such a race still exists at the rate they seemed to have been pillaging and murdering each other." Siran agreed.

"I have read about such creatures, and what explains their persistent existence are the rumors that they also breed at an alarming rate."

"The survivors said they advanced, a swarm of deadly plague upon the land. They devoured anything, everything, and anyone in their path of destruction." Anger rose within Baldur. Memories of the blood-smeared prayer house flashed before his eyes, making his skin crawl.

"I know of the promise Prince Úlftýr made to you," Siran glanced back at Baldur, who stiffened in fear that he also knew about his pledge to the prince.

"He was true to his word," Siran continued, noticing but ignoring the terror in the captain's eyes. Whatever secrets he and the prince shared were theirs to keep.

"Considering he is a young monarch, he already has the courage and honor of a seasoned leader," Siran said.

"You know that you have already received a nickname."

Baldur raised his eyebrow, visibly surprised.

"Baldur the bold," Siran smiled. "For your heroic deeds in the Ice Lands."

Baldur looked down at his hands.

"I fear I shall carry this name in a veiled shame for the lives lost under my command and the recklessness that led to it."

"To honor your fallen troops, you should not contradict it," Siran said with heavy air. "Instead, strive to live up to it, with every day gifted to you in this world."

Baldur raised his eyes. "I shall." He promised.

Silence fell between them. Siran was reluctant to reveal the genuine reason for his visit, the unspoken words lingering heavily in the room.

"Lord, why are you here?" Baldur finally asked when the silence became unbearable.

"The entire kingdom owes you a debt of gratitude, Baldur, for rescuing our people and safely bringing them home."

"You don't need to…."

Siran raised his hand. He wasn't finished. "And me in particular," He sighed. "For you had saved my daughter."

Baldur was dumbstruck. He didn't even know the Elder had any family left.

"She and her mother were always adventurous types," Siran said with a slight smile tugging at the corner of his mouth. Baldur had never seen the álfur smile before, and he realized now that he might have found out why. "I didn't want to know if she was dead or alive, for I did not want to deal with a world absent from her presence. My reluctance to approve your quest was misguided, and I am sorry."

He touched his fingers to his brow.

"We had left on such inadequate terms, and I didn't want our argument to be the last thing I remembered from her. The uncertainty about her fate comforted me. Perhaps, now that she is back, it will be a second chance for us to mend our bond."

Baldur still sat, staring at him. "I don't know what to say." He admitted.

Siran chuckled.

Another first for Baldur to witness.

"You don't have to say anything," Siran said. "I came here to express my greatest gratitude. And now, I shall leave you to recover." He turned and moved the heavy curtain away. "Oh, one more request, if I may." He looked at Baldur's puzzled face.

"You might encounter her here or in the castle. She is a healer, and I believe the young Prince might have taken a liking to her. I would appreciate it if this conversation stayed between us, and she need not know of my reluctance to help."

Baldur nodded.

"My true shameful motive will remain my own," He paused. "And her name is Elska," Siran said, and then he stepped into the open air of the infirmary and pulled the heavy curtain back into place, leaving Baldur alone with his thoughts.

CHAPTER 9

A WOUND THAT NEVER HEALED

I t took some time until Elska gathered the courage to go to her father after she returned from the Ice Lands.

She stood awhile at his door until she finally knocked, taking in the fresh air and the odor of the herb garden growing to her right. Without a doubt, it contained medicinal remedies her father cultivated himself. He took greater care of his greenery than he did his family. The heavy wood door creaked open. This fact did not surprise Elska; his door was always open. For his students.

"Hello?" She entered, taking in the musty scent of old books.

Elske's eyes dropped to the new engravings that decorated the halls. Her smile tightened, lingering her gaze too long on where the marking overlapped with his. A new companion in her father's life. Had he had any difficulty in replacing them?

Siran's house was empty save for his three massive black hounds. She loved those dogs. They were among the only creatures she came to know that gave her their love unconditionally, without her feeling that she needed to prove something to deserve it.

She recognized them from childhood; imbued by her father's ancient abilities, they too possessed prolonged lives, and even though years had passed since they played together, the hounds knew her instantly.

Fond memories of white winter days bundled up on top of a sled lashed onto her happy, hairy companions, enveloped her. She could practically feel the soft clumps of snow land on her face as they raced through the farm her father owned.

The moment they smelled her, the three mutts jumped, licked her, and snuggled up to her on the floor of the noble house. Elska remembered how she had the habit of hiding under the dining room table and calling the largest of the pack to come to her aid and protect her when her father, Siran, pretended to be a great monster attempting to catch her.

With her furry protectors, however, he didn't stand a chance. For longer than she would have cared to admit, theirs was the only love she needed to battle the gnawing loneliness in her heart. Elska believed she learned about who she did not want to become from her mother. That hunger for life—the need to see, taste, and experience everything fast before it is gone—without the genuine enjoyment of the experience. Unlike her mother, Elska wanted to enjoy the moment while it lasted. With age, Elska realized that she sought to cherish the moments instead of checking them off as done.

Something her mother had never done, not even with her. Her mother always made her feel underappreciated no matter what she did for her and expected Elska to stand by her at every beck and call.

Deep down, Elska might have caught early in her youth that her mother attempted to capture those brief moments of happiness her father allowed before his work, the council members or the infirmary staff consumed all the attention he had to give.

Elska learned the importance of how the world perceived her from her father. Appearances mattered; you couldn't reveal what was in your heart to others, for they would not share in your courtesy. And worse, they would find a way to exploit it.

According to Elska's guardians, who emotionally deserted her, you couldn't trust anyone enough to reveal who you were. It made you vulnerable; it made you weak.

By the time Elska realized that her parents' way was wrong, she could read anyone she encountered but herself.

Siran opened the door to his house, and Elska's joy-filled laughter greeted him.

"Until this moment, I was doubtful I would ever hear the sound of your laughter again." He looked at her. She sat as if no time had passed, playing with his dogs and laughing cheerfully.

"I should have come with you," he said. "I was afraid," he said as he stepped inside, and Elska stood up to greet him.

Both remained at an awkward distance, their eyes refusing to meet. Anyone who glimpsed them together at that moment would think they were admiring the wallpaper.

"I feared I would not find myself needed in the unknown land you sought to explore. My knowledge would be of no use, and I shall be a burden upon you," Siran said in a low tone.

Elska glanced at him and away again. "I didn't know who I was when I left; I thought I had no choice but to go, that I had to choose between you and Mother."

"How is she?" Siran swallowed. Until that moment, he didn't dare to ask.

"She is all right. Strong and stubborn as always." Elska laughed lightly.

"Like yourself," Siran said.

"No," Elska said, looking into his cynical eyes. "I may have inherited her appearance, but my spirit is yours. The adventure was not what drove me; the discovery was my goal, and I now realize there is still so much I have yet to discover here, in a place I once called home."

"It can be your home again," Siran said, stepping closer.

Elska smiled sadly. "The engravings in the hall—you are no longer alone here. I will feel out of place with your new companion."

Siran said nothing. He still avoided her eyes.

"Does she make you happy?" Elska asked.

"Yes." Siran finally met her gaze.

"Good."

Another moment of silence passed between them.

"I was not a dutiful father to you, and now I seem to have missed my opportunity to teach you," Siran said in the lowest voice he could muster.

"There is still much to learn," Elska said. "And we still live, so you have a chance to be my father again if you so wish."

"If that is your choice,"

"I have never denied you the opportunity." Elska stepped forward. "If you face all the things we left unspoken, I will be here to try and face them with you."

Siran allowed himself a smile. "You were always the pragmatic one."

They embraced, and Elska broke down in his arms, tears streaming down her face. She did not want to admit how much she had missed being with her father during all her time away.

As much as she wanted to put everything on the table right away between them, Elska did not pressure her father to face his feelings of inadequacy immediately following their reunion.

Instead, she decided to follow his lead and be there in the way he intended for her in the first place. She declined his offer to relocate her dwelling back under his roof but helped him create a space they could use together.

Elska and her father set up a new medical chamber in the clearing behind his house, and for a time, it remained cluttered with scrolls and large leather-bound books they needed more time to make an order of.

"You should never attempt to extract the venom of a dangerous beast in a messy environment." Her father told her while they prepared to extract the venom of the great grey snakes they captured to use in their remedies.

"Are you serious?" Elska raised her eyebrow. "Baldur built the cupboards YOU requested months ago, and your precious books are still on the floor because you wouldn't let ME decide on an order for them." Elska looked at her father, awaiting his response.

Siran blinked, shook his head, barked a short laugh, and bent down to retrieve the books. He picked up a few of the heavier tomes and set them in said cupboards.

"Better?" he asked.

Elska rolled her eyes.

"Have you prepared the glass containers?" Siran asked, shelving another book and coming over to the long, wooden counter Elska had been working atop, ignoring his daughter's sarcastic glare.

"I still need to check if the membranes are tight," Elska replied. She tugged on the knot of the string that secured the membrane over the top of the last small glass beaker she worked on. Satisfied, she returned it to the regimented line of eight other waiting containers.

The additional room was sweltering. Siran had discovered that the snakes liked the warmth compared to their cold bodies. They came alive in the heat, active and vibrant, while when he found them, they were sluggish, dormant, coiled under stones and leaves, sedated by the frost.

The nine glass beakers now stood in a row on the counter. A sheer cloth of sheep intestines, secured by tight strings, covered their tops.

"I'm just about done," Elska said.

She marked in ink on a piece of parchment the names of the snakes in their possession and the number of specimens in use.

For her, the order was vital. She held herself and the newly trained staff of the infirmary to the highest standards. Inventory required a monthly inspection, and all medicines and tools were categorized and coded according to use and skill level.

If anything was out of place in her many storage setups throughout the infirmary, you could practically read on her face that it physically bothered her. She would sometimes fall into this unsettled state, rearrange everything once in a while, and meticulously clean every surface until it satisfied her that the space functioned most efficiently.

On those turbulent days, the other healers knew not to get in her way.

She began compiling books and guides on various herbs and poisons, transferring and transcribing the ancient, nearly unreadable textbooks into a moderately accessible information base.

Elska needed to know everything. She hated surprises.

Even when she and her father first went on a small expedition to locate and collect the snakes for their experiments, she arrived an hour early to ensure everyone was ready by the time they set out. And, although some would remark on her intensity or uptightness, she had her gleeful, childish moments. She was eager to discover and eager to learn. She was excited by every fresh flower and every unfamiliar sight she had seen.

When they caught their first snake, her gleeful cheers of *"Oh yesss! Gotcha!"* echoed for quite a distance. Now, she and her father were both dressed in thick leather garments to make it hard for the snakes they were about to handle to bite through.

Siran placed a hollowed-out wooden tube on top of the snakes' enclosure they had kept under the built-in counter, slid open the trapdoor, and coaxed a snake to slither out through the tube by dangling a tiny, squeaking light-brown mouse in front of the opening.

As soon as the snake's head slathered out of the tube, Siran grabbed it at the base of its head, placed his fingers under the serpent's jaw, and gently pulled it out until he could put his other hand under the snake's long, slicked body.

"Now, you position your hand like so," Siran lightly squeezed the snake's jaw to force the reptile to open his mouth and place it on top of the venom-collecting vessel. The agitated serpent lashed out in Siran's hands, its fangs puncturing the tightly stretched membrane, and Elska watched in fascination how the venom leaked out.

"Last, you press down on the snake's head and see the magic happen."

"Where did they come from? The snakes, I mean, I don't believe such creatures are native to our land." Elska asked after they finished, and they snuggled the snake safely back inside its enclosure.

"I stumbled upon them while exploring our land," Siran admitted. Elska raised an eyebrow.

"You? Exploring?"

Siran chuckled. "It is hard to believe I would ever step away from my homestead. But I have discovered signs of ancient seaworthy vessels wrecked on the other side of the island."

Elska's eyes grew gigantic in shock. "You mean…"

Siran nodded. "I believe that the mortal beasts attempted to breach our shores before but failed and met their demise, perhaps by the elements or by their own hands. I also believe the serpents were on board with them, even though I cannot fathom why, and that is how they came to be in our land."

"Have you told anyone about your findings?" Elska asked.

"I made the King aware of my theory," Siran glanced at her. "And the royal family. Are you still infatuated with the prince?"

Elska blushed furiously. She let out an exasperated sound. "I see," Siran said in a knowing voice.

"Oh, stop," Elska was about to say something else, but a knock on the wooden door interrupted her.

"Only one will dare trot in here through the garden." Elska glanced at her father.

Siran nodded. "Let him in; I'll get his remedies prepared."

Elska watched her father pick up another pile of old books from the floor and put them in the cupboard, and chuckling, she went to open the door.

"Baldur," she greeted the captain. She didn't comment on his attire as she stepped aside to let him in. Whenever he visited her and the Elder, Baldur adorned an ordinary green robe over a grey tunic and brown earth-toned trousers.

The first time she met him at the infirmary while he was still recovering, Elska sensed unexplained animosity towards Baldur. He had never crossed her or did anything to offend her, yet her heart ached at his sight. She later learned to ignore this unnatural feeling.

"How have you been?" Elska asked as she led Baldur to a leather resting sofa by the window. Her father brought a silver tray and set it on the small wooden table beside the couch.

"I've got him," Elska said.

"Thank you, Elder," Baldur said, accepting the silver cup from Siran. He downed the simmering yellow liquid and laid back on the sofa.

He looked at Elska. Guilt sparkled inside him. Somehow, knowing her brought him unexplained sorrow.

"May I?" Elska rolled up the grey tunic, and Baldur always looked away for this part. As much as he was used to the sight of blood and injury in others' bodies, he hated the sight of his own ailment, a constant reminder of the time he let his anger cloud his judgment.

The wound he sustained at the hands of the bear man in the Ice Lands never healed—not in the way common injuries did for his people. Once in a few months, the unnatural toxin would eat away the scar, and the wound would ooze black with a foul, sickening stench.

Elska hypothesized that the poison was derived from the dark arts, but Siran failed to find a permanent remedy for it.

"You can ask me what you really want to know," Baldur said, resting his head on the padded arm of the sofa.

Elska watched him close his eyes. "How is he?" she sighed, dipping the cloth in her hand in the concoction Siran brought to clean the gash in Baldur's stomach. She didn't try to deny or correct him; by then, Baldur had come to know her too well.

"He is a good warrior; the path he chose alongside me is right for him."

"I never could imagine him joining Ingrid in a council chamber. That suits her, but he has too much fire in him, even if that's not his element." She fell silent, focusing on the wound.

"He is safe," Baldur answered her unasked question. "Even if he didn't specifically ask me to oversee his advanced training, I still would have been obliged to do so."

Elska nodded. "I am glad that you do and that he did ask you in his way. After all, you have an abundance of experience over him."

"He is advancing fast."

"Because you are a valuable mentor to him. Don't tell him I revealed this to you, but Úlftýr told me you would ensure he would not get hurt during his sparring sessions. No matter how hard he tries. Did you stop a training routine because you noticed his unfastened Armor?"

Baldur laughed and groaned, his skin tightening as new scar tissue formed, coached by Siran's elixir. "Yes, I've got several younglings calling me Mother Bal for the rest of the day after that."

"You worry about him," Elska observed. "Does it have to do with the Ice Lands? Ingrid told me how he snuck onboard. I imagine you expected as much from him."

"The King was not happy with me when we returned." Baldur opened his eyes and stared at the ceiling. "He knows that I probably couldn't have done anything to stop Úlftýr from joining us, but now, when I agreed to advance his training…" He trailed off.

"You are stuck between your obligation to your King and your loyalty to Úlftýr," Elska concluded. "You know he sees you watching him when he trains. He notices your inner turmoil even if you don't tell him about it."

Baldur considered her words. She was not aware of the real reason he kept such a watchful eye on his friend. Baldur's concern was not only for Úlftýr's safety. However, he took his role as mentor to Úlftýr seriously and hand-chose the opponents that went against Úlftýr to give him just the right amount of challenge and propel his training forward with ample time to heal after each fight, even if Úlftýr resisted his forced rest intervals.

"Úlftýr is proud of the scars and bruises he received from sparring with you," Elska said. "I met him one evening after such an occasion. I know he didn't even attempt to use his elemental abilities to ease his sore muscles after that vigorous day at the training grounds. And obviously refused any help I could offer him."

"He refuses any special treatment from me," Baldur said. "He likes that I treat him like any other qualified warrior. And the troops appreciated Úlftýr's attitude. He is reliable and easy-going. You know I caught him once making a smiley face out of his own blood while he was sewing a wound shut?"

"Oh, my, well, it sounds like something he would do." was Elska's response. "What did you do when you saw that?"

"What could I do?" Baldur shrugged. "I scolded him for his childish behavior, but that only made Úlftýr more loved among the younger Ljósálfar, so I made him train the young rascals himself."

Elska laughed. "I am sure he loved that. I know how 'eager' he is to find himself in a leadership position. How did you get him to agree?"

"Oh, I made it look unintentional on my part." Baldur had a sly smile that Elska hadn't seen before. "I told Úlftýr to keep an eye on the younger recruits while they trained in a new routine, and I casually strolled off and didn't come back, which forced Úlftýr to take responsibility for overseeing the drills for the rest of that day."

"Deviant." Elska smiled.

"Even before we set out for the Ice Lands, Úlftýr earned his rank by my side with his wits, the strength of his heart, and strenuous training. No one questions his station as both Prince and my second in command. I could step down for him, but he won't allow it, and I respect his wishes as they are."

Baldur looked at Elska. "May I inquire about something personal?"

Elska set the cloth aside. She briefly traced the newly formed scar on Baldur's stomach, satisfied with her work. "You are all set." She spoke. "And yes, of course, you can ask me anything." She got up and took the tray her father had brought back to his workstation.

Baldur looked down at his stomach and then let his tunic fall back into place. "Why do you keep your distance from Úlftýr? It can't make you happy; it certainly doesn't make him feel joy."

Elska sighed. She turned back to Baldur. "I feel I've let it go on for too long. At the beginning, our paths just parted. Úlftýr busied himself with the mastery of his body's full potential with you."

Baldur smirked. "I am sorry to interrupt you, but you know his vigorous training had a side effect he welcomed with glee. His exhausted body often made way for the clarity of his mind, so he said. And, in his dreams, Úlftýr vividly envisioned the future he desired. I am imagining a future with you. So much so that he sometimes wished to stay asleep, he told me."

Elska bit her lip. A slight tingling burned her nose. She sniffed. "I've tried to put him out of my thoughts," she said quietly. "While Úlftýr grew in strength and reputation, I took to the forests. I've tried to remedy my relationship with my father. I gained new knowledge from his old wisdom about herbs and potent remedies to help our people after what your warriors did to bring us home safely. One agreeable aspect about my father and mother was that I always received the freedom to grow in my own way." She came to sit beside Baldur.

"Look, you know that over time, the Ljósálfar around me heeded my advice as they previously did my father's. I was allowed to work on my belief that we didn't have to rely only on our elemental abilities to heal each other. Surely, I don't have to tell you how common injuries are among our people and how fatal they tend to be when they occur."

Baldur nodded. "Yes, I am aware of the reasons—hunting gone awry or a training session that got out of hand. Mostly, the long lives of the Ljósálfar make them reckless. Even my own trainees. Innately, the Ljósálfar love to explore. The wild terrains of our land call to them as I remember it calling to me and Úlftýr when we were younglings; from the underwater ice caves to the fields of lava in the mountains, our domain stands vastly rich in the adventure it promises."

"Exactly," Elska agreed, "And those less than a century old often get hurt and perish in idiotic durability contests."

"And don't forget the mines," Baldur interjected.

"How can I?" Elska agreed. "The mines also claimed their share of souls when Ljósálfar didn't make it out in time to the surface to tend to their wounds. I know from those under our care that those who perished underground and didn't make it were too stubborn to let an injury halt their work. And they paid for their stubbornness with their lives.

The healing process for injuries sustained underground proves difficult for younger, inexperienced elementals; it drains their stamina and leaves them incapacitated for days. I seek to prevent all that."

"You know," Baldur said, placing his hand on hers. "The most broken beings are those who would want to mend the world for others. I can see that something within you was somehow permanently shuttered; it's incomplete, and a great chasm now lies between your needs and your wants. I feel the same since Hoder, my brother, died."

Elska nodded. Of course, she knew Hoder and was saddened to learn of his death.

"For years before we left for the Ice Lands, I believed I needed the adventure. I was a fast-paced, curious child and a thrill-seeking, reckless youth. At a young age, I became self-sufficient. Yes, my elders hovered over me, attempting to bless me with their wisdom from the top of their stature instead of trying to be at eye level with me, where I could question their teachings instead of blindly receiving their knowledge in the form of dry law.

Their cold nature meant I could not rely on them when I needed emotional guidance. They would enter my circle when it was convenient for them, give me the thinnest of threads to follow, and slither right back out to immerse themselves in their personal growth."

Baldur squeezed her hand. "So, I gather that gradually, this behavior turned you untrusting of anyone who pledged to commit themselves to remain by your side. Is that the real reason you keep Úlftýr away? You don't have to find a way to heal the world before you heal yourself. Finding the perfect remedy to all the ailments you see around you won't mend your heart; worse, it will further shatter his."

And perhaps, with you, he can escape his fate.' Baldur thought. He knew the passage from the book clearly.

'He will face the fires of hell alone and will succumb to them until the maiden of snow will pour her life into him. Still, even then, beware of the beast unlisted, for until his mind clears, nothing will stand in the way of his thirst.'

"So, what should I do?" Elska questioned. "It's been years since we spoke of our first connection from that night on the beach when we returned from the Ice Lands, and I first laid my eyes upon him."

"Have you seen him of late?" Baldur asked.

"Of course, we keep in contact." Elska nodded. "Much more than that, our friendship endured these seventeen years. The day we met, Úlftýr offered his heart to me, but too young in thought or too fearful, I refused him."

"And I know he did not respond to your rejection well," Baldur said. "He regrets it."

Elska shook her head. "He told me he would be here when I finally decided." She sighed. "He spoke the words harshly, snarling in anger."

Baldur tapped on her hand. "His intent may have been to convey his hurt at your rejection. You know he talks about you. There was always a shroud of mystery, and you always seemed like a bright but distant star."

Elska blushed.

Baldur smiled. "He wants to find out who you are, but you keep this cold and endless space between you and the rest of us. And I think I know why."

"Perhaps," Elska agreed, "but Ingrid believes what Úlftýr sensed most was utter frustration. She confronted him about it once, and he told her she was not completely wrong. That he would do anything to be with me," Elska blushed. "When they spoke about it, Úlftýr told her he had never felt such intense emotion. No one ever came close to awakening such a call of the heart within him throughout his life."

"And what about you?" Baldur asked.

Elska looked down. "In all the time since our encounter, I could never deny that, from that moment by the bonfire, I became unequivocally and irrefutably in love with him. We both know that only my irrational dread keeps us apart."

"Dread that is fuelled by years of shattered hope and constant disappointment," Baldur didn't frame his words as a question.

And Elska didn't deny it. "You are wise." She spoke. "As the years passed, I wondered what would happen if I took that leap, I feared. The cliff of my emotional barrier keeps calling to me, telling me that I am making a great mistake and that my time is running out to fix it."

"I think that is where you are mistaken," Baldur said. "Yes, you both became infatuated with other companions over time, yet neither relationship lasted. Úlftýr sought, and still seeks, solitude from his adoring court above everything else. He skilfully avoided the courting of the other maidens, who seemed to have no pastime but fawning over him."

"I know." Elska nodded. "At one point, even Ingrid and I tried and failed to interest Úlftýr in another. Still, no matter how fair she may have been or how pure her intentions were, Úlftýr remained stubbornly unobtainable."

Baldur looked at Elska. "Because he told his sister he had given his heart away for good."

"So, you don't think I missed my chance with him?" Elska woefully asked.

"I don't think all is lost," Baldur said as he got up. "But you will never know if you don't try."

They embraced. "Thank you, Baldur." Elska smiled.

"Thank you." Baldur stepped toward the door. "I'll see you."

Elska nodded. She watched him open the door and disappear into the garden. He didn't want anyone to know about his visits to the Elder. Proud or stubborn as he was, he kept his ailments to himself and asked Elska and her father not to reveal his shortcomings to anyone.

Elska closed the door and turned. "Ohh."

Siran materialized as if out of nowhere at his workstation.

"How much of that did you hear?" Elska asked.

"Enough," Siran said, turning his attention to the glass vials. "But it wasn't anything I didn't already know." He began sealing the glass vessels in front of him with sap.

"You know, I do agree with Baldur. All is not lost. Life has a way of getting you to where you need to be," he said. "You will be surprised by where your road leads you; you just need to be open to the possibility of love, and it will come."

Elska looked at him. "It is funny to hear you say it, Father. I gather your new wife has a good effect on you."

Her father let out a tiny smile. "Perhaps. Or I have become wiser in my old age."

Elska laughed. "I do so wish for you to be right, Father," she said, the hope within her blooming anew.

CHAPTER 10
THE COURTSHIP

They met again on the eve of Úlftýr's five hundred and twenty-fifth birthday.

He marked the occasion privately with a dinner that included his immediate family and Deirdra, an adoptive sister he had never asked for and whose presence made him somewhat uncomfortable.

The guards brought Deirdra to them, an orphaned infant someone had left on the beach precisely one year after the fateful night that marked the end of the survivors' voyage home.

The King ordered a search party despite her true kin never coming forward to claim her. The King and Queen assumed her family perished in the raid on the settlement, and her appointed guardian later abandoned her, unable to withstand the grief.

Orphans at a young age were not common among their people. The Queen, missing the laughter of children in the castle and the prattle of little feet, expressed her desire to nurture another infant under her care. Especially one that had no one to care for it.

Showing his support for the Queen's wishes, Bileygr, the King's advisor, proclaimed that taking the baby in showed just how much empathy the royal family held toward the survivors' difficulties.

By adopting the girl, the royal couple adopted their brethren not just into their city but also into their home.

Úlftýr was there when the infant was brought into the throne room by the guards. Something growled within him at the sight of her, something he felt before but could not explain now.

Ingrid noticed his reaction. She had only seen this look on her brother's face once before when they were hunting for the stag.

She led him out of the room while their parents contemplated what to do with the child, and Bileygr watched them as they went.

After their first encounter Ingrid and Úlftýr regarded the child with some suspicion. And despite her humble beginning, Deirdra grew selfish and spoiled, partly by virtue of the queen.

It was more times than Úlftýr cared to count that a maiden assigned to his new sister would leave in tears. The child was an absolute nightmare to be around. She threw fits, berated, and insulted anyone who was at her words beneath her. Úlftýr felt sick whenever Deirdra acted as a saint around his mother.

And the Queen, she never denied her anything, so Deirdra regarded herself in the brightest light possible. She admired herself narcissistically like no other, a precious jewel in the crown of her land.

Maturity in body and mind brought to her attention the one she considered worthy of admiring her as she did: the tall, dark álfur that slept down the hall.

He, in turn, shut down her advances right off the bat. Úlftýr let Deirdra know that even if he reluctantly accepted her presence near him and had no say regarding her place in the castle, he had a say about her place by his side. He made sure, rather harshly, that she knew he had no interest in her in any shape or form—particularly not an intimate one. The seventeen-year-old was an infant in his eyes as he once was when he first regarded himself as capable of greatness.

Deirdra knew of and despised Úlftýr's affection for the Elder's daughter for years.

More than anyone, she caught the subtle glances between them—the reddening cheeks and the gleaming eyes. She could not understand what Úlftýr could possibly find in the redheaded álfur. Elska was, in Deirdra's opinion, too short, too full, and too plain to be considered worthy of the prince's attention, certainly not more than herself. Deirdra made the mistake of letting her thoughts be known at the dinner table in the middle of Úlftýr's birthday celebration.

"I think it is high time that you were mated," Deirdra told Úlftýr after the king toasted his health and a long, prosperous life.

They sat in the throne room, Úlftýr, Ingrid, Deirdra, and their parents. A long wooden table draped with golden silk cloth was set with the most fragrant fruits of the season and an abundance of game. Úlftýr always preferred to celebrate the passing of his years with close family instead of a spectacle-filled banquet, like Deirdra preferred doing every year. In fact, if he could, he would exclude Deirdra from his celebration, given half the chance.

Úlftýr glanced at Deirdra and ignored her, looking at his mother instead.

Deirdra did not seem clever enough to understand when her opinion was unnecessary.

"Úlftýr," she all but whined. "Listen to me. You can ask anyone who is anyone at court that my authority on the subject of a proper mate is unparalleled."

"Huh," Úlftýr let out. "Does your craving for attention know no bounds? You are very well aware that I have already pledged my heart away. I do not need to replace my heart's desire."

Deirdra snorted. "You mean the elder's daughter? She has nothing in stature save for her association with her father. I hardly see her at court, and when I do, she feigns no interest in royal affairs."

"Deirdra, " The queen warned.

Deirdra turned to her like a scolded child. "Oh, Mother, you know I am right; look, she is not even here; how is she even an important topic for conversation?"

"She is not here," Úlftýr said through greeted teeth. "Because she is hard at work cultivating medicinal herbs for our remedies in the only place that allows their growth. But of course, I understand 'hard work' is not a concept you would know anything about."

"Úlftýr," The queen sounded tired; this was not the first or the hundredth time she had witnessed their children's bickering.

"You need a mate that will always be by your side, not one that will gallivant off looking for adventure."

Somehow, this statement from his found sister made Úlftýr feel violently ill, given that he followed correctly what she suggested. "Adventure is what I seek as well," Úlftýr said without sparing her a look.

"You do have your responsibilities." His mother said.

An aura of pain lingered at the back of Úlftýr's head. "Thank you, Mother," he said, putting his utensils down. "Well, I believe I am done with this feast. I will bid you farewell, for I much rather seek the tip of Baldur's sword than sit here further."

"Úlftýr," Ingrid said, placing her hand on his. She noted that his fingertips began to take on a blue tint.

"Father!" Deirdra screeched. "Do something! You must forbid him from endangering himself; it's so unbecoming for him to still run around with swords instead of adorning the robes of the council."

Úlftýr's ire continued to rise within him.

"Deirdra, why don't you keep your thoughts where they belong behind closed teeth and stay out of my priorities? You have no business commenting on them." A red tint came down over his eyes, and his blood boiled.

Deirdra flipped her blond locks back. "If you are allowed to sort out your priorities, Úlftýr, soon we will find you playing in the dirt with that redhead dung wench."

"Deirdra!" Ingrid looked at her, appalled, while the queen had her hand over her mouth.

The next moment, Úlftýr was on his feet, his eyes ignited in blue light, his hair flew around him, and electric currents ran down his arms. The wall behind Deirdra crystallized and exploded, with sharp shards of ice aimed at her. They tore through her pretentious, sparkling dress and slashed the air on their trajectory towards her face, barely stopped only by a second wave of ice produced by the king.

Deirdra screamed and wailed, her cheeks bleeding blue from the gashes of the icicles that did get her.

Úlftýr blinked his eyes once again the color of amber. "No, no no, damn it." The realization of what occurred struck him and it angered and upset him further. His elemental abilities manifested in full power. He knew it meant his people would expect him to rule if the situation called for it.

His royal blood awakened, marking him a legitimate heir to the throne. He could now access power he had never known before. All the knowledge of his ancestors and the strength of his bloodline were now at his fingertips, ready for him to wield.

Suppose he learned to control it if he didn't lose himself to the power trying to dominate his will.

It was a burden-filled obligation he didn't wish for; for decades, he hoped the full force of his capabilities would never come to him because all he wanted was to be free.

Believing that option did not exist for him anymore, Úlftýr let out a low growl and furiously left the table.

The crisp night air welcomed him into its calming embrace. Úlftýr wandered through the valley, mourning his freedom.

He thought about what it would be like if he ran away, left all his duties behind, and disappeared into the mountains. He knew there would be nothing simple about him from that moment forward.

Úlftýr walked, wandering, the stars illuminating his path.

On a brightly lit road, as if out of a dream, Elska appeared, coming towards him, the brightest light to lift the smothering darkness. They embraced without uttering a word and stayed in each other's arms until they could both breathe again. A distraught expression was etched across Úlftýr's face.

"Would you like to accompany me home?" She asked on impulse before she could stop herself.

"Yes." He gladly accepted and followed her.

That night, he stayed in the home she had taken for herself, hidden from the world. Desperate to disregard the calling of his powers, Úlftýr began drinking copious amounts of ale during the following days and spent most of his nights up in the mountains, away from any living soul.

After he failed to return to the castle on the second day, Ingrid asked Baldur to locate him, which he did with ease.

Ingrid then asked Baldur to watch her brother while Úlftýr came to terms with his new predicament. She, too, remembered the churning of emotions when her powers awakened, although they came more calmly, not as explosive as her brother's had.

Knowing that Úlftýr had found his way into Elska's arms somewhat reassured Ingrid that Úlftýr would find his way back stronger and sooner than anyone could imagine.

Meanwhile, Úlftýr spent his nights on blades of his own making. He glided down the frozen river and jumped off its solidified waterfalls, just him and the wind that carried him forward.

Úlftýr fashioned the blades with the sharpened horns of a goat he hunted, skinned, and strapped to the bottom of his winter boots. Elska remarked that honing those bones had done a marvelous job of calming and focusing him. In those moments when his work consumed him, the events that led him to her door didn't seem to burden him.

Úlftýr didn't seem to agree with her. He was disappointed with himself and frustrated by losing his identity, which made him who he was. He was now a part of something bigger, ancestral, and he hated that he was so intertwined with the old that he was discouraged from a new discovery of self.

But Elska remained by his side, supporting him, patiently waiting until he found what he wasn't sure he had lost. It was hard for her not to pry into the personal troubles that dwelt in his mind. She was curious innately, and many years passed before she learned that, eventually, Úlftýr came around to doing and saying things in his own time and that pressuring him would most likely resolve in an argument and him shutting down rather than opening up to her.

Elska took great care not to take offense when she wished to speak or read tales of her creation to him but remained denied the attention she craved, while he only wanted to talk about perfecting his blades and mastering his magic.

She smiled in understanding when he talked about the unique growth periods of various antler structures, genially taking an interest in his discussions.

Those were trying times for both of them. Úlftýr attempted to contribute to the home they shared for a time.

He first did this by chopping the wood pile in the yard. Elska, who saw him, commented that he was not stacking the logs neatly. In retaliation, Úlftýr threw the axe to the ground and stormed off.

Elska looked after him, shrugged, and decided to leave it as is.

She thought of going after Úlftýr but instead went about her day. There were still many ingredients in her father's workshop for her to go over and label.

When she returned that night, the wood pile had been neatly arranged in the yard.

She entered her home to find Úlftýr seated by the fire.

She gladly accepted the meal he had prepared for her. They sat by the flames on a warm wool rug.

After a few moments of eating in silence, he began. "Listen, about earlier,"

Elska shook her head. "As much as I would like to dwell on the escalation of your outburst, our time is too precious to me for me to give this matter any more space. In the future, I will take care of what I see right by myself, and if I require your help, I will ask for it."

"You are mad." Úlftýr put his wooden plate down.

"I assure you, I am not." Elska discarded her plate on the floor and took his hand.

"What was is not important; let us just enjoy what is."

Úlftýr was clearly unaccepting of her answer, but he did not push the matter further.

On Úlftýr's second day in Elska's home, he awoke to find her chopping wood in the garden.

"You know," he said then as he sat on the stoop and watched her, "if you bend your knees when you swing, the movement of the axe will go down smoother." he tapped his chin. "Also, these wedges you make are too big; you will never catch a good fast flame with those. And what wood are you using? I believe I can find a more suitable tree to use for fire logs…."

He stopped rambling when he noticed her standing with the axe in her hands, unmoving and staring at him, her left eyebrow arched.

"Mmm," Úlftýr cleared his throat. "How many was that? Three critiques in a row?" he smiled bitterly and rubbed the back of his neck. "Yeah, Sorry, I will shut up now."

Elska rolled her eyes, laughed, and went back to work.

Elska understood the demons within Úlftýr's head, for she had encountered them herself and won, strengthened by his presence. She understood the weaknesses he attempted to conceal and welcomed all of them, for conquering them only strengthened Úlftýr.

She attempted to be patient and supportive; he wished he could have been a little more like her.

Less cruel and more optimistic. The road to get there had been challenging for Úlftýr, and peace did not come lightly to him, nor did hope.

Úlftýr suffered difficulties containing his powers. With Ingrid's encouragement, he returned to the castle and maintained the facade as required by his duties. Still, every time he exploded, downing another intoxicating beverage and stumbling through the town, Elska found him, beckoned him into her home, sat him by the open hearth, and braided a thin braid into his hair.

"Whenever you feel out of control and that another fit of rage is imminent," she said, tracing the braid down its length, "trace the lines of this long, thin braid; I will hide in your dark locks and think of me. Think of us sitting here by the fire, listening to the calm of the night." She said,

And Úlftýr tried to follow her advice. He valued it immensely, and he would try many of her suggestions, hoping to find himself again.

While they sat together one night, Elska put a gift wrapped in silk cloth in his lap. "Good yule, Úlftýr." She said, kissing him on the cheek.

"This gesture does make my heart flutter," he said. "But I am uncomfortable; I haven't brought you anything. I must admit I had forgotten the Yule season was upon us again."

Elska laughed.

Something resembling a smile tugged at the corner of Úlftýr's mouth as he pulled the cloth from Elska's gift. He revealed a wooden box with a lavish set of paints. When Úlftýr opened the box, he gasped.

"Oh, what wonderful colors. Have you brought the pigments from the Ice Lands?" Elska smiled and nodded. The beautiful wooden box contained a palette of dye and several brushes in different sizes made of bone and horsehair. The leather-bound book was blank but filled with parchment; she must have flayed and dried herself.

"I cannot accept such a valuable gift and must refuse your generosity." He offered her the box back.

"I insist that you do accept it, Úlftýr." She said, pushing back his hands gently, placing them atop the box she set in his lap. "Use the brushes as an extension of your fingers. Practice fine movements. Perhaps, that way, you will gain complete control over your abilities."

"Will you be my inspiration?" Úlftýr winked.

Elska blushed and nodded.

That night, he sketched her, for the first time, to the light of the fire.

He inscribed the piece with a dedication he considered too embarrassing to show her. It read:

"We met when times were dark; despair shadowed our souls. But in our hearts was born a spark, and in that darkness, hope we shared."

Later that night, while Úlftýr slept by the dying flame, worry and agitation rose again within him. He ventured outside, careful not to wake Elska, meaning to conquer another mountain peak with his blades.

When morning came, Úlftýr wasn't at the cabin. She looked outside, startled by her life-size statue of her made entirely out of ice standing by her window. It had been Úlftýr's first proper fit of control. He perfected the figure through the night; his blades lay forgotten.

In those hours he spent making the sculpture, Úlftýr realized that a world without his Elska would be a horrible and desolate place. Úlftýr didn't know that before he made that statue, Elska believed she had lost her chance with him. She thought she had waited for far too long. However, seeing her image through his eyes and realizing that, in his eyes, she was beautiful made her second guess her resolve not to pursue a relationship with the álfur she had known for so long.

That morning, while she stood outside and touched the image of her frozen duplicate, she decided to take the leap she dreaded.

Winter set upon the land.

"Come with me," Úlftýr knocked early on her door one morning, not long after Yule night.

"Úlftýr?" Elska followed him outside into her snow-covered garden. "What is this?" Elska asked.

A jewelry piece of white gold hung from a low branch. It was an ethereal snowflake threaded through a delicate white gold chain.

"What are you doing?" Elska asked.

"I want to try something I've been practicing." Úlftýr led her under the branches and sat her down on a nearby rock. "Ever since you gave me the gift that helped me control my abilities on Yule night, I couldn't stop thinking about it...."

"Oh, Úlftýr..."

"No, no. Allow me to finish. You don't have to say anything, and I am not expecting you to feel obligated by this gesture; I just want to do this."

Elska nodded, bewildered.

Úlftýr cracked half a smile, put his hands together, rubbed his palms, closed his eyes, and took a deep breath. Elska felt it immediately. The chill in the air and the surrounding temperature dropped. Úlftýr opened his eyes, and inside, the amber color of his irises ignited a blue flame.

Úlftýr pulled his palms apart slowly; electrical surges sparked between them. His face contorted. The river churned, and three grey-brown rocks the size of her fist skidded through the snow.

A surge of water followed the stones, creating an icy path.

The kimberlite rocks rose into the air inside a swirl of water, turning and crumbling under the powerful pressure Úlftýr created.

Úlftýr's hair flew around him like a dark halo, and beads of sweat appeared on his brow.

The stones shattered into numerous reflective gemstones. The water surge smoothed the rough edges and, one by one, set them into the hollows of the snowflake pendant. Úlftýr released the magic with a deep breath of relief; his hair settled down, and his eyes returned to normal.

He sighed and smiled, removing the necklace from the branch.

"For you." He spoke. "May I?"

Elska nodded and turned back. She raised her hair, and Úlftýr set the pendant against her chest. He fastened the clasp, and Elska turned back to him, her eyes sparkling. She lightly touched the snowflake, which shone like a star.

"Happy Yule, my snow maiden." Úlftýr took her hand and kissed it.

"Oh, Úlftýr. Thank you, it's perfect." Heat rose within her. She knew, from that day, she would never take it off.

The seasons changed, and spring rolled in.

One day, just as the flowers bloomed anew, Elska sent word to the castle, asking Úlftýr to meet her by a concealed waterfall deep in the forest that spread below the estate. Úlftýr had been certain that no living soul except them knew of its existence.

He had discovered it accidentally, falling while blading into a gorge concealed behind the shrubbery.

Glad to meet her, he arrived at the agreed-upon time as the sun set on a hot day.

When he got to the clearing overlooking the waterfall, he thought he was too early to arrive, but his breath caught, and his heart stopped at the captivating sight revealed to him.

Úlftýr's breath fluttered while he watched her bare body, standing under the cascading water that streamed down her curves. He blushed furiously, his eyes following the flow of the water trickling down with the outline of her body.

It didn't take her long to notice him.

Úlftýr opened his mouth to apologize; his legs were howling at his brain to rush him out of there, but then Elska did something he did not expect.

She stepped from under the stream, revealing herself to him completely, and reached her hand out.

"Join me." She spoke. And he, dazed, without saying a word, complied, took her hand, and followed her in.

They fused, tenderly, then lustfully, as neither had before. The urgency of their movements spoke of great yearning and atonement for lost time.

Under the rising moon and the night sky, they pledged one to another, body and soul, under the stars.

Neither of them had ever known such a profound and sensual connection. Such deep and elevating passion sprouted from a long friendship and blossomed into the fervor of eternal love.

Morning found them coiled into each other, gazing into each other's eyes in adoration.

There was no need to utter their devotion, and they were bound in a vow of everlasting love that would endure the boundaries of time.

CHAPTER 11

THE KING

Úlftýr proposed to his beloved Elska on the peak of the tallest summit he had ever scaled in the mountains surrounding his city. On that day, he asked to show her his kingdom from one of his favorite vantage points. As he expected, unquestionably, she agreed to climb up with him.

Úlftýr timed it perfectly.

As dawn broke on the day of their anniversary, Úlftýr got down on one knee and pulled out the rose-shaped ring he had designed for her. At first, she didn't even notice him doing that since she was so mesmerized by the scenery, but then she looked at him, and it dawned on her like morning.

"Úlftýr – " She gasped.

Úlftýr smiled and took her hand. "This land is where my life began, and for a long time, something was incomplete; I did not know what I was missing. I now know what it is; it was you, and I am asking you to join me as I want my life to start anew with you."

Elska cried, so choked she could not answer.

"Is that a yes?" Úlftýr got up and put the ring on her finger.

"Yes! Yes, of course." She laughed through her tears and gladly accepted. Now, she, too, felt complete.

Midgardr, Capital Region, Islandia. 1638 B.C.

In the early hours on the twenty-first day of Harpa month, Úlftýr and Elska enjoyed each other's company by the hidden stream.

Úlftýr lay with his head resting in Elska's lap. She leaned over him, her hair tickling his skin. Her lips brushed against his lips, trailing butterfly kisses along his sensitive ears.

"Úlftýr." She mused. Her voice pulled Úlftýr out of the sleep he longed to return to; her voice was a clear bell in his ears.

Úlftýr cracked one eye open and glanced up at her; Elska smiled.

"Are you trying to start something?" he asked her.

She blushed. "We can go…" She began to get up.

"No," Úlftýr lifted his hand and placed it on the back of her head; he pulled her down to cover her mouth with his.

Elska blushed. "Úlftýr, someone might see us!" she protested while kissing him back.

"They will have to go through the castle to get here from above, and if they come from below, we will hear them. Do not worry." He kissed her again, weaving his fingers in her hair to devour her.

"Úlftýr…" Elska breathed, her eyes half-lidded. "A lot of people go through the castle, my father…"

Úlftýr looked at her mischievously. "And?" he asked.

Elska frowned. She didn't have time to come up with a response before he lifted himself up, grabbed her around her waist with his other hand,d and smoothly laid her down in the hollow of his body, her back pressed against his chest and his arms wrapped around her.

"And what if someone sees?"

He tilted her head back. "Let them watch, they might enjoy it." He whispered as he kissed her.

She sighed, enjoying his taste of citrus and chocolate, and it clouded her mind further when he cupped her breast with his left hand. He snaked his left arm under her, grabbed her right hand, and guided it back into his pants.

Elska gasped, feeling how hard he was. Her hand traveled up and down his adonis belt, and he moaned at her touch, burying his face in her neck.

"Someone might come…" Elska breathed while he worked on hiking her blue dress up.

"Yes," Úlftýr agreed. "Me." he entered her, and Elska shuddered around him. He lifted his head up slightly and turned her head back to kiss her again.

He held her impossibly close to him; he moved with her as she backed into him and skillfully undone the front lacing of her dress to reveal her breast.

Elska would never have let anyone else touch her like that. Trust anyone to melt in the tight embrace of her lover's scorching hot body. His arm was dangerously pressed against her neck as he held her while Úlftýr's fingers twisted and pinched her hard nipples to make her tighten around him and emit little screams every time he thrust into her.

His other hand was busy traveling up and down her body, caressing every part of her he could reach.

She felt bold with him, and the world disappeared a little. She could only hear the bubbling water and his breaths as he neared his ascent.

She placed her hand between her legs and circled her fingers around him in and out in rhythm with his movements; she loved the sensation of herself dripping around him. She moved her right hand to grasp the arm that held her, pulling him even closer; the only air she craved to breathe was the one filled with his scent.

Elska stroked along his shaft and then grabbed his hip and urged him to submerge deeper into her; they rocked, propelled by their passion, lost in each other until the build-up was too great for either of them to handle. She went over the edge, and he was soon to follow, emptying his warmth into her and pulsating inside her while she came down, her heart fluttering like a butterfly trapped in her chest.

She lay beside him, breathless. Her tender fingers caressed his skin, trailing down with the lines of his body, and then she kissed him again. She leaned back, and he smelled the air. Crisp and clear.

He breathed in the fresh grass he lay upon and the fragrance of the surrounding flowers. Roses. Elska's favorite. Without opening his eyes, Úlftýr knew the beautiful colors of their royal blue bloom.

Elska caressed his cheek gently. She sighed and got up, fiddling with the lace of her dress to rearrange her built-in corset.

After she was done, she looked at the lake that formed under the waterfall.

Stray rays of light reflected in its crystal blue pool, emitting from an underground source, fresh to quench the thirst of the growing trees on its banks.

The overgrowth around the vast reservoir dipped the long-tangled branches into the water, bowing in reverence to the source of life.

Elska came closer and leaned forward over the edge. Úlftýr opened his eyes, lifted his head, and looked at her. In his eyes, she was a nymph imitating the evergreen trees, and, for a moment, he feared that she might tumble in before he would catch her. He opened his mouth to speak and call out a warning to her, but then, she leaned back, and he sighed in relief. He smiled and got up. She looked at him and came to stand by her side. He gave her his hand to help her up.

Úlftýr kissed the hand of his beloved. On her wrist, where the gashes of the mortal were still embedded in her skin, Elska drew a vine of hollyhock flowers in pink and deep crimson. Even though Úlftýr never wanted her to conceal her scars, he knew she felt very self-conscious about them.

"Oh! It is so beautiful!" She accepted the rose he had concealed behind his back and now revealed it and offered it to her. She took a deep breath of the fragrant flower with her eyes closed. The blue hue of the rose was pale, similar to the moon's color, radiant with its light. The magic bathed them both in its mystical glow.

"I fear a day will come when magic might run out from this world, and there will be no more blue roses," Elska said, a sad tone in her voice.

"It will never happen," Úlftýr assured her. "The blue rose is the symbol of my family," he proudly told Elska. "I will never let it fade from creation. On my honor, I vow to you."

Elska smiled.

Úlftýr pulled her closer to him. He was at least a head and a half taller than her, "My darling." He called her with affection.

"My beautiful love." She said and beamed up at him. Her eyes sparkled like emeralds.

Úlftýr looked down into the face that smiled at him, her arms wrapped around his body. He gazed into those big, green eyes. "The desire to kiss you blooms in my heart."

He leaned in.

"Your lips are so soft..." She murmured against his lips.

"Úlftýr!"

His eyes snapped open, and he looked to the side, still holding Elska in his arms. The álfur that spoke did so in a stern voice.

"Úlftýr." Ingrid halted a few steps away, dark hazel eyes reproachful.

"Hello, Ingrid." Elska bowed her head and smiled.

"Hello, Elska," Ingrid nodded and returned the smile.

Ingrid looked at Úlftýr, "I've been looking everywhere for you, little brother."

"Don't call me little, sister," Úlftýr growled, pulling himself unwillingly from the comfort of Elska's arms. "Age means nothing to us, Ingrid," Úlftýr stretched his body, throwing his long ebony hair back.

He brushed some stray leaves from his black cotton robe, left open over his loose cotton trousers.

He made his way to the water's edge with bare feet.

His amber-gold eyes stared back at him. It always took him a fragment to recognize his own reflection. He couldn't explain why he expected to find someone else looking back at him. His sharp-edged ears reacted to the slightest shift in the air in the cool wind of the end of summer. He kneeled at the bank and sprayed his face with crystal water.

Then, he looked at his sister.

As children, they resembled each other so much that their people believed them to be twins. Now Úlftýr grew taller and more powerful in build while Ingrid's once dark hair turned lighter, the result of decades in the sun.

All those early hours Ingrid spent outside sculpting in wood in the palace courtyard, Úlftýr could never bring himself to be out in the daylight for so long, for it would mean sacrificing his favorite time, the night.

The world came alive at nighttime for him when the sky danced with mesmerizing light, and he felt the slightest movement on every hidden path of his land.

"What do you want, Ingrid?" Úlftýr asked a little unkindly. "I thought you were sitting with the council in father's absence today."

"I was." Ingrid glimpsed the ground.

'Why won't she look me in the eye?' Úlftýr frowned.

Their age difference was merely three winters, insignificant by the standard of their long lives. Ingrid could scarcely hide anything from Úlftýr, and now Úlftýr felt that his sister had something she strived to conceal from him.

Úlftýr straightened up and looked his sister over. Ingrid wore the golden robes of their father, the King, and she had been the royal family's representative while their father was ill.

Úlftýr had no objection to the arrangement. He was not interested in the political dealings of the state; he was a warrior, not a politician. He believed his sister served that role better than he did.

Ingrid and the high council kept the news of his father's ailment a secret. However, no one is immune to gossip in court, even the King.

Úlftýr hated that fact.

It was not unheard of for an Elder to release their physical body and entwine their soul with the kingdom's delicate, magical balance. However, only their most ancient returned their essence to the earth.

The devout, centuries old Ljósálfar, the first Ljósálfar who saw this world reborn from ash and ice and grew tired by its many changes. Known to be a force of nature by himself throughout the land, that was not the álfur the King was. Their people did not get sick without letting go of their eternal life; it had to be sorcery.

Úlftýr was confident that that was what put his father on his sickbed. He knew others thought so, too. They, however, did not have a traitor in mind; he did. Whispers about spiteful gods or sick beings that might have invaded their land and poisoned their food source were spread, but his suspicion fell on someone much closer to home.

Úlftýr did not reveal his thoughts on the matter to anyone, not even to his beloved Elska. He resolved not to worry her, Ingrid, or any of his immediate family until he had solid proof or until he took proper steps toward flushing out the perpetrator responsible.

"The council wishes for you to be present in a debate concerning the future of our people, brother," Ingrid told him officially and knew from his expression precisely what he thought about attending such a sleep-inducing meeting.

"What would I have to say about our future, Ingrid?" Úlftýr asked. "We are immortal, and you will continue to be as you are, and I trust you will lead us if…." He trailed off; he would not think of that horrible outcome just now.

Ingrid let out a loud, slightly overdramatic sigh to emphasize how unfortunate she was for dealing with Úlftýr, her unruly little brother.

"Just come to the meeting," she said in a tired voice, pinching the bridge of her nose. "I come to summon you in the name of our father. At his royal command." Ingrid declared.

Úlftýr sighed. He glanced again at his reflection in the water and then turned to look at his sister.

"All right." Úlftýr agreed unwillingly.

Like herself, Ingrid knew Úlftýr could not refuse a direct order from the King despite him being his father.

"When?" Úlftýr asked, defeated.

Ingrid's mouth twitched in a malicious smile.

"Now."

Úlftýr flinched. "Thank you for the heads up, dear sister."

Ingrid smiled.

"Devil." Úlftýr couldn't help himself smiling, too.

"Do you want me to come with you?" Elska asked.

Úlftýr turned to her; she lifted her hands to fasten the wooden clasps of his robe. Úlftýr smiled, raising and kissing her hands when she finished. His first instinct was to tell her, "No." However, he appreciated how much she hated him for not including her in what she considered important events in his life.

"Yes," Úlftýr said after a short pause.

He pulled her against him, taking in her fragrance. Roses, citrus, and cedar. A mixture she prepared from pure glacial water Úlftýr brought from Eyjafjallajökull volcano, aged in a vessel of lava stone he meticulously carved for her.

She was one of the few fire-imbued redheads Úlftýr had ever encountered. He loved that she differed from the delicate, perfect, yet mundane image sported by the royal court ladies. He loved that Elska looked considerably small against his tall physique.

A thought went through Úlftýr's mind. *'Her petite size was in complete contrast to her loud and endearing personality. Sad she only ever wanted to show it off with him.'* Úlftýr smiled, and he knew he could be himself around her.

"Úlftýr, you can't enter the council chamber barefoot." Ingrid pointed at Úlftýr's grass-stained feet.

Úlftýr shook his head in amused annoyance and, with a grunt, plucked his heavy leather boots from their place on the ground and pulled them on.

"Will this attire suffice for presenting me in front of the lords and ladies of the high council?" Úlftýr asked in a mocking tone.

Elska stifled the laughter that escaped her lips. Ingrid handed him a robe he didn't notice his sister holding, similar to hers. Úlftýr said nothing but, half rolling his eyes, took the garment and pulled it on.

"Better?" Úlftýr asked.

Ingrid nodded, letting out the thinnest of grins. "Quite," she replied.

Úlftýr laced his fingers with Elska's, and together, they followed his sister on the dirt path, stepping from under the low-hanging branches of evergreen trees that lined the path leading up to the castle.

Ingrid led them up the spent stone steps. The steps turned flat the further they went, for their primary use was to accommodate the riders of the King's guard.

"Ingrid, I know this entrance is the quickest way to bring us to the council chamber. However, this path would have us going through the inner courtyard." Úlftýr snarled.

Elska tightened her hold on Úlftýr's hand. "Are you trying to relieve me of the notion that I would soon have to endure the gossiping mass of the court elite nestled between the castle walls?" He asked.

"Yes," Elska confirmed. "Is it working?"

Úlftýr had to stop himself from laughing. "I grow weary of them staring at me at every chance they get. They are not too subtle in their attempt to encounter me, and while they bow to my face, they whispered idle fabrications behind my back regarding father's ailment and my avoidance of court." Úlftýr took a deep breath.

"Then perhaps you should stop avoiding it," Ingrid suggested.

Just then, they arrived at their first obstacle. As Úlftýr had predicted, a large assembly of Ljósálfar lounged in the courtyard. He nodded politely at the bows and curtsies of the high lords and refined ladies. Some lay about on ornate wood pews, and some stood wasting their time in idle conversation under the plentiful, red-leaf trees.

The court attendants enjoyed the pleasant rays of the bright sunshine and the sweet berries extending down so low they essentially offered themselves to the lustrous Ljósálfar. Úlftýr knew what most of them were thinking. Their ears twitched in excitement, speculating among one another in poorly concealed whispers.

'Which one of the royal descendants shall it be to inherit the throne on the tragic occasion of their adored King's spirit consigned to oblivion...?'

As Úlftýr, Elska, and Ingrid made their way further into the castle, Úlftýr attempted to sense the tone that prevailed in the royal courtyard.

The Ljósálfar, who did not slump over the ornate wood pews, sat comfortably atop red sandstone benches erected from the Dryas Octopetala Alpine flowering ground.

The Ljósálfar wore an assortment of lightly colored fabrics. The garments graced their fair skin, looking like flurry and mist.

Úlftýr closed his eyes for a moment. He allowed himself to delight in the moving tune of harp and violin played by the skillful hands of his kin. He opened his eyes and glanced at Ingrid.

Úlftýr believed that, even though his sister was an artisan, spending her days methodically studying the material world around them and the spirit behind it, she would step up when and if the time came to sit on the throne in their father's stead.

"You know," Úlftýr said in a low enough tone for only his sister to hear. "I find it agreeable that you are vocal in your objection to the games of war after the awful ordeal our people went through in the ice lands. You are a diplomat and a skilled negotiator of peace among our people, and many seek you out for advice and to broker trade deals between them. No one in the kingdom is suited more to the task of ruling in father's stead; you are just and fair, and our people love you for it."

"What are you getting at Úlftýr?" Ingrid asked.

Úlftýr shrugged. "I really see no point in my sitting in the council. I speculated that your artistry is essential in running a nation, and you would use your skills wisely to run the kingdom if the worst occurrence ever came. Or so I would hope you would. Because I have no interest in it."

Just then, he had noticed how closely packed the dwellers of the courtyard were. How many of them could have listened in on their private conversation.

Úlftýr forced out a smile. They slipped through the eager crowd and up the castle stone staircase on the other side of the courtyard.

The guards pulled open the large wooden gate for them. Úlftýr, Ingrid, and Elska entered the castle gallery dotted with several corridors leading out.

"Let us hasten our step," Úlftýr said, taking the lead. They expedited their pace to clear through quickly before any other member of the royal court's nobility noticed them and stopped them in mindless conversation.

Passing the kitchen on their way out of that corridor, Úlftýr felt the heat waves coming from the furnaces. The trio had arrived at the end of a long hallway adorned by lavishly set reading nooks and descended a flight of stairs that led them to an open chamber bordered by long, pointed arches.

Úlftýr's family crest decorated the walls; a blue rose guarded by two dark green serpents coiled around it.

Legends said the two serpents were lovers entwined in each other for all eternity.

The sound of raised, aggravated voices speaking simultaneously snapped him out of his thoughts.

Ingrid opened the heavy wooden door that led into the council chambers. They stepped onto the podium, surrounded by fair elder lords and ladies adorned in crimson robes embroidered with gold serpents.

Úlftýr looked around. The door opened again, and the King himself entered. The room fell into dead silence, and Úlftýr was taken aback by the sight of his father. The King slowly sat on his throne in the center of the room, and his appearance worried Úlftýr. Not two weeks had passed since the last time he had seen him, but the king's ailment seemed to take a startling hold.

The King's once robust and assured face appeared sunken in, drained of vitality. Grey streaks were visible along his fine, black hair, similar in length to Úlftýr's. The once mighty and proud King appeared shriveled in his too-large golden robes; Úlftýr had never seen him in such a defeated state.

His mother, the Queen, came in after him and stood beside him, raising her eyes to look at Úlftýr. She wore a long, green embroidered dress under the red open robe of a council member. Her long, strawberry-blond hair was set in a halo of braids with a circlet in the shape of a serpent entwined between them.

Worry filled her gaze, and the small apologetic smile that tugged at the corner of her mouth was there to prepare him for something grand that was about to occur.

Úlftýr gulped. They had led him into an ambush. He turned to Elska, who let go of his hand and went to take her seat by the podium reserved for the closest affiliates of the royal family. She, too, watched Úlftýr with unease in her eyes.

Úlftýr wondered, "Does everyone here know something I don't?" He looked at Ingrid, but his sister remained silent, avoiding his stare.

Úlftýr looked at the throne.

Bileygr, the King's advisor, stood on the other side of his father's throne. He always appeared in silence, giving the air he could be anywhere, anytime.

He stood high in stature.

One of the few Ljósálfar Úlftýr known to have lengthy, white facial hair; it extended to his chest, intertwined with twine-holding Earl Grey marble stone runes.

He has been by Freyr's side constantly. Nevertheless, Úlftýr had never trusted him.

Only known by his nickname, Bileygr, which meant *flashing eye,* Úlftýr wasn't sure he knew Bileygr's true name. Úlftýr could never shake the feeling that his one good eye constantly followed him while, in the hollow socket of the other, he swore, flashed of malice reserved just for him.

Ingrid claimed that Úlftýr had an overdeveloped imagination. Úlftýr had never revealed his suspicions to anyone else, not even Elska. His lack of evidence and gut-tugging fear of retribution at the hands of Bileygr's followers meant he did not dare to call him out on his suspected malicious intentions openly.

Tales of how Bileygr lost his eye while he exerted himself, pouring over tome after tome in the castle's library, were common knowledge. Bileygr's followers claimed he sacrificed his eye to gain the wisdom of the ages.

He had speared it out by himself and threw it into the river that led from their crumbling world to this one in a symbolic suicide, for the power of such knowledge came at an immense price.

Bileygr himself said, *'Knowledge is power,'* and he took great pride in the wisdom he had collected over the centuries. He never was without the long staff he possessed, carved from a young mistletoe with a serpent coiled around it, its head resting on the tip of its twisted tail.

The staff was, by Bileygr's proclamation, *'To represent the great serpent who in his mighty grace had delivered us onto this land.'* He would say, but, despite his declaration, Úlftýr knew that the head concealed within it a deadly weapon, a spear infused with evil sorcery, for he had seen Bileygr use it on a wild boar while he stood hidden from sight in the thick of the woods.

By the great serpent — Bileygr referred to the legend concerning the creation of their unique landscape. They based the Ljósálfar kingdom on the banks of a magnificent blue fjord that opened into the sea. The word fjord literally meant *'where one fares through.'* The story of how this long, deep, and narrow body of water reached so far inland by their city told, *'that the great ice serpent, mighty as a colossal glacier, ferried the first Ljósálfar out of the land of Álfheimr when darkness overcame it.'*

He gave them a safe harbor and a quiet threshold to the ocean, retreating into the deep, shaping the landscape with its grand body as he left.

The wooden door creaked open again, and Úlftýr's adoptive sister, Deirdra, let herself in. Her striking, blue eyes burrowed into Úlftýr like a hungry animal. She wore the finest blush silk gown the merchants provided, in line with what Úlftýr only assumed were the latest fashions. Her corset wound too tight around her waist to give her otherwise flat figure the false appearance of curves.

She raised her jewel-adorned hand and flung her delicate, blond curls over her shoulder, winking at Úlftýr, who averted his eyes. Her goading and maliciousness spilled out of her like venom. Úlftýr could sense the foul air she held around her when she stood too close to him.

The sight of Deirdra was terrible enough without her miserable advances toward him. Úlftýr never showed any interest in them getting close, emotionally or otherwise.

The Queen stepped forward, addressing the council in a mighty, uncharacteristic voice. "My friends," she began. "We have arrived at a point where we can no longer conceal our sovereign's illness. Our public voiced their concern, and rightfully so. Their concern is fertile ground for gossip and instability, and the general morale of our people is running low. Our nation is in dire need of a capable leader."

Úlftýr glanced at Ingrid, expecting her to step forward as the rightful heir, yet his sister's eyes rested on him.

"Oh, no." Úlftýr mouthed.

Ingrid nodded.

His mother's voice cut loudly through the now silent chamber. "... A leader most fit to replace his father in his absence, who helped reunite our people. Our son, Prince Úlftýr."

CHAPTER 12

THE NEW DESTINY

Ú lftýr had time to let the word *'shite'* slip through his lips before the room exploded into cries of protest, and cheers of agreement contrasted Úlftýr's own disbelief.

Some shouted that Úlftýr needed to be more ready or mature to assume the throne, and Úlftýr agreed with their view of him.

Others claimed this was a marvelous idea, and Úlftýr silently compiled a list of those miscreants for him to strangle them later in their sleep.

Elska rose from her seat and came to stand beside Úlftýr, taking his hand into hers for support.

"Quiet!"

Úlftýr whipped his head towards the source of the booming sound, baffled at the sight of his father standing, frail as he was, still projecting the might he possessed within.

145

The room fell silent to his command and hung closely on every syllable the King was about to breathe out.

"I had given a great deal of thought to the matter," the mighty álfur Lord whispered aloud. "I have come to the only suitable conclusion regarding our predicament. Úlftýr will take the throne and rule our kingdom in my absence."

"But father…" Deirdra opened her mouth to speak before Úlftýr could do the same.

"Hush, child." The King turned to her. "I care for you and consider you my own. However, I do not believe you are suitable for this position. You have much to learn before I feel confident to entrust you with real responsibility or state matters."

Deirdra bit her lip. Úlftýr assumed she did it to keep herself from screaming at her adoptive father and King. If she did, Úlftýr knew that, for sure, she would lose all her remaining credibility in the King's eyes.

Úlftýr wished she had, though.

"For that purpose," the King continued, ignoring her burning glare, "I have decided that I shall give you a patch of land and a proper estate to govern over until you prove to be a mature, responsible, and caring álfur I know you can be."

He made a point of looking over her extravagantly lavish attire. Deirdra tensed as if someone had struck her.

"But what about Ingrid?" Úlftýr asked, filtering the words through the shock he sensed. "She is the public figure our people came to trust, father. What about the line of succession?"

Ingrid shook her head. "I am one for words, not action, Úlftýr. I wouldn't know the first thing about defending our borders or rallying our troops. They won't look up to me as their leader. They come to me for guidance on moral and legal matters, and I will be glad to continue holding my post as your chancellor."

"We shall discuss this in private," the King said, glancing at Bileygr. "It is a family matter now." He turned to the delegation of Elders. "We appreciate your counsel. I understand your concerns, which I will answer in full tonight, but for now, I dismiss you, my Lords."

The ancient Ljósálfar bowed out.

Bileygr lingered a moment longer but received no further attention from the King. Pursed lips, he bent his head, turned on his heel, and left, robe flying.

The others went ahead without another word. Úlftýr was sure that, when they were out of his sight and earshot, they'd have plenty to say about him they dared not utter in front of the King.

Úlftýr strained his neck to look out of the grandiose archaic windows at the chamber's top. He glimpsed the mountain ridge, covered in snow. He longed to rush out of this royal imprisonment and immerse himself in the freedom his blades provided him, with the wind in his face and the grand mountain, his personal playground.

The tallest summit held fond memories for Úlftýr.

They were not yet married since Elska wished to take her time to prepare their promises to each other, and then his father fell ill, and time didn't seem right. Úlftýr thought that the promise they would make to each other at the sight of witness would hold little weight for him since he had already promised his heart to her forever, bonded or not.

Úlftýr blushed at the memory, and then he looked at his father. "You cannot be serious about this," Úlftýr exclaimed once the room emptied save for his family and Deirdra.

Elska tightened her grip on his hand, and he was glad she did so, for he wasn't sure he would have been able to control himself otherwise. Sharp, icy pricks pulled at the ends of his fingers. His powers threatened to burst out, fueled by his fear and frustration.

"Your father is severely ill," the Queen told him.

Úlftýr opened his mouth to say that was not news, but she raised her hand to silence him.

"Your father is ill," Queen Gerðr repeated slowly. "More than we led anyone to believe. Tonight, we will settle this matter officially, and come dawn, we will leave by boat to set sail searching for the first blue rose."

Deirdra stiffened and gasped. "But it is a myth!" She exclaimed with a glimpse of annoyance that crossed her face.

"I hate to admit this, Father; however, Deirdra may have a point." Ingrid nodded in reserved agreement.

Deirdra glared daggers at her, which Ingrid skillfully ignored.

"It is not just a simple fable we tell our children before bed," said the King. He groaned from the toll speech took on him.

"Whispers reached us from the east of the island. Travelers weave tales of a majestic mountain, two giant stone serpents entwined as one near the summit and hidden in a cavern leading into the earth between them. They speak of the rose temple, Úlftýr, but only the great serpent who brought us to these shores can grant entry. No creature or álfur was brave enough to scale that plunging darkness, but I must try, my son. I must sail out into the great dark sea, find the serpent, and ask for its guidance once more. It is my only hope."

"Then, let us come with you, father." Úlftýr insisted. "Let us help you find the serpent and the cure you seek."

"And leave our kingdom without proper leadership?" Freyr raised an eyebrow.

"Mother, you can stay here and Baldur…." Gerðr narrowed her eyes.

"I had followed your father from the world of our ancestors through the darkest barrier in the lands of our gods. I was there when the earth opened, and the great serpent declared my beloved Freyr King." Gerðr declared. "And I will be damned if I don't follow him now. I will travel up the steepest mountain, go through a dangerous sea, and seek a cure for this dreaded ailment. Even if it takes us up the tallest summit of this land, we will find the blue rose that will make a reality of our dreams."

Úlftýr fell silent. He tried to think of a compelling argument that would rival his mother's, but he could not think of one.

"I believe in you, Úlftýr," Elska said. I think you will be a marvelous ruler." She reached out to hug him, but he shied away from her.

"Not now," he asked, apologetic. "I know you think this is for the best, but you might be blind to my faults, so I cannot trust your judgment. Moreover, I do not feel ready; I can't wrap my head around this decision. It's too much."

Sad at his blatant rejection, Elska bowed to the royal family. Before she could allow herself to cry in such a public forum, she quickly excused herself and disappeared through the same door the Elders took.

Úlftýr blinked as he looked after her; he did not expect her to take his words to heart in such a way; she must think him cruel.

"You once told me you would go anywhere and do anything to fight for our people. You crossed the sea and fought the most terrible enemy," Freyr gestured to Úlftýr to come closer and took hold of Úlftýr's arm when the latter did. "Now I ask you to fight for our people, my son. I ask you to fight for me. My mind will rest at ease knowing you are here, a guardian of our kingdom. The King your kin need."

Baldur's words echoed in Úlftýr's mind, leaving him no choice.

"I accept my responsibility, father," he said, at last, humbly turning to his mother and then back to bow to his King.

"I accept my fate and my post and will do what I can to uphold the honor of our family and the safety of our people."

The King rested his frail hands on Úlftýr's shoulders, "I can hear in your voice how you have forced this statement out for my sake, but know this, you make my heart swell with pride, my son."

Deirdra stormed into the great library and slammed the door behind her.

"We failed!" She declared in a rage. "They chose that brute to rule the kingdom instead of me! Now, what are you going to do, Father? Years of planning… Wasted!"

She grabbed a book from the nearest shelf and hurled it across the room.

"Hush, child," a deep voice answered from the library's upper level. "Is that any way for a future Queen to behave?" Bileygr smiled at her through the ornate wooden staircase.

He tucked the old book he held under his arm and, gliding, descended the stairs.

"Will you, too, reprimand me like that old fool?! Your plan failed!" Deirdra snapped at him, watching him running his hand down his beard. It sent shivers down her spine. She had seen his ravens fly out of that beard and a serpent slide inside.

"The royals are off to find a cure, and that jackanape is sitting on my throne!" Deirdra grabbed another book and flung it past her father.

"Placing me in their care all those years ago didn't pan out like you hoped, father. Better luck next time."

Bileygr's smile cracked for a split second to reveal the true darkness of his features. However, he quickly regained his composure. "You have failed, Deirdra." Bileygr looked at her sternly, and Deirdra involuntarily shrunk back. "You were supposed to warm yourself up to the one chosen by the serpent. I knew that Ingrid wouldn't take the throne, and Úlftýr seemed too detached from court to do so, too unstable in his magic and indulgent in the consumption of ale it had led him to; however, now we have to deal with the outcome of Freyr's decision."

He looked at Deirdra, who did not respond, shame coloring her cheeks.

"Disposing of Úlftýr won't be a simple task to accomplish," Bileygr said severely. "A young King cannot just wither and die following the fate of his father; that would call forth too much suspicion to a traitor in the kingdom," he sighed. "But all is not lost, girl," he announced, circling her. "The King will never find a cure for my poison, for there is none to be found. It was a toxin of my own brew."

He stroked his beard. "And, while we are on the subject of the royal succession and our new juvenile King - well, I'm sure a lovely girl such as yourself can work her charms on him."

Deirdra sneered. "We are not exactly the best of friends, father." she said, casting her blond hair back.

"He is all head over heels with that redhead creature, and I doubt killing her would warm him up to me."

Bileygr nodded. "No, I should think not. But there are other ways to get what we want, my child."

Deirdra let out a bitter sigh. "Enlighten me, then. What are those ways you speak of?" Deirdra asked in a mocking tone.

"Look here, girl." Bileygr placed the book on a large wooden stand and flipped it open.

Deirdra leafed through the yellowing pages. The book was ancient, older than any other she had encountered under the instructions of her elder.

"I don't understand…" she looked up from the encrypted writing. "What does this old book give us?"

"It gives us a new plan." Bileygr smiled. "But the first thing that we will need to do dear child," he snapped his fingers, and, from behind one of the book stacks, stepped a mortal male with a badly scarred face.

"Is acquiring an army."

CHAPTER 13

THE AMBUSH

Tvímánuður - the second to last summer month

 A short time into Úlftýr's reign, he was woken one morning by the sound of a mallet falling on wood repeatedly, coming from the direction of the library.

Curious, and after confirming that Elska was not in bed by his side, he got up and made his way through the semi-abandoned halls of the castle, all the while reaffirming that the hammering didn't seem to have been coming from the barracks but really did drew him to the great information center of the capital and Elska's favorite room.

"Elska?" Úlftýr entered the well-lit room and followed the hammering noise through the aisles to the middle of the study tables.

Sure enough, here was his beloved, standing by one of the wooden tables, in front of her laid out planks of wood and on the floor several assembled crates without a lid on them.

"My love," Úlftýr frowned. "What are you doing?"

Elska all but jumped. "By the gods!" She glared at Úlftýr. "You are like some sort of a feline predator. I can never hear you coming."

Úlftýr smiled. "I have been calling your name; perhaps you are simply hard of hearing."

Elske shrugged. Úlftýr came closer. "What are you doing?"

"Making the crates for tonight."

Úlftýr blinked. "What is tonight?"

Elska frowned. "The Lundi hunt. Úlftýr, don't tell me that you have forgotten."

When Úlftýr didn't reply but kept staring at her blankly, Elska sighed.

"There are only two months of summer left, and grain-cutting season is upon us. The baby Lundi are about to begin their season at sea, and sights of them have already begun popping out through the city. They get lost every year on their way to the ocean at this time; our city lights confuse them. Didn't you ever do the Lundi tossing of the cliffs as a youngling?"

"I have," Úlftýr confirmed. "But I was a youngling. What is this fascination with doing it now?"

"Because," Ingrid entered the library, carrying her own carefully crafted crate. "It is a time of uncertainty, and we should show to our people that even if mother and father are away, everything is fine, and any trepidations the kingdom experiences are just temporary. They deserve a night of joy, and so do we. Besides, we would be helping the helpless Lunde."

"And I, for one, love this idea." Elska beamed at Úlftýr.

Úlftýr rubbed his neck. "Yeah, I'm sure you do."

"What is that supposed to mean?" Elska frowned.

"You like all these sorts of bonding experiences and quick-passed outings. It is just not my idea of a calming pastime. So how about you go on with my sister, and I will lay out my bones to rest at home? Won't that be a great idea?"

Elska huffed. "You told me once that if I want us to do something together, I should plan it out, and you would show up and play along."

Úlftýr laughed nervously. "You really expect me to uphold that?"

Elska glared daggers at him. "Yes."

Úlftýr sight. "Ok, but let's be clear: I am doing this for you."

"For us," Elska corrected. "And you won't be alone with us, maidens; Baldur is coming too."

Úlftýr laughed. "How did you rope him into that?"

"I asked." Elska smiled sweetly.

"Ok," Úlftýr pretended to be defeated. "I see I have no option then. Would you mind making me a crate, too, then? I'm going back to sleep if you want my company to last a whole night. Wake me up when it's time to leave for the hunt."

Elska waved him goodbye. "Baldur has already made you one. Go back to sleep, my love."

Úlftýr left to the sound of Elska's and Ingrid's excited chatter.

Later that night, Elska, adorned in a deep blue cloak, led Úlftýr, Ingrid, and Baldur through the town in search of the baby Lundi.

Dozens of younglings ran around them, looking into every nook and cranny, under the houses and in the tall grass for the little flappy birds. They lay as close as they could to the ground, coaxing the little creatures out of their hiding spots.

The night grew cold, but the search was relentless, at times, in almost complete darkness, led only by the starlight; the bright white chest of the Lundi shone as a beacon to guide young and older hands to catch to tiny fluffs and set them safe until dawn in the wooden crates.

As the sun washed the land with its first rays, most of the townsfolk stood on the cliffs, baby Lundi at hand.

"You have nothing to fear, little one," Úlftýr said to the Lundi in his hands. "You are an amazing swimmer and a superb diver, almost like me." He winked. "We will meet again when you come back to hatch the next generation on our shores."

Úlftýr lifted his arms towards the sky and tossed the Lundi into the air. It flapped its wings, gliding for a moment over the waves until it finally landed, followed by its brethren, sailing away like tiny boats sent out into the open sea.

The day greeted them on top of the cliffs. They sat in the grass, sipping on the hot cider. Ingrid had her maids distribute through the many groups of kin and companions that gathered around them, watching the Lundi swim into the open sea.

"When are they expected to come back to us?" Baldur asked, lying propped up on one arm.

"About two years now," Úlftýr replied, and Elska blinked in surprise at his knowledge.

Úlftýr noticed her bewilderment and smiled. "What? I read. I also know that we might see them sooner if a great storm will be upon us and the Lundi will swim to shore to warn us of its approach."

"I appreciate you joining us tonight," Elska said, sipping on her hot cider.

"It's nice to know that you do," Úlftýr said. "But I am glad I came with you guys."

The month of Gormánuður

A heavy blanket of snow covered the previously green fjord. A blizzard wailed across the valley, binding every inhabitant of the realm to their home.

Elska pressed her nose against the massive, arched windows in the throne room. She wore a long, royal blue cotton gown with a plunging neckline and puffed sleeves. The side lacing of the thickened bodice lavishly hugged her curves.

Frost covered the glass, a mural of swirling configurations in all shapes and sizes, a musical composition created by the hand of Skadi, the giant winter goddess herself. Their people used to sing to her for fair winters.

Much of their knowledge of the gods, of these powerful beings that once dwelled in their home world, had been tucked away in dusty books on the vast shelves of the castle's library.

It seemed like the King himself had an animosity towards them. A personal vendetta that led him to erase most of the influence of the high beings from their lives for not doing their duty in preserving their ancestral home.

Elska used her fitted buttoned sleeve to wipe away some frosts to reveal the valley below. The domiciles spread under the castle, with the charming scenery of a winter wonderland. In each one of their windows, she identified the flickering lights of the fire burning in the hearth lit inside.

Smoke plummeted from their chimneys, merging with the heavy snow. The throne room was warm. They decorated the stone walls with silver shields bearing Úlftýr's family crest. The green-colored serpents, embroidered onto the heavy silk sage curtains covering the walls on either side of the shields, gleamed with fine golden threads running through them.

The threads, skillfully woven into the lines of the artwork, made the snakes come alive and move along the fabric to the light of the candles placed atop large reindeer's antlers and candle holders mounted on the walls.

There were several sets in the throne room - some ancient, some newer.

Úlftýr accounted for each of the ones he was responsible for. The ones coated in bronze. He spent many days extracting the Saffron spice from the Autumn Crocus flowers to create the deep pigment.

His father, the King, was adamant about the social education he wanted his offspring to acquire. Freyr did not tolerate special treatment in the royal court. He led by example; he took Úlftýr, Ingrid, and later, Deirdra, however unwilling, on his hunting parties and his journeys to the remotest villages on the edge of their realm.

The princes knew from a tender age how to hunt game and learned the feeling of satisfaction and gratitude for contributing to their people.

"What are you looking for?" Úlftýr asked. Elska turned towards him and smiled at the sight of him. He sat slouched over the throne, one of his legs resting over the armchair and the other dangling in the air. He gazed back at her while he spun the crown in his hand, a gold circlet etched with entwining serpents set with stones of diamond and jade.

Úlftýr threw the circlet in the air and let it bounce from his foot, catching it with a sigh.

Elska smirked and returned her eyes to the valley. "I don't think you should be doing that." She returned her attention to the snow, her brow furrowed. "There has never been such a blizzard this early in the year, at least not one I can recall. Have you ever seen such a storm?" She turned back to him. Úlftýr stopped playing with the crown and placed it on his head, tipping it to one side like a jester's hat.

"Better?" He asked.

"Much." Elska laughed. "You like being bad, huh?"

"Why don't you come here, and I'll show you how bad I can be." Úlftýr winked at her.

Elska shook her head in amusement.

Úlftýr jumped from the throne and came to the window to stand behind her.

He leaned against the wall beside her, and she looked at him, towering above her.

"Were you always this tall?" Elska breathed.

Úlftýr smirked. He placed a gentle hand under her chin and tilted her head up, leaning down to kiss her lips softly while Elska stood on her toes and sighed into his touch.

He disconnected their lips, his dark gaze holding hers. He kissed her forehead and moved to stand behind her. He wrapped one arm around her waist and glanced into the dark valley.

"You are making it very difficult to talk to you when you look like that, you know?" Elska sighed.

Úlftýr blinked, "Thank you?"

Elska chuckled. "I'm serious; my brain forgets how to form words when I take all of you in. Your image is seared on my mind forever."

Elska loved his new formal attire. He wore a long, deep blue coat of woolen fabric decorated with a trim of gold serpents, the front slit overlapping to guarantee protection from the cold. He panted his legs in double-layered cotton trousers finished with black leather boots.

"This is our coldest winter yet. The valley has never been so white," he confirmed, watching the sunset.

"Any word from Deirdra?" Elska asked, leaning back against his warm body.

"No, I haven't heard from Deirdra in months; I can't say I have the urge to complain about that fact. I have no genuine connection to her, nor do I want one. I daresay the sentiment is not about to change on either end." He sighed. "I know she still dwells in the estate up north father granted her, and Bileygr is still with her. He said it was my father's wish that he would be there by her side to advise her, and I have a nagging feeling that that was a lie." He remarked.

"At any rate, the guard I stationed to watch them has not reported of any change." Úlftýr shrugged. "Whether his reason was that he wanted to be in a place where he was in a position of power again, I welcome his absence." He tightened his hold around Elska's waist and snaked his other arm across her chest.

"But enough about her." He looked down and tipped Elska back, kissing her deeply.

Elska giggled and turned in his arms, wrapping her arms around his neck and smiling into the kiss. She refused to let him go even when he began tickling her. "No." She protested.

"Oh, it's going to be like that, is it? Don't you know that sweet maidens like yourself should never deliberately taunt the big bad wolf?" Úlftýr grabbed her thighs and effortlessly hoisted her up.

She squealed and held on to him while he carried her to the throne.

"You want me to dominate you," Úlftýr said.

"Are you invading my fantasy?"

"I am your fantasy, and you are mine."

He sat down and draped her over his knees, with her hands held in a vise grip behind her back. His other massive hand came down over her small backside.

She yelped in surprise and moaned with raw pleasure.

"Don't ever deny me." He *chastised her, rubbing her bottom.*

As his hand ventured under her dress, sliding across her skin, she gasped and squirmed, the sensation sending shivers down her spine. Her moans filled the room as his fingers dipped into her and withdrew, their relentless motion causing her nipples to ache against their restraints.

Úlftýr snickered and let her go, and shaken, her knees wobbling, she stood up before him. Úlftýr smiled mischievously. "Had enough?"

Elska bit her lip, flushed red, and nodded, too embarrassed to speak.

"I think not." Úlftýr grabbed her arm. "Turn around." He commanded.

Excited and somewhat fearful of defying his command, Elska turned around.

Úlftýr pulled her closer, put a hand on the small of her back, and guided her to bend over. Her breath caught in her throat as he threw the skirt of her dress up and pulled down her linens, revealing her blushed buttocks.

He leaned forward and licked the hot flesh. She shivered and immediately cried out as something hot and hard slid inside her, "Ah, mmm…" she moaned, writhing, her limbs shaking. He kept holding her down, her hands tightly gripping the armrests. She felt so full.

"You love it, don't you?" Úlftýr mused in her ear, penetrating her deeper with every thrust.

"Ohh...!" Elska couldn't form coherent thoughts at the delicious abuse of her opening.

"I'm hungry," Úlftýr said after several more thrusts. He pulled out of her slowly, drawing out her anguish, turned her back around, sat her on the lavish seat, and got down on his knees. He lifted her dress again and dove under it.

Elska gasped, throwing her head back. He placed her legs over his shoulders and was delighted to discover she wore no more barriers to block his path.

She grabbed hold of his hair with both hands and put to good use his ability to hold his breath.

After long, smoldering moments, he came up gasping for air and looked at her, sprawled on the throne. Lust in her eyes. "Get in me." She commanded, and Úlftýr laughed. "you're so wet for me already; don't you want me to prepare you for what's to come?"

"Allow me to taste you for a change." Elska rose up and turned him around. She pushed him to sit in her place and straddled him.

"You don't have to do anything to make me lust for you," Úlftýr said.

She leaned down and kissed him, slowly pressing him into her; she began to move in slow, deliberate circles, lifting herself up ever so slightly and back down, skewering herself on his erect phallus.

"Why don't you look at me?" she asked between moans, noting his eyes were tightly shut.

"If I look at you, I will be done in seconds." Úlftýr groaned.

"Please," Elska placed her hands on his cheeks and leaned in to kiss him. "Look at me." She whispered, remaining close.

Úlftýr's golden amber eyes fluttered open, and his arms tightened around her waist.

Holding her emerald gaze, he bucked into her, driving himself deeper, faster, and faster until she shook in his arms, and he bit down on her neck, following with his release.

They scarcely had time to collect themselves before the door to the throne room burst open.

"Úlftýr!" Ingrid rushed into the room.

"Agh!" Elska let out an annoyed moan, with Úlftýr's lips still nuzzling her neck fondly. From the corner of her eye, Elska glanced at the door where Ingrid stood, clothed in brown leather garb and silver breastplate, panting.

"Is this going to be your thing now?" Úlftýr rolled his eyes, reluctantly letting go of Elska and allowing her to stand up. "Interrupting us?" he asked, half smiling, fixing the crown on his head and his open trousers.

Úlftýr 's jest about Ingrid's impeccable timing died on his lips when he saw the frantic look in her eyes. He straightened up. "What happened?"

"Fire," Ingrid breathed out. "Someone set the Armory ablaze!"

"What?!" Úlftýr glanced out the window; he couldn't see anything in the semi-darkness of twilight and the snow coming down.

"Sound the alarm!" Úlftýr ordered the guard who stood at the door.

The guard bowed to the young King and hurried away to execute his command.

Úlftýr turned to Elska. "I have to go down there!" He looked at Ingrid. His chancellor stepped forward and handed Úlftýr a pair of ice trekkers, crafted at his instructions with a side grip of sharp carved bone for further stabilization that would enable the wearer to scale all-terrain.

"Go! I will catch up with you." Úlftýr said to his sister, strapping them on.

Ingrid nodded and ran out of the room.

"Do you want me to come with you?" Elska asked, grabbing Úlftýr's arm before he could run after his sister.

"No." Úlftýr lovingly stroked her face and kissed her. "Send a messenger to the infirmary. We might have casualties, and I don't want you to get hurt."

Elska frowned.

"I can't do my job when I'm worried about you," Úlftýr whispered gently, extracting his hand from her grip and following his sister.

The wind blew hard, fueling the blaze set upon the wooden structure. It went up to wailing as Úlftýr and Ingrid arrived at the Armory mounted on two large dapple-grey mares. The horses' coats looked embroidered by the pattern of the falling snow.

"Was this done by malice for certain? Did you catch the culprit?" Úlftýr questioned.

"We are still looking, my King," Baldur informed him when they neared the Armory. He stood, shielding his eyes from the blaze.

Distantly, the bells of alarm rang through the valley. The castle guards, who also arrived on horseback, dismounted and were now using their collective elemental abilities to crush the ice of the streams and direct it into the blaze. Ingrid exhaled and was quick to join them.

Úlftýr dismounted and joined them. He reached his hands towards the frozen waters; the roil of raw power rose in his gut, a gripping force that pulled at the very core of his being. Úlftýr closed his eyes as force built up, snaking up from the bottom of his feet through his body until it called to unleash in his mind.

Úlftýr opened his eyes. They glowed in blue fire, and a shout tore through him, a vortex of raw power violently erupting from his veins.

The ice around them burst, the explosion echoed through the valley, and the crystal-clear waters rained upon the fire and extinguished it.

Úlftýr staggered back, lightheaded. He did his best to maintain his composure and appeared poised and collected after his endeavors. The crowd gathered and cheered the young King's success, all thinking the danger had passed.

Ingrid rushed to Úlftýr's side, seeing her brother attempting to catch his breath, winded.

"Are you all right?" Ingrid asked.

"I'm fine," Úlftýr let out, his eyes unfocused.

"Come with me," Ingrid instructed.

Úlftýr waved to the Ljósálfar around him.

He let Ingrid lead him away, and when they were out of sight of the crowd, Úlftýr allowed himself to lean against a large birch tree and close his eyes, exhausted.

"You are bleeding," Ingrid pointed out. She pulled a linen cloth out of her robes and handed it to Úlftýr.

"Agh!" Úlftýr opened his eyes and put his fingers to his nose, removing them to reveal the dark blue stain of fresh blood.

"Thank you." Úlftýr took the cloth and wiped his face clean. "I don't think I ever used my powers on this scale before."

Ingrid smirked.

"Well, if you plan to be our King, you better learn to expand your strength fast, little brother."

"I know you are goading a response out of me, but I wouldn't mind trading with you. I never wanted to rule - " Úlftýr protested.

"Sire! Look out!" A black arrow whistled too close to Úlftýr's ear, followed by another that grazed his arm and struck the tree where he stood just before Ingrid pulled him down.

"Who is shooting at us?!" Ingrid roared, enraged.

Several black-clothed men with reptilian masks of overlapping black, grey scales emerged from the darkness. The masks seemed stretched over diapsid skulls that contained glazed, over-bloated, dark green eyes.

"Sire!" Baldur cast Úlftýr a sword. A flash of movement caught the King's eyes.

Another arrow whistled through the foliage.

Úlftýr whipped the sword and cut the arrow in half, then turned on his heels and sent the blade flying into the branches.

A cry came from above, and the man, previously crouching in the shadows, fell dead into the snow.

Úlftýr drew his sword out of the assassin's body, then turned to the battalion of his King's guard. "After them!" He thundered. "Don't let them get away!"

Úlftýr, accompanied by Baldur, led the charge into the forest.

The arrows kept coming, and Úlftýr skillfully avoided each one, deflecting them with his blade.

He sprinted off the ground and used his momentum to propel himself into the trunk of the nearest tree. His ice-trekker's side blade embedded into the bark, and, with his other leg, he spin-kicked another bowman, who was sniping arrows at his men from the cover of the leafage, slicing him across the face.

The archer released a dying grunt and dropped down to the ground in a tumble. A spurt of crimson spilled on the fallen leaves.

An outraged cry left Baldur's lips – Mortals!

Úlftýr's troops attempted to follow on horseback; however, the terrain forced them to dismount. Vanir instructed his crows to fly ahead and look for the enemy.

Thick woodland obscured the road — the masked killers were baiting them deeper into the forest.

"It's an ambush!" Baldur bellowed a warning, gasping as the masked monsters lying in wait in shallow pits under the cloak of blind camo leaf nets sprung from under their feet and stormed his battalion.

The mortals separated one álfur from another and attacked them using sharp blades and cut wire garrotes. Some were successful in coiling the deadly wires around the stunned Ljósálfar throats.

The roar of battle erupted around him. Úlftýr turned back, landed in the snow, and attempted to return to the battalion of his warriors only to be knocked down by the fishing lines he did not notice stretched, concealed on the ground. He crashed down, twisting with a grunt across the dirt.

"Úlftýr!" Ingrid caught up to him after he fell. "The foul creatures set the Armory blaze as a ploy to capture you. Get up! We have to get out of here!"

"Agh!" Úlftýr pulled at the thin chain twisted around his ankles.

The thermal line ignited, scorching hot when he touched it, burning his hands.

Úlftýr recoiled. He heard it before the pain could register: the shrill sound of metal launched through the air. Two hard blows to his back racked his body. He looked down at the bloody tips of the iron broadhead arrows, driven through his shoulder blades and coming out at the front from the sheer force of the impact.

Úlftýr opened his mouth, but no sound came out. Blood stained his lips, and two blades deployed inside him. He gasped, drawing in a sharp, painful breath, and more blood spilled from his mouth. The blades shattered his bones, further embedding into his flesh.

"Úlftýr!" Ingrid attempted to grab him, but Úlftýr shoved her away.

"Stay back!" He grunted; his blood splattered on the ground.

There was a violent jolt, and before Ingrid could do anything to help him, Úlftýr's captors tore him away, dragging and pulling him by the ropes that adhered to the arrows through the dirt. His body recoiled from every rock and high-growing root sticking from the snow.

"Baldur!" Ingrid shouted, and the two sprinted after Úlftýr.

"Ingrid! Up ahead!" Baldur gestured to the dug-up dirt, and the pit Úlftýr was headed towards.

Ingrid stopped dead in her tracks, raised her arms, and, with a bawl of raw power emanating from her, commanded the heavens above to obey her.

Heeding to her desperate cry, it began raining down a storm of jagged hail and frigid snow. A wall of ice rose high, erecting between them and the assailants.

The ropes attached to Úlftýr's body snapped free. Baldur bolted forward, leveling on the ground to catch him, but he was too late.

Releasing a dire howl, Úlftýr went over the edge and plunged into the abyss.

CHAPTER 14
THE ABYSS

Úlftýr opened his eyes and moaned in pain. His pounding head jumbled his vision, which took some time until his surroundings became clear.

He looked up and could only make out the shadows of the trees and the darkening sky spread above them. He attempted to rise to his feet only to drop back down with an agonized groan, his limbs burning, paralyzed.

Something slithered beside him.

Grey-black scales of a long, heavy reptile passed by him. Úlftýr gasped and attempted to scramble back to his feet. Again, he did not get far.

The throbbing of anguish in his body did not let out. A weight crushed down on his lungs, like a smoldering boulder that threatened to bury him under its weight.

Úlftýr wrapped his arms around his body; he cried out. Every movement hurt, digging the arrowheads deeper into his mutilated flesh.

A loud hiss caused him to gasp and shuffle back, dragging himself away from the impending danger. He hit the dirt wall of the pit with a thud, knocking the air out of his lungs.

He saw them all now. Giant venomous snakes, slithering and coiling around him and each other, and the largest of the den, a massive grey reptile, rose before his eyes to an ominous upright position.

The menacing, sensitive eyes of the snake sized up Úlftýr's movement, who now attempted to remain still despite the throbbing pain. The creature aggressively opened its mouth, its fangs gleaming, venom dripping to the ground. The vicious beast launched forward and sank its fangs into his outstretched lower limb.

"Agh!" A sharp pain shot through his leg.

Attempting to move farther back, Úlftýr closed his eyes and prepared for another strike that never came.

The ground shuddered as someone landed in the pit. Úlftýr opened his eyes, and Baldur stood beside him, his sword drawn. The snake tore the air as it launched forward. Úlftýr yelled a warning, and Baldur whipped the blade, slashing the snake midjump.

He raised the sword, dirty and bloody, and wiped it off on his cape. At his feet now lay the snake's corpse sans its head, its dead beady eyes staring at Úlftýr.

"Can you stand?" Baldur asked.

"I can try," Úlftýr answered with difficulty. He looked down. The snake Baldur dispatched of its head lay in touching distance. Úlftýr caught the glint of venom on its teeth, and a thought crossed Úlftýr's mind.

While Baldur sheathed his sword, Úlftýr sneaked the snake's head into the pouch attached to his belt. *Elska might need this later.* He thought.

Baldur grabbed hold of Úlftýr and heaved him up. Úlftýr moaned in pain; he slumped forward in Baldur's grip.

"The arrows…" Úlftýr groaned.

Hod's demise flashed in Baldur's mind. He wasn't there to remove the horrid arrows from his brother. He didn't get to Hoder in time to save him.

Baldur slid down to the ground with Úlftýr in his arms. The rush of his blood deafening in his ears; he had experienced this horrid sensation once before.

"Baldur, break them." Úlftýr breathed. Baldur blinked; his vision clouded; he strained to focus on the tips of the arrows protruding out of Úlftýr's back.

Baldur swallowed and pushed back the fear that filled his mind. With trembling hands, Baldur yanked the ropes out of the fletching.

The scent of dirt and blood and death filled the hole he crouched in. His eyes frantically went from his king to the remaining snakes that slithered just out of reach.

He gathered Úlftýr tightly to his chest and went to work snapping the shafts in half.

Úlftýr held his cries in, but after the second arrow snapped, he buried his head deep into Baldur's neck and released a guttural noise. His body shook as it strained to its limits.

When Baldur finished, they slowly got up, and keeping an eye on the snakes, Baldur lifted Úlftýr just enough for Ingrid to seize his coat. Then, both Ljósálfar pushed and pulled their King out of the pit and back to safety.

Baldur ensured Ingrid had a good grip on Úlftýr before climbing out, slouching in the dirt, and heaving in exhaustion. At last, they all sat, staring at each other, near Úlftýr's intended grave.

"Thank you," Úlftýr uttered, gritting his teeth at the trauma still burning through his injuries.

"I need to inspect the extent of your wounds, Úlftýr," Ingrid said, reaching out to her younger brother.

"Not right now," Úlftýr shook his head. Filled with adrenalin, he attempted to twist away from Ingrid and grimaced at the movement he had to make.

"We have more pressing matters to attend to." He ensured his pant leg was intact enough to conceal the snake bite above his ankle.

"I cannot condone this behavior, Úlftýr; you are being reckless," Ingrid said apprehensively.

"My chancellor will not reprimand me." Úlftýr spat in blood on the ground. "I am not a youngling." Úlftýr gritted his teeth. "Ingrid, I know that my anger seems unfair. Know I do not direct it at you. You do not deserve it." Ingrid's expression softened. "Besides," Úlftýr sighed, "I have to find out who attacked us." He slightly lifted his arm. "Now, help me up."

Ingrid didn't move.

"I am your King," Úlftýr intoned.

"You are," Ingrid agreed. "You are also my brother, and we are your friends; we are worried about you."

"Worry about those who mean us harm, Ingrid," Úlftýr said. "My well-being should not come before my people. You've seen how easy it was for them to lay a trap for me. Next time, they might succeed, and if I go, at least I will help you identify the threat to our people and devise a plan against it."

Ingrid's face contorted. "So, you expect us to ignore the massive bloody arrows stuck in your body," Ingrid muttered under her breath.

"Yes." Úlftýr gave her a crooked smile.

"What do you think Elska would have to say about that?" Ingrid narrowed her eyes.

Úlftýr's lips became a thin line. "That was a low blow, Ingrid, even for you." Giving up on convincing his sister enough to get any immediate help from her, Úlftýr lowered his arm, pushed himself off the ground, and stood up with visible difficulty, intending to head back to his troops.

"First, we will sort this out. Then," Úlftýr touched the tip of one arrow embedded in his flesh and winced. "I will let you drag me to the infirmary. Think about it this way: if I pass out from blood loss, it will make the task easier for you." He said, spreading his arms in amusement and regretting the action imminently.

Ingrid rolled her eyes but said nothing more. She got up and followed her brother, gesturing to the astonished Baldur to do the same.

"Imbeciles!" Deirdra growled, observing the failed campaign unfold before her eyes.

One of the filthy mortals scrambled up the cliff she stood atop, accompanied by the mercenaries' scar-faced leader. The mortal threw himself at her feet. "Help us! They're after us!" He begged, glancing back in fear.

"Agh!" The last sound the mercenary heard was the whistle of metal of an enormous blade cutting through the air and embedded deep into his head, splitting his skull in half.

The scarred man narrowed his eyes, though he knew better than to stop Deirdra. He merely kicked the corpse of his dead comrade away and bowed to his sovereign.

"We shall have another chance, my Queen," he uttered, his eyes darting to the bloody sword in her hand.

"Perhaps we should work on freeing him of his powers." He suggested, careful not to aggravate her further by referring to Úlftýr as The King.

Deirdra said nothing. With a wave of her hand, she dismissed the leader of the mortal mercenaries and dissipated in a bright orange flame.

The battle had finished by the time Ingrid, Úlftýr, and Baldur returned to the defoliated area stomped clear by the monstrous scum that ambushed their army.

Under the guardianship of the great serpent, the Ljósálfar company suffered only one death.

Baldur lifted the cloak placed upon the face of the dead warrior, lying slain in the snow.

"Sna-" Baldur couldn't utter the name. The savages sliced Snakur's throat open, and the wound appeared scourged and black at the edges.

"It was the same device used to bind my legs," Úlftýr said. Crouching beside Snakur's body, he placed his hand upon the breastplate of his fallen soldier.

"Vidar," he called over to one of his warriors. "Ensure they bring Snakur back to the castle and find that instrument that killed him. Search the dead enemy bodies for any other unusual, concealed weapons they might possess. I want to know what devices they prepared in their war against us,"

Úlftýr breathed out, and thundering pain shot through the arrow wounds. "We must be one step ahead of them from now on."

"And find Vanir before word of this gets out," Baldur added, his eyes stung. "This is his older brother, and I don't want him to find out like this."

"Vanir was among the injured," Vidar glanced back. "We were preparing to transport them to the infirmary."

Baldur looked at Vidar. "Not a word about this then. I shall deliver the news after they have treated him for his injuries."

Úlftýr nodded. "Good, so that is what we shall do."

Carrying out Úlftýr's command, they split the battalion into two parties. A few to transport the injured to the infirmary in the valley and ferry Snakur's body back, and the rest, the able-bodied Ljósálfar, Baldur took to give chase after the assassins. The Ljósálfar knew there were those who fled, still alive and scattered throughout the forest.

They disappeared into the trees, and Úlftýr turned his attention to the bloodied and mutilated corpses of their attackers discarded in the snow.

"Who are you?" Úlftýr winced in pain, crouching down next to one body.

His extremities were barely working, and he willed them to obey his brain, calling on the ice and light within him to his aid. Úlftýr grimaced, and his dark blue blood ran down his arms to mix with the vile red of the dead assassin.

Úlftýr breathed in and finally snatched the demonic mask from the dead creature's face, studying it carefully.

The mask resembled a snake's head with small metal horns emerging from both sides of its coarse features.

"A dauðadyr!" Ingrid breathed out, forever inspecting the grimace etched into the mortals' features.

The dead man's face was scarred and dirty, and tufts of mostly coarse and filthy red hair covered much of his visage.

"Thugs for hire." Úlftýr spat. "Filthy creatures. There hasn't been a sighting of a dauðadýr mercenary in these parts in decades!" he uttered, agitated. "Not since they followed our people back from the Ice Lands. I thought they were all dead!"

After Baldur's bloody battle in the Ice Lands, they discovered that some dauðadýr had pursued the refugee ships back to Midgardr. The wounded pride of the savages drove them to seek vengeance for their defeat, but greed and the promise of new lands to pillage and plunder enticed them more than anything.

They did not expect to meet the entire Ljósálfar army posted along the east shore.

Those who did not drown in their retreat or the Ljósálfar army did not beat in the battle that followed their failed attempt at conquest fled to the mountains and presumably died there.

Úlftýr always believed that a handful of these barbarians managed to return to wherever they came from, taking back the account of fertile land and fabled treasures for others to seek. It was just a matter of time, in Úlftýr's opinion, before a ruler with means and dark intentions would secure their loyalty, however brief, to attempt to conquer Islandia, the Ljósálfar land, again.

"They wouldn't travel this far north for nothing." Úlftýr crumpled the mask in his hand.

"I doubt they are here to avenge their fallen brethren from long ago. These savages have destitute memory, a brief life span, and no loyalties." Ingrid agreed. "No, someone is paying these savage monsters, funding their weapons, and feeding their army."

"Yes," Úlftýr said gravely. "And I will find out who!" Úlftýr stood up in a sharp motion.

"Agh…" He staggered forward, instinctively attempting to raise his arm to steady himself against Ingrid, who got up after him.

Úlftýr let his arm fall back down, a painful grunt escaping him.

"Úlftýr?" Ingrid helped him lower himself to the ground.

"I'm fine." Úlftýr shook his head, attempting to rid his consciousness of the mist creeping in at the corners of his vision.

Ingrid raised her eyebrow. "You are a fine liar." She looked her brother over and then inspected his clothes. She reached her hand towards his pant leg's ripped and bloody end.

"No…" Úlftýr grasped her hand, but Ingrid ignored him and yanked the garment upward.

"What the…?" She gritted her teeth. "We were not fast enough to get to you." She said,

Úlftýr looked at her through half-lidded eyes. He was familiar with the expression Ingrid had on her face.

His sister felt guilty, and Úlftýr was too weak to tell her *she* should not be the one to endure it.

"They bit you." Ingrid pointed at the bloody tear in Úlftýr's pant leg. "You need to get to the infirmary. Now."

"I gather your plan failed?" Bileygr mused when Deirdra materialized in the splendid hall of the citadel where they resided.

They set it in a magnificent timber structure modeled after the impressive temples of old. Deirdra never made it to the estate her adopted father intended for her. Instead, she and Bileygr summoned a lavish three-story building to the base of Mount Eyjafjallajökull. Large, intricate dragon heads were carved on all four sides of its roof. Its courtyard led through an ancient temple honoring the great serpents at the start of the age.

Bileygr used a massive magma chamber to feed his intentions while the powers he once possessed strained to return to further torment the being trapped within the mountain.

Reluctantly, he also allowed Deirdra to master the use of this ancient sorcery. Not because he wanted to share the glory that awaited him but because he feared his potency might not be enough.

"Ki-yah!" Deirdra threw her blade, plunging it into the wall beside the marble hearth, built to withstand the angry fire used by the stronghold's inhabitants.

"To think that urchin once infatuated me. Úlftýr... I should have destroyed his spirit in his sleep while I still had the chance." Deirdra walked up to the natural stone mantle. She blew onto the coals and set them ablaze, marveling at the sight of the orange flames.

"You know that we need him broken, not dead, but you shall have your chance, child," Bileygr said, moving a blood-red dowel piece on his Hnefatafl board game closer to the King dowel. He ran his hand down his white beard. "You must also reconsider your approach, girl." He lifted one of the white dowels, the defenders of the King. "Next time, exercise your patience. Your strategy cannot be as simple as charging into battle where you cannot comprehend the entire board." He ignored the look of utter contempt displayed on Deirdra's face.

"Wait," he continued, sliding one wooden bead down the turn counter and placing another blood-red dowel by the King, closing in on him on three sides.

"Wait until his mind resets. Wait until he gets comfortable. Wait until he thinks the danger has passed, and he will no longer be confined to the watchful eye of his royal guard." He slid another bead down the turn counter. "And then, when he least expects it…." Bileygr trapped the King dowel amidst his attacking team. "We shall have him, daughter," Bileygr said, lifting the King's dowel into the light.

Deirdra grabbed her sword, pulled it out of the wall, and ran her hand along the blade. She was only half-listening to her father's jabber.

A single drop of blood glistened on her perfectly manicured finger. She flicked the blood into the fire that blazed in a blue, bright flame.

Deirdra did not answer her father. Instead, she let the rage seething inside her like a venomous snake fuel her new plan.

Despite his initial protest after Ingrid discovered the snake bite, Úlftýr allowed his sister to help him onto her steed. Ingrid mounted the horse behind him and made haste to the infirmary, careful not to disturb the arrows in Úlftýr's back.

Ingrid knew that's where Elska would be, tending to the other Ljósálfar wounded in the battle.

She halted the mare in front of the entrance to the infirmary, helped her half-conscious brother down, and led him inside.

Trotting through the snow, the cold burrowing into his bones, the adrenaline that sustained Úlftýr seeped out with his blood.

Aware of the glances they got from the troops bound to their sick beds in the solarium, Ingrid and Úlftýr made their way through the room. Ingrid attempted to step lightly to put the minds of her soldiers at ease, but her pretense ended when she had to assist Úlftýr onto a nearby velvet cot when her brother could no longer hold himself up.

His skin pale, his body shaking, Úlftýr lay rattled by what was done to him, unable to lift his arms.

Someone called for Elska after they saw the royal siblings walk in.

Unaware that it was Úlftýr in need of her care, she rushed over, halting in shock at the sight of him.

Right away, she noticed the glinting metal in his flesh and his tight grip around his upper body. Then, her eyes traveled downward toward his pant leg, where Ingrid had ripped open his clothing to expose another gruesome, bloody wound.

"Úlftýr?" Elska moved closer and laid her hands on his. "Forgive me, but I must see what's going on." Carefully, she attempted to release his constrained muscles while he gritted his teeth agonizingly over the intense pain.

"The iron blades...." He leaned forward and whispered. "It feels like hot metal sawing through my flesh...." He panted. "I can't... the slightest movement..."

Heat burst inside him, his fever spiked, and his eyes fluttered shut.

"Eir," Elska called on a female healer who had just finished laying a mending charm on a nearby wounded soldier. The maiden turned, and her eyes widened at the sight of her King.

"I need the dried latex from the opium poppy seedpod," Elska instructed. "The screen," Elska said to the maiden that hurried over, carrying the mixed powder opiate concoction in her trembling hands.

Elska turned to Ingrid. "Help me."

Eir set the bottle down by the cot and quickly released the heavy cloth separating the sick beds. She set it down, concealing the King from the eyes of his worried subordinates.

Ingrid helped Elska lower Úlftýr onto the cot while Eir fetched the bottle and a silver blade and handed them to Elska.

"Drink this," Elska ordered.

Ingrid lifted Úlftýr's limp head off the cot, and Elska brought the crystal-clear bottle to Úlftýr's lips.

"Arrows," Elska said, glancing at Eir, and the latter nodded, departing quickly to retrieve the tools required to extract the iron blades.

Úlftýr took a big gulp, and Ingrid lowered his head back down. Elska set the bottle aside, took a deep breath, carefully lifted the cloth pierced by the arrows, and slashed through Úlftýr's garb, exposing the wounds.

Elska gasped in terror.

"That's not all," Ingrid said. She moved to the foot of the cot and further ripped open Úlftýr's pant leg.

"A snake bit him."

Elska moved closer to examine the area around the penetrated skin.

"By the Yggdrasil!" She cried out. She looked at Ingrid. "Do you know what snake it was?"

"There were many snakes in that pit…."

"What pit?" Elska raised her eyebrow, and Ingrid reluctantly told her of the trap the mortals laid out to capture Úlftýr.

Elska clenched her fists. She shut her eyes briefly and let the scorching heat of anger wash through her, then she opened her eyes and turned to Eir.

"Fetch my father. He has far greater knowledge of snake venom than I do. Meanwhile, I will attempt to find the unfinished guidebook we had been compiling, and it can be of expert use until we can summon my father." She was about to leave Úlftýr's obscured area when Úlftýr grabbed hold of her hand.

"Elska," he breathed out. "Baldur killed it," he said barely above a whisper. "The snake that bit me. Baldur took off its head."

Elska nodded and looked at Ingrid. "Can one of your soldiers find and bring us that dead snake? I am relieved there is one; devising an antidote will be easier with the offending reptile corpse in my possession."

"I'll see to it myself," Ingrid said, then she looked at Úlftýr.

"No…" Úlftýr's eyes flashed with fear. "You don't need to go down there."

"Well, you are the reason I need to go down there. You knew you got bitten before we pulled you out, didn't you?" Ingrid asked accusingly.

Úlftýr's silence was answer enough.

"Why did you hide that from us? We could have gotten the damned thing right away!" Ingrid scolded.

"It was just a little prick…." Úlftýr attempted to smile, but his face contorted in pain despite his striving for humor.

"No, you are a little prick," Ingrid said.

"I have it. I have its head." Úlftýr sighed. He was drifting in and out of consciousness. He patted the pocket pouch attached to his trousers.

Ingrid grabbed the pouch and sliced the strap with her blade. She opened it and shook the contents out on the cot. There came rolling the dead snake's head. Its eyes and mouth were wide open, and its fangs glinted in the light of the solarium.

"Why didn't you tell us?" Ingrid looked at Úlftýr, but he was already out. She picked up the snake's head and showed it to Elska. "Is this enough?"

Elska took a linen cloth from her dress pocket, wrapped the snake's head, and placed it on the bedside table. "I hope so." Elska turned back and carefully probed Úlftýr's wounds.

"I don't understand this," she muttered. "Úlftýr should be bleeding much more than this."

"What do you mean?" Ingrid asked, frowning.

"Look here." Elska indicated the skin around Úlftýr's wounds. "The snake venom curiously does more good than harm, and I am certain it did not yet reach his vital organs. Úlftýr's skin looks too healthy for that. I'm guessing the venom moves slowly, but it rapidly coagulates Úlftýr's blood at his wounds despite this. It halted the profuse bleeding of his injuries."

"You think the mortals knew what these snakes would do to him?" Ingrid asked.

"I would think so if they had used this trap before." Elska nodded.

"Why not just kill him?"

"Perhaps they knew exactly what they were doing." Úlftýr listened to Elska hypothesize, his senses engulfed by blissful darkness, safe in his beloved Elska's care.

CHAPTER 15

THE SOULS OF THE SWORD

The following day, when daylight pierced the sky over the mountains, Bileygr summoned Deirdra and the scarred leader of the dauðadýr to his private library.

He called on the dark flames of the magma chamber to produce a tome of ancient runes. Flames burst to life in his cupped hands before dying out and leaving the ancient script in his hands. He then handed it to Deirdra.

"If we cannot have the kingdom, then we shall have this world. It is time to awaken **his** powers, and if you can't sway the álfur, release him of his godly binds."

Deirdra took the book with reverence. She turned to the mortal leader. "Thunaer," she honored his station, elevating him from the horde of the dauðadýr by calling him by his given name.

"Choose three from within your ranks," she ordered. "Choose those you will dispose of yourself, for I will sacrifice them on the altar of our rise to power over this land."

Thunaer didn't dare question their motives. Deirdra did not reveal the complete plan to him, yet she ordered him to tell the three he called upon to collect their dead from the previous day's battleground.

He immediately called upon his oblivious comrades, ignoring his disdain at Deirdra's request. He knew she would reward him handsomely for each additional soul that perished from his ranks; of those, there were many.

His soldiers came at his summons, apprehensive and fearful of what the witch woman would command them to do next.

They screamed in terror when her orange flames engulfed them, whimpering and yelping as they emerged unharmed in the clearing of the forest, falling into the snow.

Thunaer barked a threat in their native tongue, his stern voice striking enough dread in the hearts of his subordinates to settle them down.

"Bring us the bodies of your dead comrades," he told them. "And be quick about it. You don't want to test our Dróttning patience."

His underlings scattered throughout the clearing where they had ambushed the beautiful, blue-blooded humanoid beings the night before.

They dug through the snow and scoured the woods, dragging back their fallen allies' lifeless, frostbitten corpses.

Deirdra called on her flames to turn the pile of bodies they gathered into smoldering ashes. She then let the fire scourge the path made by Úlftýr's body, leading to the snake's pit.

The still-alive snakes wriggled and squirmed, biting each other to escape the flames engulfing them whole until they had perished.

Deirdra opened the book she received from her father and chanted in an old rasp tongue. It was the first time Thunaer had a chance to inspect the ancient tome in her hands. The book was made of dark, crinkly leather, sewn by a golden thread, and secured by iron clasps. It resembled no kind of leather that Thunaer had seen before, and his intuition told him he would not want to know the origin of the dark-toned hide.

The ashes of both men and reptiles rose into the air, beading to Deirdra's command.

A swirl of remains darkened the daylight.

Thunaer closed his eyes, and when he opened them again, he was not looking at the same horizon.

She took them back to where it all began.

He heard the stories of this place where the beautiful unnatural beings defeated his predecessors. Blue and green hues of shimmering lights covered the skyline, dancing in the heavens to music only the gods could hear. The blue turned dark, and the green bled crimson, interrupted and converted by the blood magic his queen had called upon. The sky flashed red, and the smoldering remains of the bodies appeared in the scope of his vision, solidified, and poured down like a rain of ash, bone, and blood.

A blast of heinous power scorched the land on which they stood.

Thunaer observed the dead, setting down on the earth in a destructive, fiery mist, tainting the battleground. Their remains caused the earth to rumble and rupture open and unearth the mangled remains of past mortal and magical beings buried under their feet.

Deirdra looked at the hollows of their dead eyes. Only their heads surfaced, coming up for air from their dreamless sleep. The pain of their trapped souls and the painful death that was their everlasting prison ravished her.

They sat in a field of hundreds of skulls resembling a dead forest's stumps.

She commanded the blood and flesh absorbed by the earth to show itself in all its glory, like black gold emerging from the ground.

As Deirdra recited the spell, she uttered in the strange ancient tongue, the dry crimson blood of the mortals and the vibrant blue roses that sprouted in places where the dirt absorbed the Ljósálfar essence mixed. It crushed to a fine powder to the command of her voice akin to daggers, piercing all that once was good.

The black mixture from the ungodly union slithered through the icy landscape and cast a shadow upon the land. It swirled through the air, eclipsing the sun, and finally set a large misshapen black rock at Deirdra's feet.

"Your bones shall be my hilt and shield; your blood shall be my blade," Deirdra said, her voice carried on the howling gale, hollowing through the deserted barren soil.

"Lift that," Deirdra ordered the three disposable mortals she had brought with her, pointing at the large, misshapen stone.

They hesitated at first, looking questionably at their leader, and Thunaer merely nodded, gesturing for them to follow Deirdra's mandate. All three rounded the rock and attempted to heave it up at the order of the scarred man.

It took them more than a few tries, the mineral lump proving heavier than it seemed compared to its size but inside packed to the raptors.

The mortals could not comprehend in their primitive minds what Deirdra already knew.

The stone contained the weight of all the sorrow, grief, horror of battle, and torture of the souls whose lives were cut short in a moment, who still mourned the life never lived.

The mortals buckled under the weight of the blood rock they held. Deirdra summoned her orange blaze to immerse them in a swirl of ash and bones and take them back to the magma chamber under Eyjafjallajökull mountain.

A tall, dark blond álfur carrying a long hand-carved hiking staff watched the mortals dissipate along with the female álfur he had never seen before.

Markian did now know what he had just witnessed, but the darkness from her ancient summons still lingered in the air. The delicate purple flowers he had planted between the rocks marking his past brethren perished on the desolated ground.

The stench of death and blood rose to the surface of the barren land and threatened to suffocate him.

He knew what he had to do now. He had to warn the King of what he witnessed.

His seventeen-year-long, self-inflicted exile was over, and he had to return to Islandia and face the life he left behind.

The mortals Deirdra captured within her dark enchantment cried out in surprise and terror. They attempted to set the bloodstone down but discovered it fused their arms to the blood iron.

A rave of screams and howls filled the air, their bodies becoming one with the rock. Their death gurgles sang with the churn from the open magma pit.

Deirdra raised her hand, and a gleaming, rasping sword forge filled with magma had opened and risen from the ground along with a polished stone slab.

From within the earth came a loud rumble, and red glowing eyes opened in the liquid ground. The fire god drew to Deirdra. Sensing an ancient power residing within her, he recognized it when she called upon him from the oblivion he had been confined to.

Deirdra turned to Thunaer, grabbed him by the collar, and pulled him in for a carnal kiss. His eyes opened wide, and a fire burned within them.

"A deal," Deirdra said, pushing Thunaer on the stone slab. "Grant me your power and make me a weapon this world has never known, and in exchange, I will grant you something you desperately crave spirit. I will set you free and pull you through the veil into this corporeal body to use as your own."

"Agreed." came the rumbling answer like stone grinding rock, and the earth shook.

Thunaer screamed. A fire burned around them, flames obscuring the sky. Soon, it engulfed Thunaer in flames that did not hurt him. His clothes melted away, but his scarred skin remained intact.

Deirdra allowed the flames to lick her garments away. She climbed on top of the scarred man, drove his hardness into her, and clutched his hands to her breasts. She hunched over him and bit down on his flesh, ravishing in his screams, his red mortal blood cascading over her white creamy skin.

Something arcane awoke within him; he seized her hair and tore her off. They rolled off the slab onto the ground, and Deirdra laughed as a heavy battle-worn blacksmith's hammer appeared in his hand.

The fire god settled within him.

Deirdra stood up, her bare body illuminated by the flames that refused to die down. "Now, make me a sword of blood and bone to solidify my rightful place on the throne of both death-bound and immortal."

Thunaer's scars smoldered, and the flames set in his skin slithered into his veins and pulsated crimson. The fire whispered in his soul, guiding his hand.

He knew exactly what he had to do.

The scarred man thrust his hands into the fire. He lifted the malleable iron from the forge's heat with his bare hands.

In a trance, he placed the hot, scolding lump on the stone slab and began hammering at the metal. Not long after, it took shape under his powerful blows that echoed through the mountain.

Once the metal had taken the form of a long-sword blade, Deirdra had called on the ash and bone, still contaminating the air above them, to set as a beautifully carved-out hilt to the newly forged sword.

Runes of power and the shape of a howling wolf had burned into the handle.

The scarred man had raised his sword. The sizzling lava engraved in its polished metal. In the right angle, the tortured souls reflected, forever cast into its blade.

"Now, bring me what I desire," Deirdra commanded.

Thunaer bowed to her on a bent knee, leaning on the soul blade he had just forged.

"For you," he said, the fire still burning within his veins. "My queen."

CHAPTER 16
THE FUTHARK RUNE

Extracting the broadhead arrows from Úlftýr's body proved a far more grueling task than any of them anticipated. The dauðadýr, ingenious in their cruelty, devised a mechanism designed to penetrate the organs and lead to much more significant damage than a regular broadhead arrow did.

These broadhead arrows split into four sharp blades as they penetrated their target, slicing through flesh and embedding more, plunging into the already wounded victim.

Elska had to use a specially built tool her father perfected to remove them.

A three-piece gold forceps, fashioned with scissor-like handles, a narwhal horn, and an ivory grip.

Elska inserted the tool into the wound in a contracted position for the central shaft to grasp the arrow. Sharp edge blades facing outwards then expanded the flesh to prevent ripping through the meat as she pulled out the arrows.

The process became tedious. Even with the charms and oils Elska and Siran applied, the damage done to Úlftýr was excessive.

Twice, he woke from the sleeping potion. His screams of pain echoed throughout the solarium. Úlftýr's body battled the anguish, his high fever burning the drug away. Only with the help of several of his soldiers did Elska manage to restrain him before Úlftýr could hurt himself further.

It took Úlftýr a long time to recover.

Even now, two months after the dreaded affair, he has not fully regained his former strength. No matter how profusely he refused to admit it.

Throughout the time that passed, Úlftýr sent parties of his most fearsome warriors into the surrounding woods, searching for the mortal beasts. Later, he sent them even farther into their kingdom's known boundaries to seek the dauðadýr hidden camp he had been sure they kept.

No one dared claim the Ljósálfar soldiers were not thorough in their search. Many knew the foremost reason for Úlftýr's slow recovery was the fact that despite Elska's protest, Úlftýr would frequently join his royal guard in their quests.

At first, she attempted to use reason and her medical authority in the kingdom to convince him.

"You must let me set your arms and allow others to dress and feed you. If only for a short while so that your bones begin to mend properly from the trauma you suffered."

Úlftýr's response was always the same. "The anxiety of not finding anything drives me to act. I have no intention of making peace with the notion that, after they devised such an elaborate plan to subdue me, the mortals would simply give up and return to the godforsaken place from which they came. Without at least another attempt on my life. I know they are just waiting for me to get comfortable, and then they will attack again."

"Your insistence to keep yourself in the line of danger caused me great worry," Elska said when he was about to ride out again but knew her statement fell on deaf ears.

"I see the strain the search takes on your still injured body," she wanted to say more, but she remained silent at the look on his face. Her words of warning did nothing to penetrate Úlftýr's stubborn, adventurous heart.

"You keep telling me things I am already aware of. If you have nothing to contribute, please allow me to deal with this matter as I see fit without this attempt to hinder my resolute." Úlftýr saddled his steed, wincing at the strain he put on his arms, preparing the horse for another expedition.

Elska chose her next words carefully, mostly for his sake but also for herself since her emotions would not lead her the way she wanted to go at that moment. "I acknowledge your need always to be an álfur of action," she said when she came to stand before the horse Úlftýr intended to ride.

"Then do not make me feel incompetent."

"I know that sitting on the sidelines drives you mad." She sighed and moved closer to him. She placed her hand on his thigh before he rode off. "You are purposely ignoring my concern for you. Úlftýr, I don't know if this is stubbornness or general ignorance of your well-being, but I need you to understand me. I need you to stay safe, to stay here with me."

He shook his head and reached out to tenderly stroke her hair. "You worry too much, and I will come back. And if I don't, you'll carry on."

Elska swatted his hand away; she did her best not to give in to his inviting touch.

Úlftýr looked at her. She turned away from him, her shoulders high, and crossed her arms over her chest.

"I can practically see your expression," he said. "You always go silent when you are annoyed. I know you do it so that a fight won't break out between us."

"If I lose you, I will lose myself." Elska hissed through the lump that stood in her throat. The tears had already welled up in her eyes, and she was too proud to let him see it.

He always did this to her. Every time she attempted to express complex emotions, he laughed them off.

Úlftýr leaned down to her. "Even if I am to be lost in body, my spirit urges me to do what I can to keep us safe. You know how outraged I am at myself, how useless I feel when my broken body refuses to obey me," he confided in her in a low voice. "I cannot be invalid in my own castle, and I cannot keep sitting still while others do my work for me and take risks protecting *my* home while I remain safe in a gilded cage."

She looked up, tears in her eyes.

"Can you promise me you won't disappear?"

"I will disappear if I succumb to my fear of being absolute to you and our people, or worse, a burden. I can only promise to do my best to return to you. Besides, I know you wouldn't ask me to change because, if I do, I will no longer be the álfur you fell in love with." Úlftýr kissed her, straightened up, and urged his mare forward.

Elska wanted to yell after him about how inconsiderate he acted, but her lips remained pursed. She did not want to start a fight she could not win, and she knew better than anyone; Úlftýr's mind was set.

"I'll keep him safe," Baldur whispered to her as the procession of soldiers rode past her.

Elska watched them leave the castle, a pit in her heart.

She imagined that, when Úlftýr came back, she would have to once again forcefully sit him down with Baldur's assistance to restitch his wounds with silken threads, only to have him tear off the sutures she had carefully laid down at the first chance he got.

He came back late the next day, drenched in sweat, his back bleeding from the wounds Elska knew she would have to stitch.

"Sit down," Elska said. "I will sew your wounds for you."

"Is that the only reason you want to touch me? To poke sharp needles into my back?" Úlftýr asked.

Elska rolled her eyes. "No, I would love to touch you in another capacity if you allow it. I miss the feel of your warm skin against mine."

Úlftýr smirked, "You only say this now because I pointed it out."

"How can I ease your pain?" Elska asked and Úlftýr smirked.

"You can grab my axe, take a nice swing, and chop my head off."

"Úlftýr…" Elska grumbled, unamused.

"Oh, you're right, a better idea- use my sword, blade's sharper. You just place it between my shoulder blades and push."

Elska felt the bitterness in his voice. "Will you let me help you?" she asked.

"You must relish this," Úlftýr said. "We can now do whatever you like since I am unable to indulge in anything remotely fun. I can't glide, I can't train, I can't even swim after a long hot day in the cool water of the underground caves. All beauty is stolen from me." He looked at her. "Besides you, that is."

"I am glad to be your consolation prize." Elska didn't mean to sound so bitter herself, but she couldn't help it, no matter how deeply she understood him.

"Would you like to come sit with me in one of the alcoves? It's been so long since we sat there together, me leaning against you and you reading beautiful words to me?"

Úlftýr frowned. "I've built those alcoves for you; you can go sit and read there all by yourself at any time you see fit. Don't give me another task right now."

"I am not a chore," Elska said, her voice surprisingly calm. "Can't I just enjoy your company and you mine? It seems that every precious moment we have together is interrupted."

"I am doing everything I can to ensure we have more of those moments," Úlftýr said, frustrated. "These are my duties to keep us safe."

"Did you ever consider your duties to me? To us? When will we have something that is just ours that I don't have to share with the kingdom?"

Úlftýr frowned. "If you are referring to what I think you are, then that is out of the question. Say we do, and I will go and never come back. What will you do then? I see you fall apart now by yourself; how can you possibly think that you will be strong enough to care for another life without me?"

Tears welled up in Elska's eyes.

Úlftýr sighed. "I'm sorry, I can't pretend I don't see the immediate burst you have with your emotions. It's just not the right time, alright?"

"When is the right time then?" Elska shook her head. "When we are happy, I do not want to spoil the moment, and when I am sad it's an outburst. I need you to understand I am allowed to have negative emotions, but you seem to punish me for having them. Again, something I would never do to you. Do you not feel free to feel with me as you please without judgment?"

She glanced at him as he walked past her.

He looked at her, sitting on the bed. "What do you want from me?"

Elska sighed. "I want your affection, a gentle touch, a kiss. Our interactions do not have to be only intimate encounters to show our love for each other."

Úlftýr growled. "Well, if you intend to deny me anyway, I will seek to quench the calling of the flesh with someone else." He said and then entered the shower without another word spoken between them.

When Úlftýr emerged from the shower, after having some time to think, steam bellowing from his skin, he found Elska on the bed, half asleep. He sighed, let his towel drop, and slithered into the bed behind her.

She stirred in his grasp and tensed up. Úlftýr moved her hair up and kissed her neck. "I was trying to protect you, to keep you where you can do what you love. I was trying not to disrupt your life with the things I had to see through, and you are mad at me?"

"Do you feel safe to open up to me?" Elska asked.

"Only you." Úlftýr replied.

"Well, I no longer feel safe to even talk to you. Your default can't be closing the door to your heart in my face every time you are hurting."

Úlftýr buried his face in her hair. "Forgive me. For so long I have got accustomed to maidens wanting only one aspect of my company, for so long I had craved someone who will want to share something more with me than my bed. And here you come and you offer this to me freely, everything I ever wanted, and I am so busy with reacting explosively and rebelling against a sugestion made to me like I always do, that I don't even see that my instinct prevents me from getting what I really wanted all along. I want to be your safe place."

Elska felt a sting in her eyes. "And you were. But don't you think that something happening to you will disrupt my life?" She turned to him. "Don't you think that I lie here and think about what I am going to do tomorrow if you don't come back?"

Úlftýr sat up. "I just want to put this day behind me. Can't you see that I am miserable too?"

Elska grunted and followed his example so they could be at eye level with each other. "This is not a competition of who suffers more." Tears rolled down her cheeks.

Úlftýr looked down. "You always react like this. Too emotional. You need to get out of here too. Be social; do something that isn't your work."

"I just don't have the energy, Úlftýr," Elska choked. "I don't have the energy to indulge in anything that is not worrying. Worry about you, about our people, about the threat we face that you are so determined to face head-on without giving the slightest thought to what it does to me."

Úlftýr got up from the bed.

Elska had seen this reaction before. He was about to leave.

She sighed. "I wish I had the same degree of freedom that you possess. Sometimes, I wish that I could just go into the world and never look back."

Úlftýr stopped. "I am not free."

"At least you can escape yourself." Elska wiped her face with her sleeve. "I cannot escape my thoughts. They are stuck here; everything anyone has ever said to me grinds on a never-ending wheel in my mind for hours, for days; it never leaves me alone." She looked away from him at her hands clutching the cover. "I am exhausted from the moment I wake up until I go to sleep; I am always haunted by worry."

Úlftýr stepped back to her and sat beside her. "What do you want me to do? What can I say?"

Elska placed her hand into his. She loved his warmth; it was as if his touch was healing.

"Say anything," she said. "Ask anything. Please stop storing your emotions to air them out when you want to get even with me. You know I would do anything for you if you only asked; I would give you anything to make you happy. I wish I didn't feel like you are punishing me with your silence for the time I cost us because that is how I feel every time you keep me out."

She leaned on him, and he laid down with her.

"I couldn't stop you, but I wanted you to tell me at least to come with you," Elska said, breathing deeply. She didn't want to give him the satisfaction of knowing his touch was affecting her.

She could feel him smile. "Úlftýr, please." She couldn't hide the shudder that ran down her body right to where his hand traveled to pull her closer.

"You are always with me," Úlftýr whispered.

"That's not what I mean." She murmured, but the fight had already gone out of her. She always struggled to form a coherent thought whenever he touched her. She leaned her head back, and he massaged between her legs; the thin Shemesh she wore did nothing to hide her perked nipples. She could no longer suppress her whimpers.

She bit her lip and turned to him.

He glanced down at her lips and pulled her impossibly close, his body radiating heat. He closed his eyes and let her get lost in the softness of his lips against hers, in his tongue exploring her mouth.

She was left breathless when he pushed himself up on one arm and dove under the covers, his head disappearing between her legs.

Elska threw her head back, her hands grasping Úlftýr's long hair as she guided him to explore every crevice of hers, the same as he did with her mouth. He gasped for air, which only made her tighten her grip on his locks and pull harder. She placed her legs on his back and bucked into him.

Úlftýr chuckled, his mouth pressed tightly against the lips between her legs. A finger accompanied his tongue, and then another one followed.

Elska gasped. She pulled at his hair again and forced him to return to her. They kissed, his hands running down her body.

Elska looked at him, eyes filled with lust. "Let me-" she flipped him over and kissed down his chest, his tight stomach, into the hollow of his V-shaped muscular grooves, circled his family jewels, and kissed up his shaft before taking him in.

Her tongue lapped circles around him before she swallowed him in deeper. Delighted, she hummed. His body arched and his stomach muscles contorted, while he moaned and gasped, throwing his head back and covering his face to stifle a scream. "Ride me." He panted.

Elska chuckled around him, which only made him spasm again. She released him, climbing her way up into his arms.

Úlftýr sucked on her lower lip and then kissed down along her jaw to her neck. He lay beside her with her still in his arms; he moved her so that her back was to him, her shape fitting perfectly against his chest as if they were made for each other, two halves of a whole.

He snaked his left hand between her legs and entered her; his right hand held her in a chokehold against his chest.

Elska grabbed hold of the arm around her neck; she felt euphoric, almost floating; a wave of pulsating pleasure followed the head rush; she moaned and arched into Úlftýr, her movement making him tighten his grip around her. She closed her eyes and gave in to his thrusts. No longer able to hold back when she shuddered against him, he came inside her, filling her with warmth.

Several moments passed until she came down from the high of their encounter. When she finally turned back in his grasp to look at him, Úlftýrs' eyes were burning into hers—a deep shade of caramel. "I'm sorry that I worried you," Úlftýr said.

Elska nodded slowly. "But you are going to do it again, aren't you? Worry me like that?"

Úlftýr pressed his forehead to hers. He didn't have to answer for Elska to know the answer to her rhetorical question.

Instead, he told her what would always be true. "I love you," Úlftýr whispered.

Elska fought the lump in her throat. "I love you too."

The end of 1638 BC.
Yule month.

'As much as I love the purity the winter brings onto our land, I adore the bloom coming back to life at the start of the warmer days.' Elska thought to herself while she bent down and took in the heavenly scent.

The wonderful fragrance of the blue roses filled the air. The marvelous hue of sapphire, flowering on the bushes that covered the road leading out of the castle, looked magical.

The crisp winter had begun to pass.

The river churned, awakened under thin ice; the cold retreated, and the warmth reigned anew.

The enchanting cobalt roses were the first to rise from the frost and blossom, lifting their heads high to be kissed by the sunlight.

The timing of the life reborn, arousing from the frozen veil of deep slumber, could not have been more perfect.

It was always her favorite season. Her people's most sacred celebration, the winter solstice, marking the start of the longer, brighter days, was just around the corner.

The stream running down from the mountains began to thaw slowly; the babbling sounds it made were sweet music to her ears.

They rebuilt the armory, and the mortal assassins had since disappeared. Elska shuddered at the memories of that horrible night.

She shook her head vigorously to rid herself of the frightening images of her Úlftýr, wounded and soaked in his own blood, lying unconscious under her care on the velvet cot in the infirmary.

Elska straightened up and put her hands on her hips, scanning the surrounding scenery.

They were racing each other through the gardens. Úlftýr wanted to train his beloved because he knew he could not always be with her, and that thought frightened him.

"I beat you this time!" She announced to the air.

"Not quite." A voice filled with glee answered from somewhere above her head.

Elska raised her eyes, and her jaw dropped to the sight of Úlftýr, perched on top of one of the chiseled columns of black stone that lined the path to the castle, a blue rose in his hand.

"Oh, my love, you boasted a little too soon. I told you you wouldn't defeat me." He teased her, throwing her the rose.

She caught it, and for a moment, something resembling deep affection reflected on her face. But then, irritation replaced it, and she glared up at Úlftýr.

"Two out of three!" she demanded.

He laughed, looking on to study the road.

From up here, his land spread out before him, from mountain to sea.

The columns, ancient even by his standards, were erected with the initial stones laid to construct his home soon after the first álfur set foot on these shores.

Úlftýr's keen amber eyes reflected the infinite beauty of his kingdom.

To his right, the remarkable fjord extended into the horizon. The vast mountain ridge rose to his left, the tops covered in the most brilliant white snow. Underneath stood proudly the wonderfully soon-to-be colorful hills that, come spring, will be filled with rich aromatic groves of sweet and savory produce ready for harvest.

An immense river snaked along the path upon which they mostly traveled, lining the slope down into the valley with arteries of crystal-clear water flowing between the peaceful cottages of his kin.

At its lowest point, the river merged with the black ocean that cut a dark boundary between their land and the world beyond their border Úlftýr did not care to know. The rapids rushed into the valley beneath them.

A vision sparked in his mind.

He would have loved to shed his garments, discard the royal shackles of duty, and dive headfirst off the renowned cliffs of Midgardr to silence the stormy waves in his heart, as he used to when he was a youngling.

He used to lose himself in the current for hours, exploring the bottomless depths of the crystal-clear underwater caves.

Úlftýr looked at the dark sea again, wishing for the flickering lights to signal his father's royal vessel's return home.

In all Úlftýr's days, five hundred and thirty-six winters since his coming into this world, the land he called home has never suffered a drought.

The castle, akin to the roads that lead up to it and the base of their homes, was built of the most brilliant black sandstone.

As young Ljósálfar, Úlftýr, and Ingrid loved exploring the mines containing exceptional blue diamonds and quarries that produced the brilliant black sandstone.

Úlftýr remembered the day his father, King Freyr, took him and his sister to witness firsthand the runes and charms the pit Ljósálfar labored to place upon the stones they mined to prevent the erosion of time.

A small smile tugged at the corner of Úlftýr's mouth. He remembered his mother loudly protesting when he and Ingrid returned to the castle, their once-white robes covered in black soot.

"This is not the activity that you two should partake in!" She scolded them sternly.

Her protest, however, yielded no result, and they were right back there the next day. Manual labor never intimidated either of them. Both took great pride in the knowledge they contributed to constructing their peoples' homes in the valley and of the west wing where Úlftýr and Elska now resided.

'This is my home.' Úlftýr thought. *'I've grown up in these gardens and know these ancient stones more than my own flesh. The veins of the roses are my veins, the fragrance of flowers, vivid colors set in my soul. I could never imagine myself being anywhere else. Nor do I want to. I hiked this land back and forth, a moon of my life exploring it from shore to shore. How I long to do it again.'*

"You cheated!" Elska declared, her voice cutting through his thoughts like the ring of a bell. "How did you get here so fast?!"

"Before a challenge is presented, know who your opponent is, my love," Úlftýr smirked.

"Also, timing may be the key that will lead you to defeat or victory." He advised her.

"Next time, I suggest you try challenging me right after I consume a large meal. My honor will oblige me to accept the challenge; however, my full belly will force me to roll slowly behind you." He winked.

"And when will that be?" Elska raised her eyebrow.

Úlftýr blinked. "When will I consume a large meal…?"

"Yes," Elska stomped her foot. "Let us set a date; I suggest the yuletide feast and race right after you stuffed yourself with all the goodness our land offers."

Úlftýr laughed but stopped in sight of Elska's expression.

"Oh, you are serious about setting a date and time for my pending defeat?"

Elska smirked. "Yes. You can't expect to suggest something like that, get me all excited to spend more time with you, and then just go back on your idea. I'll feel disappointed."

Úlftýr nodded. "Ok, you pick a date, arrange it and I will follow your instructions."

He failed to read the light downward twitch of her lips before she perked up again.

"Ok. But for now, it was your notion to train me. If you are done for the day, I would be quite content to go back to our chambers to continue indulging in other activities such as the ones we partook in last night."

Úlftýr smiled and leaped from the top of the column to Elska's sudden gasp.

Úlftýr laughed, landing right in front of her. "Oh, my snow maiden."

"I could never refuse an offer like that." He reached to caress her cheek. "Are you happy?" he asked her, watching as she leaned into his touch.

"Are you?" She answered with a question.

"I am when I'm with you." He said and leaned in to kiss her.

Elska wrapped her arms around him to deepen the kiss. Right before Úlftýr closed his eyes to oblige her, a movement captured his attention at the corner of his sight.

The hairs on the back of his neck stood up. He felt a malice-filled gaze set upon them from within the shadows of the castle's woods.

"Elska." He said against her lips in an even low tone. "I need you to flee now."

"What?" Elska blinked at him. Following his glance, she started to turn her head, but Úlftýr caught her face between his palms and compelled her to look at him.

"Run back to the castle and call for the guards, then stay in the fortress until I return to you. We are not alone."

Elska's breath caught in her throat. She began to protest, but Úlftýr silenced her with another kiss.

"Remember what we agreed on?" he asked, never breaking their gaze. "If we are put in a dangerous situation and on our own, you run. I cannot act and fret over your safety simultaneously."

Elska scowled, but she unwillingly nodded. She hastily kissed Úlftýr, and took off up the road from which they came, battling the urge to turn back.

When Úlftýr was confident she was a long way off, his gaze darkened and he turned towards the trees.

"I know that you have no genuine interest in my beloved," Úlftýr said aloud. "She was only an additional perk, wasn't she? Capturing me is the main event again?"

Úlftýr stepped closer to the edge of the paved path; the crooked branches of the trees cast long menacing shadows across his face.

The air shifted from pleasant to cold. The world seemed to hold its breath, anticipating a battle. The shadows crept toward him, swallowing his own.

"Go on then!" He shouted, and the wind began picking up. "I know you are out there!"

He looked around him, his body tense, prepared for the attack.

"I can feel you," he said in a low tone. "What are you waiting for?!" He roared.

"Courageous youth," said a chilling, ominous voice carried in the wind. "Courageous or foolish…." The voice mocked.

The strike from above failed to surprise Úlftýr.

He sidestepped and landed a downward elbow that cracked the mask of the mortal, gripping the sword from the unconscious man's hand while he went down.

"Tyr!" With a battle cry, Úlftýr raised the sword above his head, and the sound of it colliding with the metal of another blade rang through the air.

The brute fell atop of him; Úlftýr skewered the man on his blade, momentarily caught under the dead weight of his attacker. He grunted, shoved the corpse off, and got up just in time to receive another blow, this time from an assailant charging at him head-on.

Úlftýr somersaulted over the assassin and slashed him open, landing behind his back.

He welcomed another black-clad warrior who came straight after the last with a rallying cry and drove his sword through him, impaling the man on his sword.

Úlftýr pulled the blade out of the dead flesh and turned to face a large dauðadýr. The man stood, inspecting him, sizing up his power. He wore the same reptilian mask Úlftýr remembered the mortals wore the night of the blaze.

"Are you the one leading this horde?" Úlftýr spat, wiping off the fallen mortal's blood from his face.

The massive dauðadýr said nothing. His eyes flashed behind the reptilian mask in anticipation, and then, he pulled off his facade and grimaced at Úlftýr with his badly scarred and disfigured face.

Úlftýr wished the man had kept the mask on. It was an improvement on his natural features.

He did not want to imagine what horrors this man faced or committed to deserve such hideous disfigurement. And then it hit him.

"No – " Úlftýr gasped and stepped back. "No, you're dead; I beat you; you are one of them; how can you still be alive?"

The dauðadýr laughed. "Luck stood at my side, King Úlftýr. Yes, you did your best to dispatch of me, but my dark lady offered me salvation, and thus I am a servant to her will."

Úlftýr's blood boiled. He had promised Elska that he would keep her safe, and there he was, standing in front of him, the demon from Elska's nightmares that he failed to defeat a second time.

"What are you doing on my land?" Úlftýr demanded, his weapon raised, "Who paid you to attack me? You have just confirmed that you answer to a powerful individual. Tell that coward to stop hiding behind your masks and face me! I demand to know who means me harm in my kingdom."

The scarred man bowed, "You will soon find out, *King* Úlftýr." He replied in a mocking tone.

The scarred dauðadýr turned back to the trees and made a sharp, shrill sound, and out they came — from the darkness, silent as death, dozens of men all clad in black, wearing slimy reptilian masks, a horde of unidentified monsters.

The scarred man drew a massive black metal blade and charged at Úlftýr.

Úlftýr blocked it with the sword he held, only to have it shatter in his hands.

He threw away the broken hilt and raised his arms, attempting to summon the river to his aid.

A blazing strike of agony thundered through his unhealed injuries, the roil of power awakening within him.

The scarred man swung his blade; Úlftýr ducked, and the black iron whistled above his head.

The scarred man kept coming, ferociously strong and more aggressive with every step, his body reinforced by hell's fire.

Úlftýr was painfully aware of the other mortals advancing towards him from every direction, cutting off his escape route. He made a last desperate attempt to call forth his powers and the scarred man's blade finally made contact, cutting Úlftýr deep across his side.

Hot blood sizzled on the cold blade. Úlftýr gasped, suffocating.

'*The black steel…!*' His thoughts screamed with revolting terror, '*A dark enchantment is placed upon it!*'

His ears rang, he tasted the blood he knew was not his own, and the dying wails of countless souls screeched in his head.

Úlftýr's powers dampened as it got harder to breathe. He was drowning on dry land. He heaved with difficulty.

"What...what have you done to me?" Úlftýr gasped, his eyes bulging.

The scarred man smiled. "The death pain of two hundred and nineteen souls, both álfur and mortal, now courses through your veins, *my King*." He said with a wide grin.

Úlftýr heaved again. He believed the scarred man. He heard them. Their horror deafening, their searing pain blinding, he felt them all, trapped within the blade, clawing at his soul to let them out and set them free.

Úlftýr experienced each one of their deaths as if it were his own. Cold steel cutting him to pieces, angry hands, and claws tearing him apart.

Each raging, fearful, shattered voice, pleading, begging, threatening in his mind, urging him to do anything just to end their suffering.

At that moment, Úlftýr wished for nothing else.

By all the gods, he craved their redemption and his own.

He stood paralyzed, unable to help even himself.

The scarred man barked a command Úlftýr did not understand in his native tongue, and his men advanced further.

With their swords unsheathed, they encircled him, ringed him in like a caged animal, and began jabbing him with their blades for what seemed like their amusement.

Úlftýr sought to fight, but he could not stand against all of them at once. His arms still hadn't returned to their former strength, his ears rang, his vision clouded, and they surrounded him, their sheer numbers overpowering him.

Someone laid a hard blow to the back of Úlftýr's knees, forcing him to go down. The scarred man caught Úlftýr's long, black hair in a painful grip and pushed the sharp black blade against his neck.

"What do you want?!" Úlftýr growled. He attempted to free himself, but two mortals grabbed his arms and twisted them in either direction, making even the slightest movement he sought to make impossible.

"Oh, it is not what they want." Úlftýr's eyes opened in astonishment. He knew that voice.

"It is what I want." Deirdra leisurely strolled out of the shadows, clothed in a fine, long, mink coat, carrying a large leather-bound book in her arms.

"Deirdra!" Úlftýr shot up to launch at her, but the mortals yanked him back.

The scarred man pulled at his hair so hard Úlftýr cried out, and he was sure the man intended to rip it out with his scalp.

"I should have known." Úlftýr let out a painted laugh. "I am an imbecile." His eyes traveled to the two cloaked figures that accompanied her. He recognized them at once – the guards he had assigned to watch his adopted sister. But there was something wrong with them, a hollow in their eyes. He stared at them, and the abyss of their absent souls stared back at him.

"What, what have you done to them?"

Deirdra laughed. "Something I unfortunately cannot do to you. And not from the lack of trying. But why divulge all of my secrets?" She looked at the scarred man. "Dispatch of them for me."

"No!" Úlftýr yelled, but it was no use. His guards put up no fight when the black blade was lifted. They crumbled where they stood, their throats slit ear to ear and their blue blood a cascading river, staining the ground where Úlftýr was forced to kneel.

He cursed himself for his reluctance to put Deirdra's actions under scrutiny like he knew his father would have expected him to do in his absence.

A realization concerning the mayhem of the past months became nauseatingly clear in his mind, all of his suspicions and speculations rapidly sorting themselves out.

"You sent these brutes to set fire to our Armory…!" He blamed her. "You… You…" A lump formed in his throat. He should have trusted his intuition.

His vision blurred further from unshed tears, and his head throbbed so hard it might as well have been split open.

"You poisoned our father?" He demanded in accusation. Rage and pain in his eyes.

"Your father." Deirdra corrected. "And no. I am afraid I cannot claim the honor for that action." She took extra pleasure in the sickened expression on Úlftýr's face. "That was the work of my true kin."

"And who is that?" Úlftýr questioned, unbalanced.

Deirdra looked at him, her eyes narrowed, her chin raised.

"You are a traitor!" Úlftýr bellowed. "He took you in! He gave you whatever you wanted! You were like family to Ingrid and me. How could you do this to him?! To us?"

"Not *everything* I wanted. Please, Úlftýr," Deirdra waved her hair back. "You have never seen me as part of *your* family; I was only another obligation in your eyes. Like the powers you never asked for and like the throne you are forced to sit on."

Úlftýr exhaled. "Well, I would have admired your intuition, except you are a hag that had gone off her mind." He breathed.

Deirdra smirked. "Don't take it to heart, dear brother; my interest in you isn't personal."

"What is it then?" Úlftýr's gaze darkened; in his mind, he still searched for a way to get free and get close enough to Deirdra to rip her throat out.

"A means to an end." Deirdra shrugged. "I won't be denied again."

Úlftýr looked at her, his gaze burning with hatred. "All I thought of when you left was - good riddance."

Deirdra stepped forward, closing the gap between them. She grabbed Úlftýr's chin and forced him to look at her. "I suspected it was you all along. The all-father doesn't know, so it can be our little secret. Awaken," she said in a low tone that resonated in his mind.

"What?" Úlftýr glared at her.

"You can save yourself. Submit. Pledge your strength to me. Awaken." Deirdra repeated.

"What are you talking about?" Úlftýr bared his teeth.

He gasped. His eyes flashed in green light. For a moment, his hair took on the color of fire, and his skin glowed alabaster. He struggled against his restraints, his body pulsating with power.

"Submit to me," Deirdra commanded.

"*Never.*"

The alabaster being growled and shifted, but gradually, the light in Úlftýr's eyes dimmed, and the amber shone anew. Deirdra smirked. "Pity. I had such plans for you." She sighed and let go.

She straightened and opened the ancient book.

"Relieve him of his garments." She commanded.

The mortals hesitated at first, but then, Deirdra's gaze flashed with orange fire. One mortal hastily ripped open Úlftýr's coat and tore down his tunic, exposing Úlftýr's bare chest. Deirdra put her hand on Úlftýr's forehead with her men still holding him down.

She sliced the skin open with her nails, sharp as claws. Muttering in a low whisper, she began to embed a futhark rune onto Úlftýr's skin.

"What are you doing!?" Úlftýr exerted himself, fighting to pull away from her, but Deirdra ignored him, her chant resonating louder.

Old words, ancient like the sands of time, rang through the air. Archaic words echoed through Úlftýr's mind.

The sun eclipsed in his eyes, and the day became night for him.

The trees grew so tall their branches obscured the sky. They fell with roots in the form of rotten dead hands reaching out from the desolate ground, attempting to grasp what remained of their fleeting life.

The blue roses and the green grass withered and died; the stream dried out.

His castle crumbled to ruins and stones marking his beloved, erected in the abandoned, overgrown courtyard.

Úlftýr's eyes burned in blazing light. He opened his mouth, and the sound he let out resembled that of a tormented animal, a pitiful beast rather than the noble King he was.

It echoed, deafening with misery, through the valley.

Deirdra's enchantment burrowed into his soul and came out, dragging away his essence. Gradually, his fair skin took on an ashen tint, his lips lost their color, the hue of his previously long ebony hair grew white, his body convulsed, and an ink-like stain bled from the rune Deirdra carved into his brow.

The ink flowed down to the middle of Úlftýr's chest and pooled there in deep blue swirls, resembling the petals of a rose.

Úlftýr no longer knew what was real and what wasn't.

Only the words, the endless stream of ancient dead words, filled his mind.

"Úlftýr!"

He knew that voice. It warmed him in his sleep; it rang clear as a bell in his dreams.

The voice from a life he was sure he had long forgotten.

"Úlftýr!"

Elska, holding the reins of a snow-white stallion, galloped down the road, flanked by Úlftýr's royal guard, with Ingrid holding the lead on her grey mare.

The uproar of approaching hooves beating the stone walkway and the shouts of the nearing battalion caused Deirdra to cease casting her dark magic upon Úlftýr.

She turned to glimpse Ingrid growing dangerously closer on her mount.

"Deirdra?" Ingrid shouted.

For a moment, Ingrid was dumbfounded at the brutality in front of her, her gaze shifting rapidly from Deirdra to the mortals to Úlftýr. A horrified understanding dawned on her.

"How could you?" Ingrid shouted, and Deirdra knew, from the twist-up motion Ingrid made with her hand and the splash of water, that she had been correct — a liquid serpent rose from the stream.

Deirdra cursed, enraged.

She grabbed hold of the scarred man and spun in her place, vanishing in a heap of bright orange flames just as the serpent launched forward at the dauðadýr, who were misfortunate enough to still hold on to Úlftýr.

The water surge blasted the assailants into the air, and Úlftýr regained his freedom. He looked up with black eyes that glowed of burning crimson.

Elska hastily dismounted her horse and ran towards him.

He raised his arms to reach out to her but collapsed to the ground with nothing to hold him up.

"Úlftýr!"

She fell to her knees beside him, turned him onto his back, and pulled him into her arms. Baldur led the King's guards mounted on silver-haired stallions past them, pursuing the dauðadýr that fled from the scene and scattered like roaches.

Úlftýr did not see the bloody battle that followed.

At that moment, all he knew was that he could no longer see anything or feel the maiden he held so dear, holding him in her arms.

He lay frozen, his body a cold stone statue, as the bitter darkness slowly claimed him away.

CHAPTER 17

THE
UNDERWORLD

Úlftýr sensed the ground move beneath him.

A low rumbling filled the air. Birds fled from the trees; the horses whined, uneasy. A shudder ran through Úlftýr's bones.

Searing hot spikes pierced through the cold darkness. Úlftýr's eyes opened; he wanted to scream.

Úlftýr knew from bitter experience the sensation of snake venom coursing through his veins. The scar tissue over the gaping holes left by the broadhead arrows shriveled away, and blood seeped through, soaking his clothes.

He lay bound to the ground, powerless, agonizing, his body an open pit lane with tortured souls destined for the inferno.

He could not move his limbs. He could not even blink. His consciousness was cast in lead, his psyche constrained by the molten lava that was his blood.

Realization trickled through his horrified mind; Deirdra had trapped him inside his own body. She made him a prisoner of the wailing demons she unleashed within his contorted soul.

Úlftýr heard the shouts of his saviors and the screams of his unsuccessful captors as they fled. However, he understood nothing; their words made no sense to his exhausted mind.

Through a veil of pulsating pain, his black eyes focused on his beloved Elska, holding him in her arms, crying for him to respond.

He broke her heart and, by doing so, demolished his.

He could not shield her from his demise.

His inability to console her drove him mad. It tore open the north-facing gates of Náströnd in his heart, the hell where he felt he was bound for.

He pledged to protect his beloved Elska but couldn't keep his promise. He was now the one causing her grief.

An oath-breaker. That is what Úlftýr believed he was, and the great serpent punished him for it.

Úlftýr's eyes fell shut, and his soul, while still tethered to his body, was no longer bound to the physical world. He became aware of the void and the waves, his being washed ashore amidst the corpses of the damned.

Purgatory.

Úlftýr got lost among myriad decaying cadavers, insignificant as a grain of sand, crushed under the weight of his guilt.

The oblivion sky rained searing venom on his exposed skin and ate at it akin to acid. Snakes slithered out of the poisoned sea and coiled around him, constricting his limbs and crushing his bones to dust only to mend his corporeal soul to repeat the vicious cycle.

The tar that flooded his soul began to cover bits of his memories. With each passing moment, a piece of the one called Úlftýr slipped away and drowned in nothingness.

A pitiful fragment of what he once was, craved to wake up, to be King Úlftýr again.

The trace of him that was still clutching to life feared that he would soon be discovered. The wolf demon, Vargr that prowled the carcass-littered shore of limbo would find what was left of him and claw Úlftýr into hell.

Ingrid detested having to be the one in command.

If it were up to her, she would have gladly continued to avoid the burden of responsibility and the heat of battle. But with Úlftýr lying in the dirt, blood seeping from the unnatural wounds Deirdra's monstrous followers inflicted upon him, his skin ashen and hair white, a sense of duty overtook her. She had to act.

Summoning the inner strength she was unaware she possessed, Ingrid hastily divided the reinforcement of her warriors, called upon from the barracks, and ordered a battalion to join that of Baldur's to make haste after the dauðadýr.

Aesir made his way to Ingrid after the troops were dispatched.

He bowed. "We found the guards Deirdra's death beasts had slain," Aesir said.

Ingrid breathed. "How bad…?" she finally uttered.

It was clear Deirdra's thugs murdered their way into the grounds, although Ingrid understood that she could have conveyed them in, using the outburst of her powers to avoid the unnecessary killing.

She wondered how she controlled the unnatural flames when it was not her element to wield.

What bothered her most was that their sister chose not to use it on the mortals. Ingrid now knew that there was no good left in Deirdra's heart.

"Their throats were garroted, and the tips of their jeweled ears were cut off and taken for trophies," Aesir replied, the tint of his skin turning green at his own words.

Ingrid felt violently ill at such savagery. She regretted asking the dreaded details of the warriors' demise, but she had to know.

The abominable creatures had stolen one of the greatest gifts the great god serpent had bestowed upon his people. The jewel shards were a reminder of their ancestral home. Grains broke off from their dying world and embedded in their souls to allow them to obtain the strength their plane provided. They were born with them. It was a part of them, the same as their blood or immortality was.

"The mortal beasts must have noticed our ears fragments and viewed them as precious rocks. Something they can bargain with." Aesir spat. "They are like mindless rodents. Just give them something shiny, and they will follow you to the ends of the earth."

"Retrieve the assailants at all costs, along with Deirdra. Alive, if possible, dead if necessary." Ingrid ordered. "As a blood sister to the King, I desire to avenge Úlftýr's suffering, and I now have the means at my disposal to make even the dead reveal their secrets to me."

She looked at Aesir. "Select a handful of your most trusted warriors and ferry the King back to the castle. I will remain behind to join the battalions hunting for the mortal scum." she glanced at Elska. "Make sure a guard remains by Elska's side at all times. Take Vidar and tell him to accompany her to the infirmary to get supplies. Then, bring her and her father back to the fortress."

Ingrid smiled bitterly. "I know Úlftýr would never forgive me if any harm came to his bride while he was confined to whichever purgatory Deirdra damned him to."

Ingrid had to protect Elska and keep her under a watchful eye until Úlftýr found his way back to them and out of his damnation.

Elska watched over him constantly, refusing to leave his side and only relenting to allow Baldur a moment of privacy with his old friend when they returned to the castle.

Baldur observed as his warriors brought Úlftýr in. They laid his mutilated body on a wood-carved canopy bed with sheets of red velvet.

If not for the faintest rise and fall of Úlftýr's chest, Baldur would've been sure that his friend succumbed to his wounds. Baldur gulped. The gash on Úlftýr's stomach looked like his own. Baldur's hand instinctively moved down to his stomach. Somehow, the same malice that kept him from properly healing now infested Úlftýr as well.

'We survived the Ice Lands; we made it back home. Did the evil we faced follow us back? Would it creep now into your heart? Would it be better if you never woke up?' Baldur fell to his knees, the horrible thoughts crippling him, suffocating him. He looked up at Úlftýr's face, blood stricken, paler than death, just like Hod's face was when Baldur laid his lifeless body in a bed of blue roses on the stone table in the royal courtyard.

The passages of Friia's book haunted Baldur. He read them so many times he could recite them by heart. 'Allow his descent into the underworld, and you will never know the touch of the cold stone.'

Baldur couldn't stand the thought of Úlftýr on the stone table with the dying light of day signaling his last sunset.

"Wake up," Baldur whispered, resolute. "I will find a way to fight destiny, or I shall forfeit my life for yours. But you must wake up."

"Baldur," he tensed at Elska's gentle touch on his back. Taking in a shuddering breath, Baldur willed his expression of sorrow and fear to leave his eyes before he got up and turned to her.

"Please, tell me when he wakes." He asked. Elska nodded, and guilt struck Baldur when she wrapped her arms around his torso in the mutual pain she thought they shared.

After he left, Siran, Elska's father, arrived to help clean and dress the bloody inflictions. They took extra care with the deep gash on Úlftýr's side.

The wound released a foul stench. A black substance oozed from it, mingling with Ulftýr's blue blood that seemed thinner than usual and had a grey tinge like his skin.

Superficial cuts adorned Úlftýr's upper body.

"These cuts look like they came from the tips of many swords thrust into him from all directions," Siran told her.

Elska didn't want to imagine the mortals surrounding him, mockingly thrusting their blades into his flesh. But the horrible vision came anyway and choked her with angry tears.

"It does not resemble any reaction from a poison I ever encountered," Siran said after they removed Úlftýr's garments and cleansed his wounds. "I am afraid Deirdra might have stumbled upon ancient magic that predates us and that she could not fully understand. I will consult with Elder Svarta. He might have come across this before. I wish we could access Friia's old writings, but even I would require time to locate them in the royal archive."

He looked at Elska's tear-stricken face and knew she was too far gone to answer him. Her body was beside him, her hands working on Úlftýr's wounds, but her heart was trapped with Úlftýr in his hell.

"He will come back to you, I promise." Siran kissed her forehead and got up. Even as he uttered this reassuring, he knew there was no solace to be found in his words.

"I shall be in the library. We will find a way, Elska. Do not despair."

Elska did not look up when he closed the door behind him.

Instead, she attempted to inspect the incision in Úlftýr's forehead closer. She knew that it was carved intentionally, and it gave her pause.

Deirdra had cut the rhombus shape precisely, a rune Elska had never seen before.

Elska reached out her hand and traced the carved skin.

The moment she touched it, the rune ignited. Elska gasped but did not remove her hand. The rune glowed on the inside, not with blood but with something that resembled burning coal.

"What…" Elska started to move away and yelped at a sudden hold of Úlftýr's hand around her wrist.

"Úlftýr?" Hope bloomed within her. She looked at his face. His eyes remained closed, but his lips slightly parted. "Oh… " Elska breathed. Sharp canines descended from Úlftýr's gums. The grip of his hand on her wrist tightened. Large, menacing claws grew instead of his fingernails.

"Úlftýr…!" she tried to yank her hand away, but even unconscious, Úlftýr was much stronger than her. "Úlftýr!"

His lips parted further.

"Please!" she cried, his claws digging into her wrist. She thrashed in his hold and fell to the floor, her arm still tightly held in his grasp.

One drop of her blood landed on Úlftýr's exposed torso, and the second it touched his skin, all animalistic characteristics were gone from Úlftýr's features. His hand relaxed and dropped to the side of his body, and Elska was released.

Elska slowly got up, rubbing her sore wrists.

"What… What is happening?" Elska whispered while the carving in Úlftýr's brow dimmed down. "Úlftýr, what is happening to you?"

Elska wanted to remove all traces of the atrocities committed to Úlftýr's body, but she could not remove the blue ink from his chest no matter how hard she tried. It was fused with his skin, a constant reminder of the savagery he endured.

She wanted to be mad at him for telling her to run. "Why didn't you let me stay and fight? I could have helped you."

Elska caressed his cheek, the winds of a freezing night howling outside.

She sighed. She didn't want to admit it, yet she knew Úlftýr was right. In sending her away, he, more likely than not, saved her life.

She just wasn't sure if his efforts would go in vain. The loneliness, it ate at her. When she was alone before Úlftýr, she had her ways to feel happy alone. She found happiness in her art, in her books, and in nature, but now all that held no charm for her. The loneliness she experienced without him felt like abandonment.

All she wanted was for him to hold her, and even if it wasn't his fault that he wasn't there to do so, she felt resentment towards him for leaving her for the hellish nightmare he was stuck in.

She had a hard time seeing herself without him. She could not remember anymore who she was without him, but at the same time she was slowly losing hope that he would ever return to her.

Late at night, in the cover of darkness, when no one but the moon and stars heard her, she confided in the only person she believed understood her.

"I wish you knew how hard it is to motivate myself to move, how much I just want to crawl to the corner of the room, ball up, and disappear to where no one can hurt me. Even walking had become difficult. I feel this pit inside my chest that craves to cripple me and pulls at my arms and legs and threatens to swallow me whole." She let out a shuddered breath, unable to rid herself of the lump in her throat.

"I need you...." She whispered. "I would have already given up on this life and came looking for you in purgatory," she told Úlftýr, watching his closed eyes for any sign that he was listening to her. "If I hadn't been such a coward if I knew I could follow where you go and bring you back or stay with you in the afterlife forever, I would have severed my eternal coils to this world, only to be reunited with you."

Neither her friends, the guards Ingrid sent to her, nor Ingrid herself managed to pry her away from Úlftýr's chambers for the briefest of intervals in those crucial days.

At first, she had books brought to her from the library, but as days went by, she had begun to run out of floor; everywhere you looked, there were open books. Eventually, she began spending a small portion of her day buried behind stacks of paper in the candlelit chamber, digging up such ancient writings that had not seen the light of day in centuries.

She poured over the ancient tomes with her father, scrutinizing every glyph, searching for the sinister charm Deirdra had exacted against her love.

"I suspect the rune Deirdra carved is incomplete," Elska told her father. "I've heard before of ancient symbols that can transform one's mind and body to make them stronger, more agile, but this carving on his brow acts peculiarly."

"How so?" Siran asked. He looked into the sunken eyes of his sleep-deprived daughter.

Elska closed another book and put it aside, disappointed at its content. "Úlftýr is not healing as fast as he should have; even the small cuts on his chest are still open. And, this time, he is confined to his bed, so he is not to blame for them remaining so."

Siran had no answer to what curse could've caused an effect so vile.

That night, Elska did the unthinkable. In the small hours of the night, in complete secrecy, she performed a blood transfusion in total confidentiality.

Úlftýr's superficial wounds finally closed.

It was a last-resort treatment that was rarely used because of the unforeseen effects it sometimes had on the Ljósálfar.

Tales of the darkness that gripped those who this remedy was used on passed down to them since they were children. Frightening stories of Ljósálfar who succumbed to bloodlust and, when healed, attacked those closest to them.

Some were even believed to have become Dökkálfar — dark shadow Ljósálfar who fed on death and were eventually destroyed.

Regardless of the stories, Elska felt she had no choice. She was willing to try anything.

Even with Siran by her side, loneliness and frustration threatened to overtake her.

She craved to open up to someone, anyone, but what could she say that they did not already know, and what advice would they give to console her with words her mind was already prepared to negate? Most of all, worry gripped her heart. Sleep claimed her from exhaustion after she did everything that came to her mind to try, performed every healing charm in her arsenal, and used every remedy her father suggested to speed Úlftýr's recovery.

When Elska finally slept, her head rested on old knowledge-filled pages she had gone through countless times before, sure she had missed the clue she was searching for.

Even in her dreams, miserable comprehension tormented her; she could not wake her lover up, and the truth of the curse upon him eluded her.

The weather mirrored her emotions.

Wailing winds and heavy snow replaced the hint of spring that briefly graced the valley. Elska knew that cold had never bothered Úlftýr. Unlike herself, she was not an enthusiast for the chilly nights.

Colder and lonelier now that Úlftýr was not there to envelop her in his warm embrace, she only ever felt sheltered from the frost that covered their land in his arms.

Fortunately, the heating system, cleverly blended with the fortress's architecture, served the residents of the royal dwelling well.

Elska was glad for it, now that the freezing winter nights had come back to haunt her and brought with them the wind that howled through the fjords and the frost that painted brilliant murals on the glass-stained windows. At another time, she would have admired them, even painted them, but now, even the beauty of nature failed to plant joy in her heart.

Elska became plagued by visions that came to her in the brief moments when sleep claimed her.

One of their last conversations played itself out in her head over and over again; Úlftýr had just assumed the throne, and he sat upon it, his face contorted. The seat and his station were the most uncomfortable place he could be.

"Dark thoughts cloud my mind," Úlftýr told her. "I fear the serpents of legend no longer protect us; their light magic has drained from the world, and my father's journey is all for naught."

Elska wanted to protest. In her dream, she opened her mouth to try and console him, but no words came out.

She drifted over the fabled mountain, and the great serpents rose into the heavens before her and fell in the form of broken stone upon the ground.

She woke with a start, realizing her head rested against Úlftýr. She watched Úlftýr's uneasy sleep. His eyelids moved frantically, his breath coming in shallow heaves.

Elska wiped the sweat from his brow with a wet cloth.

"Come back to me." She begged him, wishing she possessed the ability to dive into his mind and pull him out. But she could not follow where he went — at least, not in this life.

CHAPTER 18
THE FIRST DEATH

While his body rested safely between the castle walls, Úlftýr's tormented soul wandered in darkness.

He walked barefoot on hot soil in a cavern stretching on for miles. Only a faint, distant light gave him hope that there was an end to his quest.

The air was stale and sickeningly sweet. It weighed on Úlftýr like a cloak made of shadows. Úlftýr looked down; specks of yellow brimstone clung to his feet. The heat of the soil stung his bare skin.

Small fires reeking of sulfur burned with blue flames along the path.

Úlftýr wondered then if the netherworld claimed him and if he would ever be granted a way out. Úlftýr desperately craved to reach the distant light, but it kept getting further. *'Perhaps this was the fate the gods bestowed upon me,'* he thought, *'To travel without hope for redemption, trapped in solitude forever.'*

He walked until he could no longer walk, and just when he lost all hope of ever reaching the light in the distance, the dark cavern ended.

The path led him to a tall, ornately woven metal gate. When he stepped beyond it, an icy fog welcomed him to the entrance of another cavern set in the trunk of a large tree.

Letters unfamiliar to him were engraved in the bark of the ancient Quercus. The blue hue of the letters illuminated Úlftýr's path and the unmarked gravestones that protruded like broken teeth out of the mist obscuring the ground underneath his bare feet.

Úlftýr took in the cold air, fresh.

Revived, he stepped over the entrance to the second cavern and merged with the shadows of the dead tree.

The sound of bubbling water trickling down into vast pools made him take notice of them. They lined the wall to his right, partly engulfed in the shadows that parted for him as he walked on.

The sight of the pools mesmerized Úlftýr. He trotted over, got down on his knees, and plunged his hands into the deep.

The liquid was cold to the touch, caressing Úlftýr's burning skin, and a sudden realization hit him when he cupped his hands, intending to drink.

'Never eat or drink the fruits of the underworld, for you will grow addicted to their alluring flavor and forever remain bound to hell.' The memory struck him.

Who bestowed these words of warning upon him?

Úlftýr was grateful for their wisdom.

He looked into the water, and a young man with a rounded face, hazel eyes, and delicate mahogany-colored curls stared back at him.

A golden circlet of laurel leaves was interwoven into his hair, and a light blue tunic adorned his sun-kissed skin. His tunic was made of a large piece of square cloth held together by golden pins at his shoulders and secured by a brown leather belt around his waist.

A golden lyre rested on his shoulder, fastened on a strap.

Memories that were not his own flooded Úlftýr's mind.

"Orpheus." He murmured; that was his name in this reincarnation.

Úlftýr's consciousness was certain that what he experienced now was a glimpse into an uncertain future.

'Perhaps,' he thought, *'The gods saw fit to show me a vision of a life my spirit is destined to live if I let go of my old self. If I let the one called* Úlftýr *die.'*

A great urge to continue pushed him forward.

He looked at the cavern, and the light at the cavern's end shone closer than he realized. Beyond it lay a mound of grass and flowers. The illumination of the day blinded him. Úlftýr, in the body of Orpheus, stepped out into the sunlight.

Pangaion Hills, Macedonia, Greece
8 AD

Orpheus's ethereal beauty was known throughout the land, and his fans often discussed his appearance among them. They were many, and they doted on him and his enchanting musical skills, which he used well and often to gain favors with the local court.

Eurydice was a dryad, a tree nymph, and a daughter of the sun and earth.

They met while Orpheus sat in her meadow and played on his lyre with such passion all the flowers bloomed to perfection.

Usually shy, she left her guardian tree and came closer than ever to a mortal.

She realized then, standing so close to him she could reach out and touch him, that he was not a mere man.

A divine presence dwelt, dormant inside him.

Eurydice was unsure that the young man knew that fact about himself.

Orpheus sat, his eyes half-closed, his fingers expertly flying over the strings of his lyre.

Through lidded eyes, he noticed the young maiden, her skin pale, her red hair coming down in waves over her sheer green dress.

His heart skipped a beat.

She danced to his song, lost in his mesmerizing melody. She didn't notice him getting up until he was beside her.

The music ceased, and she fell into his arms, astonished.

Her first instinct was to flee, but something in his affectionate, amber eyes and warm smile had stayed her will to escape back into the safety of her tree.

Their wedding day was the happiest Orpheus had ever been until that moment.

He played and sang and was filled with joy like never before. A nagging feeling in his mind told him that something ominous was approaching. Yet he chose to ignore it, thinking that, for once, his intuition was wrong.

However, it didn't take long for his dread to become a reality.

While he was away playing for the royal court, a Cinnyris bird flew into the hall he played in and crashed into the wall. Heeding the deathly omen, Orpheus raced back only to find his beloved Eurydice slain on their mound, a venomous snake slithering away as Orpheus rushed to her side and attempted to revive her.

He was too late. No beast nor man rivaled his grief.
Day and night, he sat there on the hill and sang his mournful song:

"In this world where thoughts of joy are slaves.
To a usurper king named he despair
Where hope lies in a lightless grave
And agony fills the free air.
Two lost souls unimaginably combined.
Thenceforth a glimmer of hope we shared...

In this world of fog and screams
In this world where cold is God
In this world, I heard her sing.
In this world, she felt my burning blood.

Two souls destined to pain.
Found we that within this prisoning world.
Our grief we could condemn to chains.
Within each other's binding hold.

When chests as one were mended
In hearts, a flame pure was born.
Solace to the soul was commanded.
Hope in my mind had grown.

Alas,
The one who wears the tyrant diadem.
In this endless absolute abyss
Thoughts of hope and joy condemned.
And wished our bond to be deceased."

Distraught by his words and sharing in his grief, all the nymphs and dryads of the land came to mourn with him. The flowers of the land died, and the trees lost their leaves.

Fearing for his kingdom's fate, the King convinced Orpheus to attempt the impossible, to breach the veil between the living world and that of the damned, and to bring his wife back from the dead.

With nothing to lose, Orpheus begged the deities of the land to lead him to the entrance to the underworld.

Eurydice's father warned him he might suffer the same fate his bride had for his insolence in taking on the gods. Still, Orpheus ignored his warning and only received his wisdom to refuse the call of hunger while underground.

Led by the dryads who loved him, Orpheus came to stand at the river's start that ran under his mound.

Miraculously, Orpheus gained entry by charming the undead guardians at the entrance with his song. The rock surface parted before him, and he went under a waterfall of lava that did not burn him and closed right after he stepped inside.

Dead souls reached out to touch him, he thought he recognized their faces, but he had to ignore them and surge forward.

As Orpheus walked, he shed the garments they tore from his body with their bony dead fingers. He ventured forward with only a perizoma; a loincloth remained to cover his decency.

Orpheus stepped onto a path of pomegranate red rubies that led to the feet of a raised throne. The throne was made of white bone and red volcanic rock set upon a mound of bone, ash, and black grave dirt. On it sat Despoina, Queen of the dead.

Orpheus's breath caught in his throat, his heart thundering in his chest at the sight of her. She sat before him, her demeanor striking and her dark lavender gaze sizing him up. She held herself, one who knew for certain that her strength lay in the fear she inspired. She fed on, nurtured, and encouraged it in all her subjects, both living and damned.

She had radiant bronze skin, blush pink lips, and flowing golden hair that contrasted with the dark cavern she dwelt in.

Honoring her godly station, Orpheus tried and failed to avert his gaze from her body.

Extravagant, highly ornate gold top armor adorned her frame with rose windows to cover her breasts.

Attached to the armor lay a cape of rich emerald arranged upon the throne she sat on. When she stood to greet him, he noticed her slender shimmering figure unmistakable under the sheer metallic chain-mail fabric draped from the chest piece and pooled on the floor.

Orpheus knew that, despite her beauty, Despoina led countless mortals to sign over their souls to her with trickery and deception.

They believed in her many promises of riches, glorious warrior status, and even the hint of the godhood she had the power to bestow upon them. Slaves to their many cravings of fame, fortune, and bliss, Despoina made them her playthings, their souls forever tormented for her pleasure by her endless cruelty.

Those lucky enough to make her sick of their insipid wailing faced the wrath of their final punishment.

By her word, she decreed the execution of spirits under her rule, a feast for the beasts that prowled after their prey in the underworld. But by the time the monsters slew them, most of the dead welcomed the nothingness. The void was their release from torment and their salvation. They preferred simply not to be.

Orpheus bowed low.

"My lady of twilight, Queen of souls, ruler of spring, I come before you to seek your favor, to beg for the release of my one true love back to the land of the living." He kept his eyes firmly on the ground. "Please release her from this land of the dead and allow hope to take root in my heart once more."

Despoina looked at him from the height of her throne and smiled. "You speak well, warrior poet. I wonder if you can play and sing as sweetly?"

"Yes, my Queen." Orpheus closed his eyes, straightened up, raised the lyre close to his chest, and began to strum up the most beautiful melodies accompanied by his passionate voice.

"And for you, my beloved dear.
Fate gloom and cruel was no less.
You were lost below in cold, cold drear.
And frost had built where once ruled my warm caress.

Tar black tears you cried.
For in freezing darkness, you drowned
As your aura withered and died
Bestowed upon you, the black heart crown.

World of yours in dark ice cast
Warmth upon you was forbidden.
Buried from you was the sun to rest.
The sight of light from your eyes was hidden.

As hope descended to past
Spirit in your heart deaden.
You wore the icy Chiroptera crest.
You came to be known as the sorrowful snow maiden.

And as grief infinitude
Upon you was bestowed
In tears of cold solitude
You found your loyal abode."

As Orpheus's finger masterfully strummed the golden strings of the lyre, Despoina slowly stepped down from her throne. She circled Orpheus intentionally as a hunting animal would, and ever so slightly, she leaned towards him to take a whiff of her prey.

Orpheus breathed deeply as he attempted to ignore her advances and was careful not to show his disgust.

Despoina's smile grew wider. She reached out and caressed his toned body, so warm to the touch and different from the dead surrounding her. She couldn't help but whisper sweet nothings in his ear.

"Dear poet," she mused. "The beauty of your music and voice might have persuaded me to indulge you, but, you see, Aidoneus, my leash and master, ruler of the heavens at dawn, lord of the underworld, leave me so lonely here in this vast kingdom when the night falls upon the earth. In his absence, I am desolate, akin to this land in which I dwell. Join me, son of Kings, and I will grant you riches beyond your wildest dreams; join me, and I will crown you lord of mortals and bestow upon you eternal life."

The godly presence within Orpheus stirred. He knew better than to believe the enchantress's lies.

"You shall never perish in battle," she continued, ignoring the flash of green in his eyes.

"You shall never become feeble and die. You shall never crumble to dust."

She produced ruby red pomegranate seeds from her breastplate and offered them to him.

"May you feast with me on the fruits of spring, young warrior?" she asked in her enchanting voice.

"I thank your generosity, my Queen of spirits, yet I rely on my music to nourish me here so far from the nurture of the sun," Orpheus said, reserved.

He bowed and remained so, careful not to offend the Queen of the underworld. He knew it took but a taste from the fruits of hell, and he shall be bound, a prisoner of their alluring sweetness forever.

Just as the Queen herself once was foolish enough to be enticed by their lure and the lord of the dead.

"Very well," Despoina sighed. She waved her hand, and the fog took shape, and Eurydice materialized, summoned to them from whichever hell she was confined to in death.

"Eurydice!" Orpheus launched forward while Eurydice reached for him, but all he could touch was the cold air that made up her vision.

"Ah-ah, you can only look." Despoina mused. "I tell you what. If you want the opportunity to touch, I will allow you passage through my kingdom. You must walk without a glance back even once, and all the while, you must play for me on your lyre. If I like what I hear, I will let both of you go. If I don't or you look back even once, your beloved will remain here, and I will reunite you in death. Do you agree to my terms?"

Orpheus gazed into the eyes of Eurydice.

She shook her head, warning him from striking any bargain involving the Queen of deceit, but he had to try even for that fragment of hope.

"Yes," he said. "I agree to your terms."

"Then, off you go." Despoina once again waved her hand, and the cavern opened before them to reveal a long tunnel going straight up and, at the end of it, the blessed light of day. Orpheus did not hesitate. Whatever happened next, he was about to try to leave hell with his beloved.

He held his golden lyre tight with fear that the many anguished souls around them would try to snatch it away from him, turned to the tunnel, and began to play, willing his legs to take him forward.

He strummed on the lyre, his fingers expertly flying over the strings, keeping his gaze fixed ahead.

They walked on the dead black ground through the low, cool fog on a path that led them between deep dark pools and blue flickering sulfur fires.

His feet blistered, and his throat choked from thirst, but all Orpheus did was ignore his discomfort and step forward on the yellow brimstone road.

With the light of day in sight, Orpheus quickened his pace, desperate to reach the surface. He was just about to step out of the cave when his fingers slipped, and immediately after, the terrified screams of Eurydice sounded behind him.

Orpheus knew at that moment that he had nothing left to lose anymore.

He had failed her. He turned.

Eurydice was planted in place at the mouth of the cavern with massive black serpents coiled around her.

Orpheus roared in miserable anger and flung himself onto the snakes.

Before he reached her, Eurydice dissolved, and Orpheus fell into the tangled mess of obsidian reptiles that coiled and hissed around him.

His first instinct was to fight.

He kicked, slashed, and tore into the serpents with his nails and teeth until he emerged covered in his and the reptiles' blood.

Orpheus's lyre, which had fallen from his hands in the struggle, snapped in half, the wail of the golden strings breaking, filling the air with mournful wailing, the saddest sound imaginable, and then dying out.

Orpheus grabbed the pieces in his calloused hands and staining them with blood, plunged the two sharp, gold-colored spikes into the closest serpents, piercing them through.

Dying but with a fighting spirit still within them, the snakes launched into his sensitive organs and sank their venomous fangs into his skin.

Orpheus yelled in pain and agony. He tore the now-dead beasts from his weakened limbs, pushed himself sharply away, and tumbled out of the mouth of the cave.

He lay on the ground while the radiant sun renewed his strength.

The living serpents slithered out of the darkness after him.

Orpheus grunted, rolled to his stomach, and slowly rose to his feet. His slippery pursuers changed as they entered the world of the living.

They grew legs, took on a curved female form, and came to stand tall before him.

Dark-skinned women, their nightshade-long hair a mess adorned by green vines, dead leaves, and snake skulls.

Snake skin was embedded into their arms and cheeks, a remnant of their recent origin. Bullhorns sprang from their heads.

They wore garments of fawn, fox, and rabbit skins messily sewn together, and, with their dirty hands, they held onto coiled sticks wrapped in ivy and tipped with sharpened pinecones.

"Maenads! Raving banshees!" Orpheus cried out to them, recognizing the mythical she-demons.

"Why do you torment me? Why do you seek to destroy me?"

"Join me, son of Kings." Despoina's voice emerged from the largest maenad.

"I offer you so much if you join me. Grant me your heart, body, and soul, and I shall make you King among mortals."

Orpheus laughed so maniacally that he did not recognize himself. "I refuse your generous offer, Queen of deceit!" he yelled in vigor.

The maenad bared her teeth.

"Heed my words, son of none. One day, you will be mine, and I shall feast on your soul that day."

As her laughter died out, the she-demon returned to normal, as normal as a maenad can be.

Orpheus stood shaking. He watched them groaning and snarling at him. Pomegranate juice was smeared on their faces; it ran down with their saliva and stained their skin in the color of mortal blood.

Orpheus knew that Despoina sent them into an intoxicated frenzy brought upon by the fruits of hell she attempted to entice him to consume. There was no reasoning with them in this state.

"I'd rather die than succumb to eternal slavery as you have."

Orpheus charged forward into the inevitable battle.

Aidonneus's underworld demons surrounded him. In his weakened state, they overpowered him quickly. They smashed the pinecone spears against his flesh, piercing his arms, legs, and abdomen, and it seemed they had no intention to halt their attack before they ripped him to shreds.

But just as it began, it was over.

"Last chance…" Despoina's voice rang thoughtfully.

Orpheus ignored her. He ignored the demented Maenads, too.

They, in turn, lost interest in his mangled body.

They reverted to snake form to Despoina's laughter and slithered back underground.

With his arms wrapped tightly around his body, Orpheus dragged himself with what remaining strength he had to the river that ran under the hill he emerged atop.

He looked at his reflection in the water, beaten and broken; he no longer possessed the rounded face, hazel eyes, and delicate mahogany-colored curls.

Who greeted him was a frightening creature. At some point amidst the battle, Orpheus changed back to Úlftýr again.

The same Úlftýr that was cursed and corrupted by Deirdra and more dead than alive.

Blue blood stained his white hair, and his eyes stared dim and bloodshot.

"Elska…" he whispered.

Her reflection appeared in the water. Her mouth was moving, saying something to him, but her words were muted.

Úlftýr opened his mouth, and quite mournful words floated down to the netherworld:

"And so, my vigor they reaped.
On pain of mine, they thrived.
Blood of mine in pleasure they sipped.
Prayed I for graceful death to arrive…."

The void called out to Úlftýr, and he eagerly listened. He closed his eyes, let his torn-up body fall, and tumbled into the stream.

As he slid into the deep, the water began to cover him, suffocating him but simultaneously cleansing his soul.

The water turned dark blue, colored by his blood, the surge pulling him down.

A bright vision played in his dying eyes; Elska's face shone above him in the light of the rising moon.

Snakes slithered across the water's surface, preventing him from coming back up.

The vision took Úlftýr back to their hidden stream. Elska stood before him in the shallow water, dressed in a sheer green dress—a curious glow emitted from her. Úlftýr heard her heartbeat. The realization was almost at his grasp, but a bawl of deadly power howled within him before he uttered the question or speak her true name.

The waterfall behind his beloved Elska crystallized and exploded, burying her underneath.

His mind screamed in misery, and in the west wing of the Blackstone castle, King Úlftýr opened his eyes.

CHAPTER 19

THE RAMPAGE OF THE BELOVED

The earth moved beneath him.

He lay on his red velvet sheets and felt the restless stir of something big beneath the ground.

Through the large arched window, the bright moon shone in to arouse him from his death slumber.

Úlftýr opened his eyes, shot up, and sat, panting in his bed. He still felt the torturous sensation of water filling his lungs, clouding his sight, smothering him as he went down, bound to return to the underworld.

Úlftýr finally awoke but was still suffocating; water splashed inside his lungs. He coughed, tumbling out of his bed, disoriented.

His surroundings were strangely familiar, a distant memory of a previous life.

The snakes!

Úlftýr's eyes snapped down; he felt them coil against his skin, slithering, twisting, and was sure they were moving under his skin.

"Aggh!" He clawed at his arms to tear them out.

Without thinking, he sank the newly grown canines he didn't realize he had into his arm and bit down.

Bile rose within him, and the metallic taste of his blood grew prominent in his mouth. The pain made him recoil; he stumbled back against the bed. He coughed and spat, attempting to wipe the blood away, but smeared it all over his face.

An unacquainted feeling grew inside him and gradually became louder, overpowering all other senses. It took him a moment to recognize this gut-wrenching craving; hunger was all he thought of, such a horrible desire for sustenance he had never known before.

Úlftýr stepped back, crouched down, and doubled over by the emptiness that grabbed hold inside his stomach.

He staggered, his head throbbing with unnatural agony. It obscured part of his sight with pounding, blinding, hot flashes. Swaying, he made his way toward the wooden door. His claws scratched the wood surface, and he pulled the door open and stepped outside into the hall.

"Sire?" The warrior, Vidar, who Ingrid stationed outside Úlftýr's door, looked at his distraught King.

Úlftýr's hair was white and came down in clumps around his face. The rune still glowed in the strange, red gleam on his forehead, and his eyes glowed the same.

Úlftýr looked at Vidar, blind to his true identity; instead, a shadowy being stood before him with pulsating blue veins.

'The Queen of the underworld must have sent her demons after me to bring me back under her reign.' Orpheus whispered in his mind, enraged.

Úlftýr felt the fangs cut into his lips, protruding further from his shredded gums. He clenched his fists, and the claws curled into his skin.

Úlftýr tasted his blood again, and it set his mind reeling. At that moment, Úlftýr only knew starvation, and the shadowy demon stepped closer through the red tint that covered his eyes.

'Protect yourself!' Orpheus's consciousness persisted. *'You can't let her drag us back to hell!'*

Úlftýr's body felt confined, his movement restricted by the cloth attached to every part of his torso. Úlftýr growled and began clawing at the bloody bandages. He had to take them off; he had to get free.

"No! King Úlftýr, you must not do that!" Vidar grasped his arms.

The shadow demon seized his arms, and Úlftýr gasped. He wouldn't let the creature hurt him.

Úlftýr snarled and pushed the shadow demon away. He shook his head to rid it of the headache that refused to subside and enraged; he unleashed upon the offending creature before him.

He slashed, gnawed, and tore into the demon until the pulsating veins running through his body were faint lines, and the creature lay vanquished at his feet.

Úlftýr pushed at the dead guard, his hands coming into contact with something sticky. He moved his hand to his mouth, sniffed at it, and then licked it.

Immediately, he felt rejuvenated.

He grumbled in agreement and plunged his face into the sticky mess before him. His fangs cut through soft flesh and mangled tissue, and the sweet taste of nectar hit the back of his throat.

He drank until the satisfying gulps turned into trickling drops. Disappointed, he growled. He had to get more.

Úlftýr grabbed an outstretched limb of the dead creature he fed on.

'More... I need more.' he thought, walking down the hallway, dragging Vidar's mutilated corpse by its arm behind him. Warm candlelight and familiar voices beckoned him to a large wooden door.

Úlftýr propped Vidar's body, half slumped against the wall. He stood momentarily, watching the shadows move under the doorway, seeing them through the crack under the door.

Several shadowy figures with pulsating, beckoning veins stood around a large wooden table.

"We cannot let these savages hinder us from celebrating one of our most sacred days." a shadowy figure said.

"With the earthquakes and the ambushes, do you think it is wise to allow large gatherings at the moment?" asked a smaller shadow.

"Úlftýr is still on the mend. What do we tell our people?"

"What we have been telling them," said the shadow sitting on the throne across the table. "Deirdra's leashed monsters injured him, and I took over until he recovers."

Úlftýr... *I know this name...* 'Úlftýr thought.

'*The queen of the dead is clever in her deception,* ' Orpheus whispered in his head.

"We cannot live in fear in our land," The one on the throne said, her veins shining brighter than the others, and a purplish glow emitted from where her eyes should have been. Úlftýr's mouth watered.

"It's what Úlftýr would have wanted," Ingrid said. "I know what is in my brother's heart; it is similar to mine."

Úlftýr lowered his gaze and pushed the heavy wooden doors open.

He hissed at the bright firelight reflected from silver plates mounted on the walls and shone in his eyes.

He entered the throne room, slouched, his eyes averting from the light. When he glanced up, he hissed again, louder, while shielding his eyes.

"Úlftýr?" Ingrid rose from the throne. She glanced at Baldur, who stared at Úlftýr, gob-smacked.

Ingrid focused her gaze on Úlftýr.

Her brother looked distraught. Úlftýr stood, his torso exposed, the inked stain prominent on his pale grey skin and fresh blood that didn't seem to belong to him, smeared all over his face and upper body.

"Úlftýr?"

The mesmerizing shadow stepped closer. Úlftýr didn't dare to move.

"You're awake… How do you feel?" The shadow demon touched him. "Whose blood is this?"

Úlftýr wanted to recoil; the demon's touch scourged his skin, yet a strike of arousing lightning went through him.

'This! This is who I need to drain to be whole again. Its essence shall make mine complete.'

The rune on his forehead glowed in bright red.

He ignored the other shadowy figures. The fangs cut through his gums again, and his claws slashed through his skin, growing out.

With a pained cry, Úlftýr threw himself at the glowing demon and caught her in his claws.

"Úlftýr! Stop!" Ingrid yelled.

Úlftýr strangled the trashing shadow demon in his grasp and smashed her head against the stone floor. The devil stopped moving, going limp in his arms, her essence still shining with inviting vigor.

"King Úlftýr! Unhand her!" Young Vanir attempted to grab him, but he could not subdue Úlftýr.

He jumped up, threw Ingrid on the floor, and caught the offending demon by its throat.

Vanir screamed, and tears welled in his eyes, *'This is not happening!'* went frantically in his mind.

The snapping sound of Vanir's neck echoed through the chamber.

Aesir fell to his knees, gaping at Úlftýr. This was not their King. A manic beast emerged instead of Úlftýr.

"King Úlftýr, please! Return to your senses!"

Úlftýr snarled at Aesir and advanced toward him. He slashed at Aesir with his claws; his nails made contact, and Aesir yelled in pain and astonishment.

"Whoever you are," Aesir got up and stepped back from him, "you are not my liege."

Úlftýr looked at him with eyes of burning red fire.

"King Úlftýr, stop." Aesir drew his sword. Úlftýr kept advancing.

"The King is dead." Aesir struggled to find the air to fill his lungs.

Úlftýr growled and slashed at him again.

"Forgive me. Tyyyrr!" The battle cry tore through Aesir. He swung his sword, Úlftýr ducked, and, in the next moment, he was on him.

He seized Aesir by his shoulders and, in one swift motion, tore him in half.

"Úlftýr." Baldur stood before him; his gut twisted with revolting sickness as Úlftýr tossed Aesir aside.

"Úlftýr, you must fight this. If you are still in there, please, I beg you to wake up."

"I am awake," Úlftýr said in a low snarl and launched at Baldur. "You won't take me back to the underworld, demon!"

"What? What underworld? What demon?" Baldur shook his head, but his questions went unanswered.

Baldur raised his sword, but it was a futile attempt to stop the inevitable.

All the fight had left him at the sight of Úlftýr, quickly blocking his sword with his arm. The deep gash in Úlftýr's flesh closed instantly. Úlftýr grabbed the sword by its blade, tore it from Baldur's grasp, and threw it aside. He lifted Baldur by his neck with one hand.

"Úlf…" Baldur gulped.

For a split second, the light of the rune diminished, and Úlftýr's kind, amber eyes shone through.

"Úlftýr…" Baldur mouthed.

His hope desecrated when the rune in Úlftýr's forehead reignited, the fire that burned within his eyes visibly reclaimed Úlftýr's thoughts, and the starving beast returned.

Úlftýr grimaced and hurled Baldur into the wall where the bronze-coated antlers skewered him, finally dimming the offending light in the room. Something deep inside him registered the painful gasp, the sigh, the gurgle.

It hurt, an internal scream begging to get out, but only a moan escaped the savage beast. Úlftýr watched the veins of the shadow demon pulse for a moment longer before they, too, were extinguished like the dying light.

'Finally.' The thought of the sweet nectar that awaited him filled his body with morbid happiness.

He turned back to the glowing shadow still on the ground where Úlftýr had left her.

With no one to stop his ghoulish deeds, he got down on his knees, sank his fangs into the warm flesh, and began to drink.

The ruckus coming from the throne room startled Elska awake.

She stared at an open rune book before her and the black ink covering part of her hand.

'I must have fallen asleep while reading.' She thought to herself.

Another crash, followed by battle shouts, echoed through the corridor outside the great library. She jumped to her feet.

'Had Deirdra breached the castle to hurt Úlftýr *again?'* Elska swung the library door open and ran into the warrior Garuk, who was about to run in to protect her.

"What is this?! What is happening?"

"I don't know, but I must get you to safety." Garuk attempted to grab her hand, but Elska recoiled.

"Call for help!" Elska ordered and ran down the hall to Garuk's shouts of protest.

"Úlftýr!" Elska's heart pounded in her ears. She ran, winded, into the throne room.

"Úlftýr!" She stopped dead in her tracks.

The blood was everywhere, screaming at her from the floor, from the walls, and smeared lover's face, who sat hunched over another álfur on the floor.

At the sound of her voice, Úlftýr let go of his prey and raised his burning red eyes at her, and then, he slowly got up.

That was when she saw the bodies.

"No…" Elska put her hands to her mouth, tears stinging her eyes. "Baldur…" she looked at his bloody corpse, pierced through and mounted on the wall like a trophy.

"Aesir…" his eyes were still open in permanent horror. She looked away with a mournful cry.

And Vanir, poor Vanir, his neck twisted in an odd position with streaks of tears staining his contorted face. She stepped back. "Úlftýr, what is happening?"

Úlftýr shook his head.

'That voice! I've heard it before in another place. I've known it for eternity; it guided me out of the dark shadows of my life.' The pain of loss struck him, and the agony of separation and longing threatened to overpower him; that voice belonged to the one person who always stood by him.

He reached for her.

The rune on his forehead that had burned in bright red until that moment was dimmed to have a low glow. The menacing energy that emanated from him had subdued completely.

Úlftýr screamed in pain; his fangs retracted, and his claws disappeared. He breathed hard, his eyes darting to the bloody wall.

He blinked again and again, waking up from a bad dream. His eyes flickered, first in amber and then back to glowing red. He looked down at his hands and the blue blood that covered them.

Bile rose in his throat. "Elska…? What is going on…."

He glanced down at the unconscious álfur that lay on the ground at his feet.

"Ingrid… what…? Elska," he looked around him in terror. His eyes stopped on Baldur.

"No…!" He whispered frantically. "No, no, no! Baldu…r."

Broken images surfaced from his inner beast's dim memory to play out in his head.

His own hands grabbed hold of Baldur.

The astonishment, the sad look on Baldur's face that quickly turned to horror and betrayal in his dying eyes before the light had gone out of them forever crippled Úlftýr.

Úlftýr looked at Elska.

"Have I done this?" His voice trembled.

"Úlftýr," Elska stepped towards him, but he staggered back.

"No! Stay there! It isn't safe! I'm not safe..." He couldn't bear to face her. "I'm sorry. I'm so sorry." His eyes rested on the window. He had to get out of there.

"Úlftýr, no!" Elska screamed, but it was too late. Úlftýr bolted to the arched window with godlike speed and crashed through it, falling with a frenzied shout.

"Úlftýr!" Elska ran to the broken window and looked down; she feared she would see Úlftýr lying on the ground, but he was gone. Only his bloodied prints remained in the snow.

Elska didn't notice her hand slipping into the broken glass until the sharp pain pierced her palm.

"Aghh…" She winced, removing the broken glass from her hand and clutching it under her other arm to stop the bleeding; she stumbled over to Ingrid.

"Please, please be alive." She put her uninjured hand on Ingrid's neck and felt Ingrid's pulse strong beneath her fingers. "Ingrid!" She hastily patted her pockets and pulled out a vial filled with the spirit of hartshorn, a liquor made of shaved deer horns and water that emitted a potent odor to wake the senses. She used it earlier to keep herself awake while she read into the night.

She put it to Ingrid's nose, and Ingrid coughed. She opened her eyes and groaned in pain.

"Elska…? Where... where is Úlftýr?" she asked, attempting to lift her head but failing miserably, weakened by the blood loss Úlftýr inflicted.

"He left." Elska gestured to the broken window. "I am going after him."

Ingrid's eyes focused on the scene before her. Her mouth opened in horror. Baldur's dead, wide-open eyes stared at her from the mount on the wall.

"Who... By the Yggdrasil! Did... did Úlftýr...?" she let out a whimper. "Elska... Elska! It was Úlftýr! He's gone mad! You can't go after him." she protested, her thoughts becoming clearer.

Ingrid turned her head. From the corner of her eyes, a bloody hand lay flat, but from the angle she lay in, she couldn't see who it was. "Aesir, Vanir, they were here with me." Ingrid cried out. "He is dangerous," Ingrid grabbed Elska's sleeve. Elska winced in pain, but Ingrid pulled her closer. "He will kill you!"

Elska wanted to cry out; she craved to scream, but she forced herself to take in a shuddering breath instead. "He was gone for nine days, and I felt my world crumble around me. I am not willing to lose him forever. Besides, he already had the chance to end me. He didn't even try to attack me." She managed. "I am still alive. And so are you. I have to go after him." She began to get up, but Ingrid still held on to her.

"He won't hurt me," Elska said with her reassurance directed at herself. "I am going to bring him back,"

"What are you going to do when you find him?" Ingrid breathed.

"I will find a way to get through to him. I have done it before. You don't understand; he cannot be alone now. I am sure he is scared and confused, even more than we are. I don't think he knows what is happening or what he is doing, and he might hurt himself or others."

"All the more reason not to go!"

"All the more reason I *have* to go."

"And what about Deirdra?" Ingrid was grasping at straws to keep Elska safe.

It didn't work. Elska's gaze darkened. "Let her come. She did this. If the great serpent is on our side, her path will cross with Úlftýr, and I hope no one stops him from taking his vengeance on her."

Ingrid gaped at her. "Never have I heard you wish harm on anyone before."

Elska extracted her hand from Ingrid's grip, got up, and hastily approached the door.

"No one ever hurt the one I love like that before. I will send for help; just try not to move." She said before she disappeared down the hall.

Ingrid swallowed hard, tears streaming down her face. She closed her eyes and wept, wishing the gruesome deaths around her to be but a nightmare she would soon awaken from.

Úlftýr landed in the snow. He looked up at the light shining from the broken second-story window he had just jumped out from. The icy cold seeped into his bones, his breath misted in the frigid air, and his racing heartbeat thundered in his ears.

And then it all suddenly stopped. The cold no longer bit him, his heart slowed, and his breath all but stopped, as if he were a frozen statue bereft of life. The world loomed in front of his eyes, covered in a red tint he could not wipe away.

Úlftýr's head spun, images of blood and shouts of horror filling his mind. Shards of glass littered the snow beneath him, and some large pieces were embedded deep in his arms.

For a fraction of a second, Úlftýr was sure that two emerald-colored, malice-filled eyes blinked at him from the shadows.

In a flash, they were gone.

Úlftýr heaved, pounding the ground. "No! No! It didn't happen! It didn't…!" The scourging pain of guilt bore into him. "I didn't! It wasn't me!" he screamed.

'Away! I have to get away!' Úlftýr staggered up to his feet and ran.

The darkness seemed brighter than daylight in his eyes.

Úlftýr's mind went blank. He halted; the sound of trickling water led him down into a crevice under the castle. Through thick shrubbery, he emerged on the rocky shore.

In front of him, the waterfall lay nearly frozen over. Above him, a million lanterns shone in the sky.

Úlftýr dropped to the ground, and he seized the shattered fragments that stuck out of his flesh and began carelessly pulling them out.

The bloody wounds rapidly healed, and the gashes in his skin knitted together and closed until no trace of them was left.

Deirdra observed the whole ordeal unfolding before her eager eyes through the flames that burned in the fireplace of the throne room.

She was glad she had the insight to implant her blood in the fireplace structure and candleholders in the main chambers of the castle right before she left.

She had found an ancient sorcery that allowed her to feed upon the fire's essence while it was lit and see everything the fire reflected through her mirror of flames.

She watched Úlftýr now while she hid in the shadows at the edge of the crystallized waterfall.

At first, she was furious that she could not complete her ploy, but the interruption to her spell yielded an exciting result.

His new, savage behavior intrigued her.

'Perhaps I can control the beast.' She thought. *'Persuade him to rule by my side after all.'* Her eyes shone with malice.

"Sleep now, my King," she whispered, her dark spell already taking hold of Úlftýr's tired mind.

"Sleep and dream of the possibilities."

CHAPTER 20

THE FINAL RESTING PLACE

E very part of him ached; his limbs screeched in exhaustion, and cold sweat formed on his brow. It wasn't long before his eyes fell shut, and he collapsed in the snow.

The snowfall came down on Úlftýr and covered him in a thick white blanket. Only where he lay, he stained the ground in bright blue.

Úlftýr was not bothered by the cold. He was safe. Laying there, hidden from the world beneath the soft covers, he got the sense of a sturdy wood bed underneath his tired body, and, gradually, memories of silk sheets became his reality.

Castello di Fossa, province of L'Aquila, Abruzzo, southern Italy 1346 AD

Their castle stood overlooking the village on the eastern side of Circolo mountain.

The circular tower in its apex was Vincenzo's favorite vantage point.

The castle's square structure had high thick walls that protected the estate sitting prominently against the green landscape, flanked by four tall square towers built before his home was even there.

Two towers, located close to the gated entrance, served as living quarters for the hired workers in his noble father's service.

An arched stone entrance welcomed the visitors to the castle through large double wood doors.

Vincenzo knew of another hidden passage by the north tower that only the constant dwellers of the castle knew about, and even they, besides Vincenzo, rarely used it. It was a bright morning. The birds chirped outside his window in the garden, and the air was filled with the bustle of the servants outside, who had been undoubtedly awake since the early hours of the morning.

The sun shone through the heavy, red curtains that covered his arched window, and after a knock and a brief pause, a female servant opened the great wooden door to his room.

The maiden bowed, bringing in the dish with the freshwater and the washcloth to cleanse his face from the hold of the night.

Slow to get up, Vincenzo pulled himself out of bed.

The female servant blushed and averted her eyes. He was, after all, stark naked. It was the middle of summer, and it was no wonder he slept in the nude. Outside, there were only a few more good hours of pleasant weather before the sun started beating the earth relentlessly with its heat. By the time he got up and a male servant came in and helped him into his attire, his family was already up.

Vincenzo wore a black doublet embroidered with pearls. He sighed deeply, looking himself over in the great mirror that stood by the window. Close to nothing at all had changed in his appearance in the past decade. Everyone said that time was kind to his family. Still, he bore the same sun-kissed complexion and the same long black hair.

He grew somewhat of a mustache and a beard that his little sister absolutely hated, but it made him feel older and more mature.

He knew now he would have to go down to where his family gathered in the grand sitting room.

'At least,' he thought. 'It would be filled with delicious odors from the meat cooking in the kitchen beyond the great hall.' He decided then that he would try his luck at sneaking past his family to get himself free and clear out into the gardens to enjoy what was left of this beautiful day.

He had no genuine desire to hear his father again boasting about their royal guest and how uncourteous it was of Vincenzo not to bless her with his presence and how he should charm her with his grace.

She certainly did not charm him with hers.

Dabria. A daughter of a lord that arrived not two months back in the middle of the night. She entered the castle soaking wet, caught in the last rainstorm before the beginning of summer, and Vincenzo was sure she brought the storm with her.

His parents were infatuated with her immensely. They were honored that a lord sent his daughter as a potential bride for their son, so they could get acquainted over the summer and eventually married and multiplied their family's wealth.

For Vincenzo's father, the prospect of a high station was everything. But Vincenzo did care for her.

Her immediate interest in him, though, was apparent, and so was the suspicion she raised in the eyes of his younger sister, Amelia. "She is always watching you." Amelia once told him when they were alone. "So intense, it is like she wants to devour you whole."

"Vincenzo!" His father's voice reached his ears. Vincenzo cringed.

Sadly, he couldn't make the swift escape into the gardens he hoped to accomplish.

Vincenzo took a deep breath to maintain his composure and, with the brightest smile he could master, turned and entered the grand sitting room.

"Father." He greeted him while he took in the wonderful fragrances from the kitchens that rose with the high wooden ceiling and filled the room with a pleasant aroma.

"Mother, Amelia." The hair rose on the back of his neck, and a chill ran down his spine.

Dabria. There she was. She wore a Florentine-style deep red velvet dress decorated with pomegranates along the bodice and expertly trimmed by expensive fur.

"My lady." He bowed before her.

"Oh, Vincenzo!" She stood up from the velvet cushions of the window seat and closed the distance between them.

Vincenzo had to stop himself from recoiling at her touch.

"I feared you wouldn't grace us with your presence this day." She ran her hand down his back. Goose flesh covered his body.

He thanked the heavens he wore the long black brocade doublet and tunic to hide his genuine aversion to her touch.

"Lady Dabria." Vincenzo stepped forward and turned to her, quick to escape her brush against him.

"I fear I shall not be good company to you, my lady. I am, in fact, on my way to the gardens to use this fine morning for training."

"Training?" Dabria's face contorted in mild disgust. "Why on earth would you allow your noble son to dirty his hands in matters of war?" she demanded in accusation of his father, who had gone pale with embarrassment.

"My father does not control my actions. And our family always served in times of war. We do not shy away from a righteous fight." Vincenzo's blood boiled in his veins.

"Won't you give your sword a rest for one day to entertain our guest?" his father, Lord Monsonego, urged him. "You are not being a gracious host."

"I'm sure you and mother are accommodating and hospitable enough." Vincenzo let out through his teeth. "But our enemies surely do not rest, and neither can I."

Vincenzo glanced at Amelia, who sat with his mother at a mahogany ladies' writing desk, quill in her hand and parchment before her.

When she caught him looking at her, she nearly toppled the inkwell over but seized it at the last moment, stiffening the laugh that slipped from under her breath.

She was fourteen — old enough to marry but young enough to be still but a playful child, and Vincenzo loved her with all his heart.

He took note of her pleading eyes.

"Would you care to join me in the garden, sister?" He asked her. He knew she didn't want to be there any more than he did.

"Yes!" Amelia jumped up, her pale peach Lucrezia dress dragged behind her, and hurried to Vincenzo's side.

"Amelia!" Their mother cried out, appalled. "Calm yourself! Is that any way for a young lady to behave? "

"I am sorry, mother." Amelia went red in the face; she curtsied hurriedly and nearly fell off her feet.

Vincenzo caught her under her arm and laughed." Oh, let her be, mother. It is too beautiful a day to spend inside."

"And who will help me write the invitations to our banquet?" His mother inquired.

"Lady Dabria can assist you." Vincenzo took hold of Amelia's hand and pulled her after him.

"I am sure she has the most delicate penmanship." He smiled towards Dabria, bile rising in his throat. "Come along, Amelia."

They were out the door before anyone else could insert a protest. Amelia laughed. "Oh, thank you! Thank you!" She exclaimed, overjoyed when they were out of earshot. She kissed Vincenzo on his cheek and, gathering the hem of her dress, ran into the garden before him.

Vincenzo followed her into the little training arena he had built on the grounds, to his mother's dismay.

He grabbed hold of a wood long-sword from the racks he had put together and made his way to the pell - a wooden post Vincenzo planted in the ground with grooves he added for targets.

The wooden sword was twice the weight of his regular long sword to ensure that he could build up his upper body and arm strength when he wielded his real weapon.

"You could not get out of there fast enough," Vincenzo smirked as his sister flopped down on the grass.

"I cannot stand her!" Amelia let out a little too loudly; at once, she looked around to make sure traitorous ears had not heard her.

"It's 'Amelia, look at lady Dabria and how skillfully she dances' or 'Amelia! Cover your shoulders! Can you see how modest Lady Dabria is? And my favorite, Amelia! Riding does not become a proper lady; lady Dabria should teach you how to play a skillful game of cards. Aggh!"

She huffed, and Vincenzo laughed. He turned to the pell and swung at it hard with the wooden sword.

"Do not taunt me with your laughter, brother! Am I to dwell alone in my misery?" Amelia scorned him. She picked up a small pebble from the trail, laid down throughout the garden and threw it at him.

The rock hit his neck. Vincenzo yelped. He turned to his sister and grinned.

"Forgive me, Amelia. My words were only in jest." He smiled. "Consider me a company to your misery."

Amelia beamed at her brother. She leaned back as he resumed his training.

Vincenzo's skill with the pell was apparent. He spent rigorous hours in training, alone and with the village's teenagers, perfecting his thrusts, acquiring dexterity in the precision of slicing motions, and showing true artistry in his focus and agility in his maneuvers.

He had just hoisted the wooden sword up and brought it down on the lumber with such force it left a permanent dent in the timber when a familiar, repulsively sweet voice rang behind them.

"Vincenzo! Amelia." Vincenzo flinched.

"Amelia, I wonder if you allow me to speak to your lovely brother privately." Dabria smiled at his sister.

Now, it was Vincenzo's turn to plead to Amelia with his eyes. He knew that she wanted to stay and assist him, but he also knew that he had to deal with Dabria's unwanted advances once and for all on his own.

"Of course, my lady," Vincenzo put the wooden sword away.

"Walk with me." Lady Dabria stepped onto the path. Vincenzo rolled his eyes, and unwillingly, he followed.

They walked silently until Dabria was confident, they were both out of earshot of Vincenzo's sister.

"The banquet is imminent," Dabria said. "I am sure you are aware of my initial purpose in coming here. My father is interested in strengthening the ties of our families' friendship and influence by the marriage bond."

When Vincenzo did not reply, Dabria continued a bit more sternly. "I had hoped, Vincenzo, that you would be the one to take the necessary steps towards our union by now, but I see that you are reluctant to do so."

Vincenzo's stomach twisted in a knot. He knew what was coming next.

"If you agree, I would very much like to make the happy announcement at the banquet," Dabria concluded.

"No," Vincenzo said and stopped.

Dabria halted her step and turned to him in a sharp movement.

"No?" Her face contorted; Vincenzo had not yet encountered this dark side of her.

"No, "Vincenzo repeated, and he stepped back. "Forgive me, Lady Dabria, for I did not intend to mislead you. However, at the banquet, I do plan to announce my happy engagement; only it will not be to you."

Her facade of proper manners cracked under the insult of rejection, and, more than ever, he knew he had made the right choice.

"Forgive me." He repeated and turned back towards the path they came from, leaving Dabria to seethe with ugly anger on this beautiful day.

A moment later, when she regained her senses, Dabria called out to him and demanded to reveal his beloved's identity.

Vincenzo politely but sternly refused and, instead, thoroughly prepared himself to be reprimanded by his father once Dabria revealed Vincenzo's plan to him.

However, in the time that passed from their conversation until the evening of the banquet, she unexpectedly remained tight-lipped regarding his plan.

And, until then, Vincenzo did his best to avoid her. While his household labored over the party's preparations, he preferred to distance himself from the castle.

The village still dealt with the storm damages from the night Dabria appeared on their doorstep. Vincenzo preferred the manual labor of putting up livestock enclosures and repairing the roads over Dabria's company at any given moment.

And so, too soon, the night of the banquet rolled in. Lords and Ladies from all parts of their province had arrived by carriage to take part in the grand event.

Dabria emerged from her chamber, fashionably attired in a red velvet and gold-trimmed gown, her bosom nearly defiling all modesty in her tight-laced-up corset.

"Vincenzo," she stepped up to him while he stood at the entrance to the great hall, half-hidden behind a heavy curtain that obscured the path to the kitchen area and the respected visitors who took their place at the dinner table.

"Lady Dabria." Vincenzo nearly jumped out of his skin. He didn't notice her appear beside him and kept his hand from accidentally striking her.

"I presume you had time to reconsider this evening's announcement?" Dabria asked, her voice restrained, while she took his arm.

"Reconsider?" Vincenzo glanced at her. "I am sorry, my Lady, but my heart remains true to my beloved, and my decision will not be swayed to your liking. I shall announce my engagement tonight. I suggest you enjoy the festivities and perhaps attempt to give your heart to another suitable suitor." He politely extracted his arm from her grasp, moved the heavy curtain, and stepped into the great hall.

Dabria stormed away in anger.

The table was set with polished silverware and lavish wine.

Odors of nutmeg, cinnamon, and juniper enhanced the rich meats' flavor at the table.

As Vincenzo called it, a lively conversation of fashion, literature, current events, or gossip bubbled in the air accompanied by the wine glasses' clunk. The intoxicating spirits that night ran free.

Vincenzo sat by his father, Lord Monsonego, who was deeply immersed in a profound conversation about the country's military advantage with Dabria's father.

"Mother, where is Amelia?" Vincenzo asked, looking around the table.

"I have sent her to see what is keeping Lady Dabria." His mother replied.

A sinister feeling arose in Vincenzo's heart.

He took a deep breath. It was now or never.

"Mother, father," he called for their attention, "I have something that I wish to tell you."

"Lady Dabria?" Amelia knocked on the door to her chamber. "My Lady?" The door creaked open as she leaned against it. Careful, Amelia stepped into the dark chamber.

The room was in shambles. Lavish gowns were scattered on the floor in piles of torn fabric. The bed had been stripped of its covers, and one of the wood bedposts was snapped in half.

A large trunk lay overturned by the window. Candles, herbs, and an assortment of bottles, blades, crystals, and books spilled out on the strangely damp floor.

Lady Dabria sat in the middle of a drawn-up circle she had etched into the floor with what appeared to be her blood. Strange runes were marked along the brims of the circle, and Lady Dabria was hunched over, chanting, while a large, ancient book lay open in her lap.

Amelia yelped in fear. Dabria's head snapped up. Her eyes glowed with madness. Red fire flashed in her previously blue irises.

"What… what are you doing?" Amelia asked in horror, stepping back.

"You shouldn't be here." Dabria rasped. She got up from the floor, the book tightly held in her arms, and stepped out of the circle.

Strange wind began to blow in the room, although the windows were tightly shut. Red eyes gleamed in the shadows, and the darkness gathered into beastly forms that reached for Amelia with sharp, curved claws. Amelia screamed, turned away, and ran.

Her terrified scream echoed through the hallway.

"What was that?" Vincenzo rose sharply from his seat.

At once, the conversation at the table had ceased.

Amelia screamed again.

"Amelia!" Vincenzo pushed his chair out of the way and ran to the staircase. His sister stood at the top of the stairs with a menacing shadow looming behind her.

"What the…?" He staggered when Dabria stepped into the light.

"No! Stop!" Vincenzo sprinted to the bottom of the staircase. Dark force exploded from Dabria's screams, knocking Amelia off her feet, and she tumbled down the stairs. Dead.

"Amelia!" Vincenzo held her tight. His little sister lay still, her eyes staring on, open in horror.

Vincenzo wanted to weep, cry, and shout. For a moment, he wondered why no one was doing the same, and then he realized. An eerie silence spread in the banquet hall.

Vincenzo lifted his head, a horrifying sight revealing to him. All the guests, his parents, even the one he thought to be Dabria's father, still sat at the table, but their faces were slumped against their plates or tilted back in an unnatural form. Froth came from their mouths, and their eyes were hollow and open.

Poisoned.

Vincenzo looked at the table; the wine goblets spilled and seething on the cloth. She poisoned the wine.

He hadn't drunk the wine yet.

"What have you done?" Vincenzo choked out.

"I told you," Dabria slowly descended the bloody stairs. "I do wish you would reconsider my proposition."

"You are out of your mind." Vincenzo spat.

He carefully laid down Amelia's body on the floor and got up to face Dabria.

"I'd rather die." He said.

Dabria smirked. "Again? That can be arranged." She said,

"Again?" Vincenzo stammered.

Dabria raised her right arm, and blinding light engulfed the castle. The thunder roared above their heads.

Red mist descended upon the banquet hall. It crept on the floor, came down from the ceiling, slid along the table, and the bodies scattered around it and engulfed them until they were gone.

A moment later, Vincenzo heard the unmistakable hiss of snakes. The mist rolled away, revealing the monsters in all their glory to him.

Giant reptiles took the place of the nobles' corpses. Beasts resembling humanoid crocodiles, vermin, and serpents emerged instead of those Vincenzo once knew.

Vincenzo yelled and stepped back. All at once, the venomous beasts turned on him.

They were on him before he took another step. They pinned him down under their claws, burrowed their fangs and talons into his skin, piercing his flesh, directly injecting their venom into his bloodstream.

"Your death will be slow and your suffering prolonged unless you accept my offer to join me," Dabria warned him. "Be mine, Lord Monsonego."

Vincenzo shivered, revolted, at being given his late father's title; something about this situation sparked a familiar feeling inside him. He experienced this horrible situation once before.

The numbness slowly spread inside his body, the poison taking its hold.

"Never." Vincenzo breathed.

"I know what will change your mind," Dabria said.

She smiled, turned in her place, and disappeared in a bright orange flame.

A terrified scream came from the garden immediately after.

"Carina!" Vincenzo's eyes widened; his love, his light, he knew she was coming.

He didn't have the chance to warn her to stay away.

Vincenzo stumbled, broke through the beasts that clawed at him, and ran outside.

"Carina!" He yelled.

His beloved, the red-haired maiden, ran, her blue dress billowing behind her. She screamed while one of the stone horses once stationed at the castle entrance galloped after her, animated by Dabria's dark spell.

"Carina!"

The sound of her fall was unmistakable, another blood-curdling scream, then nothing. The rain began pouring down, and Vincenzo's body failed him.

"Now you have no one," Dabria said. Vincenzo fell on his knees beside his slain beloved. He took her into his arms, his hot, salty tears mixed with the rain. Her bright red blood stained the middle of his shirt, pooling in deep swirls in the shape of a rose.

"You will pay for this," Vincenzo uttered, his blood seeping out of his mouth. He was dying.

Dabria laughed maniacally at his threat.

"I will avenge her! Do you hear me, monster? Vincenzo yelled.

Dabria shook her head, dismissing his empty threat.

"Last chance," Dabria warned him. "Be mine, and I will save you from the venom now coursing through your body; it will soon claim this life."

Vincenzo groaned loudly. He gently put Carina down and got up. He coughed and staggered forward. "I refuse to yield to your wishes; I am no more eager to be with you than to gauge my eyes out so I won't have to see you any longer. I'd rather succumb to this poison and meet the woman I love in the afterlife than spend another moment in this life with you."

Dabria sighed. "So be it, then. I will just have to try again. But, for now, you will know only suffering for defying me, Úlftýr."

Her red flames engulfed her, and she was gone again.

Vincenzo dismissed her rambling. Weakened and hurting, he grabbed a sword from his training rack and ran after her.

"Until my dying breath," He promised, "I shall fight you, demon, your poison may claim my body, but you will not have my soul."

He burst into the banquet hall, and the humanoid reptiles awaited him.

Dabria watched from the top of the stairs.

Vincenzo lifted his sword and charged at them. He managed to lobe off the head of a sizeable snakelike monster with the head of a cobra and the back feet of a lioness.

Vincenzo attempted to follow Dabria but was repelled by her fire. He dodged the immense blaze, and instead, it scorched the wall where a moment before he stood. Another flame leaked the sealing, and a fireball exploded a hair's breadth away from his face.

Dabria raised her arms and began to chant in an ancient tongue; the air shimmered and crackled above her, and in her outstretched arms glowed the blade of a large sword.

Vincenzo fell to his knees, the venom reaching his heart; his chest tightened, and his pulse slowed.

He glared paralyzed at Dabria, who descended towards him, the sword in her hand.

*"The death moment of two hundred and nineteen souls…" he whispered. He breathed hard. He couldn't understand how he knew this. Or what **this** was.*

He yelled in agony when the blade went into his gut. His cries of pain were replaced by erratic breathing and gurgling heaves.

"Eventually," Dabria said, "you will understand that you don't have a choice but to surrender to me." She took his face in her hands. "Even if I must haunt you for a thousand lifetimes. All you need to do is to wake up and yield to me."

She kissed him maliciously, cutting his lip with her teeth, forcing her tongue to explore his mouth.

Vincenzo let out a painted groan, unable to stop her.

With the sword still embedded deep in his stomach, two reptiles grabbed hold of Vincenzo and lifted him.

They carried him out into the garden and down to his family's crypt behind it.

The sound of two heavy stone slabs grinding against each other echoed in the damp chamber.

The reptiles moved the lid out of its place and threw him into the tomb. All air was knocked out of Vincenzo's chest, his body hitting the bottom of the tomb with a thud, crashing against the bones of his ancestors.

"Goodbye, for now, sweet Prince. I do hope you will have pleasant dreams."
Dabria mused.

Vincenzo tried to move, but it was hopeless.

By her order, the stone slab of the tomb was moved back into place, and the mausoleum was sealed shut, condemning Vincenzo to darkness.

He lay surrounded by death and decay, trapped in a fetal position while the voices from inside the blade that was driven through him howled in his head. Their agony was his own; their voices brought upon him relentless torment.

Vincenzo yelled, screamed, and shouted until his throat was hoarse, and he lost the ability to breathe.

He let out another loud, painted grunt, gripping the sword's blade with his trembling hands.

Hot blood coated his fingers. Vincenzo gasped while he twisted the blade, wishing this horrible existence would end.

His eyes opened wide, and, in the suffocating darkness, the blazing green light came from his widened orbs. At that moment, he remembered — he was Úlftýr again.

Úlftýr's spirit soared above the crypt, and he remained chained to existence, a shadow upon the earth as the years passed.

Vincenzo's castle sat abandoned, the tales of the banquet massacre spreading far across the land. People whispered that he was to blame, that he murdered everyone because his body was the only one that had not been found, and so his name was remembered in infamy. The castle was slowly overgrown by large trees and crumbled, and the monarchy's seat of power was reduced to dust.

He witnessed the spirit of his love, Carina, the reincarnated Elska, reborn across the centuries.

She reincarnated and died repeatedly, and he could not prevent her suffering. He tried to save her, but every time he came close, the vengeful spirits of his past had gotten to her first.

He watched in wretched helplessness as a wild horse struck her dead in a desert town. He watched, unable to look away, while a man she rejected followed her through white stone streets. Her blood stained the steps in red when he pushed her down to her death after she refused him again, and Úlftýr was granted a moment with her bright spirit. She recognized and reached for him for a fleeting moment before disappearing to his tormented cry.

He begged the gods to allow him to pass from the world, for his soul crumbled with every death he witnessed.

The deaths only became more brutal with cruelty as the centuries rolled by. In a particularly terrible vision, a group of young men dragged her, kicking and screaming, into his ruined castle after they caught her reading within its grounds.

They left her broken and violated to die alone under a large tree, and in his miserable existence, he was denied the ability to even so much as comfort her when she took her dying breath. Úlftýr wanted to remember her the way she was for him, his Elska. His red-haired maiden, beautiful and peaceful, sitting and reading in their great library.

As a spirit, he followed her once as a court maiden. She sat and read, perched atop a wooden spiral staircase, and through her window, the gold castle lit the night sky.

That was the only time their spirits connected. Úlftýr took her hand when she died in that lifetime and danced with her by a lake alive with black swans.

Mostly, though, Úlftýr was her dark shadow. He followed her, and his presence built walls around her heart.

She sensed his spirit beside her, and she craved to find him.

Not knowing what banished the love from her heart, Elska's fear summoned her demons out of the abyss his spirit created within her.

Her panicked tears stained his heart. He watched her curled up in the corner of a red room with bars on the windows and a metal bed.

Úlftýr knew she feared death but was also curious about what waited for her on the other side.

She tried to hide her light, but he easily found her even when her hair was darker than night, and she hid her glow beneath heaps of black paint around her eyes.

'No more...' his spirit whispered. *'No more can I watch you die.'*

"No more." The reincarnated Elska whispered. She stepped into the road.

"No!" Úlftýr grabbed her and yanked her back just as the metal carriage roared past her.

Elska breathed hard. She turned, and her mouth made the sweetest sound he dared hope for.

"Úlftýr?"

With a pained cry, the tormented King woke up.

CHAPTER 21

THE BATTLE CRY!

***Midgardr*, Capital Region, Islandia 1638 B.C.**

lftýr woke covered in fresh snow. The cold, frozen water sizzled against his hot skin. Steam rising from his body, he jumped and lashed at the rocks and trees surrounding him.

He kicked and punched and clawed at everything he laid his hands on, leaving carnage in his wake. But his real enemy was long gone.

Úlftýr fell on all fours against the cold ground, panting. His hands were smeared with blue blood, but the wounds he inflicted upon himself in his rampage were already healed.

'*Vincenzo... I remember you.*' The abominable visions he had just experienced flooded his mind. '*Had that man ever existed? Is he going to?*' Úlftýr asked himself.

He wasn't sure, but now Úlftýr was himself again, craving to remember his real álfur life.

An irrational fear gripped him. Úlftýr couldn't understand why he felt the memory could hurt him so much.

"What is happening to me?" He whispered aloud.

'Midgardr.' He thought. *'My Midgardr.'* In his common tongue, it meant *'Smoke deviation.'*

It was named so by virtue of his land's magnificent hot mineral springs, which were said to hold miraculous healing properties.

Unfortunately, even this natural wonder had contributed nothing to his father's health.

'Father...' Úlftýr *thought. 'I wonder where you and mother are now....'*

A vision of ice flashed before his eyes. Úlftýr pressed his palm to his forehead in a losing battle against another wave of splitting headaches.

"I have to get out of here," Úlftýr said. *'But where can I go?'* he thought.

He vaguely remembered this time in the past as one of the festivities. The winter solstice was nearly upon them, and the Jol month ushered in the longer days. His people should be celebrating.

Úlftýr got up slowly with visible difficulty. His ears twitched, voices came from the direction of the beach, further down the valley. He sniffed the air. There was an unmistakable odor of fire. Úlftýr was drawn in by the dry-scented warmth, and their inviting heat prompted him to venture into the woods.

He walked solely on instinct; odors of roasted meat and the warm blood of his people ushered him on.

He emerged from the shrubbery, struck by confusion. His people and the fires were there, and the moon shone on shimmering silk and embroidered gold garments. But the silence, the suffocating, tense silence that lingered among them, could drive anyone mad.

It was a time of celebration, but no one sang, danced, or praised the moon, stars, and the Earth for another well-lived year.

The faces of everyone told of a horrible truth. They were all in mourning.

Sunken eyes and crestfallen expressions, pursed lips, and tear-stricken faces appearing more prominent were illuminated by the light of the flames.

"King Úlftýr?"

Úlftýr hissed and whipped around. A young álfur, not older than Vanir, stood behind him with gathered logs in his arms. He blinked, confused, but Úlftýr was already gone.

"A mirage…" The young álfur mumbled to himself. He soon disappeared into the crowd.

Blood.

Úlftýr shook his head. *That* he did not want to remember. His hands were still stained by the remnants of the innocents he killed.

He gasped at the sight of two emerald eyes flashing in the darkness.

The demon, his tormentor, was here.

Blinded by rage, Úlftýr followed Deirdra's image straight into the middle of the mournful gathering.

Intoxicated by the prospect of laying his hands around her neck and squeezing the breath out of her, Úlftýr failed to notice the flames until he was nearly upon them. The heat that wouldn't bother him in his normal state scorched his skin.

Úlftýr yelped and turned to the flames. He couldn't cover his eyes fast enough, and the light from the bonfire blinded him, and his sensitive eyes burned.

Surprised murmurs rose around him. His fangs cut through his gums; his claws curled out. If he did not restrain himself, he knew he was about to hurt someone again.

A startled shout from a nearby álfur sent him bolting for the dark cover the trees provided.

In the darkness, he fell to his knees. His mind tightened around the dark beast that craved to burst from inside him, the beast that craved to devour more blood.

Úlftýr put his head into the snow. *There has got to be a way to rid me of this pain!'*

In desperation, he didn't notice Deirdra appearing in front of him in a swirl of orange flames.

"Hello, Úlftýr." She said when she was too close.

Úlftýr whipped his head up and attempted to launch at her, but the rune in his brow pulled him down, his head weighing like a boulder.

"Release me, you foul creature," Úlftýr growled, which only elicited mocking laughter from Deirdra's throat.

She approached him and slowly circled him. Then, crouched behind him, she placed a scorching hand on his steaming skin.

Úlftýr screamed.

Deirdra removed her hand, and the burn mark healed instantly. "Why, Úlftýr? I do marvel at your new abilities." she stroked his back in a manner meant to arouse him. The scorch marks appeared and healed, drawing further shouts of anguish from Úlftýr.

"I can take your pain away so easily," she whispered in his ear. "All you have to do is let me complete the ritual your sister so rudely interrupted."

"What ritual? What have you done to me?" Úlftýr hit the ground with his fist, unable to lift his head. "I will not succumb to you, beast."

"Oh, Úlftýr," Deirdra stood before him and waved her hand. Some of the invisible weight lifted from him, and Úlftýr managed to look up at her.

"How low you must think of me," Deirdra said in false sadness. "I will not leave you vulnerable. I will allow you to retain and enhance your new powers, for I know their origin. Don't you crave to know?" Her eyes flashed. "What do you say, Úlftýr?"

"I'd rather die."

Deirdra blinked. "You really should thank me, you know."

"Thank you!?" Úlftýr yelled, and, for a fraction of a second, he managed to sever Deirdra's bonds on him and launch at her. He got a little too close for comfort before Deirdra's enchanted restraints back on him, and he fell to the ground, froth and blood staining his lips.

"You stripped away what I am!" Úlftýr shouted, unable to get up.

"I made you better," Deirdra dismissed his outburst.

"You made me a monster," Úlftýr spat.

"That is remarkably hurtful, Úlftýr." Deirdra sighed. "Now, listen to me, dear brother. Give yourself to me, and I will grant you your freedom." She said,

Úlftýr's skin crawled with disgust." You are entirely deranged."

"Well, I was going to offer to let you keep your redhead pet, too, but I see there is no reasoning with you." Deirdra shrugged and moved closer. "I hoped we would do it the easy way, but the hard way works just fine for me."

The weight of her spell returned in full, crushing his essence under it. Úlftýr yelled.

Deirdra laughed, turned around, and dissipated in a swirl of bright orange flames. She released Úlftýr from her deviant magic, but he had no strength to get up. He lay in the snow for what seemed like a long while, but no more than an hour passed in reality.

When he came to, an all too familiar smell hit Úlftýr's nostrils. He lifted himself and, dazed, followed the scent. It led him back to their lake, back to the crystallized waterfall.

The snow fell around him, and the waterfall under the hill gushed with specks of crystal. Through the mist that rose from the ground, Úlftýr watched as two white horses trotted gracefully across the water of the un- usually shallow lake. Mesmerized by them, he didn't see her right away, but she was there, and Úlftýr knew she was the only one he wanted to be there.

The horses stopped, observed him, and then continued on. And Úlftýr followed Elska closely. He knew she was aware of his presence, for she strolled to allow him to catch up to her easily. When the lake appeared before them, Elska stopped, and Úlftýr stepped up to the water's edge and looked down.

He gasped. "Is that...me?" He whispered.

"I don't want to believe it; what evil sorcery changed me so?"

His eyes were deep red, and his hair had turned white. His grey skin stretched over his bones, almost transparent. Úlftýr traced the blue rose-like stain in the middle of his chest with his fingers.

"Úlftýr." A forceful voice, strange and unfamiliar, startled him. "Úlftýr, *I can help you. Grant me control.*" Úlftýr's mouth opened. He glanced at Elska, and she didn't react.

"Who... who are you?" Úlftýr whispered.

"*Grant me control,* Úlftýr; *let me guide you.*" The voice demanded. "*Release me, and I will smite our enemies!*"

"I..." Úlftýr began.

"Úlftýr?"

Elska's voice broke through the darkness that enveloped him.

"*Ignore her!*" The voice commanded him.

"No, leave me be!" Úlftýr shook his head. The dark voice grumbled angrily and disappeared.

A tremor shook the earth.

"Úlftýr?" Elska stepped closer to him.

Úlftýr recoiled when she put her hand to the stain on his chest.

"Are you real?" Úlftýr whispered. He observed her delicate touch.

"Real?" Elska frowned. "Úlftýr, do you know where you are?"

"I know where I hope to be," Úlftýr said. "I know where I want to be, but I fear I might be dead." He gulped. "I fear you might be too."

Elska took a deep breath. "Úlftýr, I don't quite understand what is going on, but allow me to try and help you see the truth." She took his hand and guided it to her chest.

"Can you feel it?" Elska held his hand against her chest, and she placed her other hand on his cheek.

Úlftýr closed his eyes and leaned into her touch. The steady beat of her heart pulsated against his hand, and his own heartbeat a little faster to her touch.

She stepped closer, and he traced his fingers against her lips.

A bittersweet smile appeared on her face, and then she embraced him, settling against his hot chest.

For a moment, the weight of uncertainty lifted from both of them. Elska suddenly tensed up in his arms. "Elska? Did I do something wrong?" Úlftýr let go of her and looked down at her face, but Elska wasn't looking at him. Instead, she narrowed her eyes.

"Stay where you are!" She demanded the guards that entered the clearing, her features harsh.

Úlftýr began to turn to where her gaze was pointed. Elska took his hand and guided him to stand behind her.

Elska stepped forward.

The rune in Úlftýr's brow ignited. Fangs cut through his gums, and his claws began to curl out.

Two guards of the royal guard stood at the edge of the clearing, their expressions visibly frightened and their long bows drawn.

"Don't you dare come any closer. If you take another step, it might be your last," Elska warned them.

"My lady," Úlftýr recognized the warrior; his name was Garuk, and his weapon was still drawn. "Queen Ingrid - "

"Queen Ingrid shouldn't have sent you. I told her I could handle the situation." Elska fumed. "Away with you! You are putting yourselves in danger by being here. You can tell Queen Ingrid I shall have some choice words for her when I return."

"But…" They lowered their weapons, "My lady…." Garuk tried again. "Look at him… King Úlftýr is not himself. Our lady, Queen Ingrid, ordered us to protect you."

"I told Ingrid, and I am telling you," Elska interrupted him. "Úlftýr will not hurt me; now leave!" She stood in front of Úlftýr; her smaller frame shielded him from the frightened, armed guards.

Úlftýr slowly let himself slide down to the ground behind her. He did not look at the guards but knew what they were thinking.

"My lady," they murmured before they bowed and disappeared into the shrubbery.

"Undoubtedly, they prepare themselves to return later for your lifeless body," Úlftýr said, the rune in his brow extinguished.

"Is that what they are going to find?" Elska glanced back at him.

Úlftýr shuddered. "Better me than you."

"You are not going to hurt anyone else today," Elska said.

Úlftýr frowned. "I wasn't planning on it even without you commanding me not to."

Elska raised her eyebrow. "Did I attach some demeaning word to the end of my statement to make you think I am commanding you to act a certain way?"

"You didn't have to for it to sound like it," Úlftýr said, and Elska rolled her eyes but didn't indulge him in continuing such a pointless discussion.

Elska waited until she was sure the guards were gone, then she turned and sat down next to Úlftýr.

"I can still smell them," Úlftýr said. "They are keeping close."

Elska blinked at his new heightened sense but decided not to comment. "Ignore them." Elska moved in closer. "Focus only on me."

They remained silent while Elska completed a thin braid in Úlftýr's hair. When she was done, Elska laid the plait against Úlftýr's shoulder.

Úlftýr looked at it and then turned his caliginous crimson eyes to her.

He gradually became aware of a strange scent that didn't come from animal blood remaining in the guards' weapons.

He took it, and it smelled honey-like with a hint of sulfur. It had to be Elska's blood. The sweet nectar enticed him.

Úlftýr's eyes flashed. "You…" he rasped. "I smell your blood?"

Elska blinked. "You smell…? Yeah, I cut my hand on the window you jumped out of." Elska said, raising her palm to show him.

Úlftýr's mouth watered. He breathed hard and shuffled away from her. "You need to get out of here. Now!" He demanded.

"What? Why?"

Úlftýr looked distraught. "I... I need... I want...I am ashamed."

Understanding dawned in Elska's eyes. "You need to feed." Elska forced herself to lean closer to him. "Úlftýr," She took in a shuddering breath. She didn't want to admit that she feared him, but a pit of anxiety opened within her. "It's better you take what you need from me than an innocent that will be caught in your path." She offered him her hand.

"I... What if I lose control?" Úlftýr asked, though his eyes glazed over with lustful hunger.

"You won't," Elska whispered, reassuring herself.

"I... Can I...?"

Elska nodded and extended her hand to him once more.

The call of savagery awakened within Úlftýr, and fierce darkness took him over, manifesting in his blazing red eyes. Without another word, Úlftýr snaked one arm around her waist and, with the other, lifted her hand to his mouth.

Elska closed her eyes, and he plunged his fangs into her arm. She whimpered while he took in her sweet nectar.

Úlftýr tensed up at the sound she made, but Elska nodded, biting her lip, encouraging him to go on.

She breathed deeply, a blush coloring her cheeks. Elska's eyes fluttered open, a sudden wave of sexual rapture stirring within. Her lips parted. A strange sense of excitement rose within her. She had to admit she was aroused by the danger she put herself in, so fragile in Úlftýr's powerful arms.

The fever struck him. Úlftýr's conscious mind battled against the blissful beast that had taken residence within his body.

Elska's body began to go limp in his arms. She was losing consciousness.

He had to stop. Úlftýr tore away from her hand with difficulty. Her chest went up and down while she struggled to catch her breath. Slowly, a lively tint returned to her skin.

"I... Are you all right? " He asked in a low tone, still holding onto her.

He looked at Elska, who opened her eyes and focused her gaze on him; her face flushed, and her eyes sparkled. She reached for him.

Úlftýr froze when she pulled herself up against him and kissed him. His heart thundered in his ears. He slid lower on the ground, and she settled against him.

Úlftýr kept his hands gently wrapped around her. She aligned her body with his, reached her hands into his hair, and gently pulled him towards her. Heat sizzled between them when their lips met.

Elska shuddered, and Úlftýr detached from her lips. He looked at her and then got up.

She seemed puzzled.

She yelped when he effortlessly picked her up and carried her behind the waterfall.

No one knew of the sheltered stone alcove inside the rock face of the hill, which was lined with furs Úlftýr had set up for them long ago. The scent inside was fresh and alluring, and the clear water beat against the rock outside.

Úlftýr laid Elska down on the furs and sat, guiding her legs to straddle his hips.

He listened to the sound of her heart quicken, perhaps with fear, perhaps excitement, and a slightly sweet smell like freshly harvested honey called him forth in between her legs. He reached down and slowly undid the lacing of her dress, revealing her breasts. She lifted herself and kissed down the crevice of his body, her lips traveling down from neck to navel.

His smell—citrus and dark chocolate — hardly changed with his transformation.

The rest of both of their garments were quickly discarded along with their inhibition. Úlftýr shuddered as he entered the hot, wet heaven between her legs while her hands slid down to the small of his back.

Úlftýr kissed her lips, and then he kissed down her neck.

She threw her head back when he sucked on her breasts, one then the other. He cupped the smooth orbs, his claws digging into her flesh. Elska took a sharp breath while their movements started slow but soon picked up the pace, and with every thrust, Úlftýr went deeper, his breath erratic, the crimson in his eyes darkening while he slowly lost himself to pleasure.

Captivated at the moment, he felt her reach euphoria, and Úlftýr couldn't hold himself any longer when she tightened around him. He growled and sunk his teeth into Elska's neck, right above her clavicle. He bit down, breaking the skin, and Elska screamed, and her reaction only made him more savage.

His fangs piercing her neck were anything but elegant. Not the fabled "chiropteran kiss" but something carnal and coarse. Her blue boiling life source sprayed his face as he tore into her, covering it all but his wide open, raging eyes.

He growled low and pressed her harder against him. He drank his fill, and Elska moaned in rapture and pain while he rode on his climax and reached nirvana.

This time, when she went limp in his arms, he did not detach from her. As he watched her fluttering eyelids drop and he faded from her vision, Úlftýr held her tight while she succumbed to the dark in his claws.

CHAPTER 22

THE ROAD BACK
HOME

They stayed at the lake, Úlftýr's body an inferno against her cold skin. He fell asleep wrapped in her embrace.

At dawn, Elska woke up to the sound of Úlftýr's voice.

"No… Ugh!"

She opened her eyes and found she lay alone on the furs. She pulled herself up, dizzy at first, as she tried to stand up. '*Úlftýr must have drunk more than I realized.*' she thought, holding her hand to her head and waiting for the world to stop spinning. She eventually swallowed enough air to make a second attempt at getting up. This time, she dusted off her dress and made her way out of the cave. She looked around, and there was Úlftýr, just a few feet away.

He cowered under a nearby tree, his back firmly pressed against the large trunk.

"Úlftýr, what is it?" She stepped closer to him. His eyes were closed, and she just caught a glimpse of a superficial burn mark vanishing from his cheek.

Úlftýr opened his bright red eyes and looked at her. "The sun," he said. "It burns me."

Elska frowned. "It's your skin; it's different. Deirdra did something to alter you." She took a breath, anger, and sadness bubbling within her. "Come home with me. We need to find a way to change you back." Elska extended her hand to him. "We can use the trees for cover and get inside through the merchant entrance of the castle."

Úlftýr looked at her outstretched hand. For a moment, Elska feared that he would bolt again.

"I can't go back there," Úlftýr whispered, his eyes wide.

Elska bit her lower lip. "What happened wasn't your fault. Deirdra was the one that made you ki...."

"Don't!" Úlftýr yelled and shuffled back, his back crashing against the tree trunk.

His scream startled Elska. She stepped back.

"I..." Úlftýr's breathing quickened. "I don't... I can't remember... I don't want to remember..." tears stood in his eyes. "It wasn't me." Úlftýr put his face to his knees, his hands tight against the back of his head. "It wasn't me... I couldn't stop..." he heaved and wept.

Elska's hands balled into fists; a lump grew in her throat. She had to regain her composure. She couldn't fall apart; she had to remain strong for him.

"No." Elska walked up to him and got down on her knees. She put her arms around his shuddering form. "No, it wasn't you. You don't deserve this. Come home with me, don't let Deirdra drive you out of your life."

Úlftýr slowly raised his head and looked at her.

"Please, don't leave me again," Elska whispered, kissing him.

His salty tears stained her lips.

"Please." Elska got up and extended her hand to him once more. "Come home."

Úlftýr sighed. He fell deeper into oblivion in his mind, but in real life, he took her hand and pulled himself up.

"All right." He finally said, letting her lead him out of the clearing.

They climbed up the narrow dirt road and through low, thick shrubbery that hung on the ancient stones that made the tunneled path. The path let out close to the food cellar on the castle grounds.

Elska knew their way would be empty. The night before, their people had spent time at the beach, and most would be sleeping it off this early in the morning of a new day.

Two guards were stationed at the back entrance. Elska and Úlftýr emerged out of the shrubbery. The guards drew their swords at the sight of them.

Úlftýr growled. The rune in his brow ignited, and his eyes flashed red.

"It's us," she said to the guards, holding Úlftýr's hand tighter to restrain him.

The guards shifted their gaze from her to Úlftýr.

It took them another moment until they sheathed their blades and bowed to her. Elska let out a little sigh.

Despite keeping their appearances, the guards were visibly shaken at the sight of Úlftýr.

Elska understood their reaction. They barely had time to deal with the attack on their castle, and now they had to face the darkness that seeped from the eyes of their dethroned King.

The rumors of Úlftýr's unimaginable horrific deeds swept over the castle, and seeing him the way he was only enhanced their fear.

"Let the Queen know we are back," Elska said.

"Yes, my Lady." The guards bowed their heads in unison, their eyes fixed on Úlftýr.

"I shall accompany you, my Lady." One of the guards said, "At her majesty's request."

"They are not the enemy," Elska reminded Úlftýr.

Úlftýr blinked, the rune in his forehead extinguished. "But in their eyes, I am." He continued to walk in uncertainty, echoes of spilled blood calling to him from within the castle walls.

Úlftýr wrapped his arms around himself.

Elska placed a guiding hand at the small of his back.

A maiden briskly walked towards them, her eyes meeting with Úlftýr's. She whimpered and pushed her back against the wall at the sight of him.

Elska pressed her hand firmly against Úlftýr's back and led him on.

They rounded the corner, and Úlftýr noticed that the guards outside the throne room had ceased their activities immediately when they walked by.

A low murmur passed between them while Elska encouraged Úlftýr to keep walking.

"Don't stop," she said, and he knew better than to deny her.

Úlftýr and Elska quietly climbed the stairs that led to the west wing.

They were both aware of the guards that followed them, joining the one that accompanied them inside.

Úlftýr glanced back at their entourage.

Elska did her best to ignore them.

Blue streaks of blood were visible on the floor. Úlftýr's stomach did a somersault. "Does the blood trail lead to our bedroom?" Úlftýr asked aloud.

Elska did not respond, but the tight grip on his hand was his answer.

They emerged at the end of a long hallway. Elska guided Úlftýr into their bedroom.

The guards stopped outside their door. "Queen Ingrid requested an audience with you if you returned, my Lady." One of the guards said. "We have orders to guard and prevent her brother from leaving again."

Elska frowned. "You will do so at your own peril. I will talk to the Queen, but hear me when I tell you — if your former King wants to leave, let him and do not stand in his way. I beg you not to appear under my care in the infirmary or on the stone slab in the courtyard."

She entered after Úlftýr and closed the door. Elska knew the message would be passed on.

Besides being an Elder's daughter, she built herself a reputation as a skilled and respected healer and a royal family member, even before she had the merit to claim her place in court.

"What happened here?" Úlftýr asked when he sat on the bed.

"You don't remember?" Elska asked as he lay down.

"I don't remember much from last night," Úlftýr confessed. "Just broken flashes of blood and hunger."

"It is for the best." Elska took his hand. "We can talk about what happened after you rest." She looked at him.

"If you need to wake me up," Úlftýr murmured, "Do it from far away and, preferably, from the direction of my head." He warned her, "I might lash out violently when I wake up. It's Deirdra; she inflicted horrible visions upon me."

Elska nodded.

"Don't give up on me." Úlftýr closed his eyes.

"I never would." Elska remained seated on the bed by his side. She looked him over after he fell asleep.

The blue rose-shaped stain was still prominent on his skin, but the marks the mortals inflicted with their swords were nearly gone. Even the unnatural wound in his side closed and was now no more than a prominent, white scar against his grey skin.

She inhaled and made her way to the washroom. She stood in front of the silver mirror and slowly undid her corset; then, she pulled down the top part of her dress. She moved her hair back and inspected her neck.

Úlftýr's teeth left blue punctures and blue grazing marks on her skin. Elska took a washcloth, dipped it in the stone water basin, and wiped the remnants of the blood away from her neck. Next, she inspected her body. She was glad no one could see the aftermath of her night with Úlftýr, for no matter how much she enjoyed it, only now did she begin to understand exactly how dangerous her endeavor was.

Amidst the pleasure of their passion for each other, she ignored his rough touch, his sharp claws, and the power he now possessed that could easily end her life.

Elska took in a shuddered breath. She let the cold water of the washcloth soothe her skin, and then she put her garments back on, wincing at the sudden tightness of the corset on her raw skin.

Outside their window, the sun had shown to chase away the horrors of the night when Elska quietly left the room.

The guards kept vigil by the door, and Elska warned them again not to stand in Úlftýr's path if he tried to leave. She hoped her warning carried enough strength to sink in.

Elska made her way out of the west wing. The door to the throne room was opened for her and shut immediately by the guard stationed outside after she entered.

Elska looked around the room.

The blood had primarily been scrubbed off the floor, the bodies of the dead taken away, and a cloth in a deep blue shade covered the antlers Baldur was impaled on the night before, obscuring from sight the blood that remained on the wall.

Ingrid sat on the throne and leaned to the side.

Her father, Siran, stood next to her. He had set Ingrid's right arm in a sling against her chest. A linen bandage Elska knew her father infused with a cooling agent was wrapped around her head. Her father now worked on carefully laying a leaf bandage on Ingrid's neck.

"Let me," Elska stepped up to Ingrid.

Siran nodded and handed her the bandage. Ingrid looked up at her with bloodshot eyes. "You didn't get any sleep. I am not surprised." Elska shifted the leaf bandage to a better position. "How do you feel?" she asked quietly while she worked.

"Is Úlftýr back?" Ingrid answered Elska's question with her own, involuntarily shuddering when Elska nodded.

Elska noticed but said nothing. She finished laying the bandage on Ingrid's neck and stepped back.

The door opened again, and Elder Svarta walked in.

Ingrid looked at him. "We can begin," she said. Ingrid attempted to straighten herself on the throne, but the movement significantly hurt her. She winced, and Siran stepped towards her.

Ingrid raised her arm to stop him. "I am alright," Ingrid said and looked at Elska. "The four of us here, apart from my brother, are the only ones who know precisely what happened here last night. Úlftýr's involvement in the deaths had been played down. We will issue an official proclamation regarding Deirdra, her attempt to reclaim Úlftýr, and seize the throne...."

"Why are we protecting him?" Svarta interrupted. "Forgive me, my Queen, but with what you told us last night about your brother's transformation, we cannot allow his deeds to simply pass from memory."

"Deirdra cursed him," Elska said sharply. "Deirdra is responsible for his actions."

"Cursed or not, my Lady," Svarta looked at her with pity. "The former King, Úlftýr, must answer for his crimes. I cast my vote that he stands trial before the council."

"It will not be a fair trial while Úlftýr is not responsible for his actions," Siran said before Elska had a chance to lash out at Svarta.

"So, what do you suggest we do with him?" Svarta questioned.

"We can lock him up," Ingrid suggested.

"Ingrid!" Elska looked at her, disgusted. "Don't you realize that imprisoning him will only make matters worse? He needs our help right now, not condemnation."

"We can't stand by and do nothing while he is free to kill again," Svarta said, ignoring her outburst. "The truth of what happened here will come out...."

"And who will let it out? You?" Elska glared at him. "We can turn him back! I know I can find a way to negate Deirdra's magic."

"Elska, if my father were here, he would tell you that immersing yourself in the dark arts is madness. Madder still than what you did last night," Ingrid said, and Siran raised an eyebrow at that statement.

Elska blushed, looked at her father, and then at Ingrid. "If your father were here, he wouldn't give up on Úlftýr so easily. And what I did last night worked."

'Did my blood turn him?' Elska immediately hated herself for dwelling on such a thought.

Ingrid rested her good hand against her forehead.

Elska looked at her wounds. "You can admit how you really feel, Queen Ingrid. I know fear resides within you. I bet you see Úlftýr's red, wild eyes just like I do, and they are burned into your memory. You can't even bring yourself to go talk to your brother or stay alone here while Úlftýr is free. Your guards have never been so alert, undoubtedly by your order."

Ingrid smirked bitterly. "You're insightful, I'll give you that, but we cannot be sure this outburst of savagery was a singular event," Ingrid said. "Elska, you cannot guarantee Úlftýr will remain in control and won't attack anyone again. You can't even be sure he won't attack you."

"Give me time, Ingrid," Elska said. "You owe him that much; he was injured by enemies we all share. Allow me ample time to try and heal him."

"How much time?" Ingrid asked, her lips a thin line. "Enough time for him to kill again?"

Elska took a sharp breath, and her father stepped forward. "Might I make a suggestion?" Siran asked to calm the spirits, and Ingrid gestured for him to proceed. "While I do not agree with putting your life on the line, Elska," she opened her mouth, but he continued. "I understand your need to protect the one you love, and I admire your determination to do so." He looked at Ingrid. "I propose an agreement. You will grant Elska time to heal Úlftýr. The duration of this period shall be determined later. We will limit the access to the castle, and the gates will be closed save for the required staff and produce delivery. Several guards will be assigned to watch Úlftýr at all times and will be allowed to subdue him if the situation calls for it."

Ingrid looked at Elska. "The moment Úlftýr reverts to the animal he turned into last night, I will have no choice but to restrain him by any means necessary, Elska. Do you understand?"

"Yes." Elska spat.

"Are we in agreement?" Siran asked.

Svarta crossed his arms, not pleased with the outcome of their conversation. "I will agree to your terms, Siran, if the Queen agrees to grant the warriors assigned to guard Úlftýr a kill order."

"What?!" Elska whipped at him. "You…"

"He is right," Ingrid said, and Elska looked at her, her mouth open in shock. "Elska, if Úlftýr attacks anyone of my people, our pact is done. Without a trial to determine his fate, I cannot prevent my soldiers from defending themselves. You must understand that."

Elska let out a low cry but sharply nodded. "So be it." she agreed.

CHAPTER 23

THE REMAINS

When Úlftýr closed his eyes, his dreams claimed him instantly. He dreamt of the warmth of the sun he once loved and feared he might never again feel its tender touch on his skin.

He didn't know that orange flames burst from the smoldering ashes of his fireplace while he slept. The fire crawled onto his skin, licked across the cursed mark etched into his chest, and slithered into his open mouth.

A dark shadow closely followed.

Rays of light played across his vision. In his dream, Úlftýr stared into dancing flames.

Nomadic Gers, dwelling camp. Mongolia.
1692

Úlftýr *opened his eyes inside the dream and stared into the fire. He wanted to scream and call for help, but the dancing flames pulled him in.*

Úlftýr *heaved, his eyes bulging out. He leaned forward, and then the sound of a loud drum pounded.*

Ezelj blinked. He leaned back and looked around. He sat by an open fire that burned in the pit of a large ger. The nomadic structure was easily assembled wherever his people went, providing a sturdy, natural dwelling.

Ezelj's mind cleared of the one called Úlftýr, the apparition vanishing like a bad dream. He found himself sitting in the large ger, listening to the holy man, the renowned Shaman who led his people.

The holy man, a large man with wrinkled dark skin, long black hair, and adorned in furs, told the young warriors of the tribe the story of the two lovers and the jealous witch who would not let them be in their life and the next.

Ezelj's ears pricked up, listening to the Shaman telling the familiar story.

"Over three centuries have passed since the dreaded day." Began the holy man. "In a land ruled by a conflicting monarchy, a sorceress lied her way into the home of whom she knew possessed hidden godly powers."

The shaman blew into the fire. "The young man she desired was unaware of his remarkable abilities." The holy man continued. "The sorceress, called Dabria in that incarnation, tried desperately to claim the soul and body of the godly youth to claim his strength for her own. The young man refused her, for his heart belonged to another." The shaman blew on the coals again. "After being rejected repeatedly by the youth whose name was Vincenzo, the devious sorceress, Dabria, brought to life a stone stallion, found his beloved, his bride-to-be, and ordered the stallion to stomp the life out of her." The holy man sighed.

"As for the young man, the sorceress slew everyone he knew. She then poisoned Vincenzo to persuade him to heed her request to join her in exchange for his life, but the young man refused again. He escaped outside his death-filled manor and found his beloved dead in the garden. He held her in his arms for the last time; her blood stained his clothing in the shape of a rose, and the young man departed this life." The Shaman looked straight at him. Ezelj gulped.

"The young man chose to succumb to the poison before the witch had a chance to claim him." The Shaman concluded. "Love makes one's heart stupid and careless. In the ring, you must consider your honor, purpose, and place in this tribe before the call of your heart." Ezelj sighed. Every year, at this time, when the hard earth thawed, the warriors of his tribe gathered to compete in armed combat to prove themselves worthy of the glory and of going up in rank in the tribe.

Some even reached a position in the personal service of the clan leader.

This year, the title of the champion came with the invitation to court the chief's older daughter, Kara, the red-haired maiden who came of age and was obliged to give the winner a chance to win her heart.

Ezelj knew that any competitor in the tournament would strive to claim her as his prize.

"Ezelj, you're staring." Kara nudged him.

Ezelj blinked; he didn't even realize he was gawking at the young woman sitting beside him by the flames. He caught himself, looked away, and back at the holy Shaman, hoping no one else noticed their exchange.

They were familiar with each other for many moons, exchanging stolen kisses and care-filled embraces hidden by night. Approaching Kara before the combat trials were done was strictly forbidden.

They were permitted to meet at official gatherings when Kara, the leader's daughter, participated in the briefings and schooling of the warriors who came to compete.

"You know there is an earlier version of the myth about Vincenzo," Kara told Ezelj when they left the shaman tent.

"Oh?" Ezelj stole a glance at her while they moved forward.

Kara looked at the sky. "According to the legend, the witch pursued the young warrior through his many incarnations for her to find him at his weakest state and convince him to join her or give her the strength that resided within him."

Ezelj clutched his shirt; the birthmark on his chest burned like it always had when he imagined the young man's encounter with the sorceress.

He never told Kara that he suspected Vincenzo might be him in this life. He never revealed the mark on his chest to anyone but his totem animal. And no one knew his totem animal spoke to him.

Ezelj wanted to learn more about the power he might possess without revealing his suspicions.

If the stories were true, then the sorceress, like himself, had reincarnated into this life. So, he was reluctant to trust anyone.

"In the myth," Kara continued, unaware of Ezelj's inner dialogue and struggle. "A young man named Pyramus was to marry a maiden from a powerful family by an arranged marriage, but fate had other plans. He fell in love with a girl he met by chance. Her name was Thisbe."

Ezelj's ears rang. He had never heard this story before but somehow remembered it.

"The two lovers discovered they lived in joint houses with only a thin wall to separate them from each other." Kara glanced at Ezelj. His eyes were distant, and Kara figured he must have thought of going back to bed.

"Go on." Ezelj prompted when Kara fell silent.

Kara smiled. "Every night, the young couple whispered words of love and devotion to each other through the fissure that formed in the plaster that connected their two houses until finally, they made up their minds to elope."

"I'm guessing that didn't go well," bile rose within Ezelj.

Kara shook her head, a bitter smile on her face. "They were to meet under the white mulberry tree on the tallest hill in the city to celebrate their promise to each other. But they could not hide from the witch woman who pursued them, and that was betrothed to the young man once again. When she learned of the lovers' plan, she turned herself into a lioness and slashed Thisbe across her neck when she arrived first at the tree, eager to meet Pyramus. Pyramus came up the hill, and Thisbe's blood-stained shall greet him, and then he found her body, waiting for him."

"And then, the lioness stepped from behind the tree and turned back into the sorceress," Ezelj said in a trance.

Kara blinked. "Oh, you know the story?"

"No, just a guess." Ezelj caught himself and shrugged.

Kara narrowed her eyes. "Ok… Well, the sorceress offered Pyramus to take his memory of Thisbe and be happy with her in blissful ignorance.

And Pyramus refused.

The sorceress raised the sword she held in her hand, a sword of black steel. The weapon reeked of death, giving out a dark, foul aura. Pyramus knew he wouldn't stand a chance against the lioness when she turned again.

With his heart broken, he also knew he wasn't interested in his life anymore, and he wasn't going to give the witch the satisfaction of control over his fate. He chose then in what manner he would depart from this world. Pyramus stepped up to the witch, pretending to accept her, grabbed the sword from her hand, and fell upon it, dying instantly."

Ezelj's breath caught in his throat, and he stopped, feeling the black steel embedded in his gut.

"Are you all right?" Kara reached her hand to touch him, but he involuntarily recoiled.

"I'm fine; finish the story." He growled.

Kara swallowed. She nodded sharply.

"The pure blood of the young lovers seeped into the ground. The witch had no choice. She dissipated in orange flames, promising to get to him in his next life. The white fruits of the tree forever became dark red, a lasting reminder of Pyramus and Thisbe's eternal bond."

Ezelj heard his blood calling from under the ground. He knew it was true.

"I need to go." He said without looking at Kara, urging his feet to carry him far away.

Ezelj avoided Kara in the weeks that followed.

He told himself that his focus had to be on the competition and the many battles he fought and won in the village arena.

Unknown to his opponents and Kara, Ezelj's totem animal, a black bankhar dog with violet eyes named Tögsgöl, attempted to convince Ezelj to unleash his powers so Ezelj could rule over his tribe.

"Release me from the bond of guardianship." The giant animal urged him when they were alone.

The myth of the totem spirits was vastly known among the warriors. Yet, Ezelj never knew of another like him born with an animated guardian attached to his soul.

Like many things about him, Ezelj kept this a secret. He knew that, on some level, his guardian could imbue him with its strength, but he was reluctant to test out just how powerful both of them could become together. Ezelj was too afraid to succumb to a beastly transformation and lose himself in a power-hungry rage. He felt such a situation had happened before.

In fact, the older Ezelj got, the more powerful his totem grew, and on far too many occasions to count, the large dog attempted to convince Ezelj to let him possess his master. Every year, Ezelj refused, and every year, it became harder to resist, especially when the mark on his chest began growing.

Besides his ability to speak and the long life he possessed compared to other animals of the kind, Ezelj's totem possessed the ability to change form. He transformed from dog to falcon to wolf, but Ezelj knew that most saw Tögsgöl as he wanted to be seen, a loyal mutt with unusual violet eyes who trotted everywhere along with his master.

"I will fight with honor."

Ezelj told him when he finished another successful battle and winced as the blue rose mark on his chest claimed another skin patch.

Ezelj did his best not to gaze at Kara when she announced him victorious, but his guardian was smart enough to catch on to the nuance of his stare.

"Your love for her makes you weak,"

Tögsgöl remarked angrily when they walked back to the warrior's part of the village. "The closer you get, the faster your curse will claim you. Let me rid you of her. I swear it shall be quick."

Ezelj stepped in front of his guardian; he didn't care how this stance looked from the side.

"Hear me, monster, if you have my best interest at heart, I forbid you from hurting anyone without my direct order. When you first spoke to me, you swore not to claim a human life without my direct order. Will you break this oath now?"

Tögsgöl remained silent. Ezelj nodded with satisfaction and resumed his walk by the dog's side.

"Are you ready to admit now that I was Vincenzo?" Ezelj raised an eyebrow.

"I've never denied it. Are you ready to claim my strength now?" Tögsgöl dismissed Ezelj's smirk.

"Better the poisoning claims my body than my soul," Ezelj said. "I will remain me for as long as I have. I assume your honesty means I am coming close to the end of my days." He ignored the annoyed look in Tögsgöl's violet eyes and forged ahead. Ezelj hated to admit it, but his health deteriorated fast.

In the arena, he still held his own.

After, though, when he retired to his chamber in the wooden structure built specifically to house the many warriors who arrived at the tournament, his rest was anything but easy.

Ezelj kept waking up, suffocating. At first, he felt like a drowning man, and then the cold, constricting anguish of poison took over his body.

Ezelj knew death was calling him home.

The deity that took on Tögsgöl form was running out of time.

Soon, the life of his master would end, and he had accomplished nothing. He couldn't hope luck would also be on his side in the next incarnation.

He worked too hard to get Úlftýr's spirit in Ezelj's body to trust him. This incarnation was the first life he found Úlftýr's soul at birth.

Love had no meaning in his eyes. Only power mattered.

Tögsgöl waited until Ezelj fell asleep that night. He then turned into a dark wyrm only seen by those he allowed the true sight of himself. His actual shape in this life was a dark serpent with many tails and wings, a blaze around him. His skin reflected the images of empires that rose and fell and will rise again, only to crumble to nothing.

With this intimidating body, he flew to the ger, where he sensed Kara sleeping. "Kara," Tögsgöl called to her in Ezelj's voice, willing the surrounding mortals to remain dormant.

She appeared in the doorway faster than he expected.

At first, only darkness reflected in her eyes, but then the creature allowed her true sight. Kara stifled a horrified cry because she recognized his unusual eyes.

"Tögsgöl?" She asked uncertainty and stepped back.

Tögsgöl blinked, his violet eyes flashed. Clever girl. "Now you see my real form," he hissed. "I came to warn you, Kara. Keep your distance from my master. The closer you get to Ezelj, the closer he will come to death."

"I will not," Kara said, standing her ground before the menacing creature. "No man or beast may command me to go against my heart."

"The will of your heart will be his downfall!" Tögsgöl was upon her in a heartbeat. His great paw caught her in a tight grip.

A long, sharp talon curled under her chin.

Kara's heart thundered, but her expression remained determined.

Tögsgöl let out an enraged cry. "If only my master allowed me to slay you, mortals, at will!" He shook her in his grip but not vigorously enough to harm her. "Know this to be the truth," he said, lifting Kara to eye level. "If Ezelj fights in the final battle, he will die." Tögsgöl let out and put her down.

Kara looked up at the dark creature. "Then, he won't fight. I will see to that. Take me to him."

Tögsgöl hesitated a moment, not expecting her to take his side. In every incarnation, she got a bit closer, and in every embodiment, his master's death came that much faster when she was around, but he couldn't kill her. The struggling soul of his master never stood her demise.

Until the spirit called Úlftýr surrendered to him, he had to do everything to keep him alive in every life he found him in and gain his trust or be doomed to repeat the cycle until darkness prevailed and all was lost.

"All right." He relented and picked Kara up again, gently this time.

He flew over the settlement with enormous wings that shimmered like a mirage in the night sky. Tögsgöl set Kara down on the ledge of Ezelj's window. Kara knocked on the glass and let herself into the dimly lit room. Ezelj lay on the bed, drenched in sweat. He kicked the fur covers off himself and remained bare. Kara found herself unfazed by his appearance. In fact, she rather enjoyed it.

"Ezelj?" Kara stepped closer. She carefully sat on the edge of the bed, discreetly pulling the covers over his lower half.

Kara looked Ezelj over. Swirls of blue pigment on his chest caught her attention. They were visible now that he had shifted the covers while kicking his nightmares away.

Kara reached her hand and carefully moved his long, black hair out of the way. The petals of a blue rose were revealed to her, etched into Ezelj's skin.

"Ohh!" Kara yelled; Ezelj opened his eyes and jumped up, so suddenly she didn't have time to react.

He grabbed her wrists and pinned her down, his expression mad.

"Ezelj! Ezelj! It's me!" Kara screamed.

At once, Ezelj's expression softened. He blinked, confused, released Kara, and backed away from her.

"I…" He breathed hard. "What? What are you…?" He glanced down, realizing he had revealed his mark to her.

Ezelj hurriedly attempted to cover up, but Kara stayed his hands. "No, don't," she pulled his arms down.

"You are - him. You are, aren't you? I knew it." She smiled.

Ezelj looked at her, mystified. "You…you are not afraid?"

Kara chuckled. "No, why would I be? This is amazing. I knew there had to be something extraordinary about you."

His relief at her reaction did little to banish the bitterness from his heart.
"I am cursed," Ezelj said. "No matter what I do, death will claim me young."

"No," Kara put her hand on the mark etched into his chest.

Ezelj hissed, and Tögsgöl howled outside the window.

Kara removed her hand.

"Owe...it's..." Ezelj's eyes bulged in astonishment. "The mark! It's shrinking!"

Tögsgöl growled. 'Impossible!'

"That has never happened before," Ezelj muttered, dumbfounded.

Kara held his hands. "Run away with me." She begged him.

Ezelj blinked. "What?"

"Don't fight tomorrow. Come away with me. We can both leave this place and be happy."

Ezelj shook his head. "No, Kara. We have a responsibility to our tribe, to your father. I swore on my honor to uphold our sacred rituals, and I cannot leave before I'm done."

Kara glanced out of the window to where Tögsgöl took on the form of a falcon. His piercing eyes followed her from the ledge.

"What if you get hurt?" Kara asked, desperate to convince him. "What if this is how you die?"

Ezelj raised his hand and lovingly caressed her face. "Now that I know your touch can heal me, I must give this life a chance and not shy away from its challenges. Perhaps now I will finally experience the eve of my days and the peace I crave."

He leaned forward and kissed her. "Besides," he sighed. "I have pride, Kara. I won't allow myself to be seen as weak and won't run away from a challenge after I have already accepted it."

Kara kissed him back and then glanced at the falcon. She did what she could. Now, all that remained was hope.

The next morning found Ezelj in the arena. It was now down to him and to his most powerful opponent, a brute called Thunaer.

Ezelj was damned if he let such a malicious animal win a chance at Kara's hand.

Tögsgöl sat by his side, having taken on the form of the large dog again. He nuzzled Ezelj's arm.

Ezelj petted him absentmindedly while Thunaer entered the arena. Seeing his scarred face from the many illegal battles he conducted in the warriors' village made Ezelj sick.

"Bring me victory today and grant me life to enjoy it," Ezelj whispered.

Tögsgöl knew Ezelj's prayer was not meant for him, but this was an opportunity he could not pass on. He needed this entry, and Ezelj just granted it to him.

With Ezelj's hand still stroking his fur, Tögsgöl's violet dog eyes emptied, and Ezelj stiffened, his eyes glowing violet and then settling into dark green.

No one noticed the possession taking Ezelj over. Although his movements were a bit mechanical when he moved further into the ring, to the spectators who arrived to witness the final battle, Ezelj seemed full of confidence. He even uncharacteristically waved to the gathering crowd.

Kara raised an eyebrow. It was very unlike him.

But she had no time to ponder it, for the time of battle drew near. Both warriors chose the battle axes for more skill required to wield them than a sword. It was over faster than anyone anticipated.

No one saw the dark energy that enveloped Ezelj.

No one but Thunaer, and he saw his axe ricochet off Ezelj's body. To the gathered villagers outside the ring, it looked as though Thunaer missed Ezelj completely when he swung the battle-axe at Ezelj's gut.

Ezelj, with no control over his body, ducked another attempt Thunaer had made at his neck and then at his head and struck the brute warrior down with the butt of his axe.

Thunaer went down like a rock. Ezelj used his disoriented confusion and jumped on top of him, grabbing Thunaer's axe and putting it to the warrior's neck.

The crowd's gasp and stunned silence turned into cheers.

Thunaer thrashed under Ezelj, unwilling to admit defeat. He drew a blade of sharpened animal bone from his position on the ground and thrust it into Ezelj's chest, failing to draw the slightest remanence of blood.

"That's impossible! What are you?" Thunaer whispered. Then, he saw it — Ezelj's shirt fell open, and the blue rose was visible momentarily etched into his radiant skin.

"You!" Thunaer breathed.

"Do you yield?" Ezelj demanded in Tögsgöl's voice, bearing down on Thunaer's neck with his axe.

Thunaer growled.

"Yield!" Ezelj commanded, pressing the sharpened axe down and spilling first blood.

"Aagghh!" The warrior struggled, but at last, he relented.

"I yield!" Thunaer rasped.

"Louder so everyone can hear you!" Tögsgöl taunted.

Thunaer glared at his tormentor, he didn't want to surrender, but the axe was becoming heavier against his jugular.

"I yield!" He let out a choked cry.

Ezelj blinked.

He looked down at Thunaer, beaten and bloody beneath him.

"Get off me." The scarred warrior said through gritted teeth.

Ezelj breathed out, sheathed his axe in his belt, and got up, extending his hand to Thunaer, who batted it away.

"This is not over." He hissed as he staggered up and left the ring, ignoring the people who came flocking, cheering Ezelj's victory.

They shook his hands, patted his back, and yelled, "Champion!"

Ezelj breathed hard. He looked around for Kara and saw her slipping away towards the wood structure that housed the other warriors.

"Thank you... Yeah, thanks... I..." Ezelj tried to ignore the glaring gaze Thunaer still held for him. "I'm sorry... I have to..." he distanced himself from the crowd, but it was still a while until he got away.

After extracting himself from the excited spectators, he hurried in the direction Kara had taken.

Rounding the corner of the wooden structure she disappeared behind, Ezelj came to a halt with his back pressed to the wooden wall, panting.

"That wasn't you." Kara appeared by his side.

Ezelj closed his eyes and shook his head.

"No, it was...."

The sound of approaching paws made both turns. Tögsgöl prattled up to them, once again an obedient dog to his master.

Fury rose within Ezelj. "Don't ever do that to me again!" He shouted.

"I gave you what you wanted." Tögsgöl calmly answered, neglecting his discretion in front of Kara.

"There is no honor in deception." Ezelj punched the wall and left a small dent. "Never again. Do you hear me?" Ezelj looked deep into his guardians' violet eyes. "Stay away from me. I order you to leave me."

"You are vulnerable without me," Tögsgöl growled, baring his teeth towards Kara.

Ezelj ignored him.

He took Kara's hand and led her away to the sound of Tögsgöl howl.

They walked together in silence until Ezelj realized that Kara was leading him.

The scent of sweet, woody, sappy green fragrance alerted Ezelj to the Birch trees ahead. The woods were a rarity in their land but a welcomed sight to behold.

They entered the forest surrounding their encampment and walked until the sound of falling water reached their ears.

They stepped into the dimly lit grove, which led them on a stone path that ended in a waterfall. At the end of the stone path, an altar laid with fruit, dried meat, and sealed jars of wine stood, before the path itself winded behind the waterfall.

"What is this place?" Ezelj asked. He had never seen this part of the village before, yet his spirit was drawn to it.

There was something familiar in this setting.

"As my champion," Kara said, ignoring his question, "I invite you to join my family." She stepped up to a stone altar and brought back a rare and expensive gift. A lavish coat, magnificently done with the fine fur of the black sable.

"This is too extravagant, Kara. I have no need for such gifts." Ezelj grazed the coat with his fingers.

Kara chuckled, unfolded the coat, and draped it over his shoulders. "Well, consider this an engagement present."

Ezelj bowed his head and took her hands in his. "All I have to give is my heart." Kara smiled. "There is nothing in this world of greater value to me." She stood on her toes, threw her arms around him, and kissed him deeply.

The tingling sensation of the rose mark residing pulled at Ezelj's chest.

Kara detached from him and gestured to the waterfall.

*"Here lay the bones of Pyramus and Thisbe," Kara said. "Your first **human** life, Ezelj. What you were before, we do not know, but whatever that being was, he was powerful, in body and soul."*

Ezelj's eyes widened, "I feel it," he admitted. "That is why I feel such a magnetic attraction to this place."

Kara nodded. "My family had them in our possession for generations," She explained. "And everywhere we went, prosperous grazing fields and abundance of fruit and water came our way."

Ezelj placed his right hand on his chest. "I feel the need to mourn the life I lost, all the pain that followed, and the fact that my restless soul is unable to find peace. However, I have to try and live this life now." He looked at Kara.

She took his hand. "We can, together."

They kissed again and then, with one final glance at the altar, left the hidden shrine. They stepped out of the clearing to the banks of a small lake, and Ezelj was about to suggest a formal meeting with Kara's father when a mad, blood-curdling shout came from their right. Ezelj whipped his head toward the scream and saw Thunaer charging at them.

"You abomination!" He bellowed and raised a mistletoe spear in one hand and an axe in the other "You may deceive the village, but you cannot pour sand in my eyes! I see what you are... You foul beast!"

His attack came in a blitz of aggressive assault.

Kara yelled at him to stop and attempted to pull Ezelj away from the crazed warrior, but Thunaer caught her arm and threw her aside.

The sound of her head colliding with the smooth rocks on the banks of the small lake echoed through the forest.

Ezelj gaped at his beloved. She lay on the ground; her blood ran into the water.

Her eyes stared at him blankly.

She was gone.

"No…" Ezelj fell on his knees by her side. "What have you done?" He pulled her into his arms and looked up at Thunaer.

The brute breathed hard. "You stole my place in the tribe." He growled.

Ezelj said nothing. The blue rose stain crept up his skin to his throat. It was already over for him. With or without Thunaer's murderous intention, Ezelj only had moments.

"Now, you can join her."

Ezelj looked up at Thunaer.

The brute raised his mistletoe spear and unceremoniously plunged it into Ezelj's heart.

Hot blood spewed out of Ezelj's mouth and down his chin.

He coughed and closed his eyes, holding Kara while his strength allowed it until the last drop of life abed from him, and the darkness took him.

Ezelj's death thundered through Tögsgöl as if it was his own.

The guardian arrived at the lake to find his master and Kara lying in a blood pool by the tainted water. Their limbs entwined in a last embrace.

Tögsgöl hissed, he was too late. The skin of the canine fell away, and a great ice serpent with violet eyes emerged.

"All this time I attempted to keep you two apart, I thought she was your weakness." He bellowed. "Now, I see she is your reason to fight; she gives you strength." The serpent diminished his size until he could slither across Ezelj's chest without crushing his body.

"Awake now, Úlftýr," Jörmungandr whispered. "Awake, and I give you my word I will not make this mistake again."

The snake opened his mouth, and his fangs gleamed in the sunlight; swiftly, he sunk them into Ezelj's chest.

Ezelj's dead eyes opened; they glowed with green electricity, and up on the hill, in another time, in the west wing of the black stone castle, Úlftýr screamed himself awake.

CHAPTER 24

THE TOP OF THE MOUNTAIN

Midgardr, Capital Region, Islandia 1637 B.C.

 lftýr gazed down onto the inner courtyard. He stood hidden behind the heavy dark-blue curtain covering his bedroom's arched window.

His crimson eyes followed the guards. They placed Baldur and three others, Aesir, Vanir, and Vidar, on a stone slab.

Silk draped over Aesir's body, an azure-colored shrub. His body seemed to be misshapen somehow; one leg bulged out, longer than the other.

Deep in his shattered mind, Úlftýr knew why they laid him out like that, but the dominant part of his mind refused to remember the gruesome reason.

A blank veil obscured the faces of the dead in Úlftýr's memory, and only Baldur's face shone through brightly, persisting with vigor to force Úlftýr to deal with what he did to him from beyond the grave.

Úlftýr didn't want to evoke the sights of the previous night or recall what he had done to the one who had been his friend and mentor for half a millennium.

In his mind's eye, Úlftýr saw the blood running down the wall and his hands trembling; the claws retracted back into his skin.

Vivid memories of sharp pain as the change wrecked through his body refused to leave his mind. His skin tore where his claws burst through and retracted back. His gums were half numb and shredded by the horrible fangs that sprouted without his control. The sensation of snakes slithering under his skin and his head pounded as if an axe split it open. It hurt relentlessly even now.

"Who killed them?" Úlftýr asked Elska, who stood behind him, a lump of agony forming in his throat. "I believe I know the answer, but I must ask to know my mind does not deceive me." He added quietly.

Memories he would've happily forgotten floated back to torment him. Úlftýr stiffened when Elska pressed against his back and wrapped her arms around his torso.

"I'm sorry…" Elska said, reluctant to reveal the truth to him. "It was…"

"Me," Úlftýr said.

He once again looked down at the courtyard. Amongst the maids tending to the bodies stood a fair álfur; his long, golden locks shone in the light of the sun. His body was clothed in the finest, shimmering, cobalt-blue silk robes that moved in the light breeze, and blue blood seeped from the open gaping wounds in his chest.

The fair warrior looked up at Úlftýr. They stared at each other, and Úlftýr felt planted, frozen in place, his breath refusing to restart.

"Úlftýr?" Elska's voice broke the spell on his body, Baldur's image shimmered out of existence, and Úlftýr breathed free. He let the curtain fall back against the stained-glass window. His action plunged the room into semi-darkness. A dozen candles remained to provide a dim light, burning in the hung crystal holders.

Úlftýr twisted in Elska's embrace. He turned to face her. "Do you fear me?" He asked her, his bright red eyes gleaming.

Elska looked hard up into his crimson orbs. "Yes. There is no point in lying to you and saying that I don't, but my love for you is stronger than my fear." She said, and Úlftýr knew she meant it. "If I can't restore you and spend this life by your side, my life might as well not be worth living."

"I hate what I am doing to you," Úlftýr said. "I hate that my curse falls upon you. You stand so close to me now; only with your presence and warmth can you save me," Úlftýr snaked his arms around her petite frame and pulled her closer.

"But my love might not be enough to save you. I already hurt you." He murmured against her citrus-scented hair.

"That wasn't you… not completely," Elska said. "Know I will endure much worse for you."

Úlftýr buried his face in her shoulder. They embraced, and Elska laid her head against his feverishly hot chest. She glanced at the blue swirls etched into his bare torso.

"I can hardly remember who I am. How can you still trust me?" Úlftýr murmured against her neck. "How can I be sure I remain in control with you?" Úlftýr saw his reflection in the window. He saw his clawed hand drawn against her back and willed the claws to retract back into his skin.

Elska shivered, his talons grazing her dress; she moved her head to the side, exposing her neck further. She gasped as Úlftýr pressed a claw to her outstretched neck. Hot blue blood welled up from the wound, and Úlftýr lapped at the sweet nectar.

Elska breathed hard, but she remained firm in her decision. "Trust in me. I will find a way to undo what Deirdra did to you. I promise." she vowed.

"I know." Úlftýr managed to let out, begging his strength to restrain the beast inside him that craved to burst out and devour Elska whole.

Baldur, Aesir, Vidar, and Vanir were interred alongside the warrior Snakur and Baldur's brother in an underground cave on the cliffs of Krýsuvíkurbjarg.

The day before the funeral procession was to set out, Ingrid sat alone in the throne room, her eyes fixed on the empty space on the wall where a set of antlers had been just a few days before.

"You won't find the answer to what happened here on the wall."

Ingrid jumped when a low voice spoke from the shadows beside the window.

"Úlftýr? Where are…" Ingrid's eyes darted to the door, but it remained closed. "How did you get in here?" Ingrid got up and involuntarily stepped back.

Úlftýr casually strode over to her. He was dressed in his usual leather attire, his white hair held in a messy tie, and his eyes were dim, but the unnatural red tint still glowed deep within them.

"I'll show you sometime," Úlftýr smirked. "Did you mean to ask where the guards are?" He came closer. "Do you fear me, sister? You haven't come to me since I returned." Úlftýr reached out to touch the bandage on Ingrid's neck.

Ingrid recoiled from his touch, moving back until she hit the wall behind her and closed her eyes.

Úlftýr looked at her sadly. "I am sorry," he said. "Truly. I don't remember much from what I did to you, to Baldur…. to…. but Elska told me I was… A beast."

Ingrid opened her eyes.

Úlftýr's glance lingered on her neck. He turned away and walked up to the already mended window. "I don't blame you for fearing me right now, Ingrid," Úlftýr pressed his forehead against the cold glass. "I fear myself… There aren't many I can turn to. Father…"

"Father would have known what to do," Ingrid said bitterly, too ashamed to raise her eyes. "Úlftýr, I have wronged you; I-"

"Yes, you have," Úlftýr said, cutting her off. "I am almost glad that you are finally in this position. It is only fair that you would put your life on hold for the sake of our land like I have."

Ingrid frowned. "Haven't I been here by your side in all of it?"

Úlftýr smirked. "You can't really compare your contributions to mine. Don't even try it; you won't like the result."

"Why do I even need to compare us?" Ingrid stepped closer. "Why do you always need to get even?"

"Because none of you have sacrificed as much as I have; none of you had to shoulder the burden of the responsibilities that were thrusted upon me." Úlftýr's voice kept rising. He clutched his fists. "I want to come with you when you go to the cliffs tomorrow," He finally demanded.

"Are you out of your mind?" Ingrid clamped her uninjured hand over her mouth, immediately regretting her outburst.

Úlftýr nodded. "I know what you think of this, sister," he said, turning to Ingrid and pressing his back to the window. "I know what you think of me. You think that this is a foul proposition, that this is an indecent move on my part. Elska said you would consider my actions abominable as you should, but I cannot-" His voice broke. "The thought of him gone - I know he did not give up on me until the last moment. His dying breath will haunt me always… and the others." He added an afterthought. "I need to be there when you bring them to rest. To see Baldur off to where I cannot follow."

Ingrid looked at Úlftýr's distraught face. "Úlftýr, you understand that for you to be, there is to spit in the face of everyone that would gather to mourn them. However," Ingrid sighed, and Úlftýr looked at her, surprised and hopeful. "I also believe that for you not to be there would be to soil Baldur's memory." she paused. "Are you aware of my pact with

Elska and the remaining Elders? Although I am uncomfortable bringing that horrid bargain up, I must ensure our agreement's terms are upheld even outside the castle walls."

"Yes," Úlftýr answered simply. "Elska told me."

Ingrid sighed. "Yes, I expected she would. And you agree?" Ingrid stepped forward.

Úlftýr looked at her with red eyes dipped in darkness. "If the beast inside me threatens your well-being, the cliffs of Krýsuvíkurbjarg shall become my final resting place."

The cliffs were located past the lava fields, some thirty rost outside the capitol. In the summer, the cliffs were home to thousands of winged creatures that migrated there systematically year after year to nest, with their numbers growing exponentially over the centuries.

At one point, it seemed there wasn't a spot to be found in the sky unfilled by a colorful swirl of song and rainbow-colored feathers.

Unfortunately, the march made the trek up the backbone of the mountain during the dead season, and had they been any other creature, the snow blocking their path would have wholly buried them underneath.

As it was, a squad from Baldur's platoon forged ahead of the main party to clear a path for their horses and the deceased they were transporting, utilizing their elemental abilities.

They thawed the snow to create a path and solidified the water on each side to prevent anyone from straying from it.

From the moment Úlftýr left the castle, he kept his pale face and white hair concealed under a black linen hood etched with his family's crest.

It draped over a long wool cloak topped with a coyote fur capelet. Úlftýr, along with Ingrid, Elska, Baldur's first battalion, and a handful of the court's high Ljósálfar, including council members, journeyed up the mountain on horseback.

The bodies of Baldur and his slain comrades were drawn after the main party by their saddleless horses, resting on top of fully rigged and intricately carved wooden stretchers.

The snow crunching under the feet of the horses was partially covered in ash. The road to the cliffs of Krýsuvíkurbjarg led through a ridge of active volcanoes and took nearly two days to complete.

On the first night, the company rested by Kleifarvatn Lake, located on a fissure zone south of the peninsula.

Nobody knew where the water was coming from or where it was going out, and many believed it connected to the same underground reservoir that served the capital. The Ljósálfar took advantage of the simmering hot springs to unwind and De-stress from their tedious journey.

Úlftýr chose to stay away from the assembly when they halted for rest. He and Elska sat by themselves on a fallen tree trunk, their faces illuminated by a makeshift fire Úlftýr built.

"This setting makes me reminisce of the first night we met," Úlftýr said, and Elska allowed herself a small smile. "However," Úlftýr continued immediately, "The circumstances we are in now are dire." He raised his eyes from the fire. "I am grateful for your presence here. I seem to have lost my appetite for anything that is not you. Your company is my only current pleasure. However, I am painfully aware of the fleeting glances and the downright stares cast in our direction."

Elska sighed and scooted closer to him. "Most of the Ljósálfar who travel with us are unaware of…" she trailed off. "My guilt?" Úlftýr offered. "And what was the exact role in the events that led them and us to such a morbid setting?"

Elska did not answer but merely took his hand as he went on.

"I know what the official tale is of the tragedy that befell the kingdom; Ingrid told me that she proclaimed that Deirdra had gained entrance to the castle undetected. Then, she and a group of her sinful, mortal assassins broke into the throne room, killed – " he took in a shuddered breath. "Killed Baldur, Vanir, Aesir, and Vidar and proceeded in their attempt to overthrow my sister." He let his head drop lower; the flames danced in his eyes. "The warriors, it seemed by her tale, with their final breaths, managed to fight the mortal assassins off, but not before the brutes injured Ingrid."

He straightened his back. "I was, by the same account of the royal guard, still recovering from my encounter with the traitorous wench more than a week before the murderous night happened."

"But you were," Elska said, and Úlftýr laughed.

"How I love your twisted sense of reality, my dear Elska. But regardless, only a fraction of the court believes and trusts these stories. Whispers of the savage howl that echoed through the valley when I was attacked are widely spread, and I can't even remember it. I was told that no one had ever encountered such a sound of pain and horror within the borders of our peaceful shores. And don't think the extent of my injuries is such a closely guarded secret; many Ljósálfar know that even the most potent charms were insufficient to wake me up after my ordeal with Deirdra. Not even Siran, your father, an Elder with immense power known for his healing and mending rituals, could revive me."

Elska blushed. She still could not bring herself to tell Úlftýr of the blood ritual she performed to get him back.

"Perhaps I should show them," Úlftýr said. "Perhaps they should see what was done to me, how I fair now that I have returned from the brink of death, no one had laid eyes upon my face save for my closest relations. And you know the court dwellers are forbidden from discussing my appearance outside the castle walls at Ingrid's command."

"Then, perhaps we should introduce you back to our people, bit by bit if you want to avoid the shock it might cause. Keeping you hidden had only contributed to the mysterious air surrounding your current condition. Speculations of your state of mind and body are wild and vary from horrible disfigurement to mental loss due to dark spells." Elska sighed.

Úlftýr's expression hardened. "Unfortunately," he said through grritted teeth, "Their conclusions are close to the truth."

When the first light of morning illuminated the cliffs of Krýsuvíkurbjarg, Baldur, Aesir, Vidar, and Vanir were interred alongside the warrior Snakur and Baldur's brother, Hoder, in an underground cave on the cliffs.

Úlftýr kept his distance. He didn't tell Elska that when they sat by the fire the night before, they were not alone. Baldur sat beside them, staring into the flames. At this point, Úlftýr could not be sure if Baldur was as real as he was, a ghost of his past truly hunting him, or his fractured mind playing tricks on him.

At any rate, the phantom was gone by morning.

They lowered the bodies into the ground, with Baldur being the last to go into the crypt. They clothed his body in the finest, shimmering, cobalt blue silk robes that moved in the light breeze of the morning. They placed blue roses on his body, the last honor his people bestowed upon him.

Úlftýr waited until they sealed the mouth of the sacred cave, and the procession moved away, beginning their descent down the mountain.

"I will catch up to you." He told Elska, who nodded in understanding. She kissed his cheek, saddled her horse, and slowly ushered it after the others.

Icy winds caressed Úlftýr's skin as he gathered the courage to approach the sealed crypt. The sound of the procession gave way to the melancholy sounds of crying crows and rustling branches. The air felt as heavy as his heart. Not a moment after Elska rode off, Baldur was before him. Clothed in the same garb he was in when Úlftýr put him to death, his angry ghost seized Úlftýr by the neck and slammed him against the stone covering the crypt.

Úlftýr didn't cry out, didn't try to claw Baldur away from him. Baldur opened his mouth in a scream, but only a low moan came out.

"I'm sorry," Úlftýr whispered.

Baldur grunted and released him. He looked up into the sky and shimmered out of existence.

Úlftýr turned and leaned against the cold stone. "There are no words to describe how sorry I am. There are no actions I can take to restore the life I took from you, including offering up my own. Believe me, I tried." Úlftýr whispered. "Your death is a nightmare I can't wake up from, and this life is a torment I did not expect to endure."

The stone crystallized with blue ice under his fingers. Úlftýr growled and tore his hand away. The rune on his forehead ignited, and his claws grew from his shredded skin.

"No…" Úlftýr willed the change to remain dormant, "No! For you, I cannot lose myself to rage. I cannot let it take over me again." He clutched his foreign hands tightly to his chest, bent over in anguish as he focused on his breathing. As soon as the wave of red receded from his sight, he stood up and approached the tomb, but he dared not to touch it again to keep his ire from rising. "Rest well, my friend, forgive my actions if you can, for I was in a world of torment or condemn me when we meet at last, and I shall endure your punishment, but for now, guide me down the path I must take to avenge us-" he paused. "And tell Hoder to take good care of you where I can't," he said while scorching tears burned down his face.

CHAPTER 25
THE WRECKAGE

The ancient bronze bells on Engey Island rang in sharp alarm.

"A wreckage on the beach! Bodies on the shore." The guards shouted frantically, running through the castle hallways not a fortnight after their precession's return.

A crowd gathered on the shore to help.

When Queen Ingrid arrived, the guards had already pulled three dead álfur out of the water and laid them alongside the wooden wreckage that washed ashore.

The Elder, Siran, was there, too. A handful of his trained healers were casting their magic in the form of a net across the water, hoping to sense anyone who had miraculously survived the nautical disaster.

"Over here!" Came the shout everyone anxiously hoped for.

Ingrid regarded the unconscious álfur carried out of the water. The álfur's long dark brown hair covered half his strong-set face; however, Ingrid immediately recognized him. They were nearly the same age and often saw each other in court.

It was Murtagh, captain of King Freyr's flagship.

Before Ingrid had the time to react or ponder on the meaning of this catastrophe, Siran hurried past her and headed to Murtagh's side. With skilled hands, he assessed Murtagh's still body. His eyes narrowed when his hands rested over his shoulder.

While Murtagh lay on the sand, Siran sat down by his side and firmly grabbed Murtagh's hand. In a slow, steady motion, he conducted it horizontally away from his body, and then he settled his foot against Murtagh's side and drew his hand to him.

A satisfying popping sound resonated in the air as his shoulder popped back into place, followed by a scream.

Murtagh opened his eyes, panting. "The lightning! The light… " He looked around him, breathing hard. He attempted to get up. "The ship! Aagh…" He dropped his head back on the ground.

"Stop! Calm down," Siran ordered. "You are safe now."

Ingrid, her mouth agape, shook her head, breathed, and walked up to the distraught captain. "What happened?" Ingrid crouched down beside him, gesturing to her warriors to stay away. She purposely obscured Murtagh's view from the bodies on the beach.

"I saw him," Murtagh whispered, his eyes wide, the complicated truth intended for Ingrid's ears only. "He came in the lightning; his battle cry was the thunder; he intended our destruction." Murtagh closed his eyes. Siran glanced at Ingrid, got up, and pulled Ingrid along. "The sea drove him mad," he said gravely.

"My father… Mother… " Ingrid uttered, still in shock.

"I am sorry, majesty," Siran said. "For now, do not ask for more revelations of this ill-fated voyage," he advised. "For its outcome is scattered here before your eyes."

Ingrid looked at the dark ocean beyond their borders. She wondered what evils lurked out of her sight that caused this terrible grief.

Ingrid ordered Murtagh to be taken to the infirmary. Five more crew members of his lost ship surfaced, all claimed to the afterlife.

At first, Ingrid had been reluctant to divulge the information regarding their parents' demise to Úlftýr. She feared that the state her brother was in would drive Úlftýr to commit more atrocious acts.

Úlftýr's reaction, however, was both surprising and unsettling. "The throne is henceforth yours, Ingrid," Úlftýr said when Ingrid summoned him to the throne room to deliver the news in person, with two guards stationed on either side of her. "You can call off your guards, Ingrid; I am controlling my faculties," Úlftýr said, his dark red eyes holding Ingrid's gaze firm.

Ingrid looked at him; she nodded and gestured to the warriors at her side to get out.

"The other two you have stationed outside can go, too," Úlftýr said.

Ingrid gaped at him, ashamed and astounded. Úlftýr stepped forward and laid a hand on Ingrid's shoulder. His sister's heart skipped a beat at his touch and then thundered frantically, her breath caught in her throat, her body tense under Úlftýr's palm.

Úlftýr closed his eyes. "I am aware of your fear, sister, and I deserve it." He didn't tell Ingrid; he only knew of the warriors outside because he smelled them. He sensed their beating hearts and almost tasted the essence hidden in their blood on his lips.

"I am sorry for invading your solitude, but I find myself in want of your company. We are blood; besides Elska, I have no one closer because I…"

He didn't have to finish; they could never forget what he had done in this room.

"You are allowed to fear me, and I must respect the distance you choose to put between us for the time being."

"Would you like to talk?" Ingrid asked, and Úlftýr opened his bright red eyes and glanced at her.

Ingrid involuntarily shuddered and shrunk back.

"I can hear your heart when you are close to me. It is nearly bursting out of your chest. I know that you feel an obligation to humor me, but it seems you have grown so scared of the beast I have unleashed upon you that you cannot stand to be near me."

Ingrid did not reply; her whole being craved to flee. Her body was involuntarily shaking.

"I need to know that I can trust you, that you can trust I will not hurt you again, and that I can lift this curse from my soul. And I will if you are with me," Úlftýr said, hopeful. He sighed. "The look in your eyes when you look at me shatters my heart, sister."

"As much as I may want to, I cannot promise that Úlftýr," Ingrid whispered. "Can you swear to me that you will not kill again?"

"I will kill again," Úlftýr replied to the astonished look of his sister. "Of that, there is no doubt. Our enemies shall perish by my hand." The rune on Úlftýr's forehead ignited in a faint glow. "Courage, sister," Úlftýr looked at his claw-drawn hands. "Now, more than ever, you shall be the light to guide our people, and I remain to grieve in the shadows that my tormented mind casts."

Úlftýr's claws grazed Ingrid's tunic before Úlftýr removed his hand from her shoulder, turned, and walked the room length without glancing back. He opened the door and steadily walked out, ignoring the alarmed guards.

The guards ran into the throne room.

"Calm yourselves; she still lives." Úlftýr threw into the air before he disappeared around the corner.

That night, Ingrid lay in her bed and listened to the low grunts and fists meeting stone from the cellar beneath her as her brother unleashed his anger and frustration on the underground walls.

Time moved excruciatingly slowly for Úlftýr in the following days and weeks.

A month has passed since they placed the stone lid on the tomb that held Baldur. His peaceful features, as they laid him to eternal rest, were forever etched in Úlftýr's memory. Along with it, the image of his dying breath haunted Úlftýr.

Baldur's eyes, filled with betrayal and sadness, bore into him from the shadows, whether he was sleeping or awake.

Úlftýr knew he was not right, not in his head or body. A dark entity residing inside him continuously craved distraction and blood. His waking hours were hell, and his dreams were purgatory.

Ingrid and Elska warned the court dwellers never to enter Úlftýr's bed chamber unannounced and unescorted by Elska.

Rumors of his night terrors spread beyond the castle inhabitants. A well-known story told of a maiden who came into his bed chamber to try and wake him after his shouts became particularly frightening. When she touched him, his unnatural red eyes opened, the rune in his forehead ignited, and he lashed out of his nightmare, kicking her across the room.

Elska found her towards morning, and she still lay, recovering in the infirmary.

Daylight proved to be another issue Úlftýr had to deal with. His condition meant he had to avoid the sun at all costs. The slightest rays that flickered through his bedroom's heavy curtains were enough to cause stinging agony to his sensitive eyes.

And that wasn't even the worst of it. Upon exposure to daylight, Úlftýr's pale grey skin crumbled in patches and peeled off, shedding like the scales of a snake.

Candles were always lit inside his dwelling. Their warm glow was the only light that didn't hurt him. Úlftýr used the flickering flames to fight the smothering darkness that enveloped him, inside and out.

At night, Úlftýr took comfort lying in a marble tub with ice water drawn in an adjacent chamber to his room. This was one of many such nights when he lay in the tub, his head resting on a cold, wet cloth and his eyes tightly shut.

Úlftýr's body of late had only one temperature — searing hot. He could barely feel the ice; the cold water was pleasant against his skin.

"Úlftýr," Úlftýr kept his eyes shut. "Úlftýr, you need to listen to me."

"Go away," Úlftýr growled. "You are nothing but a memory of a dream invading my waking hours."

"Úlftýr, open your eyes." The low voice insisted. "Úlftýr!" It hissed. "*Look at me!*"

Úlftýr's eyes snapped open, and he gasped. In front of him sat a giant silver-green serpent the size of a grown man.

The snake's violet eyes gleamed in the semi-darkness, and its face was inches from Úlftýr.

Úlftýr held his breath.

For a long moment, none of them moved, and then the serpent retreated, shrunk down, and, in its place, the silhouette of a humanoid figure appeared. The two-legged creature sat between the shadows of what appeared to be two slabs of stone, his arms and legs bound in heavy chains and clearly without any clothes on. The dark figure took a deep, ragged breath.

Similar to the rest of the room, darkness obscured him, and only his red eyes, not unlike Úlftýr's, gleamed in the candlelight.

"*Release me.*" The being said. His voice was both demanding and pleading. "*Release me.*" The being hissed in pain, but Úlftýr could not tell what hurt him.

"How?" Úlftýr gulped.

"*Unleash the beast within you and set us both free.*"

Úlftýr shook his head vigorously. "No!" He looked down, and he shrunk away from the chained deity. "No! I cannot hurt anyone else! Don't ask me...."

A wolf howled inside the chamber.

Úlftýr placed his palms against his ears and shut his eyes, keeping his head bowed until the agonizing sound died down.

When he finally opened his eyes, all traces of the serpent and the chained being were gone. Úlftýr slowly lowered his arms to the tub's sides and pushed himself up and out. He breathed in the cold air and silently approached a great wooden mirror that leaned against the far-end wall.

He looked at the creature that stood before him.

Úlftýr felt detached from him, like he felt detached from himself. His skin was foreign to him, his claws and fangs refused to retract, and his own red eyes haunted him in the darkness.

Úlftýr didn't bother to dry off or get dressed. He stepped into his room, his image from the mirror still fresh in his mind.

Gold amber eyes stared at him from a portrait hung on the wall above his wood-carved writing desk.

"What are you looking at?" He grumbled at his image. "Don't you think I know what I am?" He yelled at the prince, who gazed back at him, silent and perfect. Úlftýr growled. "Your gaze is filled with pity I don't deserve." The prince in the painting was what he once was, preserved in every brushstroke over the stretched canvas.

"Agghh!" Úlftýr couldn't take these eyes anymore. They watched him, judged him, and stared him down.

"Don't look at me!" He lashed at the canvas, his sharp claws leaving deep slashes in the painting, but the amber eyes remained intact, watching him.

The hairs on the back of his neck stood up. It wasn't just his eyes that followed his every movement. Úlftýr whipped his head back, and a sob escaped his throat.

Baldur stood by the window. Úlftýr could not see past the blue blood that covered Baldur's chest. "Please," Úlftýr whispered. "Please, I'm sorry."

Baldur looked down at the wounds in his chest. He reached for Úlftýr with hands covered in his own blue blood. Baldur opened his mouth, but no voice came out.

A crack, a screech, another crack, and suddenly a crystal candle holder exploded, and another, and another.

Úlftýr screamed and fell to the floor; he covered his head while the shattered crystals rained around him, slashing his skin as they went down.

"Please, please stop," Úlftýr begged.

"Úlftýr." The voice from his nightmares persisted in returning.

"Leave me alone!" Úlftýr bellowed. "Why do you torment me? Who are you?" He stumbled back to his feet, slashing, tearing, and punching at everything he could put his claw-drawn hands on.

Half the ornate bedpost flew across the room, the splinters raining on the floor. Úlftýr grabbed onto and overturned the heavy wooden desk that came crashing to the ground with a loud racket.

He punched the wall, leaving a deep dent in the limestone; some crumbled to the ground, mixed with the blue blood dripping from his broken hand before it quickly healed and the gash in his skin vanished.

"Úlftýr?" The door to the room cracked open, and Elska walked in. She heard the noise of crushing furniture and Úlftýr's anguished shouts from down the hall, yet she did not expect to find him, naked, covered in dust, blood, and wood chips, standing in the middle of their destroyed sanctuary.

"Úlftýr, what happened? What is going on here?" She came closer. "Úlftýr? Can you hear me?" She touched his arm.

Úlftýr's bright red eyes flashed with rage. Before she could step back from him, Úlftýr turned on her.

He seized her shoulders and drove his claws deep into her flesh.

"Úlftýr!" Elska screamed." Let go!" She tried to wrestle herself free. "Please! Let go! You're hurting me!" Her attempts to wriggle free only widened the wound Úlftýr caused her; rivulets of blood trickled down her skin.

Úlftýr looked at her, yet Elska could tell he wasn't there. The beast that took over her love snarled at her, his fangs dripping with saliva, and his grip on her tightened.

He dragged her closer.

"Please..." A sob escaped Elska's throat.

Úlftýr blinked. His red eyes dimmed, and, in a moment, he regained his senses, released her, and pushed her violently away.

Elska hugged herself, her hands pressed against the wounds Úlftýr left in her shoulders.

"I…" Úlftýr's bloody claws retracted; his fangs slid back into his gums.

"Are you all right?" He reached for her but recoiled when she looked up at him with a tear-stricken face. He wanted to go to and comfort her, but he no longer trusted himself around her. He couldn't bring himself to look at her wounds. He had to get out of there. Shame filled him. Shame and rage. "Consarn it!" he shouted. "I'm sorry! I'm… Just stay away from me, okay?"

He didn't wait for her to respond. Instead, he grabbed his discarded pants and a single dusty tunic from the floor and pulled them on.

Ignoring the mess he made, Úlftýr stepped to the broken wardrobe, pulled the halfway-attached door off its hinges, threw it aside, and got his Ice blades out. He slung them over his shoulder and walked out, slamming the door to their room behind him.

Elska slid to the floor, her hands firmly pressed against the bleeding wounds in her flesh. Her heart, however, bled harder than her body.

Úlftýr burst outside and stopped in his tracks, fully expecting the searing pain of daylight to claim his senses. To both his delight and surprise, that did not happen. A sort of darkness enveloped him, and the light seemed dimmer around him. The sunlight was still unpleasant, but the pain was manageable, like constant pressure on his limbs.

He saw the wolf's shadow follow him up the mountain.

No matter how fast he went, how loudly he yelled at the being that pursued him, the shadow remained settled on his heels.

"Is this what you wanted?" Úlftýr asked angrily, sliding down the ridge. "For me to drive away the only person still by my side? For me to hurt her so, I won't have anyone to turn to but you?!"

"*All I want is your help, and I am offering you mine.*" The dark voice answered in Úlftýr's mind.

"Your help comes with a very steep price." Úlftýr threw back. A low rumble followed his statement in his head. "Who are you, or should I ask what you are instead?" Úlftýr demanded, but the voice fell silent. Úlftýr looked back; the shadow of the wolf was gone.

"Finally, I can relax, glide down my beloved mountain, pretend I am myself again, the álfur I was before the curse tore my world apart." He closed his eyes, letting the wind blow in his face. He was not afraid of collision; he knew these slopes like the lines of his palms.

"Aggh!" An arrow whistled past his ear. Úlftýr's eyes snapped open. He skidded to an abrupt stop and turned around, his blades sending the snow flying.

Two mortals, clad in black, stalked up the mountain. Úlftýr saw the three dead rabbits they slew, strung up by rope from their belts.

Rage filled him. Those filthy mortals hunting? On his land? He would not stand for it!

The mortals nocked their weapons and aimed at him again.

"Surrender!" One of them bellowed in the Ljósálfar broken tongue, and Úlftýr snarled. Deirdra must have taught them their language, but for what purpose?

He ducked, two more arrows shrieking past him. The mortals drew their swords and advanced toward him.

Úlftýr whipped around and saw three more black-clad figures climbing the slope from the other side, attempting to ambush him. He growled and charged at the creatures who were sniping arrows at him. One hit his shoulder, the other embedded in his gut. Úlftýr snarled, pulling the last arrow out.

Instantly, he closed in upon the hunters. Without a weapon to assist him, Úlftýr blocked the strike of their swords with his arms. He grabbed the closest man by his neck, wrestled the sword out of his hand, and launched it at his companion.

The latter fell dead in the snow. Úlftýr looked back at the terrified mortal in his grasp.

"I shall use every part of you to serve me. " Úlftýr mused in a trance." I shall use your ribs for my blades to glide upon the ice, and your spine will be my soles to pierce through the snow, and the red sludge in your veins shall quench my thirst."

The advancing dauðadýr shouted incoherently.

Without warning, he snapped the grave-bound creature's neck that was in his grasp. "***Let me help you.***" The thundering voice insisted, the urgency of the words striking at Úlftýr like lightning.

"This means nothing," he warned.

"***Understood.***"

The rune ignited, Úlftýr's claws came out, and the fangs cut through his gums. A familiar red tint came down his eyes, and from that moment on, he knew nothing of the one called Úlftýr.

CHAPTER 26

THE DEATH SENTENCE

Hurting and distraught, Elska sat on the floor of the wrecked room. Blood seeped through the deep gashes in her shoulders, but the pain wasn't prominent to her senses. She was numb to the world. She fought against the will to shut down.

The urge to remain crumbled on the floor was bested by the need not to be alone.

Elska pushed herself off the floor and made her way to the door. She left the room with the door ajar and went down to the supply entrance. She had no intention of trying to explain her appearance to Ingrid or anyone in court.

She stopped before the first guard that crossed her way. "Have someone go by our room and clear the wreckage out of there," she told him. "Just discard anything that is broken." She saw the puzzlement on the guard's face, and then his eyes traveled to her shoulders. He opened his mouth to speak, but the look on Elska's face stopped him from attempting to question her. He bowed, his movement restrained, and followed her orders.

Elska slipped out of the castle without another unwanted encounter.

She went to her father's house and found him in the conservatory, hard at work on their serpent's guide.

"Elska?" he raised his eyes at her when she entered.

"Hello, Father," Elska closed the door behind her. Her father's mutts, which until that moment lay on the ground by his feet, jumped up and began licking her palms and rubbing against her legs.

Elska crouched down to pet them, and Siran saw her dress, bloody at the shoulders.

Siran got up at once. "What happened?" He asked her, opened a cupboard, and pulled out the linen wraps.

"Úlftýr," Elska said, her voice strained from holding back her tears.

Siran gestured to his seat. Elska petted the large black dogs once more and got up. She made her way to the seat offered, pulling down the sleeves of her dress.

Siran inspected the wounds. He glided his hands along the gashes, calling forth his elemental ability to rise from the earth. The torn flesh began pulling back into place, the first layer of the deep wounds sealed.

Elska breathed a sigh of relief.

Siran bandaged her upper arms, and Elska pulled the sleeves of her dress back on, concealing the dressing her father had made for her.

"Would you like to speak about it?" he asked her when he was done.

Tears came to Elska's eyes again. Her father looked at her. He nodded understandingly, took her hand, and gently led her inside the house. They sat in the privacy of the Elder's home while Siran brewed an infusion of leaves and berries.

"Talk to me," he put the blue pottery mug before her.

Elska traced her hand along the wolf carvings on the side of the mug and then lifted it off the table and sipped on the soothing concoction.

"I thought of a moment like this many times while we lived in the Ice Lands," she said.

"So did I," Siran admitted. "But don't attempt to lure me away from the subject. I know how dangerous Úlftýr is now, even if he doesn't mean to be. Did you consider leaving the castle? You are always welcome here…" Siran said carefully.

Elska looked into her cup. "I can't just leave when it gets tough," She looked at Siran. "I have to stay for him."

"I would have told you to run at the first sign of trouble; however, I understand you want to fight for the one you love." He sighed and took his seat across from her. "I should have run after you when you left. The regret I still feel for the lost time I have wasted haunts me. But your situation does not mirror the circumstances that led me to the error of my ways."

Elska set her mug on the table. "Maybe not. But the truth is that I have already wasted years in which Úlftýr and I could have been together. And for all the time lost because of my indecisiveness… I feel now I must make up for it."

"Perhaps I should relocate my things into the castle. At least, that way, I will be close if anything else happens." Siran said.

"I don't need to be protected, Father. I do not think Úlftýr will…." Elska's voice trailed off. She didn't want to face the possibility that, in his rage, Úlftýr might kill her, no matter how close their relationship was. She had to remind herself that being close to him played no significance when he killed Baldur.

Siran put his hand on hers. "At least, promise me you will think it over. I want to be there for you."

Elska patted his hand on hers, extracted it from his grip, and got up from the table. "I will," she promised. "Thank you, Father," She said, and Siran nodded.

"Anytime." He said, feeling both hopeful and anxious for his daughter, trying not to think of the possibility that the next time he sees her, she will be in a bed of roses.

When Úlftýr opened his eyes, he sat on the ground. His head rested against a large snow-covered boulder, and a foul, muddy substance was prominent in his mouth.

Úlftýr wiped his face with his hand of the red blood he tasted.

Bodies of dead men littered the surrounding ground, staining the white snow red. He attempted to get up, but his leg refused to obey him. He looked down. His ankle was twisted in an awkward position, and the bone of his fibula protruded out of his mangled flesh.

Úlftýr frowned; he felt nothing. He took hold of his foot and rewound it into the correct angle, then pushed at the protruding splintered bone until it retreated with a pop. The wound the bone created closed up and healed.

"Thanks," he said to the shadow that slithered into the ice behind him in the form of a snake.

Deirdra marveled at Úlftýr dragging the dead dauðadýr to him and removing the flesh from their bones with his claws.

At first, she didn't understand what he was doing, but then she realized he would attach the mortal's bones to replace the animal ones strapped to his boots.

Awe and admiration filled her. She wasn't about to turn away from a sight that would alarm anyone else.

Until then, she could not figure out exactly what went wrong when she attempted to extract Úlftýr's powers besides Ingrid interrupting her.

Besides the spell not being complete, it affected Úlftýr in a way she did not anticipate. Now, she was eager to see exactly how deep the darkness she mistakenly awakened within him took him over. Perhaps she would sway him to her side in his current state, with the deity inside him still bound.

"Úlftýr."

He whipped his head towards the voice, his body contorted and tensed up with the need to let the beast in him take charge.

Deirdra approached him slowly; she regarded him - as a wild animal in his current state.

Úlftýr remained seated on the ground, the dauðadýr bones tightly held in his grasp.

"Are you awake?" she asked.

His eyes flashed green. His body tensed up, and without looking up, he taunted her. "**Let me tell you a story. Now your pets are part of his story, and he made them history.**" he laughed at his joke. A flat, malicious laugh. His eyes turned red again.

Deirdra visibly relaxed.

"I see you've met my hunting party," Deirdra said casually.

"Yes, they were a delight." Úlftýr tossed the unused bones at her feet. "Here, you can have them back."

"No, thank you." Deirdra smiled. "Have you reconsidered my offer?" Deirdra stepped over the bones he tossed as if they were nothing more than an inconvenience, a branch stuck out of the snow.

"Join me, Úlftýr." She said, "I will make you the King of men and Ljósálfar alike."

Úlftýr looked up at her. "Why don't you come closer?" he murmured.

"What… ?" Deirdra hissed at the toxic green mist rising around him. The grey tint of his skin was temporarily replaced by radiant alabaster. The misty smoke coiled around his limbs and settled against his back.

It rose, growing, taking the shape of a giant hissing snake. The violet eyes of the beast flashed along with Úlftýr's, and both of their mouths opened.

Úlftýr's fangs descended. The reptile launched forward, its fangs dripping with venom. Deirdra shrieked and dissipated in a bright orange flame.

When she was gone, the snake slowly detached itself from Úlftýr. Its head hovered a moment before Úlftýr's eyes; its venom dripped, searing the snow until it disappeared.

His new power was unsettling, and Úlftýr had to admit he liked the fear it invoked in his tormentors' eyes. He was also sure that, knowing Deirdra, she retreated to devise a way to exploit his new abilities.

He knew she wasn't done with him.

Úlftýr returned to the castle.

He climbed up through the supplies' entry Elska had led him in once, and the same guards met him. The warriors wanted to say something; their minds seemed to reel at his appearance, and their hands clutched their swords, but they did not remove them from their sheaths.

"*Not as enjoyable as scaring Deirdra, is it?*" the voice in Úlftýr's head mocked. Úlftýr growled and didn't answer. He avoided the guard's gaze and walked past them, the air between them heavy with tension. Drenched in blood, Úlftýr made his way to the castle's west wing, a path that took him past the throne room where his sister sat.

"*Tell me you didn't like being so powerful.*" the voice continued drilling. Úlftýr clutched the leather cords of his ice boots tighter while he had them slung over his shoulder.

"*I told you I could help you defeat your enemies,*" the voice said matter of factly. Úlftýr stopped and looked at the wall. The shadow of the wolf was back to taunt him.

"And I thanked you for it. Now, go away," Úlftýr said and continued walking, purposely ignoring the shadow.

"*I can restore you. I can give you your life back. Isn't that what you want?*"

Úlftýr stopped dead in his tracks, part of him wanting to believe the monster. "How can I trust you when all you do is torment me?" Úlftýr questioned the wall.

Ingrid narrowed her eyes. The reigning Queen of Islandia watched from the throne room's entrance how her little brother, covered in mud, red blood, and what had to be mortal remains, addressed the wall as if someone was there, speaking back to him.

Terrified at the meaning of Úlftýr's actions, Ingrid retreated to the brightly lit chamber where she felt safe.

Úlftýr returned to his bedroom, startled to see Elska seated on a freshly made bed waiting for him.

"Úlftýr." She got up when he walked in, and her eyes widened. She took in the blood and grime that covered him.

Úlftýr didn't answer straight away. Instead, he laid down his blades on the floor and looked around the room.

While he was gone, Elska had their bedroom cleaned out of all the debris and destroyed furniture, his rampage-crazed hands broken.

"Úlftýr, what happened to you?" Elska swallowed. "Were you… Are you hurt?"

Úlftýr raised his red eyes at her and stepped forward. "Not anymore."

Elska flinched from his sudden movement, her heart thundering frantically.

He heard it, and regret filled him for what he had done. "I shouldn't have come back." He said, turning away.

"No, stop." Elska barred his way.

"Didn't I hurt you enough?" Úlftýr asked.

Elska bit her lip. "You will only hurt me if you leave now. I would never do this to you. I would never turn away from your ailments. I will see all your hurts, all your bruises, all your pain, and I will be here to help you tend to it. I only want you to do the same."

"It's hard for me to see you hurt," Úlftýr confessed.

"It's hard for me, too," Elska answered. "But it's manageable when I can rely on you."

"Maybe you shouldn't do that."

Elska weighted his words. "It will be too easy for me to close off my heart; I have done it before. I can survive on my own. To convince myself that I don't need you and that I may learn happiness without you in time, but the loneliness, the hollow that your love will leave behind, will never go away. I am always willing to fight for us. Can you see a brighter path we both can take?"

"May I embrace you?" Úlftýr reached out, and, sighing, Elska reached back. He took her hand and gently pulled her closer. He wrapped his arms around her and held her, his face buried in her hair.

"I'm sorry," Úlftýr whispered.

Elska stifled a sob against him. She shook her head and wrapped her arms around his torso, holding him tight. "I'm sorry," Úlftýr whispered again.

They stood like that until Elska calmed down and was ready to show her face to him. She looked up, and Úlftýr leaned down and kissed her, hoping she didn't taste the blood on his lips.

"I - I dirtied you," Úlftýr grazed her cheek where a smear of red blood remained, transferred from him.

Elska rubbed her face in the spot Úlftýr indicated. "Do not be concerned with such trivial things," Elska said. "I shall take a bath after you are done. Now, please, let me help you." Úlftýr nodded. He let her help him remove his pants and tunic and lead him to a bath she had drawn up.

He lay back in the marble tub as she began to remove the crusts of the red substance from his skin with a cloth. She moved carefully up his neck and to the corner of his lips.

Úlftýr looked at her and put his hand on hers. "You smell divine…" He kissed her hand and pulled her closer to lean over the tub; the front of her dress dipped into the water.

He nuzzled up and down her neck, and Elska gasped. "You haven't fed on me in a while," She whispered.

"I tasted the mortals," Úlftýr said darkly. "Their blood was foul,"

Elska breathed out. They looked at each other and kissed. Úlftýr asked with his eyes, and Elska gave the tiniest nod of agreement. The next moment, she was lost in his arms, and euphoria clouded her thoughts when he drained her life force. She came out on the other side of their encounter dazed, and he slumped back, satisfied, his mind finally free from the rage he felt after his encounter with the mortals.

"Don't stand too close…." Úlftýr warned her when she finished scrubbing the mortal blood off his skin, and he settled down in his fractured bed.

Elska nodded and kissed his cheek. "I love you." She whispered.

"I love you too." Úlftýr closed his eyes. *'I'm not alone. she still sees me as I was.'* Crossed through his mind before he fell asleep.

She stayed with him until he fell asleep.

When dreams claimed him, she, too, cleansed herself from the blood that stuck to her from Úlftýr's embrace. Then, she left the room and headed to the library.

Now more than ever, determination led her. She had much to do. She couldn't give up until she found a way to restore Úlftýr.

No bells sounded an alarm when he arrived as the sun was abandoning the day.

Favorable winds brought Markian to a small alcove near the Blackstone barracks. He dismounted the old dory boat and left it swaying in the water under the steep side hollow of the rock face as he climbed on shore.

His earth-toned robes were drenched in dirt and leaves as he silently walked on the line separating his people's dwellings from the forest.

They caught him then, several leather-clad warriors he did not know that bore the mark of the serpent.

"Halt, you are not known to us. Where do you go in such an hour?" One of them asked, his hand lingering against his sword.

Markian's green eyes darkened. "I am a véfrétt of the serpent, and I am here on a most important matter. Take me to Baldur at once." He said.

His words had an immediate effect, and he recognized grief when he saw it. "No," he said, refusing to believe it. "No, please, not him too. How? When?"

"You better come with us," The one favoring his sword said. "Queen Ingrid will be interested in what you have to say."

Elska rubbed her eyes in exhaustion. She had lost count of the number of ancient tomes she leafed through in her search for the mysterious rune carved into her lover's brow.

She sniffed; the dust had hung in the air, unmoving, stinging her airways.

A loud knock startled her. It came from the wooden door that led into the upper chamber of the library.

She huffed, closed the large book before her, and got up to open the door she had locked earlier, wondering who would be so bold to disturb her.

"My lady." The warrior called Garuk, wearing the silver armor of the royal guard, bowed low before her.

"Her Majesty, Queen Ingrid, requested an audience with you at once." Garuk gestured towards the stairs. "I am to escort you to the throne room without delay."

Elska sighed. It was like Ingrid using a royal decree to compel her to talk to her. Admittedly, she had been avoiding Ingrid of late, and with good reason. Ingrid did not support her theory that Deirdra's spell backfired when she dabbled in charms, she had no business to invoke or even know about.

She nodded reluctantly and followed the warrior. The long, arched hall that accommodated them was built with intricately sculpted columns half spiraling into the ceiling and the occasional alcove carved into the walls, each tastefully decorated.

Elska remembered longingly how Úlftýr would discover her in this hall, propped against the comfortable pillows in one of the arched nooks, lost within the mystery of the pages of a large book.

Under the heavy brocade, crimson-gold curtains covering the alcoves, she would sit and read the ancient leather-bound editions she brought from the castle's vast library.

It was a privilege and a gift to be granted an open invitation to explore such a wide array of knowledge, all available at her fingertips.

Most books bore the royal family's emblem, the two serpents coiled around a blue rose.

The story told of two giants that roamed the lone world. They searched for a blue rose that granted everlasting love and incomprehensible happiness. They did not know that the blue rose was never discovered but could only be created.

Eventually, after a long and tedious journey, both serpents arrived at Mount Eyjafjallajökull and found each other.

Enveloped in great love and happiness, they forgot what brought them to the mountain in the first place.

Centuries passed, and the giants returned their spirits to the ground. Their devotion to each other, untouched by the continuance strokes of time, endured, and from their ashes, bloomed the first genuine blue rose.

Its powerful, pure radiance brought magic and prosperity to the kingdom, embedding its light into the first Ljósálfar who set foot on its shores.

Garuk pushed the heavy wooden doors open. Like most of the castle's entryways, the royal family's crest decorated the throne room's doors.

The two magnificent serpents coiled around a beautifully sculpted rose were masterfully carved into the wood.

Ingrid stood by the large arched window, her hands behind her back, and her brow frowned, her gaze fixed on the valley.

She was dressed in the Queen's long, deep blue linen tunic with golden brocade accents on her chest plate.

Elska smirked.

Úlftýr hated royal attire. He preferred to wear black fur and leather garments. Practicality over fashion, yet he still looked unbelievably handsome in every garment that graced his body.

"Thank you, Garuk," Ingrid said to the guard.

"Majesty," Garuk replied. He placed a closed fist on his breastplate and bowed out, pulling the doors closed behind him.

"He came back drenched in blood," Ingrid said without taking her eyes off the valley.

"Human blood," Elska said. She should have known something like that wouldn't escape the Queen's ears, not when she just expected news that would set her brother up for failure.

Elska sighed, annoyed. "They must have attacked him again. You can't blame him for defending himself."

"He talked to the wall!" Ingrid whipped back at her sharply, her fists clenched.

Elska blinked but strived to hide her astonishment. "Perhaps there was something there that you couldn't see. Have you even bothered to ask him? We can't be sure what Deirdra's curse invoked within him." Elska grasped at the shards of sanity she could master to explain Úlftýr's erratic behavior.

"Elska." Ingrid looked at her, pity reflecting in her eyes. "I know you love him and would do anything for him, but please try to see the reason. No one wants to admit this, but he is no longer the Úlftýr we knew. My brother has become a Dökkálfar - a dark shadow álfur that feeds on death."

Elska remained silent.

"I know he fed on you. You were seen at the lake." There was no accusation in her voice, only sadness.

"I let him feed on me," Elska said, defiant. "He needed me. He needed to know he was not alone. I felt a piece of him come alive when he tasted my essence, Ingrid, and I would have gladly let him quench his thirst further if I thought that would restore him."

"The light of a Ljósálfar gives life to the world -that is how it's always been. The Dökkálfar - take it away. If we let the darkness spread, it will destroy us like it destroyed our home world, and the sacrifices of our Elders would be all for naught." Elska remained unconvinced. Ingrid sighed. "You don't understand that the Dökkálfar will always crave more; it is in their nature. Life itself is meaningless to them; only in death, Úlftýr finds satisfaction now. The empty void in his heart will devour you."

"You are wrong," Elska protested. "His heart still beats. I know he loves me."

"That is not love," Ingrid said through clenched teeth. "What you perceive as affection is nothing but lust. A creature with no soul cannot love. It is an urge, a survival instinct. He now has the most basic needs, like those of a starving animal."

Elska looked at her in disgust. "I am truly disappointed in you, majesty. Even if you are unwilling to fight for him, Ingrid, I will sustain Úlftýr until my dying breath."

Ingrid nodded with understanding. "That is the point, isn't it? That it will be your dying breath that will seal his fate."

Elska huffed. "If you are so sure that Úlftýr is beyond redemption, why am I still alive? Do you think that he keeps me as his pet? A plaything to torment?"

'Is he so attached to my blood that he keeps me alive only to feed on?' The thought sickened Elska as it crossed through her mind.

Ingrid glanced out the window at the darkening sky. "Perhaps putting him out of his misery will be a mercy. I fear only the gods have the power to reverse what Deirdra had done and return him to us."

"Deirdra is no god." Elska spat; that name seared like venom in her mouth. "Deirdra is a despicable creature with no morals and little regard for the world around her. She messed with forces beyond her control. She took Úlftýr's freedom, and if I don't stop her, she will destroy our future."

Ingrid nodded. "Yes. She used blood magic, Elska. Besides the fact that blood magic is forbidden by the Elders since a great deal of them perished summoning the ice serpent to our aid, if you try to undo her curse, it will destroy you."

Elska looked down; she could not deny the fear festering in her heart. *She* used blood magic to revive Úlftýr and keeps using it to sustain him. She might as well admit to herself that she was responsible for his madness as much as Deirdra, to herself, but not to Ingrid.

"Tell me something, Ingrid," Elska said. "Do you think that Deirdra intended to give Úlftýr more powers — to make him so strong he can now fight off an ambush by himself, walk unharmed from a high fall, and heal instantly? Whatever she did backfired, and when we find the right rune she used to invoke whatever changed him, we will find a way to reverse her spell and bring him back."

Ingrid pinched the bridge of her nose. "You checked every book. We have no way of knowing."

"Then, I'll write the book I need myself!" Elska reddened; her blood boiled. "I don't understand you, Ingrid! What exactly do you suggest we do?" She looked hard at her contorted expression, then she understood. The simplest solution and the most terrible one. "Oh."

Ingrid sighed. "I don't know how much longer we can keep his condition concealed. It's no longer a guarded secret that he was responsible for Baldur and the other warriors' deaths. Our people will demand justice when they undoubtedly find that out, Elska. They will call for blood, a life for a life. Even now, I hear the whispers in the halls. The castle maidens are scared to go anywhere near your quarters. Everyone heard Úlftýr scream in the night." She closed her eyes, and when she opened them, they were filled with sorrow.

"Baldur was more than our captain. He was a mentor and friend to many Ljósálfar. You know he was well-loved, not to mention a war hero.

You, too, owe a debt of life to him. I can't let his and the brethren of his platoon's demise go unpunished."

Elska took in a shuddering breath. "Do you mean to have Úlftýr executed?" Elska asked in a low voice.

"No! I don't… I don't know." Ingrid admitted. "I am still hopeful we won't come to that. If the truth does come out, I will do what I can to save him; even exile will be better than death." Ingrid felt a pang of guilt. "Either way, I won't let my brother become a spectacle for the whole kingdom to see and especially for Deirdra to marvel at. If something is done, it will be dealt with in private-" her voice broke; she put her hand to her mouth and placed the other on the wall for support. "I don't want to have to do this, but we have to consider at least the possibility of locking him up." She looked at Elska. "In his current state, he is a danger to himself and the Ljósálfar around him. As Queen, I must put the good of my people first, even at the expense of my own flesh and blood."

Elska clenched her fists, her body trembling with rage. "He was only the *King* because you refused the position in the first place, *Queen Ingrid*." She yelled, startling even herself, but she did not pity the Queen.

Tears began streaming down her face, "*You* ignored your responsibility then, and now Úlftýr is suffering for it," she choked out. "And instead of coming up with a way to help him, you try to make the problem disappear. And Úlftýr along with it."

Elska's tone was stern and accusing. "I won't let you treat him like an animal even if you think he acts like one. It's still him inside, even if you refuse to see it." She took a breath. "I understand that it would have been easier for you if he died in his long torturous sleep or became a savage beast, uncontrollable and ferocious; then, all you had to do was hunt him down. But he is here under your roof, hurting and trusting that at least his family will be by his side."

She turned and marched to the door. She stopped her hand on the handle and turned back to look at Ingrid.

"You underestimate the lengths I will go to save him," Elska said darkly.

She turned back to the door and swung it open. Ingrid knew better than to try and stop her.

"I hope for both our sake that I won't ever have to find out exactly how far," she said.

CHAPTER 27
THE VISION OF MURTAGH

I would have laughed if the situation wasn't this dire," Markian said bitterly.

He still sat behind the throne as he had done throughout the emotional exchange between Ingrid and Elska. "I advised you not to include her in this decision," Markian said, getting up. He stepped into the candlelight, his once bright eyes sunken, a look of sadness etched on his face.

"And I told you that I had to consult her, Markian," Ingrid said, her step heavy while she made her way to the throne. "She is the only person Úlftýr lets anywhere near him right now."

"Love blinds one to the truth," Markian said. "You didn't really expect her to agree with you. To lock your brother up means to give up to him, and this strong-headed maiden is unwilling to do both."

Ingrid sat down and looked at the darkening valley outside the window.

Markian sighed. "If I had a chance to bring Hoder or Baldur back, I would have taken it in a heartbeat - Elska will not relinquish her fight."

Markian looked at the wall. Ingrid told him what was up there until Úlftýr went mad. Where once there were antlers, now loomed the discolored shadow of the mount they were on.

When Markian returned from the Ice Lands and learned of Baldur's death from his troops, he demanded Ingrid tell him all that transpired between Baldur and the chosen King before Ingrid assumed the throne.

"My Queen, you have an obligation to make the right choice for our people," Markian said. "You did not see what I saw in the Ice Lands, and you did not feel the end of all life in the air. If the darkness I witnessed is within your brother now, this kingdom, your kingdom, is no longer safe. Not until Úlftýr is gone. I cannot fathom a scenario where he lives and we remain out of harm's way. Especially if the means invoked to curse Úlftýr shall sway him to that witch's side."

Ingrid looked at him grimly. "I acknowledge your council, Markian. I will not insult you by diminishing the time you spent in exile to heal the cursed land standing so close to our borders. I know the journey you endured to make it back and your desire to stop our home from being desecrated by the blood of our people hardened you to see our predicament ending in any positive way." Ingrid sighed. "However, it is my right and obligation to take charge of the situation as I see fit, and the decision of what to do with Úlftýr shall ultimately be one that I will have to make and live with for the rest of my time" Ingrid concluded.

"Forgive my insolence, but I do not see you take charge of your brother, my Queen. He remains free to roam around the kingdom and kill at will."

Markian bowed his head to Ingrid, knowing he walked a thin line between council and insult. "Baldur almost perished when he rescued us from the Ice Lands. Then, he died to protect you in Islandia, where our people were meant to be safe." Markian clenched his fists. "And the one who did it, I know, was both a companion and a protégé to Baldur."

Ingrid shook her head. "Without Úlftýr standing by Baldur's side, the voyage that took our people to safety would not have been possible," she said.

"I do not diminish the involvement of the prince had in our salvation. I am sympathetic to his circumstances. I remember him. I know there was honor in his heart. But tell me truthfully, would you have permitted anyone other than Úlftýr to live after such a crime, no matter the good he did before, *Queen Ingrid*?" Markian lashed in anger and immediately stopped; he had gone too far.

The answer, however, was evident in Ingrid's eyes.

"Úlftýr owes this kingdom a debt of blood." Markian declared, deciding he had nothing to lose now. "I do not want to think that the colony I sent back here would have been better off taking their chances against the mortals in the Ice Lands."

Ingrid glared at Markian. "Make no mistake, scholar. The only reason I allow such insolence from your lips is in Baldur's memory and your undoubtful grief." She let her right hand rest against her forehead, and her shoulders quivered.

"Elska is right," Ingrid muttered.

"What?" Markian blinked.

"She is right; I am to blame," Ingrid raised her eyes to meet Markian's. "I neglected my duty and supported Father's decision to put Úlftýr on the throne when my brother didn't want the position. Even though I knew how destructive his powers were, I thought I could keep his abilities in check. I know that if it were me, Deirdra had cast her dark spell on, none of this would have happened. I would have just died. That is why," she got up, "I will not put my brother to death. I must believe; I must try to save him, even if I must take his place in the underworld as I should have done from the start."

Elska sat in the great library. Being there among the books had become second nature to her.

Cream and crimson-colored candles bled on the wooden table she sat by, illuminating the mountains of books she had combed through repeatedly in search of what Elska was sure she had missed.

"Mmm…" She looked at the dancing flames, the fire mesmerizing, the shadows the candles created in the dark corners of the library, watching her with ominous eyes. "This is wrong, this is all wrong," Elska muttered, "I cannot concentrate here."

She placed three of the smaller candles into an iron lantern, gathered a few of the hefty tomes, and decided to set out to the one place she felt at peace. Besides, in the arms of a past Úlftýr, her favorite reading nook on the bottom floor invited her with its warmth, promising to shield her from a dark world.

She was about to close another book from the pile before her when she saw it.

"By the Yggdrasil!" She exclaimed and put the lantern close to the yellowish pages. There it was — The Othala rune. "A rune of heritage and strength." Elska read. "She *was* interrupted!" Elska banged her hand against the table, triumphed. "Deirdra didn't finish the spell just as I thought." It all made sense now.

Elska was sure that Deirdra attempted to seize Úlftýr's powers, his essence laced with King's blood. Through his vitality, she must have planned to take possession of the Kingdom. But she was interrupted — the spell was incomplete; the rune was broken.

The misshapen symbol Deirdra had carved into Úlftýr's skin had divided his soul, removed the pure portion of his abilities, and awakened the embodiment of corruption within him.

"I must let Ingrid know!" She turned to leave in a rush and screamed. The fire from the candles in her lantern grew before her eyes. A surge of bright orange flame emerged, and Deirdra, along with a large, scarred mortal man, materialized before her.

"Hel…!" Elska endeavored to yell, but the scarred man moved forward at an inhuman speed to stop her.

He drove his fist into her stomach, knocking the breath out of her. He circled Elska while she was doubled over and seized her hair.

"You…!" The scars on Elska's arm burned.

The scarred man. While she only saw his flitting image as he grabbed her, she knew him instantly. He haunted her nightmares even now after years had passed. A cold sweat washed over her; she could hardly force her limbs to move. Shaking, Elska turned her attention to Deirdra. "How…?" Elska rasped. "How did you know I am on to you?"

Deirdra smiled. She gestured to the lanterns hung from the balconies of the library.

"My little flames told me."

Elska opened her mouth to scream, but the brute holding her clamped his other hand on her mouth while she attempted to claw herself free. The scarred man yanked Elska's head up and forced her to face Deirdra.

"Before I left, I made sure to leave my mark in blood on every fireplace and torch in the castle. You would know something about blood magic, right, *Snow Maiden*?" Elska bit her lip, her eyes aflame with pure hate.

"Now, Princess," Deirdra spoke in an ominous tone. "Why don't we agree you won't be divulging your discovery to anyone." Deirdra raised her hand and opened her palm.

Elska was allowed a glimpse of the white powder she held before Deirdra moved her hand closer to Elska and blew the crushed seeds into her face.

Unable to move or cover her nose, Elska felt the toxins force their way into her airways. Tears streamed down her face.

"Don't cry, Princess," Deirdra brushed her hand against Elska's cheek. "I will not take your life in such a cowardly manner. It is but Devil's Breath." Deirdra laughed at Elska's widened eyes. "You know what the drug is about to do to you, don't you, Princess? Don't fight it. Soon, you will have no choice but to obey my every command."

Little by little, the fight diminished within Elska until she was completely drained of her free will. Elska's hands dropped to her side, and her face, still wet with tears, went blank.

"Hmm…" Deirdra hummed. "Don't think I haven't tried this on your lover. And so many times on the king while they slept. Unfortunately, the great serpent protects them; the royal blood dipped in legend prevented them from falling under such a spell."

She looked into Elska's eyes. Her pupils were dilated, completely obscuring the jade of her eyes. In places where her irises were still visible, it looked as if her pupils bled in red human blood.

Deirdra gestured to Thunaer to release Elska.

"Lucky for me, you are still not bound to him, so you have no such protection. Now," Deirdra said and kissed Elska's slightly parted lips. "Let us see if, with this Princess, we can catch a Prince." She snaked her arms, one around Thunaer's waist and one around Elska's, and scourged her path out the way she came.

Úlftýr woke up with the scent of human blood still prominent in the air. He knew that he should not reveal the origin of his new blades to Elska or Ingrid for the time being. Or ever.

There was no need to worry them further regarding his behavior. One that even he could not fully understand.

The castle was eerily quiet when Úlftýr left his bed chamber and stalked down to the inner courtyard.

He walked up to the stone table. Before the horrific events that had made this a place of mourning, the Ljósálfar would gather the first harvest of the season here. The music would play, and the maidens danced, rejoicing in another year of blessed harvest.

Úlftýr traced his fingers along the cracks in the stone slab. An image of Baldur, dead in a bed of roses, brought tears to his eyes.

"Why do you intrude on my solitude?" Úlftýr asked and turned.

Murtagh stepped out of the shadows. "We need to talk," Murtagh, the captain of the King's ill-fated ship, said as he walked along the wall's perimeter.

Úlftýr looked up - Ingrid was watching him from the throne room window. *'She would not be able to see Murtagh from where she stood,'* Úlftýr thought. *'I wonder if Murtagh knows this.'*

Úlftýr nodded to his sister and stepped into the castle's shadows, disappearing from Ingrid's sight. Murtagh stopped and gazed at him.

A pulse of recognition thundered through Úlftýr, an image that came alive from within his nightmares. A snake slithered across his memory.

"Your eyes, I know your eyes," Úlftýr muttered, meeting the radiant violet of Murtagh's irises. "You are not Murtagh."

"No, not in the way you might have known him." The strange álfur confirmed.

"Is the real Murtagh dead?" Úlftýr asked.

"Yes."

"Did you kill him?"

"No. But he pledged his body and soul to me before he perished, so I was granted the window I needed to claim his form."

Úlftýr breathed and asked the question weighing on him since he had begun to suspect something rotten was amid Murtagh's miraculous return.

"Are my mother and father gone?"

"Mmm…" Murtagh tapped his lip. "They are in the realm of the great serpent now." He answered.

'Well, that wasn't a yes,' Úlftýr frowned.

"Who are you?" Úlftýr narrowed his eyes.

"You know who I am," the creature wearing Murtagh's skin replied. "You have known me for centuries."

"I do not know you. Quit playing games with me and tell me the truth. Now!" Úlftýr stepped forward, his shadow growing against the wall. Úlftýr was not surprised to see it took the shape of a wolf.

"This is no game, Úlftýr," Murtagh replied, unfazed by Úlftýr's threat. "However, you are not yet ready to fully accept the truth, and we are running out of time."

"Ready for what? What is going to happen? Answer me!"

Úlftýr launched at him, and Murtagh didn't even attempt to move. Úlftýr grabbed Murtagh by the neck, lifted him from the ground, and thrust him into the bricks behind him, leaving a deep dent in the Blackstone from the force of the impact.

Murtagh looked at him, Úlftýr's assault not bothering him at all. He was expecting this sort of reaction.

"Tell me," Úlftýr said in a low tone.

"I won't tell you, but I will show you." Murtagh extended his hands to him; one covered Úlftýr's eyes, and the other rested against his forehead.

Úlftýr's half-lidded eyes emanated a blinding light, and the rune carved into his brow ignited. He opened his mouth to shout, and then his consciousness soared. He was no longer in Islandia.

"The Ice Lands?" Úlftýr found himself hovering in place over the seemingly barren land.

He looked to his left and gasped - Murtagh was beside him, but he was different somehow. Pale blue scales shone through his skin.

"You..."

"Do not be alarmed." Murtagh's voice rang in his mind.

"I know you," Úlftýr whispered. "Why? Why, if you were still here, seeing everything, knowing everything, why haven't you saved Hoder??"

"I wanted to come to his aid," The serpent, wearing Murtagh's face, replied. "Before your awakening, I was drained of my strength. I could do no more than guide his way home through the waves and stump the loss of his blood until he was back into familial hands."

Úlftýr cried out. He put his hand to his mouth, his eyes wide open. How cruel fate can be?

"Watch." Murtagh raised his arm. Úlftýr followed his gaze.

Not far from where they stood mid-air, a golden figure appeared.

It was a large warrior who wore a gold-winged helmet. The helmet was conical in shape with a nose guard, so Úlftýr couldn't quite make out his face.

Clad in metal-plated lamellar armor made of small rectangular plates of gold and adorned by a crimson cape, the golden warrior welcomed a number of mortal-filled boats coming into view on the waves. His seeing left eye flashed in golden light.

Bronze-skinned dauðadýr occupied the sea-bound vessels. Most had pale red hair and thick beards, some fairer than others. They all wore fur capes and tweed and linen pants bound by leather straps, topped with makeshift armor of thick padded leather tunics.

The mortals were casting their nets. Through the waves, Úlftýr recognized what it was that they were hunting. Walruses, they were after the sea creatures' ivory.

"Land!" One of the grave-bound savages shouted, spotting the elevated coastline. The ships docked by the shore of the Ice Lands shortly after.

They broke camp and scouted the island. For a while, the mortals seemed content spending their time on the beach. They sent out several parties daily to fish and hunt the areas around them and regarded the Ljósálfar settlement as a part of the land when they stumbled upon it.

That all changed with the arrival of the golden warrior.

Úlftýr took note of his patience. The golden warrior let the Ljósálfar settlement get relatively comfortable with the strange, somewhat similar creatures that roamed the coastline.

The golden warrior seemed to have been waiting for Úlftýr's people to lower their guard before he revealed himself to the men in the camp on the beach.

Several weeks into the mortals' expedition, the golden warrior appeared out of the fog. A flash of golden light from his left eye foretold his arrival. He was mounted on a large black steed whose muzzle was smeared with blood after it had feasted on the walrus carcasses the dauðadýr had piled up some way out of their campground. To his saddle was lashed a wooden shield with intertwined serpents.

He rode into their encampment, a giant warrior with a gold winged helmet, conical shaped with a nose guard, followed by two large growling hounds.

His long, white beard bellowed in the wind. He dismounted, and Úlftýr took note of the two mistletoe spears that were strapped to his back.

Two massive black crows appeared and were soaring above them in the sky.

All the dauðadýr fell to the ground and bowed to the golden warrior. They called him the all-father, lord, and God. The golden warrior removed his helm. Úlftýr gasped. He already knew Bileygr was a traitor by choosing Deirdra's side but could not fathom that Bileygr had orchestrated the attack on the settlement.

'*Who was this being?!*' Úlftýr was distraught at how much he still could not understand.

Bileygr's one eye flashed regarding the mortals. They bowed to him and worshiped him. The mortals built a giant pyre and hunted for a fresh game of bear and wolf. After the animals were caught, the grave-bound slaughtered them and burned their remains as a tribute in a pyre.

Bileygr raised his arms and commanded the ash of the sacrifices made to him to rise from the flames and seed the ground.

Yellowish, bell-shaped blossoms with purple threads in the stamp and fuzzy leaves sprouted from the soil, followed by small mud-colored mushrooms with a mucked damp finish to their caps.

The mortals were thrust into a frenzy. Climbing over each other, they grabbed at the magical plants that sprouted before their eyes, pushing and fighting each other, their filthy hands reaching for the poison.

Those who remained standing or sprawled on the ground after they ingested the substances did so after they shed their clothes, pulled on the wolf and bearskins they had slain earlier, and growled like the animals they felt their spirits had become.

Bileygr ordered the abominations to rise and follow him. With malicious intent clear in his eye, he led the mass of neither man nor beasts to the Ljósálfar settlement.

In Úlftýr's vision, the scholar Markian sat by a roaring bonfire in an outdoor communal fire pit.

Alongside him, several others were busy with different activities; some made food and carved utensils.

Markian held a wood slab in his hands, and on it, Úlftýr recognized his family crest etched in color: two green serpents intertwined around a blue rose.

He was showing it to a group of younglings.

A Ljósálfar resembling Baldur walked past them with his livestock, intending to lead them to their grazing field.

He smiled at Markian.

For the quietest and the most horrible moment, the dauðadýr faced the pale-faced, tall, beautiful humanoids, and then, the one-eyed álfur bellowed at them to attack, to claim this land as their own.

"Markian, the younglings!" Hoder shouted. He was the first to notice the mortals at the edge of the camp.

Chaos erupted. The Ljósálfar fled their attackers while the dauðadýr pursued them—butchering, slaughtering, slaying, and cutting down any Ljósálfar that got in their path.

Úlftýr was horrified to witness the dauðadýr slaughter not only the grown males of his people but females and their offspring as well, the innocents who begged for their lives and were unable to defend themselves.

Bileygr directed his horse into a blood-tainted field. The snout of the animal was soon coated by the blue blood that covered the ground.

Those who remained alive after the slaughter fled their settlement, and the Ljósálfar journeyed into the mountains.

Úlftýr wanted to shout for Hoder to turn back when the courageous warrior volunteered to return home for help.

Úlftýr understood why he volunteered to go. Hoder had to ensure the safety of those who followed him, a true sign of a leader, and he had to ensure Markian was safe. For the briefest of moments, he was also secure in his lover's arms, and then it was over.

Úlftýr watched Hoder saying goodbye to Markian. They embraced, and Markian mouthed words of love to Hoder while their heads were bowed against each other. Úlftýr's heart clenched when Hod kissed Markian's tears away. Úlftýr knew that this would be the last time Markian saw Hoder alive.

Úlftýr didn't want to see the mortals capture Hoder. He didn't want to see him roaming through his cabin, searching for a map Hoder knew he had to bring if he attempted to return to Islandia.

The dauðadýr pursued him to the beach. Their arrows pierced his flesh. Miraculously, he endured several direct hits to commandeer one of their small boats and propel it into the sea. Úlftýr almost missed the sharpened axe flung at his outstretched exposed leg.

He averted his eyes when the blood poured from the severed limb. Still, he could not drown out Hoder's cries of horrified surprise and then heartbreaking anguish and his collapsing, his body hitting the bottom of the boat with a sickening wet thud while the waves carried him home.

They followed him, attempting to crash into Hoder's vessel before he made port, but something took them from the deep; something large in deep purple and shimmering blues slithered from under the waves and took out most of them before they had a chance to pursue Hoder further.

"You protected him… You brought him home." Úlftýr said.

"I've had enough." Úlftýr breathed. "Release me! I don't want to watch anymore."

"You must." Murtagh's voice rang in his mind. "You have to know the truth."

Úlftýr turned to Murtagh, but instead of the youth he knew, a silver serpent with purple nebulas shimmering through his scales lay twisted in front of him.

The heavy serpent coiled around Úlftýr, pinning his limbs with the force of its massive body.

Úlftýr's vision blurred, and the following vision he witnessed petrified him.

The sunset left the survivors exposed to the elements. They broke camp in the mountains, wounded and distraught. Many were lost, and many more grieved for their lost loved ones.

The golden warrior changed his form to an unfamiliar álfur. Wearing the new face, he stepped into the camp with the rest. In the cover of darkness, he made his way to a blond female that strangely resembled Deirdra, sitting isolated in deep mourning, some ways from the fire the survivors built.

Her eyes widened with recognition when she saw the golden warrior in his new form. Úlftýr understood Bileygr had changed his appearance to resemble a loved one she had recently lost.

The blond álfur took the hand he extended to her, allowed him to pull her up, and followed him, dazed into the tree line.

In the form of her husband, Bileygr grabbed hold of her dress, yanked her forward, and crushed his jaw against hers. She only had time to yelp as he bruised her lips, forcing his tongue into her mouth.

He tore away from the kiss and turned her. The one-eyed warrior thrust the female's body against the cold ground. Firmly pressed against her, his hands pulled at her clothes and groped for her skin.

He took her then.

The warrior's hold on the woman was rough and unkind, his movements erratic, one hand clamped harshly over her mouth to stop her from screaming while the other held her down.

Bileygr left the blond female unconscious where she lay. Later, she would be among the survivors that Baldur's expedition brought home.

That night on the beach, Bileygr had ordered his followers to seize the female, and Úlftýr was horrified to find out that she was held in his private chambers inside the castle. She was subdued and pregnant.

"Deirdra's mother…?"

Still a captive, she went into labor. Even then, the golden warrior didn't see fit to release her from her chains.

An eerie luminous form hovered over the female as her laborers progressed.

The deity flashed Úlftýr a knowing smile as if she knew he was there, trapped inside this atrocious memory.

Something in Úlftýr growled and screamed at the sight of her. It was like a feeling of acid that burned his soul. A prominent part of Úlftýr's being knew this malicious creature.

The newborn in the memory was pulled out of the chained woman, and the little girl made her first cry, announcing her arrival into this world. The luminous spirit swept past Úlftýr, entered the child, and settled within her. The girl went quiet, her eyes flashing green.

Horrifically enough, her mother's body gave out the moment it was over.

Bileygr cradled Deirdra in his arms in a rare show of affection and left with her.

His followers dragged her dead mother away and burned her body in the woods to leave no trace of the atrocities they committed.

Unable to breathe, Úlftýr was pulled forward in time to another memory of the serpent.

He found himself on a boat. He looked up and beheld Bileygr in the sky, adorned by his golden armor, sitting on his horse.

The sky darkened, roaring thunder like the march of a thousand soldiers ripping through the air.

Úlftýr screamed when what Murtagh had made him witness became clear to him.

Using powers Úlftýr didn't understand, Bileygr raised his arms, summoned the lightning, held it above his head, and finally released it. The blinding light engulfed them, tearing King Freyr's ship apart.

Markian arrived at the courtyard just as Úlftýr bellowed in pain.

He witnessed a shadow envelop Úlftýr in its dark grasp, coiled around him like a serpent, and then released him to fall to the ground.

In a moment, the dark figure that held Úlftýr captive vanished, taking on its corporeal form, and Murtagh helped Úlftýr back to his feet.

Úlftýr's shadow grew into that of a wolf while Murtagh's stretched on the ground in the form of a serpent. "Do I have your trust?" Murtagh asked.

Úlftýr did not answer.

Markian drew his sword, stalking closer.

"Release my master before it is too late."

Markian heard Murtagh say. *'Whatever this dark entity desires, I will not let it come to pass!'* Markian thought and charged.

"Úlftýr! Behind you!" Murtagh yelled at the sight of Markian advancing toward them.

Markian hurled his sword at Úlftýr, the blade stopping mid-air before it made contact, repelled by dark green energy that surrounded Úlftýr.

Úlftýr growled; the rune on his forehead ignited in crimson light. His fangs descended, and his claws came out. With an explosion of power, he threw Markian back.

Úlftýr advanced towards him, snarling.

"Don't."

Úlftýr whipped back at Murtagh, who laid a calming hand on his shoulder. "Don't kill him," Murtagh repeated.

'Please,' the whisper was barely audible, but Úlftýr knew Baldur's voice instantly.

Úlftýr's fangs retracted, and his claws diminished. The dark energy surrounding Úlftýr deemed to have a dull glow along with the rune on his forehead. He nodded sharply and shook the hand off his shoulder.

He stepped forward, stood over Markian, who looked at him terrified, grabbed his tunic collar, lifted Markian's torso off the ground, and punched him hard in the face.

Markian went limp.

Úlftýr bent down and picked him up, throwing Markian's unconscious form over his shoulder. With Murtagh in tow, Úlftýr carried Markian into the throne room. No one dared to stop him when he kicked the door open.

"What the…?" Ingrid got up from the throne.

Úlftýr walked into the chamber. He dropped the scholar at Ingrid's feet. "I thought I asked you to have courage, sister." Úlftýr looked hard into Ingrid's astonished eyes. "Have you sent this warrior to do the dirty work for you? This álfur has just attempted to take my life." He gestured at Markian, who lay unmoving on the floor.

"Is he…?" Ingrid gulped.

"He lives." Murtagh stepped forward.

Ingrid looked at Murtagh and drew her sword. "You are not Murtagh. Úlftýr! Step away from him!" Úlftýr looked at Murtagh; he didn't move.

"Úlftýr! Look at his eyes!" Ingrid gestured frantically. "There is something wrong with him. Murtagh never had violet eyes!"

"I know," Úlftýr answered.

Ingrid stumbled back in astonishment. "You… And you still trust him?! What has he done to you?" Ingrid shouted.

"How about what you tried to do to me?" Úlftýr looked at her. "How about the fact that I gave everything for our people? Where are the thanks I never received? Where is the appreciation? Instead of shaming my actions, you could thank me for keeping all of you ungrateful people safe?"

Ingrid stared at him.

Úlftýr rolled his eyes. "Thank you, Úlftýr, for putting your life on the line to keep us safe."

"Thank you, Úlftýr-"

"Save it." Úlftýr cut her off. "It has no meaning when I have to guide you to acknowledge my contributions."

"Why do you do this?" Ingrid asked. "Why do you need to make me feel unappreciative of your deeds and sacrifices?"

"Well, aren't you?" Úlftýr raised his eyebrow.

"No." Ingrid shook her head. "Not everything is as bleak as you make it to be. Just because you are in this dark place right now doesn't mean the whole world is. I love you, and I appreciate you. I am grateful to you for stepping up when I was too weak to do it."

Ingrid could see Úlftýr no longer paid attention to her. Judging from his expression, she could have been talking to the air for all he cared.

The lit candles in the throne room flickered.

"Are you doing that?" Úlftýr asked Murtagh.

"No." Murtagh's eyes were focused on the throne. "She does."

Flames danced across the room, bouncing from candle to candle until they settled on the throne. Deirdra appeared in a swirl of bright orange flame.

"Hello." She smiled.

Ingrid stepped forward. "What are you doing here, you wench? Don't you value your life?"

Deirdra's smile widened. She ignored Ingrid and instead looked at Úlftýr.

"I see my charm agrees with you." She got up and slowly approached the fireplace.

"If you are here to make me an offer, you are wasting your breath," Úlftýr growled, and Deirdra chuckled.

"Oh no, dear Prince, I accept your rejection except... Aren't you missing something?"

Úlftýr narrowed his eyes. "What are you saying?"

Deirdra gestured towards the fireplace. "Aren't you missing *someone?*"

The logs burst into blue and orange flames. An image appeared in the fire. A white temple stood in an open area under what seemed to be the maw of a volcano.

"The rose temple." Ingrid recognized the large serpent columns.

Only the Elders were allowed entrance. Built at the command of the great ice serpent, the temple stood as a monument to the creators of the first blue rose; only there could the great serpent be summoned in a time of dire need.

As the image of the temple drew near, an easily recognizable figure appeared before them. Úlftýr gasped. He no longer paid any attention to his sister. The one image he was focused on was Elska's.

She stood chained by iron shackles to one of the serpent columns. Her hands were lifted above her head, the chains that bound her held in the mouth of the great snake, and her eyes stared blankly forward.

"What have you done?" Úlftýr demanded.

"Nothing that can't be remedied," Deirdra assured him. "If you are willing to do as I say."

"What do you want?" Úlftýr shouted.

Deirdra laughed. "Such a temper. It's simple, Úlftýr. Elska and I will be waiting for you at the top of Eyjafjallajökull mountain. If you are not there in three days - I know you, you will be there." She said, laughing. She disappeared in a swirl of bright orange flames.

The image of Elska burned out along with her.

Úlftýr screamed in rage. The rune on his brow ignited, and green mist coiled around him like a snake.

"We are leaving. Now." He told Murtagh in a deep voice that was not his own.

"Úlftýr," Ingrid blocked his path. "You are better than this! Stay, and we will find a solution together."

Úlftýr snarled with bitter laughter. "No, I tried to be better for her. But now, Deirdra is going to get exactly what she desires. She will see how much worse I am going to become."

"I would advise you not to bar his way, Queen Ingrid." Murtagh briefly bowed to a distraught Ingrid and went to the door.

Ingrid glared after him. "Please don't trust him, Úlftýr; we must discuss this." Ingrid implored her brother.

"You should have trusted me, how I wished for you to see me, your kin, your blood, and not this monster Deirdra made of me," Úlftýr said, his eyes burning like the fire in the hearth. "Still, hope dies last."

"Guards!" Ingrid yelled, desperate. "I will not let you leave!"

The door burst open, and four armor-clad warriors ran in. They trained their swords at Úlftýr.

"Tell them to let us pass," Úlftýr warned, glancing at Ingrid.

"Do not let them leave!" Ingrid ordered.

Úlftýr sighed. "This is on you."

He looked back at the guards. The form of a massive green snake grew around him. The guards stepped back, the hands that gripped their swords visibly shaking. Úlftýr's eyes flashed angrily, and the energy surrounding him exploded, knocking the guards into the wall outside the throne room.

They crumbled, a heap of barely breathing bodies on the ground.

Úlftýr cast one last look at his sister and walked out, leaving Ingrid to tend to Markian.

CHAPTER 28

THE WILL OF THE OPPRESSED

Úlftýr and Murtagh rode out shortly after. No one else attempted to stop them.

"In different circumstances, I would have enjoyed the journey through my kingdom." He told Murtagh when they exited the city's borders and took to the open road.

The route to the mountain took them through a beautiful valley set in a green gorge covered with wildflowers.

The lush meadow, teeming with wildlife, let out behind an impressive crystal-clear waterfall.

Despite the scenic and open road they were taking, Úlftýr felt confined.

"I have a strange sensation," he rubbed his wrists. "I cannot fathom the feeling slowly taking over my ankles and wrists." He looked at his companion.

"Murtagh, the closer we get to the mountain, the heavier my limbs become. I am familiar with this feeling. The sensation reminds me of cast iron shackles despite me never being restrained in that manner before."

Murtagh kept his silence.

"Is this my past life calling to me?" Úlftýr's eyes flashed in green light.

"You shouldn't take over him like that." Murtagh looked at the being sitting on the horse in Úlftýr's stead, his red hair and green eyes glowing as if engulfed in flames.

"*I am running out of time.*" The being growled.

"If you force yourself upon his soul, both of your minds will shatter under such duress. Allow me the time we need to sway him. Allow him to call to you of his own free will. Release him. Now."

The deity groaned. "*If Úlftýr does not submit to me soon, we and everything else will be lost.*" He breathed in the fresh air as if it was the last time he could do it, and the glow left Úlftýr's body. He slumped forward atop the horse, knocked out from the strain the deity exerted on his body.

When he woke up, Úlftýr looked around him. They had arrived at the mountain's base faster than should have been possible. "How did we get here?" Úlftýr asked, confused. "We just left the city; I-" He looked at the ice-covered cap tower above them. A long chasm led up a rocky terrain into the mountain. "The sky...it's morning? Did we ride through the night?"

"You have, majesty," Murtagh confirmed, a knowing look in his eyes.

Úlftýr decided the matter wasn't worth questioning further.

Shrugging off the haze in his mind, they released the horses by the stream at the foot of the mountain and started the rest of the way up in a steep climb.

"This mountain is alive. Can you feel it?" Úlftýr rubbed his wrists, leaning against the rock face of the mountain, the binding sensation tightening.

The earth quivered beneath their feet. The rune in Úlftýr's forehead ignited, yet he remained in control.

With the red tint over his eyes, Úlftýr observed the lava surge under the ground beneath their feet as if the earth was made of clear glass.

The shape of a man appeared in the rocks. The very same figure he had previously met in a vision while in his ice bath. The giant writhed in pain underground.

The cooled magma rocks in their path all seemed to take the shapes of humanoids. Some Úlftýr recognized from previous lives, some he never encountered before his future.

"Is he the one causing the earthquakes?" Úlftýr asked, looking at the man's form carved into the rock, shifting in and out of existence. He didn't expect Murtagh to give him a clear answer.

"Who is he?" Úlftýr staggered. "Is he-" the name sat on the tip of his tongue, but his memory hadn't allowed him to utter the words.

The solidified magma rocks around him looked like a field of bodies. A limbo opened within him as if he descended back into the underworld. The numerous corpses that lay one atop the other with no identity, no name, reached to him, calling him to join them. A backdrop to hell was there awaiting his shattered soul. "Úlftýr, we are here." Murtagh hissed loudly.

The rocky path ended at the mouth of the volcano. The white serpent temple of the rose lay before them. The sound of stirring lava in the pit beneath the temple churned with indecipherable voices.

"Elska!" Úlftýr bolted forward before Murtagh could stop him.

She stood bound to the column with her arms raised above her head, true to Deirdra's fire vision.

Úlftýr moved close. What he thought were chains turned out to be entrails; actual human entrails solidified to rock. "Elska," Úlftýr cupped her cheeks and gently lifted her face. "Elska?"

She breathed deeply; her eyes fluttered open. Her gaze was unfocused, searching; she raised her eyes, and they seemed to clear when she met Úlftýr's.

"N...o!" She rasped. "No!" She pulled at her restraints, frantic. "No, Úlftýr! You must leave!"

"Úlftýr...!" Murtagh hurried to him.

A loud uproar rose around them. A crush resonated, sounding like an avalanche, followed by a thunderous blast.

Úlftýr turned.

All the stone statues that stood at the base of every column save for Elska's were detaching from the marble, coming alive.

"Murtagh!" Elska called out to him. "I found it! I found the rune Deirdra used! It was incomplete."

Murtagh glanced at Úlftýr and made his way to Elska. He grabbed the bonds that held her but was struck back by an invisible force. "I cannot free you." He panted.

The sky darkened. The air grew hot around them. A deafening sound, like gushing water, roared under their feet. The temple floor split and lava spewed from the cracks.

Elska bit her lip. "Give me your hand." She spoke.

Murtagh raised his hand above hers, and she used her fingers to outline two shapes inside his palm. "Complete the rune and then negate it," Elska said. "Hurry."

A rumble sounded too close to them. Murtagh turned back.

"Úlftýr! Look out!" Murtagh yelled.

In the next moment, he screamed in pain.

Úlftýr whipped his head to where Murtagh stood, but he wasn't standing anymore.

Murtagh lay on the ground, eyes open in shock. A puddle of shimmering blue blood slowly formed around him.

The scarred man, who previously captured Úlftýr at Deirdra's command and unleashed the souls of the dead within him, stood over Murtagh, his massive black blade oozing with blue blood in his grasp.

Úlftýr drew his sword and was met face-to-face with a humanoid statue twice his size. The stone warrior stepped in front of Thunaer. The stone giant swung its massive fist at Úlftýr, who ducked and swung his sword. The metal grazed off the giant, erupting in sparks that rained like falling stars on the temple floor.

The animated statue swung his fists again, colliding with the column Elska was bound to.

Elska screamed.

"No!" Úlftýr jumped to her aid, shielding her from the falling rubble.

"Aghh!" A large rock struck his forehead, knocking him down.

"Úlftýr!" A trickle of blood formed on his brow. "Úlftýr!" She once again pulled at her restraints. She desperately wanted to help him.

Úlftýr pulled himself up, struggling to his feet; he swayed, his mind a haze; he landed on one knee and placed a hand against his forehead. He closed his eyes until he was sure the world stopped spinning and then made another attempt to get himself up again. He glanced over at Murtagh and found the latter staring at him. Clearly, Murtagh couldn't move, yet his violet eyes flashed, and a surge of energy engulfed Úlftýr.

Murtagh coughed and closed his eyes. The familiar green mist rose and set against Úlftýr's skin. The stone giant attacked. The roil of power rose within Úlftýr, Murtagh's icy force flowing through him. Úlftýr sensed a surge of lead in his veins. His skin solidified like a glacier; he felt heavier but simultaneously more resilient.

Úlftýr jumped up, landed on the advancing creature's head with a bellow, and wrenched the giant's head off.

The beast crumbled into a pile of rubble. Úlftýr didn't have time to celebrate his victory.

The sound of stones grinding against stone alerted him to the serpents from the other columns slithering, coming to life. A marble reptile made a rumbling sound, zeroed its cracked eyes at Úlftýr, and launched at him. The snake's sharp stone fangs crashed into his body and tore at his skin. Another serpent launched at him with such ferocity it rammed its head into Úlftýr's stomach and sent him flying, skidding to a stop at Elska's feet.

Elska was crying.

Light-headed and disoriented, Úlftýr attempted to stand up. The green mist that somewhat protected his body had dissipated completely, ebbing little by little with each of Murtagh's dying breaths.

Úlftýr spat blood on the marble tiles. He stood his back against Elska, surrounded by stone serpents.

The mountain began to smoke, and ash covered the ground. Thunaer advanced towards him.

Úlftýr looked around him. He had one shot.

His sword lay some way away among the rubble. He launched at it and yelled in pain and surprise.

Bileygr appeared in a mass of blinding lightning, illuminating the temple with his golden armor. A large wooden spear soared out of the light, giving Úlftýr no time to react.

Úlftýr fell to his knees, Bileygr's mistletoe spear embedded deep in his abdomen. He opened his mouth to shout, but no voice came out to relieve him.

The spear paralyzed Úlftýr. His limbs refused to budge, but he felt everything.

One of the stone serpents coiled its tail around Úlftýr's neck and flung him onto a stone altar in the middle of the temple, knocking his breath out from the force of the impact. Úlftýr groaned.

Familiar footsteps alerted him to her arrival before her vile face loomed over him.

"Hello, Úlftýr," Úlftýr wanted to cry out when Deirdra's hand caressed his cheek.

Deirdra smiled. She showed him a chained iron neck restraint, holding it before his face and marveling at his disgust before she fitted the manacle on him.

Deirdra screwed the clasp tighter until Úlftýr gasped for air.

She then took hold of his wrists and ankles and bound them with heavy steel cuffs. When she was done, she pulled his limbs apart until he laid a spread eagle on the stone table and sealed the remainder of the chain under the slab.

The scarred man handed Deirdra a small, intricately carved dagger with a bone handle. She raised it in front of her. With nothing to do but lay with his mouth open in a silent scream, Úlftýr felt her carve additional lines into the symbol she previously etched onto his forehead.

Bileygr stepped forward, an ancient tome in his hands. He opened the book and began to read.

Old words, ancient like the sands of time, rang through the air.

Archaic words echoed through Úlftýr's mind. The sun eclipsed in his eyes, and day became night for him.

Úlftýr's eyes burned in blazing light; he opened his mouth, and the howl of a tormented beast echoed through the mountain.

Elska screamed, fighting her restraints, blood trickling down her wrists.

The earth began to shake once more. Úlftýr's blood seeped through the wound in his stomach, and it filled the stone table's cracks through the mosaic set on the temple floor and continued trickling down into the stream underneath the mountain.

Fumes of rot and decay rose into the air. The blue roses that grew in the valley withered to ash.

Úlftýr opened his eyes to reveal the darkness. The red orbs of his pupils, along with the radiant white of the sclera, were completely gone. He looked on with the black hollows that were his eyes.

Úlftýr's shadow stretched from him on the temple floor. It grew until it reached Elska. She looked down through tearful eyes at the outline of a great wolf.

Bileygr shed his robes to reveal his golden armor, and the one-eyed warrior pulled his spear out of Úlftýr's stomach. Deirdra stood beside him; she had also undergone a transformation. Her golden hair was set around a crown of antlers. A short white dress, the color of luminous snow, adorned her body. A silver armor topped with grey fur was set on her breasts, and her skin glowed with a bluish sheen.

"He is getting restless." Deirdra mused.

"Soon, this mountain will erupt, his prison chamber will be flooded with magma, and he will be gone," Bileygr answered in a voice that sounded like thunder.

The earthquake intensified, responding to their words. The temple floor split open, and green smoke billowed from the cracks.

Deirdra laughed, the torment of her prisoner amusing her.

"*Úlftýr,*" the deep voice called him out of limbo. "*Úlftýr, you won't save anyone like this. You are going to fail.*"

Úlftýr tightened his grasp around himself, his consciousness craving to close up. He lay in a fetal position, lost in the pit of his mind—gods, how he yearned to stay there.

"*Úlftýr!*"

Inside his consciousness, Úlftýr put his hands over his ears and shrunk into himself further.

"*Úlftýr,*" the voice insisted a little softer. "***Deirdra won't have my powers as she intends. She will accomplish the destruction of the serpent that holds the world from being remade anew.***"

"It hurts," Úlftýr choked. "It hurts; please, just let me rest."

"***Your kingdom is in peril, Úlftýr,***" the voice sounded desperate. "***And when this mountain spews destruction into the sky, evil will prevail.***"

Úlftýr shook his head. "Please, just let me die. I don't want to fight anymore."

"***When this mountain goes, so will we, and so will the one you love.***" The silhouette of a being not too different from himself stood before him in his mind. Úlftýr could not determine if the creature was álfur or mortal. A redhead deity with alabaster skin and bright emerald eyes crouched beside him in the cage his soul created.

"*Úlftýr,*" the being said in his head, his lips sewn shut and wrists bound in heavy shackles. "*Úlftýr, you must decide now. The one you call Deirdra is my tormenter; my warden possesses the body,* **you know. She kept me captive for centuries but could not wield my powers. I will die,**

Úlftýr, and the soul of this world will die with me. Her reign will be one of chaos."

A swirl of orange mist circled Deirdra and Bileygr. The temple began to crumble around them.

Elska's screams borrowed into Úlftýr's tortured mind. He knew all that Deirdra and Bileygr craved was power. They did not care if the rest of the world burned in their wake. "Úlftýr."

Úlftýr felt a grasp on his hand attached to his natural body outside the oblivion.

Murtagh, still alive, had crawled and pulled himself up with difficulty against the stone table Úlftýr lay on, his legs barely holding him up.

Deirdra and Bileygr, caught in a summoning trance, paid him no attention.

Murtagh grasped Úlftýr, his hands warm with blood. One held his shackled hand, and the other rested against his forehead.

"Úlftýr, listen to my master; heed his request. Trust in your strength. Together, we can save this world, set the master of your powers free."

"*Watch your future unfold before you*," The deity trapped within the mountain willed the last of his strength into a powerful vision.

"See the truth written in the stars," Murtagh said. He put his bloody fingers on the rune on Úlftýr's forehead. He completed the rune as Elska instructed, and Úlftýr stopped breathing; in the next moment, the mark lifted from him, and Murtagh outlined a different shape. It glowed bright green as the new rune embedded in his forehead, and Úlftýr gasped for air.

Úlftýr screamed, the rune ignited, and a supernova exploded inside the hollow of his eyes.

Úlftýr floated above the ocean. Underneath him stood a metal structure with a rickety platform set on four columns in the middle of the sea. A massive blast rocked the compound, sending waves of metal pieces and debris flung into the air.

Tar-like substances began bleeding into the water, spreading fast. Any animal caught in the vicious vial substance wavered and perished, unable to move or escape. The fish drifted dead to the surface; the birds suffocated on dry land, their wings and bodies glistening with the toxic viscous substance.

Without a way to stop it, Úlftýr was thrust into another place. A live city spread before him.

Large cooling towers stood before him with smoke that bellowed out into the sky. Inside, the water boiled, red flashing lights indicating the pending catastrophe.

He sensed the energy rising before the middle of the structure imploded. A whole city around the blast area shook and was encased in virulent energy he felt to his core.

It greatly affected mortals, sparing no age. They rapidly became sick, vomiting, defecating, and losing consciousness as the poisoned air penetrated them. Their skin degraded. Inside their bodies, the blood became thinner, red patches of blistering ulcers appeared, their hair fell out, and unusual growth began to appear and spread inside them, slowly claiming their lives.

Nature was not spared in this manufactured disaster; the forest around the infected city changed color, a noxious orange tint claimed the trees, and the animals became large and crazed.

Úlftýr knew nothing good could ever survive there. "Please…" Úlftýr whispered, "Let this nightmare end." But it wasn't over.

Another vision pulled him close.

Another city, another two more major explosions, but these were different. Evil pulsated within them. The force emanating from them didn't feel like anything he had seen before—the rapid release of energy followed by a raging fire and two massive mushroom clouds. Blinding light imploded inside the limits of two busy cities. People were petrified, and those that remained planted on the spot turned to dust. Their shadows remained etched into the ground. Ash covered every visible surface.

A nightmare scenario. Half the first city was gone in seconds, with rubble and destruction visible everywhere. The second city was flattened, its population perished, and monuments were destroyed. Where there was life a moment before now lay a wasteland of nothing.

'This is war,' Úlftýr thought, 'A war for survival, but who would want to survive to see the aftermath of such a fight?'

In front of his eyes, soldiers marched on the battlefield and sat behind the killing machines in flying metal birds; they attacked with ships and weapons blazing. They died by the millions in trenches and closed-off camps, buildings filled with toxins, behind metal bars and barbed wires.

Úlftýr could not comprehend the sheer number of them that had to be born, so these many would die unnoticed by their human brethren.

The piles of bodies burned on pyres; the stench of death became the thick air you breathe. In front of his eyes, millions lay injured, suffering, and starving while their leaders looked on, their brisk hands signing papers that sent young men to their deaths.

Úlftýr choked from the tears that came and the weight on his chest. He was deposed in different places where the air itself was toxic. These areas were so foul that, instead of air, there was smog. It stung like acid and reeked of sulfur. Úlftýr came to know hell on earth.

Deirdra turned to Murtagh, who stood, barely holding himself up beside Úlftýr. She marched forward and grabbed Úlftýr's other hand.

"You are too late, Jörmungandr," she hissed, enraged. "His fate is sealed, and so is yours."

"I will not let you tear this world apart, Skadi." Murtagh breathed. "It will not be a wasteland akin to his ancestral home."

A green mist shaped like a giant serpent rose from his body to meet the orange haze surrounding Deirdra. It collided in the air and settled on Úlftýr.

"Now, we shall see," Deirdra said in a deep, booming voice.

CHAPTER 29

THE FINAL LIFE

An explosion of color greeted Úlftýr. He stood in a beautiful city; around him were large green trees, black curved rooftops of red-colored shrines in front of him, and behind him, the reflective surface of high glass towers.

Kamo, Aira City, Kagoshima, Japan, 1999

Akira watched the glass towers. The last time he'd been there was right after he left the army.

He stared at his reflection. Most things have stayed the same since then. Ten years. His hair was longer now, black silk he tied back in a ponytail. His face was narrow, with high cheekbones, big honey-colored eyes, and flawless, smooth skin.

The long scar on the side of his face tingled, but the skin still hoped to heal. Akira thought back on the night that changed his destiny. They came for him after sundown and left him no choice.

Singled out for his strength or perhaps in accordance with his family's connections, his older sister delivered his first kill order a few months into his enhanced training and pleaded with him to get it done fast.

At first, he was reluctant to complete his mission. He had met his intended target before, a former friend who had defected from the service, and now Akira knew why.

Akira's hesitations brought a swift retaliation upon him. Orders of this sort were expected to be carried out without question or delay.

They came for him in the night, in the cover of darkness, and dragged him out of his bunk to a shed behind the military compound. When they grabbed him, he didn't yell, didn't attempt to flee, or arouse his bunkmates, for there would be no use in his resistance. He let them gag him with a wet cloth, tie him up with his wrists to a supporting beam, and beat him until stars danced before his eyes and the taste of blood became prominent in his mouth.

When they were done, they cut the ropes that held him up without warning. Akira fell to the floor and spat the wet cloth out of his mouth. He looked up, blinking the tears and dust out of his eyes. A masked man thrust a tanto blade into his hands and whispered an address into his ear.

They released him at the crack of dawn out of the tinted window SUV they drove him in.

The moments after were vivid in Akira's memory.

His former friend, Tatsuo, looked shocked when he opened his door to find Akira on the other side.

"Akira san!" He called with somewhat of an awkward enthusiasm. "I - I wasn't expecting you. What - what happened to your face?" He gestured towards the bruises adoring Akira's cheeks and swollen eyes.

Akira ignored the question. "Good morning, Tatsuo san. Please excuse my rudeness," Akira said, bowing low to acknowledge his Impertinence. "It's just that something came up, and I have to talk to you urgently," Akira said, head still bowed.

"Of course," Tatsuo said and opened the door further, letting his killer in. He was a little shorter in stature compared to Akira, with short brown hair,

a rounder face, and brown eyes. "I don't remember ever telling you where I lived?"

"No, I don't believe you have," Akira confirmed.

A dark shadow passed Tatsuo's face.

"Please forgive my intrusion," Akira said; he took off his shoes and left them at the entrance.

Tatsuo sat on a dark brown mat by the low table in the modest living room. "Are you in some kind of trouble?" He asked.

"Yes, and so are you," Akira replied, his posture tense. "I am ordered to eliminate you." Tatsuo pursed his lips, his expression frozen. "What do you intend to do?" He choked, the answer was clear.

Akira frowned. He sat down before his friend and embraced him. "I am sorry."

Tatsuo tensed up in his grasp. "No, please," he tried to struggle, but Akira was much stronger.

"Please," Tatsuo cried. "I will disappear, I will vanish. You don't have to - "

Akira didn't let him finish. He didn't hear what his former friend was saying anyway. From the moment he walked in, he was in a tunnel; in the end of it was death. All sound rushed out; the lights seemed dimmer. The knife he drove between them was deep in Tatsuo's rib cage, and it carved out a hollow inside Akira's chest.

Tatsuo gurgled, his final words incoherent, and he passed in Akira's arms. After the deed was done, Akira knew that more than one man had died that day.

The initiation of his innocent soul into darkness was complete.

He sat with the body for a while, then put his dead friend on the floor, removed any trace of his visit, and trashed the apartment. Just another unfortunate robbery gone wrong.

The day he met Hikari, he sat in his employer's club, "Mizutamari," on the third floor between the three the club occupied, save for the penthouse where an important family member resides.

The club became a desired hangout for Japanese and foreigners looking for a good time.

It offered delectable cuisine, a world-renowned variety of drinks, and a whiskey lounge on the first floor. The second floor was reserved for dancing and a never-ending party. On the third floor, isolated from the noise, the silver lounge offered private booths and exclusive lavishly decorated rooms for relaxation and private affairs.

A rooftop bar was available only to those in the know, and Akira knew but had no desire to visit.

The large booth he occupied along with several of his comrades, fit for ten people, welcomed the hostesses in minimal Lolita outfits. They entered, carrying trays of meat and meads, dressed in revealing chiffon tops, tiny skirts, and high, over-the-knee socks.

The woman set down the trays and catered around them, but Akira only had eyes for one.

"Come sit by me," Akira beckoned the redhead over. "You're new here, right? I've never seen you before. What is your name?"

The red-haired maiden looked at him, blushed, and whispered, "Hikari, " through lips painted crimson.

They talked for hours, long after the others around them departed either to the private rooms or each to his own home and business.

Hikari told Akira that this was her first time in the big city. She grew up on a farm some five hours away, and after a massive drought that sent half the country scrambling for food, she decided to catch the first train heading toward a better future.

Their relationship began innocently enough. A touch of the wrist when she brought him a drink, the caress of her cheek when she leaned closer, a stolen kiss in a dark hallway until a day came when he revealed to her what he did for a living.

To his surprise, Hikari did not reject him. In fact, from then on, she spent her waking hours worried about the danger he was putting himself in during his missions, wishing for him to find a way to quit.

Akira craved to take her away from the service of the family he worked for and give her the life she deserved.

Akira's many hours spent in the club where Hikari worked caught the eye of a mighty woman.

She kept him on a short leash, controlling him from the shadows, sending him on grueling missions in her service whenever she thought he got too close to the new maiden she employed. The woman, whose name was Dara and who was the daughter of the highest-ranking member of the family, wanted Akira on the street, as her personal bodyguard, and in her bed - to warm her body with his. Dara offered a merger tied by the bonds of marriage between the two families, and when it neared fruition, Akira turned his back on his duty and ran away with his love.

Akira became a Ronin, an outcast who lost the favor and privileges given to him by his master.

He knew the family wouldn't stop looking for him, but he fooled himself into thinking he could keep him and Hikari safe.

His own family tried to convince him to return and ask for penance. They sent messengers pleading to answer their requests. Quickly, though, those requests turned into threats of bodily harm.

Three years have passed since they escaped together and eight months since the last messenger called him home.

Akira wanted to start believing the family had forgotten all about them, but this was not the case.

"Someone is following us," Akira told Hikari one day while they drove through a large city. Akira maneuvered through the streets, but the black car remained persistent on their trail.

Soon, another vehicle joined the pursuit, cornering them into a high parking lot ramp overlooking the bay.

The first car hit the side of their old Chevy, and Hikari screamed. Akira floored the gas pedal but had nothing to do but maneuver them against the wall up to the third floor of the stone compound, sparks flying.

The second car hit them from behind, sending them spinning. They lurched forward, Akira's head meeting the steering wheel before the airbag deployed. He fought against the airbag, attempting to clear his view of the wall looming before them. Akira hit the brakes and broke the wheel hard left to stop them before the concrete barrier did it for them. The car screeched to a stop. Smoke rose from the hood of the Chevy.

Dazed and in pain, Akira tried to hold on to Hikari when she was dragged out of the car. He lost his grip on her, and then it was his turn.

Their captors pushed them against the wall. A fist met Akira's stomach. He spat out blood and doubled over on the ground. Hikari cried out.

"Let her go. It's me you want!" Akira shouted. He launched but was struck down with a kick to the side of his head; men wearing reptilian masks wrenched his arms to the sides. Only one man stood with his face revealed. Akira knew him; he was a snake wrangler the family employed.

"Please, Akira... Run." Hikari whispered. Akira yelled. The wrangler held up an Inland taipan snake in his hands, dangerously close to Hikari's throat.

"No, please!" Akira breathed. "I'll come back with you; just let her go."

The wrangler smirked; he didn't spare Akira a glance while the beast in his hands lashed out, embedding in Hikari's throat.

She fell to the ground, her eyes wide open and unblinking. The wrangler collected his pet and looked at Akira.

"Madam Dara sends her regards. She will not stand for anyone getting away with her property. And now, you will be returned to her service."

"You can tell her I will see her in hell!" Akira screamed and tore himself from his captor's hold. The last sight his eyes met before he plummeted off the ledge of the parking lot was Hikari's eyes, dead and staring at him.

His body met the river below, and he sank, unwilling to swim to try and save himself. He wanted to die, to join Hikari in the afterlife, but fate had other plans.

CHAPTER 30

THE FINAL DECISION

A fishing boat passing by caught him in a net of paddlefish and brought his beaten body onto the deck.

At first, they thought him dead. The crew opened his shirt to discover a large blue rose-shaped bruise on his chest.

The fisherman said his appearance with the fish was a sign of impending doom. Akira vowed that he would bring ruin to those who wronged him.

Not long after, while still in hiding, recovering from his fall, Akira learned that Hikari's body had been found. Despite the danger he put himself in by coming out in the open, he had to see her one last time.

He bandaged his face, armed, and with his senses alert, he stood in a dark hallway of the hospital; her image through the window overlooking the morgue planted him in place, and the feeling he experienced was that of his own soul leaving his body. It was the first time in years that he cried.

Akira left the hospital with one thought: kill the wrangler and, after that, take his own life. He knew he would never get close enough to kill Dara, so this tiny satisfaction of watching the breath leave the body of the man who murdered his love was all he had.

He knew where to find the wrangler and waited for him, obscured by shadows. The man he ambushed drank his health in the old club Akira frequented - 'Mizutamari.'

Half inebriated, the wrangler left the club in the small hours of the morning, and Akira grabbed him with no intention of letting him escape alive.

"Point out your car." Akira shoved a gun into the man's side, nudging him forward. The wrangler gulped and opened the driver's door. Akira slammed the butt of the gun across the back of his head, rendering him unconscious.

He shoved the man into the back seat and drove to a bad part of town. There, he carried his captive downstairs into a small, run-down basement apartment he had rented under an alias the day before.

Locked deep underground from the world, in the one-room apartment, Akira began to torture the murderer. He started by slowly slicing away small bits of the wrangler's body. The grueling process promised the man lived long enough to suffer as Akira did.

He let out all the hate that burned within him towards the snake wrangler. After the first night, when the man's screams rose to high heaven, and Akira took out his lights, he had sectioned off a small space in the back of the apartment, constructed drywall around it, and connected the ventilation system into the cramped space to drown out the wrangler's screams.

There, he held the man, with the light on at all hours of the day and night and with the temperature never above that of a cold desert night, fitting for the snakes he was so fond of.

As for meals, Akira fed him a substance of his own making. It contained blended animal food laced with a fertilizer that Akira knew would poison him and eventually kill him, but that would happen slowly, and by that time, the wrangler himself would beg for death.

At night, with the hollow screams and cries of the man sealed behind the drywall, Akira dreamed of a voice that came from the tattoos that adorned his skin.

The snakes on his chest spoke to him, promising to return his love if Akira agreed to bond with their master and let the deity use his power to remake the world. Akira awoke from one such dream, covered in a cold sweat, on the third night the serpents came to haunt him.

He sprinted up from his bed and ran to the mirror, and there they were, the hissing snakes, moving and alive, slithering across his skin, circling the blue rose-shaped bruise that would never go away since Akira hit the water.

"Aghh!" Akira grabbed a kitchen knife and plunged it into his own chest. He struck at his flesh, attempting to carve the snakes out.

Every time the knife went in, gliding over his skin and exposing fatty tissue, blood, and muscle, the wound closed off immediately, but the pain remained.

"**You cannot banish me from yourself.**" The snakes hissed while Akira watched, terrified at their mouths moving in his reflection.

"**I will forever be a part of you. But if you willingly join me and merge your essence with mine, we will forge a new world. Let me give you everything you ever wanted.**"

"That. Is. Not. What. Hikari. Would. Have. Wanted!" Akira panted, plunging the knife into his chest with every word, screaming in agony.

He blacked out then, the blood loss becoming too much to bear. When he woke, Akira found himself on the floor, panting, bloody, and alive; the knife lay useless by his side.

That day, his prisoner died.

Akira left the basement apartment open. 'Someone would eventually sense the smell and call for help, but it would be too late.' He thought.

It didn't matter at that point if the police traced the murder back to him; he wouldn't be around to stand trial for what he had done.

"**You have to stop.**" The snakes whispered, frantic inside Akira's tattoo. "**There would be no more chances.**"

Akira gathered the being that possessed him sensed his suicidal intentions. He figured that when his body died, the demon would perish, expelled from the world.

"I will not allow you to blight my soul. I would rather forfeit my right to heaven, for I will not become a messenger of hell." Akira answered and forged ahead.

The dark road loomed before him. It was not long until he stood near the edge of the glass tower, and life streamed below, unaware of him. The enticing call of the void rang strong in his mind, and at that moment, he listened.

*"**No! Stop!**" The demon screamed in his head.*

Akira closed his eyes, held his breath, and stepped forward.

He fell.

He soared through the air. The wind blew into his face, and his eyes watered, but he did not close them. He wanted to see this.

The green leaves of the trees passed him by. The ground got closer.

He fell.

His arms stuck heavy at his sides; he did not attempt to stop his impact with the concrete.

Akira lay on the searing black ground, unable to move. Pain invaded his senses; He hurt from the inside out.

Not from the bones he must have shattered but from something much deeper within. From the torment, he knew in this life and from an ancient scar on his soul. He had been hurting for a long time; he knew the agonizing pit ripped out of his heart.

His limbs refused to move. He lay on the ground and stared up at the heavens.

The clouds passed slowly overhead; the rustles in the green trees were familiar music to his ears.

'I recognize the dark roof tower over me.' He thought. 'A moment ago, a lifetime ago, I fell; I leaped and plummeted down like a comet.'

He knew now why he did it. He remembered what brought him up there. His eyes were closing of their own accord; would he be granted peace at last?

The sun shone through his fluttering eyelids, blinding him, and he had no strength to fight to keep them open. Patches of light gleamed through the tree canopy on Akira's skin.

The thundering pain in his heart wouldn't ebb, a gaping hole he could never fill, not in this life or the previous or even the one that would follow. A loss he knew through the ages.

His senses got duller; his eyes refused to open.

Nothing existed but the darkness and the rustling foliage in the evergreen trees.

And the sun, the scorching sun with its bright burning light that forced its way through the leaves to caress his broken body.

The pain was real now. It wasn't a dull calling to him from a future that may never come.

The time to be warned had passed. The anguish was him.

Úlftýr woke up, trapped in Akira's body. It wasn't a vision anymore, and he knew why he was there. He knew that if he stayed bound to the altar, powerless to prevent the curse his captors were about to invoke using his blood, this would be his destiny — to die again and again while the world crumbled around him, and evildoers won.

"Úlftýr." He knew this woman's voice. He recognized the name. His name! Lost to the ages, scourged out of his soul, burned, beaten, ripped apart, and scattered over the sands of time.

"Úlftýr." He squinted through the blinding light.

There! There she was! He found her, the one calling to him out of the darkness. Was he dreaming again?

He wished to wake up in her arms, but the nightmare refused to be over.

"Úlftýr."

"Hikari?" he gargled, choking on his blood. "No... Elska." he rasped.

She stood before him in her blue dress, bathed in light. Her red hair was a halo framing her pale face, and her striking green eyes burrowed into the depths of his soul. Úlftýr felt a deep tug in his gut, and his shadow rose, obscuring his view.

Murtagh reached his hand to him, shimmering in and out of existence, as both the álfur and the snake that tormented him.

"**Will you set me free?**" The serpent asked.

"No." Úlftýr couldn't tell if the warmth sliding down his face was blood or tears.

"**Will you become one with me to save yourself?**" The wolf's howl rose to a crescendo.

"No...!" Úlftýr's voice cracked.

The snakes slithered across the pavement and rose above Elska's form. She stood radiant and alive, her hair moving gracefully in the wind. Adorned with flowers, her dress unfolded like the petals of a rose, translucent in the sun. As time passed, the light of her soul began to fade. Fear and pain took over her face.

She opened her mouth, but no words came out. She mouthed Úlftýr's name.

"**Will you unmake the world for her?**" Jörmungandr, in Murtagh's form, asked. He stood over Úlftýr and offered him his outstretched hand.

This time, Úlftýr did not hesitate. He reached up and said, "Yes."

And inside the mountain, a long time ago, a great god with alabaster skin and hair of fire opened his eyes.

CHAPTER 31

THE RAGNARÖK

Eyjafjallajökull mountain, Islandia 1639 B.C.

Úlftýr, still bound to the stone table, opened the hollows of his eyes, two orbs of bright embers materializing out of the darkness.

Inside the mountain, the massive god vibrated with power. His shackles disintegrated; he shook them off, and they crumbled to dust.

Úlftýr sat up; his bonds dissolved. He tore the iron ring from his neck, and the metal melted in his hand.

The air crackled with dense energy, and Úlftýr's eyes blazed in bright green light.

Úlftýr looked at Deirdra and inhaled deeply. The call of raw strength pulled at his gut, a gripping force merging with the essence of the god awakened inside him.

Úlftýr closed his eyes. The alabaster god's power snaked up from the bottom of Úlftýr's feet through him until it asked to be released in his mind.

Úlftýr opened his eyes, and Deirdra shouted. "No! What have you done?! You've set the trickster free! This is not the end, lúka."

"He is not your prisoner anymore," Úlftýr whispered. He now knew the true name of the God under the mountain. "Loki, I welcome you." They were together now, Úlftýr and Loki, and they glared at her as one.

"You lose Skadi." The god said through Úlftýr, and the earth rumbled.

A scream tore out of Úlftýr, and a blast of great might violently erupted from his veins. The vortex emanating from Úlftýr threw Deirdra back. She collided with the columns, resonating with a horrible crunch. The stone cracked, tipped, and collapsed on top of her.

He thought she perished under the rubble, but no such luck. A moment later, the stones on top of her cracked and crumbled, and Deirdra burst out, only she did not look like his adoptive sister anymore.

The antlers weaved into her hair grew, her skin seemed as if it was made of frost, and her eyes shone in silver. She reached out her hand, and a staff forged in ice appeared in her grasp.

"You cannot defeat me; you are a foolish child, and I am a queen."

"You are no sovereign of mine," Úlftýr said.

"That is where you are tragically mistaken." Deirdra raised her staff, and Úlftýr gasped. A collar made of sharp ice stuck to the skin around his neck. It tightened as Deirdra laughed.

The ice thickened, icicles hardening into his flesh; they penetrated the first layer, and as Úlftýr struggled for breath, a sudden fiery burst released him from Skadi's icebound grasp.

Skadi howled in frustration and turned on Elska; her hands, still shackled, radiated heat, and her hair shimmered like a fever dream around her.

Skadi drew the staff on her.

"No!" Úlftýr yelled. He charged at her, a brutal animal, his spirit struggling to reconcile with the new power he now knew.

They clashed like wolves; she slashed through him with claws of ice, and he tore into her with fangs as hard as iron. She drove her nails into his chest, clawing for his heart; he yelled and grabbed the antlers on her head, breaking them clean off.

She had no time to react to his savagery. He drove the antlers into her neck, his hands coated with her tar-like blood. He screamed when the liquid burned him, but he held on.

"This is for Baldur." He said, driving the antlers further up.

He let go then and staggered back.

Skadi yelled, screamed, her face distorted, the skin melting off her bones in globes of reeking mess.

The deity residing within her howled as it was forcefully expelled, separated from the remaining black bones that crumbled to the rubble. The stone statues she previously revived followed suit, crumbling where they stood. The land was free from her dark magic.

Úlftýr's core blazed anew. He trained his eyes to where Elska stood, shackled to a column. Úlftýr raised his hand. The temple ceased to crumble around them.

Úlftýr raised his other hand, and Elska's shackles froze over; she looked up, tugged on them, and they snapped in half, releasing her. Elska fell to the ground, exhausted. She remained sitting, staring at Úlftýr.

Úlftýr let out a half-smile and turned to face Bileygr.

The golden warrior lifted the black-blade sword and struck him with all his might. The weapon halted against the green shield of energy that surrounded Úlftýr, but then, the shimmering barrier gave in, and the sword went through, cutting Úlftýr's left arm clean off at the elbow.

Úlftýr yelled in pain, rage blazing in his eyes. He tumbled back from the stone table onto the floor.

Bileygr pursued him, the golden form of the god Odin illuminating his body. The massive black blade rose and fell; Úlftýr dodged, and the blade sent sparks, grazing the ground, missing Úlftýr by inches.

"Call on the souls of your warriors!" Loki commanded in Úlftýr's mind.

The sword fell again, directed to the top of Úlftýr's head. He deflected, grabbed the blade with his remaining hand, and drove the sword into his own shoulder.

The screech of dead warriors exploded in his head. They clawed at his soul, begging to be set free, and, this time, he gave himself to their demanding call.

"Rise within me, my brethren!" Úlftýr called to them, his bloody hand staining the metal, refusing to allow Bileygr to pull it out. "Help me cure this world with the life stolen from you!"

The pain of the warriors' last breaths stopped; instead, their craving to live shone through, and their urge to matter again prevailed over the smothering darkness that consumed them. Úlftýr launched forward, allowing the blade to slide in deeper.

"I know who you are! I can see you, Odin!" Úlftýr roared in Loki's voice. **"The soul you expelled prayed to you to save his people. You used his prayer to gain control of a nobleman. Once he perished summoning the serpent, you rode this body out of his dying world."**

He grabbed Odin and crashed with him against the ground, tumbling when they fell, the blade slicing his torn muscles.

"You poisoned the Ice Lands, but you are nothing more than an apparition that followed me into this world from the one your thirst for power destroyed," Úlftýr pinned the golden warrior to the ground, the stump of his arm raised. "Taste the foul infection you summoned; let the illness you created be your undoing."

Loki's blood flowed from the stump in sick gulps of black matter.

"Call on my wolf protector. Call on the one I named Fenrir."

Úlftýr fell back with the blade still in his shoulder. He spread his arms.

Bileygr heaved and pulled himself up. He grabbed the black sword, and a massive ebony wolf leaped from within Úlftýr's chest in the form of a shadow, solidifying as it struck Bileygr down.

Úlftýr kneeled, pulling out the sword from his flesh.

The massive black wolf closed its powerful jaws on Bileygr's arm.

Úlftýr stood up, the rune in his brow ignited. Fangs cut through his gums, claws grew out of his fingertips, and the raving howls of the spirits trapped within the blade called for his soul.

"Úlftýr!" Elska gasped. The dead surrounded him, both Ljósálfar and mortal, their hands reaching for Úlftýr's throat, confused by death's grasp at who was their true enemy.

Elska staggered forward but managed to get up. Uncertain on her feet, she inhaled deeply to steady herself.

"Úlftýr! Let go!" Elska ran to him and wrapped her arms around his torso. "Let go of this sword!"

Elska stared at the touch of the dead as it began to corrupt him, the aura around him snuffing out the light.

'Me!' She reached her arm towards the spirits, willing the warmth of her inner flame to draw them in. 'Focus on me! Let him be.' She willed the angry ghosts to direct their vengeful touch on her, to burn them out and her along with them.

"Úlftýr!" Elska gasped, choking; the dead swayed to her will.

Úlftýr breathed hard. He swung the sword over their heads and smashed it against the ground.

A massive wave knocked him and Elska off their feet, sending them toppling back.

The dust slowly settled, and the shattered blade lost its hold on the spirits within who were finally set free.

The souls of mortals descended like wraiths on the golden warrior in an angry swarm. The dark cloud tore at his skin, clawed at his armor, and gnawed at his soul.

The mayhem of vengeful spirits entered the golden warrior, his body falling to pieces. The angry spirits dragged out the god's essence and ate it alive.

While Elska and Úlftýr lay unconscious, the human souls passed, and a fog lifted from the land. The Ljósálfar shimmering spirits settled around Úlftýr. Gradually, the rune faded from his brow, his fangs retracted, his claws disappeared, his skin became lively and radiant, and the stump of his arm healed, rejuvenating into a whole arm. Úlftýr's long, white hair became ebony again, save for one silver strand to remain there forever.

The dead Ljósálfar stood, surrounding Úlftýr a moment longer; one álfur stepped forward, his pearl blond hair blowing, his azure eyes shone, he bowed his head, and then they all dissipated into an airy silver mist.

The mist lingered a moment over Elska, and then, it glided down the mountain, into the crevices of the rock surface, and down the churning stream. Everywhere it went, the blue roses bloomed. Even in the Ice Lands, the desecrated battleground began to flourish.

Loki restored Jörmungandr's powers. The serpent, who lay dead by the stone altar, breathed deep and opened his violet eyes, wearing the form of Murtagh. He rose, eyes glowing in blue ice and hair the color of lilac. There was no sign of the wound Bileygr inflicted upon him.

The earth rumbled. Úlftýr woke up. He turned his head to the side. Elska lay beside him, and Murtagh stood above them.

Murtagh reached his hand to Úlftýr, and Úlftýr took it. Murtagh pulled him up.

"Is it over?" Úlftýr asked.

"It's about to begin," Murtagh replied. "Look."

On top of the mountain, two giant serpents rose over a single blue rose in the maw of the volcano. They slithered down, gathered the remains of the golden warrior, and disappeared in the ash spewing from the mountain. The earth rumbled, and lightning struck inside the billowing smoke.

"The mountain will erupt," Murtagh said urgently in his voice. "You have to stop it."

Úlftýr looked down at Elska, and Murtagh followed his gaze.

Murtagh went down to his knees beside her. "I will look after her." He promised. "You have to stop what is coming. Don't let this mountain destroy your world. Let Master Loki guide you."

Úlftýr spread his arms and called to the god within him. The alabaster deity appeared before him.

"**Fenrir**." They both proclaimed.

The massive shadow wolf burst out of Úlftýr's chest and stood in front of him in anticipation. Úlftýr grabbed onto its coarse black mane and straddled the great animal. It was bigger than the finest horse in his stable. Instantly, they were in the air.

Fire and rock shot up from the maw of the volcano. A noxious gas filled the air, Úlftýr covering his nose and mouth with his hand. Fragments of lava and ash threatened to burst, spreading a river of death down the mountain.

Through Loki's eyes, Úlftýr watched the remnants of Bylegr's torn-up soul battle inside the mountain, surrounded by giant serpents and flames.

"Lend me your strength now," Úlftýr told the monster he straddled.

Fenrir opened its mouth, and a vortex of green flame shot out. Úlftýr called on the alabaster god to help him. Loki's strength fused with his own, and a wave of ice and hail erupted from his veins.

He thought he might lose himself by tapping into so much of the god's power, but he came too far to stop.

The two forces, fire and ice, imbued within each other, flashed inside the mountain, swept away Odin's remains, covered the smoldering opening of the volcano, and slowly sealed it shut.

Their combined power crept on and burrowed deep into the earth and into every crevice and magma chamber under the temple. The excess of the rasping lava sizzled, slowly leaking from a fissure Úlftýr opened in the side of the mountain, draining the purified mist to come down as rain upon the sea. The earthquake ceased, and the smoke dissipated. Two giant snake spirits rose to meet him. There was something familiar about them. Light snow began to fall.

Fenrir landed in a clearing right under the temple. He let Úlftýr down, and the snakes coiled around him. "Mother? Father?"

Their essence surrounded him, their love, their pride in him, and then words whispered in his father's voice: "The rose could never be found; it had to be created. It will bloom anew now for you, my son."

Their spirits settled around him, a shield around his soul.

He looked down; the cursed ink stain on his chest bloomed into a radiant blue rose, and the image of the serpents coiled around the cobalt rose on his skin, identical to his family's crest.

In ecstasy at his victory, Úlftýr's heart clenched.

Something went wrong. Úlftýr looked at Elska and Murtagh, where he had left them, and his breath caught. Úlftýr knew she was gone the moment he laid eyes on her gray skin and slightly parted, discolored lips.

He didn't want to come back, didn't want to be right. This was not another possible life, another possible future he could escape from. Úlftýr was home. If he took another step forward and touched her skin, his future would be set: a life without her, no more chances to make it right.

He was not ready for it. He wanted to run. The wolf howled beside him, mimicking the dire cry of his heart.

His future refused to let him stall the moment.

"I'm sorry," Murtagh said. He rose from her side when Úlftýr stepped closer.

"You lied to me again." The green aura around Úlftýr glowed with intensity. *'What a fool I am to believe in a happy ending.'* "That's what I get dealing with a serpent." Bitterness leaked from his sarcastic tone. "You knew she was about to pass before I took flight on Fenrir's back."

"I had to mislead you," Murtagh confessed, but his sincerity held no weight for Úlftýr. "If you knew, you would have let the world burn."

"I will if it gets her back; I see nothing stopping me now." Unnatural heat emanated from Úlftýr.

"She would not want that," Murtagh said.

"And how would you know what she wanted? I bargain her wish was to remain by my side. Alive." Úlftýr's eyes flashed red, and he raised his hand. "Begone serpent." He growled.

Murtagh opened his mouth to speak, but he wasn't given a chance to utter a single syllable before a blast of angry energy knocked him to the ground.

Úlftýr stepped forward, his dark aura growing with his rage, "You have spent centuries and countless lifetimes in a futile attempt to separate us before you realized your mistakes. Now you and your god can watch the fruits of your labor crumble to dust like my heart."

Murtagh opened his mouth to speak, but Úlftýr charged him. They crashed to the ground, and Úlftýr pounded the latter's face and body, screaming in rage. Úlftýr heaved and shook, seemingly growing bigger, his skin stretched impossibly thin over his cracking bones.

His heavy limbs slowed his movement, and the horrible sound of tearing and ripping filled the air. Úlftýr howled. Black coarse fur poking out through the gashes, his transformation ripped open in his skin.

"*Free me.*" The booming whisper came from the mountain.

Úlftýr's eyes flashed red.

"Don't," Murtagh choked. "You mustn't succumb to his treachery."

"You mean like I succumbed to yours?" Úlftýr asked, his voice distorted by his growing canines.

"*Free me, and she lives.*"

Úlftýr laughed, a sickening bitter laugh. Murtagh moved under him to escape, but Úlftýr pinned him down by his neck, his claws digging into his veins. "Trying to wriggle out like the snake that you are?" Úlftýr looked at the mountain. "I've had enough of your bargains."

He looked down, his eyes ignited in a green flame. "NO," Úlftýr growled while Loki sought to gain dominance. "No, I will no longer relinquish control of my destiny."

He seized Murtagh's neck and hoisted him up. Only not the body that so resembled his remained in his hand. A shimmering essence of the great serpent in purple and green squirmed and writhed in his fist.

The snake seemed to pulsate, to attempt to grow larger in Úlftýr's grasp, but his power was diminished, parts of him crumbled, and in the end, when the deity saw there was no escape, he wrapped his tail around Úlftýr's wrist and burned him with all the power of the dying stars he still possessed. It made no difference.

"Úlftýr."

Úlftýr's eyes snapped up; a pain, a gaping hole in his chest, left him winded. "Baldur," Úlftýr felt weakness creeping up his limbs. "Why?" He could no longer hold on to the burning essence. Why do you seek to protect him?" Powerless, he let the serpent go.

"I spared Markian for you. Do not ask me to release the serpent responsible for my pain. Hoder is dead, a mere casualty of his master's war." Úlftýr pointed accusingly at the serpent. "It was all for nothing!"

Fenrir howled. Úlftýr ignored the sound of tumbling stones. Loki stirred inside him. "All for nothing," Úlftýr said. The mountain released a foul cloud of black smoke.

Under the rubble where Deirdra's body lay, thin gray vapor slid out. Fenrir howled again, but Úlftýr ignored him. "I have nothing to fight for anymore." He said.

The serpent lying on the ground shimmered and dissipated. Murtagh stood up. Purple blood trickled from his nose. He seemed to have lost the vigor to fight or argue. Or perhaps he knew there was nothing he could say to change Úlftýr's mind. He bowed to Úlftýr and left, hunched over and limping. It seemed that Úlftýr broke something when they fought, but he couldn't master the will to care about what he's done.

Úlftýr sat on the ground, pulled Elska close, and held her in his arms. Around them, the field bloomed in royal blue. Úlftýr bowed his head and whispered words of love to her. "I didn't live through this anguish to lose you," howling winds rose in the valley. "I refuse to accept a world where you are gone." The surrounding atmosphere sparked with electricity.

"I agreed to remake this world for you. I have no need for it." He kissed her lips; the earth rumbled, and the air shimmered, crackling and bursting like fireworks.

"I'm sorry I left you behind, again and again. I'm sorry I didn't cherish the time we had together. I know you tried to tell me, tried to show me, and now it is too late."

He looked at the mountain. "I am going to let it all go now. I know this isn't the ending you hoped for; I know that you would tell me to go on, but I can't, I don't want to. Let the humans have this world; let it be as dark as their hearts, as dark as my heart."

CHAPTER 32

THE LIFE AND
DEATH

oki's mesmerizing form materialized before him. Úlftýr raised his eyes. They glowed dark red.

"You promised you would give her back to me. You promised she would live." Úlftýr accused his maker.

"I didn't expect her to draw all this death into her to save you."

"To save *us*. Now give her back." The aura that had settled around Úlftýr grew dark again, the snakes on his chest hissed, the flowers began to wither, and his ebony hair grew white.

"**Stop**," Loki commanded. The alabaster god placed his burning hand against Úlftýr's chest. Úlftýr gasped at the scourging touch.

"I don't have the power to restore her. I wished to spare us both a fate worse than death; mark my words, there will come a day when you choose to lose everything for her, and I won't be there to give it

**back. But if you insist on fighting destiny, call on her soul on her way
to the netherworld. Use my power and call forth the might you took
from our tormentors. Reach into the earth's crust where you sealed
the wicked god you defeated. Drain him of his brawn. This world
will listen to your true desire, so you better make your wishes clear."**

The great god shimmered out of existence. The scorching handprint
on Úlftýr's chest faded away, Úlftýr's eyes glowed in bright green and
then returned to amber, and his hair darkened with every breath he took.

Finally, the shadow of a red-haired maiden brushed against his heart.
Úlftýr looked down. "You are the maiden of my heart; your spirit and
beauty reached me beyond time and death. This land of magic means
nothing to me; neither the sun, the sea, nor the views of the vast fjord
can quench my heart's calling. You are the one I need, and I've always
known that. Come back to me, my snow maiden." He kissed her and
leaned back.

Her spirit was there; he could feel her, but something held her from
coming back to him.

Úlftýr laid her body on the ground and stared at his scourged hands.
He didn't heal as fast as he did when he sipped on the madness of Loki's
power.

Her spirit called to him, and in the corner of his eye, he witnessed
Baldur leading Elska away.

"No, stop, I beg you!" Úlftýr scrambled to his feet; he grabbed the
bloody antlers he snapped from Deirdra's head and offered them up
to Baldur's ghost. "Please don't take her away from me. Have your
vengeance, end my life, and let us be together."

Baldur stopped; he looked at Elska; he pulled her back, and she
resisted.

She said something, looking distraught, and Baldur shook his head.
He pulled her hand and led her to Úlftýr. They both sat before him,
Elska's spirit burning brighter than before.

Úlftýr offered Baldur the broken antlers again. "Do it."

Baldur took the broken antler from his hand. Elska grabbed his arm. "No!" She mouthed. "Don't!"

Úlftýr fell to his knees, bent down, lifted Elska's body, and cradled her close to his heart.

"It's alright," Úlftýr whispered. He searched Baldur's dead eyes. "We never had long. Perhaps now we can have forever. I'm ready, Baldur." He closed his eyes.

Elska cried out in the distance; the sharp edge of the deer's bone grazed Úlftýr's skin when his blue rose bloomed and went in.

Úlftýr gasped and opened his eyes, but just as it appeared, the sharp pain was gone.

Baldur threw the antler aside. He touched Úlftýr's chest, where he stabbed him, caught a few drops of his blue blood, and flickered them onto Elska's lips.

Baldur's shimmering form grew brighter. He grabbed Úlftýr's arm, placed it on Elska's, and held them both.

Úlftýr's eyes flickered with green light. "**You finally remember who you are**."

Úlftýr looked confused at Loki's statement that poured from his lips. And then the darkness took all of them, the stars exploded behind their eyes, and they were swept away into the heavens, through the tear in the universe and spat out in the darkest corner of their old world.

Not too far before them, Úlftýr, in the form of Loki, was caught in a vicious fight with the golden warrior. Below them, their world crumbled, and Loki, with the last of his strength, was struggling to keep it from falling apart while the golden warrior drained his power.

When Loki fell, Baldur appeared bright and radiant like the sun. His golden locks shone like the stars.

Loki reached out to him, but Baldur turned away, Odin, the golden warrior, pointed the blaming finger at him.

Other deities, silver and bronze, followed Odin's example. Loki was caught, brought before Skadi, and held down by darkness as she poured venom into him. He screamed and burned, and their world kept crumbling.

It was only at that moment when Skadi relished his anguish that Baldur, in the memory, decided to act.

He came before the gods that surrounded Loki and blocked his escape. He demanded they avert the punishment to rebuild their planet, but they soon realized how powerless they were to stop Odins' madness.

Loki waited for this moment. As the gods berated Odin for his deception and mourned their own demise, Loki charged Skadi and plummeted with her from the heavens. They fell and fought and thrashed, and the more Skadi tried to drain his powers, the weaker she became.

They toppled through the rift, and Baldur couldn't tell what became of them. The stars went out, and for centuries, darkness ruled.

She found him first. Sigyn, his destined confidant, the red-haired maiden with the alabaster skin, the snow in his winter, the softness and light he needed in the dark hardstone prison Skadi confined him to.

Skadi's dark magic bound him to the mortal world, but she lost him under the earth that swallowed him when they crashed through the rift their battle created.

When Baldur finally reached them, Sigyn's demise was nearly upon her. She did everything she could to keep Skadi's venom from reaching Loki, but she herself had succumbed to it.

Loki begged and pleaded with him to take Sigyn away, and Baldur obliged. Too drained to resist, he took her to the beach under the mountain her husband was imprisoned in and, by Loki's instructions, called forth the great serpent to save the people Loki strove to protect.

Sipping on the last of his power, Baldur opened the rift between the worlds once more and let the serpent through, carrying the Ljósálfar people.

The massive serpent crossed the ocean of space and water and rolled the land inward, creating the great fjord.

As the last of his passengers had reached the safe shores he had created, the serpent retreated into the ocean, taking Sigyn's body along with him to guard it in the depths.

And Baldur - he returned to Loki under the mountain, carrying with him a mistletoe spear, the only substance that could penetrate his godly body.

"Let my blood be your shield," Baldur said as he held onto Loki's numb hands and drove the spear into his own stomach. "Let it run into the earth and protect you until you find a way to wake up."

The blood coated Loki's hands and then perforated the ground and up his body. Loki breathed for the last time before the crust enveloped him whole.

Baldur could not free him from Skadi's enchantment. Wherever she was, her sorcery ran deep. But he could prevent Loki's suffering. Put him into a dreamless slumber, hidden, protected until his strength returned.

Baldur perished there under the mountain, holding a vigil over Loki's stone form. But Loki didn't allow his soul to wander. He pushed it out of oblivion and sent it to the people Baldur saved to live among them as one of their own. A fragment of what Loki was detached from the broken deity, and Úlftýr came into this world, unaware of the pain he endured.

Some years later, his soul called out to Sigyn, a beacon, to lead her out of the deep, and the serpent released her; he, too, gave of himself before he sunk into a dead slumber to allow the fated lovers to find each other again.

Úlftýr inhaled as he came out of the vicious memory. He was at a loss for words. Tears stained his face, tears of rage and loss and gratitude. Baldur still sat before him, but Elska's spirit was gone.

"You – " Úlftýr choked.

Elska stirred in his arms; the menacing energy that surrounded them faded. The flowers bloomed anew, and Baldur's spirit faded; the broken antler coated with Úlftýr's blood remained steaming on the ground.

Úlftýr looked at Elska's body. "Perhaps the universe makes bargains after all," Úlftýr whispered.

Elska opened her eyes.

"That's my girl." Úlftýr whispered.

"Úlftýr, you're back." She smiled, raising her hand to caress his cheek.

"I am, and so are you." Úlftýr got up, helped her to her feet, and took her into his arms. They stood embraced, breathing in each other's scent, gazing into each other's eyes.

Fenrir howled, startling Elska.

"What…? Elska turned and stepped back from the beast.

"It's all right," Úlftýr held onto her hand. "Trust me." He beckoned her forward. Elska took a breath, her eyes wide. She nodded and let Úlftýr help her climb onto Fenrir's back.

Úlftýr sat behind Elska, holding her tight. Fenrir jumped and soared into the air. Murtagh shed his álfur skin, and the giant ice serpent slithered across the land back into the sea.

A man wrapped in a yellow flame came to stand in the middle of the temple ground.

Fenrir touched down on the cracked mosaic floor. Elska remained on his back while Úlftýr, enveloped in a halo of pulsating green mist, walked up to the burning man, Thunaer.

The man balled his fists and launched at Úlftýr, but Úlftýr easily caught him mid-jump and plunged his hand into Thunaer's chest.

His hand clasped the sizzling angry spirit inside, and, baring his teeth with a great effort, Úlftýr dragged the thrashing fire god out.

Úlftýr held the volcanic being while his mind screamed at him to let go, his hand burning, but he relentlessly fought through his instincts. He squeezed the god's essence in his clenched fist and finally released him, a rage-filled, roaring, bodiless red cloud.

Thunaer blinked, his mind waking up from deep slumber. He let out a long breath.

In his freed eyes lay the heavy burden the god's presence had left on his already damaged soul.

His hand healed. The pressure of servitude faded away from the man before him. Thunaer put his hand on his chest. Finally, he could breathe again.

Elska dismounted Fenrir.

Úlftýr walked over to her and took her hands in his. He kissed her. "I will take him to his people and come back for you. Don't leave; you are safe here now," he told her.

Elska kissed him, and Úlftýr looked at Thunaer. "Get on," he said, gesturing to the wolf.

Thunaer looked apprehensive at the monstrous beast.

"If I'd intended to end your miserable existence, I would have done so already," Úlftýr said.

Thunaer let out a ragged breath and carefully climbed on the wolf.

Fenrir moved his massive head sharp from side to side, ruffling his mane.

Thunaer gasped and attempted to get off, but Úlftýr sat behind him and held him in place. "Calm down." He hissed.

Fenrir leaped into the air. They flew over the land and beyond the capital.

Úlftýr didn't need Thunaer to tell him where his human camp lay. He sensed them now, walking his land on the far side of the island.

Úlftýr summoned his serpent shadow to rise around him. They landed in the middle of the mortal encampment to the gasps and screams of the terrified mortals who dwelt there. Úlftýr let Thunaer dismount, and then, with eyes blazing in green light and the spirit of a serpent hissing at the dauðadýr above him, Úlftýr began to speak.

"I banish you from this land," Úlftýr's voice boomed throughout the camp. "You have nine days to leave our shores. A boat and provisions will be waiting for you on the other side of that ridge." He gestured to where he wanted them to go. "Those who will stay will do so at the cost of their lives. Once you leave, you will not be able to remember how to find this realm again but know this: I will watch you wherever you go. I will deal with all wars you engage in against each other that will involve the loss of innocent lives with the utmost severity. Do not test my wrath."

A second serpent spirit rose above Úlftýr. It hissed, descending before the mortals. It drew them to it. They all came forward, their eyes glazed over in green mist.

"**You will forget us.**" Loki and Úlftýr said in unison. "**When you leave, you will know this land is a barren wasteland. Here is where your brothers perished, nearly a century ago. These are your cursed Ice Lands.**"

Úlftýr engraved the information into the mortals, scourging his fruitful land from their memory.

"Wait!" An older woman stepped forward, her lengthy hair braided and white, wearing a red ankle-length strap dress. On her shoulders was a long wool cloak, and beads of bone and glass decorated the front of her apron dress. "I beg my lord to reconsider this cruel fate you wish to bestow upon us," she said.

She signaled two warriors to seize Thunaer and bring him to his knees.

"I am Rhagetla, and on behalf of my people, I implore you to hear me out."

Úlftýr gestured to her to proceed. "I cannot erase the atrocities our predecessors made against your people, but many of us here believe in moving forward. That was not the life we wanted to lead." She looked at the angry man who sat on the ground, glaring at her.

"I shall banish him and those like-minded from our tribe and send them to our homeland to face judgment against the crimes they committed. We who remain ask that you grant us this patch of land to grow, live, and, in time, put down the ties of trade and friendship between our people. We left a land of turmoil, searching for a better life and the promise of prosperity. Disease and wars had taken our children and led us to this depravity-driven existence."

Úlftýr frowned. "Experience taught me not to trust your kind. Your feeble, brief lives allow little growth in mind and acceptance of the world around you."

Rhagetla nodded. "We shall not deny our kin made mistakes throughout the decades. I see now we followed the wrong gods. They led us on the path of death and darkness, and now we ask that you grant us the path of light. Erect a barrier around this land but allow us a small passage. We shall help protect your borders, establish trade, and spread the stories of your generosity."

"And who shall lead you on this path? Not him," Úlftýr looked at Thunaer.

"No. After he is gone, I shall take over here to lead my people and see that our bargain stands. I have strong ties to the leadership of our homeland, and I am sure that, in time, we can build a world to benefit both our races." Rhagetla said. "We cannot erase the past, but I beg you to grant us a chance at a better future." she implored.

The two warriors that held Thunaer down wrenched him up and led him away, kicking and spewing profanity.

"And you, who stand witness, do you agree to uphold our bargain?" Úlftýr asked the mortal villagers standing around him in awe.

Murmurs of agreement and even cheers passed through the crowd of onlookers.

Loki's shimmering form appeared beside Úlftýr. The mortals remained oblivious to his presence.

Loki nodded.

"A millennium," Úlftýr said. "This shall be our premise. You are not to enter my city unless specifically invited. You are to hunt on this side of our land and stay clear of our central coast. A battalion of my warriors will guard the passage I will open, and an expedition with my men shall accompany you to establish the trading route. Heed my word, and soon, we shall revisit the restrictions I have laid upon your settlement. Are my terms acceptable to you, Queen Rhagetla?"

The mortal woman bowed. "They are my lord."

Úlftýr straddled Fenrir and soared into the sky. He came for Elska. Together, on Fenrir's back, they arrived back at Midgardr, back to the beach where it all began.

The great ice serpent waited for them when they dismounted. Fenrir became a shadow and disappeared, settling in a hidden corner of Úlftýr's soul.

"I will create a barrier of ice and fog around Islandia to shield your land from unwanted visitors. I now have the strength to do so." The serpent's intelligible voice echoed in his mind: his voice, the sound of crystallized light.

"Did you do this?" Úlftýr raised his tunic to reveal the two snakes wrapped around a blue rose tattooed on his chest.

"No, they did," Jörmungandr answered. "The serpents chose you to be the guardian of their magic. They have settled on your skin to grant you their power and protection for all your immortal life."

The cool mist of Jörmungandr's voice shifted around Úlftýr.

"I am grateful to you. I remember what you did throughout my many lives. Tell me, why the games? Why not just tell me who you are? Who *I am*?"

Jörmungandr's violet eyes flashed. "Would you have willingly merged your soul with master Loki if I told you? You had to see. You had to feel it. When Skadi attempted to corrupt the path, your soul was destined to take; I followed your visions to show you the truth."

"Skadi?" Úlftýr raised an eyebrow.

"Loki's tormenter. The spirit that lived within your adoptive sister from birth. She was the one who imprisoned him, but it drained her powers. She, too, was a shadow until Odin, the one you knew as Bileygr, offered her a body for her prisoner's whereabouts. He failed to find him. Skadi's magic, meant to hide him from any who would have tried to rescue him, also shielded him from the gods that craved to destroy him. Only through his death could they rearrange the world as they saw fit."

"And they needed me because I am Loki's incarnation," It wasn't a question. Úlftýr suspected this much since he merged with the great god.

The giant serpent nodded. "I was too weak to release him myself or awaken you. My power had not been replenished since I brought your people to these shores."

"Loki sent you to do that." Úlftýr looked at his hands.

"He sent a part of his soul to come into this world to set himself free," Jörmungandr confirmed. "Odin sent the stag Oakthorn after us," Úlftýr's eyes widened; Jörmungandr continued. "Without my protection, the passage between the worlds corrupted him. He came out on this end, mad, and you have faced the result in your youth. After that, Odin waited, biding his time, waiting for his might to grow after he crossed, riding Bileygr's body. The opportunity to act came when he sensed Skadi's essence in this world, and then he acted."

"Is Lord Loki going to take over my consciousness now he is free?" Úlftýr asked. "Is he going to claim me as part of himself?"

A calming breeze graced Úlftýr's face. "You are still you and him. You are both. He will call upon you again when the magic of your world dwindles thin. Peace is a fragile notion, but you will keep the immortal life of Úlftýr if you so choose."

Úlftýr allowed himself to smile.

"What would have happened if I'd lost?"

Jörmungandr looked into Úlftýr's eyes. Images played out in Úlftýr's mind while Jörmungandr spoke. "The eruption infused by his essence at Loki's death would have poisoned the sky. It would have taken the light of this world, and men would have relied on their war machines in darkness. They would have strived forward to build great weapons to protect themselves from the evil in their hearts, and their future would have been what you saw."

Úlftýr took a breath, the horrible images of the human capacity for war and destruction still haunting him. "What will happen now? Will it never come to pass? How am I to proceed with the new life Loki granted me?" Úlftýr asked.

"I cannot answer all your questions, Úlftýr. I am afraid no one can. My advice to you would be to speak with my master. He might have sufficient answers to put your mind at ease."

"Why do I sense there is still something hidden from me?" Úlftýr asked. "Are you concealing something from me? Even now?"

Jörmungandr bowed his head. "I am concealing only pain, my prince."

Úlftýr fought to control his anger. "What is it?"

Jörmungandr looked into the sea. "Hope I fear to give you."

The earth quaked beneath their feet, and the water darkened.

A surge of waves rose into the air, as high as the serpent, and crashed onto the beach, leaving behind it a tall crystal embedded in the sand.

"Úlftýr!" Elska grabbed his hand, and they both ran to it.

"Let them out!" Úlftýr struck the crystal that kept his parents captive, imprisoned in a frozen state.

"I cannot." Jörmungandr's sad voice in Úlftýr's mind sounded sincere, but Úlftýr refused to accept it.

"You said they were gone when I asked you!" Úlftýr accused the serpent.

"And so they are," Jörmungandr said.

"How can you still cling to your lies when I see them here before me?" Úlftýr whipped around at the serpent.

"If I release them now," Jörmungandr whispered, "They will be truly gone forever, Úlftýr. Odin's charms run deep. His poison is still potent, and I have no cure."

Úlftýr fell to his knees. "So, what do I do?"

Jörmungandr did not respond.

Elska sank to her knees by her lover's side. "We will find a way." She promised. "I will not rest until we will find a way to give them back to you."

Úlftýr swallowed. He sat there unmoving; his hand rested against the icy surface. "Please, keep them safe." He finally let out.

Úlftýr raised his eyes and watched as the crystal holding his parents dissipated along with the serpent. The sea stilled, and the water cleared.

Úlftýr wiped his eyes of unshed tears. He looked at Elska, and she took his hand. "I am ready to go home now," Úlftýr said.

Úlftýr stood before the body-length mirror in his bed chamber. A shimmering figure strolled the depths of the glass. When the figure walked closer, his face leveled with Úlftýr's.

Loki stood before Úlftýr.

They greatly resembled each other, except Loki's skin was radiant alabaster, his hair red fire, and his eyes bright polished emeralds.

He wore a white tunic embroidered with a trim of gold. A cape of dark brown fur was draped over his shoulders.

"You gave me my life back," Úlftýr said. "Thank you."

"**You gave us our lives back**," Loki replied. "**By your will, my chains are broken, and so are yours. We are both free now. You still did not taste the full extent of the power you can possess.**"

"How come you had such powers to gift me? Deirdra and Bileygr seemed contained within their offered bodies, but I feel released from servitude."

"**They were not offered freely.**" Úlftýr felt Loki's anger. "**They were innocents expelled from their bodies by vengeful gods. I was already here, exiled from beyond the veil of our plane to this earth and kept here a prisoner. You were my last grasp on our dying world, and when I released my hold on my homeland, you came into existence, a free being.**"

Úlftýr nodded, "I understand less than I wish, and doubt still eats at me. What will happen now? I know my future has changed, but mortals can still bring destruction upon this realm."

"You restarted the world for millennia of peace," Loki said. **"When next you hear the call of war, I will be by your side**."

"Thank you," Úlftýr said. Loki's image faded from the mirror, and Úlftýr stared into his own eyes again.

Thunder rolled in the distance, lightning illuminated the sky, and Úlftýr doubled over; his left eye flashed in a golden light.

"Úlftýr,"

Úlftýr gasped and straightened up. He blinked a few times, his eyes a warm amber color. He turned. Ingrid stood in the doorway. "Was that...?" She stepped forward. "Is he gone?"

Úlftýr laid a hand on his chest. "No, he will always be with me now, a part of me like he was from the very beginning. Or rather, I was a part of him."

Ingrid nodded. She inhaled. "Úlftýr, I came to beg for your forgiveness."

"You have it," Úlftýr said, and she blinked.

"Regardless," she said, shaking her head. "I should have stood by you. My fear was my weakness. And I am still afraid. The crown should return to its rightful place on your head."

Úlftýr looked at her, his expression one of peace and resolve. "I have no aspiration for the throne, Ingrid. I never have. I only warmed the chair for you until you were prepared for your rightful place."

"But I am not prepared – " Ingrid protested.

"But you are." Úlftýr cut her off. "You were prepared to do what is right, to put our people first. Before me, before your own blood. And I know you did not reach that decision lightly. I trust your judgment and will stand by your side if you have me."

Ingrid smiled; tears welled up in her eyes. "Of course."

CHAPTER 33

THE WEDDING

On the twenty-first day of Einmánuður month, just as the summer began giving its first signs in warm air, churning streams, and groves of flowers, Úlftýr and Elska stood at the altar in the inner courtyard of Blackstone castle.

Blue roses and banners with Úlftýr's family crest adorned the inner walls.

The entire court stood around them with Queen Ingrid by Elska's father, who officiated the ceremony.

For once, Úlftýr dressed in his official garb. The colors of the royal family, crimson cape draped from a silver armor etched with his family's crest.

Elska wore a long, silk gown of radiant blue snow pattern. It shone like a jewel against her skin. The dress had a wide neckline and full-length sleeves. A pattern of blue roses finished the trim.

Siran stood before them in his golden Elder robes.

"Úlftýr, I believe you wanted to present your vows."

Úlftýr nodded and turned to Elska.

"In yore, there was no light. But then camest thou, the brightest star in my desolate universe. Thenceforth, my soul illuminated, and thee became my goddess for all eternity. Through our many lifetimes, I knew our souls would always recognize each other no matter where fate led us. You are the one who understands my inner demons, the one who loved me so much you were willing to put your life on the line to restore my happiness.

I hope I have created a better world that will be worthy of the light you bring into it through your presence," he inhaled.

"Since our first meeting, we have experienced a world of adventure. From the mundane to the exciting, painful, and joyful moments, we were heartbroken by one another—and mended years later.

It feels like we've been together for lifetimes, but this year was exceptionally challenging. I would say that this year has tested us on every level, from being a couple to just individually trying either one of us, stretching us in what felt like different directions.

It felt like a year that was set to break us. I would say we've been on the edge, a space where we had to make difficult choices, choices difficult to even consider for two souls so truthfully united for so many years.

We've seen the brink, a dark place where everything ends, and we've also prevailed over it, no matter how hard it was.

I would also say - that no matter how low it was - we've ascended above it all.

No matter how bleak, dark, harsh, gloomy, ugly it was - you've stayed so beautiful, ever growing so beautiful by the day."

Elska wiped away a tear. "Úlftýr," she looked into his amber-colored eyes. "Fate had brought you back to me at every point of my life when I was lost to give me purpose. You were there when my life in this land began anew. You were there when I stood petrified on the edge of a cliff, fearful of my emotions, closed off to my heart's desire. You showed me that, in your eyes, I am beautiful. I owe you my happiness. I love you."

"I love you too." Úlftýr smiled.

"We who stand here before you," Siran said aloud. "Are witnesses to this union of soul, heart, and body. Your meeting was fate; falling in love was destiny. May your life be fruitful and your future bright. Úlftýr, you may kiss your bride."

The crowd erupted in shouts of cheer, cries of glee, and bursts of laughter.

Úlftýr and Elska shared a kiss for the ages that resonated in the darkest depths of the loneliest mountains, enough to bring light to the most desolate hearts.

Úlftýr found himself overwhelmed with joy. He wished that with everything he was, Baldur was there to see the happiness he had found.

And in an underground cave on the cliffs of Krýsuvíkurbjarg, the lid of Baldur's crypt split open.

A new beginning…

Made in the USA
Las Vegas, NV
21 September 2024

95444276R00236